It was that voice again . . . only this time the strange high singsong wail seemed to come from *inside* the vault.

My heart began to beat fast; my hand on the gate trembled. I looked about me but I seemed to be alone with the mist.

I went down the stone steps. "Who's there?" I called.

There was silence. Because of the light from the open door I could see the ledges with the coffins on them; I could smell the dampness of the earth. Then suddenly I was in darkness and for a few seconds I was so shocked and bewildered that I could not move. I could not even cry out in protest. It took me several seconds to understand that the door had closed on me and I was shut in the vault. . . .

By Victoria Holt
Published by Fawcett Books:

Bride
of
Pendorric

by Victoria Holt

FAWCETT CREST • NEW YORK

A Fawcett Crest Book
Published by Ballantine Books
Copyright © 1963 by Victoria Holt

http://www.randomhouse.com

ISBN 0-449-21507-5

This edition published by arrangement with Doubleday & Company, Inc.

Manufactured in the United States of America

First Fawcett Crest Edition: January 1965
First Ballantine Books Edition: December 1982

50   49   48   47   46   45   44   43

1.

I OFTEN MARVELED after I went to Pendorric that one's existence could change so swiftly, so devastatingly. I had heard life compared with a kaleidoscope and this is how it appeared to me, for there was the pleasant scene full of peace and contentment when the pattern began to change, first here, then there, until the picture which confronted me was no longer calm and peaceful but filled with menace. I had married a man who had seemed to me all that I wanted in a husband—solicitous, loving, passionately devoted; then suddenly it was as though I were married to a stranger.

I first saw Roc Pendorric when I came up from the beach one morning to find him sitting in the studio with my father; in his hands he held a terra-cotta statue for which I had been the original, a slim child of about seven. I remembered when my father had made it more than eleven years before; he had always said it was not for sale.

The blinds had not yet been drawn and the two men made a striking contrast sitting there in the strong sunlight: my father so fair, the stranger so dark. On the island my father was often called Angelo because of the fairness of his hair and skin and his almost guileless expression, for he was a very sweet-tempered man. It might have been because of this that I fancied there was something saturnine about his companion.

"Ah, here is my daughter, Favel," said my father as though they had been speaking of me.

They both stood up, the stranger towering above my father who was of medium height. He took my hand and his long dark eyes studied me with something rather calculating in the intentness of his scrutiny. He was lean, which accentuated his height, and his hair was almost black; there was an expression in his alert eyes which made me feel he was seeking something which amused him and it occurred to me that there might be a streak of malice in his amusement. He had rather pointed ears which gave him the look of a satyr. His was a face of contrasts; there was a gentleness about the full lips as well as sensuality; there was no doubt of the firmness of the jaw;

5

there was arrogance in the long straight nose; and mingling with the undoubted humor in the quick eyes was a suggestion of mischief. I came to believe later that he fascinated me so quickly because I could not be sure of him; and it took me a very long time to discover the sort of man he was.

At that moment I wished that I had dressed before coming up from the beach.

"Mr. Pendorric has been looking round the studio," said my father. "He has bought the Bay of Naples water color."

"I'm glad," I answered. "It's beautiful."

He held out the little statue. "And so is this."

"I don't think that's for sale," I told him.

"It's much too precious, I'm sure."

He seemed to be comparing me with the figure and I guessed my father had told him—as he did everyone who admired it: "That's my daughter when she was seven."

"But," he went on, "I've been trying to persuade the artist to sell. After all, *he* still has the original."

Father laughed in the rather hearty way he did when he was with customers who were ready to spend money, forced laughter. Father had always been happier creating his works of art than selling them. When my mother was alive she had done most of the selling; since I had left school, only a few months before this, I found myself taking it over. Father would give his work away to anyone who he thought appreciated it, and he needed a strong-minded woman to look after business transactions; that was why, after my mother had died, we had become very poor. But since I had been at home, I flattered myself that we were beginning to pay our way.

"Favel, could you get us a drink?" my father asked.

I said I would if they would wait while I changed, and leaving them together went into my bedroom which led off the studio. In a few minutes I had put on a blue linen dress, after which I went to our tiny kitchen to see about drinks; when I went back to the studio Father was showing the man a bronze Venus—one of our most expensive pieces.

If he buys that, I thought, I'll be able to settle a few bills. I would seize on the money and do it, too, before Father had a chance of gambling it away at cards or roulette.

Roc Pendorric's eyes met mine over the bronze and, as I caught the flicker of amusement there, I guessed I must have shown rather clearly how anxious I was for him to buy it. He put it down and turned to me as though the statue couldn't hold his interest while I was there, and I felt annoyed with myself for interrupting them. Then I caught the gleam in his eyes and I wondered whether that was what he had expected me to feel.

He started to talk about the island then; he had arrived only yesterday, and had not even visited the villas of Tiberius and San Michele yet. But he had heard of Angelo's studio and the wonderful works of art to be picked up there; and so this had been his first excursion.

Father was flushed with pleasure; but I wasn't quite sure whether to believe him or not.

"And when I came and found that Angelo was Mr. Frederick Farington who spoke English like the native he is, I was even more delighted. My Italian is appalling, and the boasts of 'English spoken here' are often . . . well a little boastful. Please, Miss Farington, do tell me what I ought to see while I stay here."

I started to tell him about the villas, the grottoes, and the other well-known attractions. "But," I added, "it always seems to me after coming back from England that the scenery and the blue of the sea are the island's real beauties."

"It would be nice to have a companion to share in my sight-seeing," he said.

"Are you traveling alone?" I asked.

"Quite alone."

"There are so many visitors to the island," I said consolingly. "You're sure to find someone who is as eager to do the tours as you are."

"It would be necessary, of course, to find the right companion . . . someone who really knows the island."

"The guides do, of course."

His eyes twinkled. "I wasn't thinking of a guide."

"The rest of the natives would no doubt be too busy."

"I'll find what I want," he assured me; and I had a feeling that he would.

He went over to the bronze Venus and began fingering it again.

"That attracts you," I commented.

He turned to me and studied me as intently as he had the bronze. "I'm enormously attracted," he told me. "I can't make up my mind. May I come back later?"

"But of course," said Father and I simultaneously.

* * *

He did come back. He came back and back again. In my

innocence I thought at first that he was hesitating about the bronze Venus; then I wondered whether it was the studio that attracted him because it probably seemed very bohemian to him, full of local color and totally unlike the place he came from. One couldn't expect people to buy every time they came. It was a feature of our studio and others like it that people dropped in casually, stopped for a chat and a drink, browsed about the place and bought when something pleased them.

What disturbed me was that I was beginning to look forward to his visits. There were times when I was sure he came to see me, and there were others when I told myself that I was imagining this, and the thought depressed me.

Three days after his first visit I went down to one of the little beaches on the Marina Piccola to bathe, and he was there. We swam together and lay on the beach in the sun afterwards.

I asked if he was enjoying his stay.

"Beyond expectations," he answered.

"You've been sight-seeing, I expect."

"Not much. I'd like to, but I still think it's dull alone."

"Really? People usually complain of the awful crowds, not of being alone."

"Mind you," he pointed out, "I wouldn't want *any* companion." There was a suggestion in those long eyes which slightly tilted at the corners. I was sure, in that moment, that he was the type whom most women would find irresistible, and that he knew it. This knowledge disturbed me; I myself was becoming too conscious of that rather blatant masculinity and I wondered whether I had betrayed this to him.

I said rather coolly: "Someone was asking about the bronze Venus this morning."

His eyes shone with amusement. "Oh well, if I miss it, I'll only have *myself* to blame." His meaning was perfectly clear and I felt annoyed with him. Why did he think we kept a studio and entertained people there if not in the hope of selling things? How did he think we lived?

"We'd hate you to have it unless you were really keen about it."

"But I never have anything that I'm not keen about," he replied. "Actually though, I prefer the figure of the younger Venus."

"Oh . . . that!"

He put his hand on my arm and said: "It's charming. Yes, I far prefer her."

"I simply must be getting back," I told him.

He leaned on his elbow and smiled at me, and I had a feeling that he knew far too much of what was going on in my mind, and was fully aware that I found his company extremely stimulating and wanted more of it—that he was something more to me than a prospective buyer.

He said lightly: "Your father tells me that you're the commercial brains behind the enterprise. I bet he's right."

"Artists need someone practical to look after them," I replied. "And now that my mother is dead . . ."

I knew that my voice changed when I spoke of her. It still happened, although she had been dead three years. Annoyed with myself as I always was when I betrayed emotion, I said quickly: "She died of T.B. They came here in the hope that it would be good for her. She was a wonderful manager."

"And so you take after her." His eyes were full of sympathy now and I was pleased out of all proportion that he should understand how I felt. I thought then that I had imagined that streak of mischief in him. Perhaps mischief was not the right description; but the fact was that while I was becoming more and more attracted by this man, I was often conscious of something within him that I could not understand, some quality, something which he was determined to keep hidden from me. This often made me uneasy while it in no way decreased my growing interest in him—but rather added to it. Now I saw only his sympathy, which was undoubtedly genuine.

"I hope so," I answered. "I think I do."

I still could not control the pain in my voice as I remembered, and pictures of the past flashed in and out of my mind. I saw her—small and dainty, with the brilliant color in her cheeks, which was so becoming but a sign of her illness; that tremendous energy which was like a fire consuming her—until the last months. The island had seemed a different place when she was in it. In the beginning she had taught me to read and write and to be quick with figures. I remembered long lazy days when I lay on one of the little beaches or swam in the blue water or lay on my back and drifted; all the beauty of the place, all the echoes of ancient history were the background for one of the happiest existences a child could know. I had run wild, it was true. Sometimes I talked to the tourists, sometimes I joined the boatmen who took visitors to the grottoes or on tours of the island; sometimes I climbed the path to the villa of Tiberius and sat looking over the sea to Naples. Then I would come back to the studio and listen to the talk going on there; I shared my father's pride in his work; my mother's joy when she had succeeded in making a good sale.

They were so important to each other; and there were times when they seemed to me like two brilliant butterflies dancing in the sunshine, intoxicated with the joy of being alive because they knew that the sun of their happiness must go down quickly and finally.

I had been indignant when they told me I must go away to school in England. It was a necessity, my mother pointed out, for she had reached the limit of her capabilities, and although I was a tolerable linguist (we spoke English at home, Italian to our neighbors, and, as there were many French and German visitors to our studio, I soon had a smattering of these languages) I had had no real education. My mother was anxious that I should go to her old school, which was small and in the heart of Sussex. Her old headmistress was still in charge and I suspected that it was all very much as it had been in my mother's day. After a term or two I became reconciled, partly because I quickly made friends with Esther McBane, partly because I returned to the island for Christmas, Easter, and summer holidays; and as I was a normal uncomplicated person I enjoyed both worlds.

But then my mother died and nothing was the same again. I found out that I had been educated on the jewelry which had once been hers; she had planned for me to go to a university, but the jewelry had realized less than she had hoped (for one quality she shared with my father was optimism) and the cost of my schooling was more than she had bargained for. So when she died I went back to school for two more years because that was her wish. Esther was a great comfort at that time; she was an orphan who was being brought up by an aunt, so she had a good deal of sympathy to offer. She came to stay with us during summer holidays and it helped both Father and me not to fret so much with a visitor in the studio. We said that she must come every summer, and she assured us she would. We left school at the same time and she came home with me at the end of our final term. During that holiday we would discuss what we were going to do with our lives. Esther planned to take up art seriously. As for myself, I had my father to consider, so I was going to try to take my mother's place in the studio although I feared that was something I should never be able to do entirely.

I smiled remembering that long letter I had had from Esther, which in itself was unusual, for Esther abhorred letter writing and avoided it whenever possible. On the way back to Scotland she had met a man; he was growing tobacco in Rhodesia and was home for a few months. That letter had been full of this adventure. There had been one more letter two months later. Esther was getting married and going out to Rhodesia.

It was exciting and she was wonderfully happy; but I knew it was the end of our friendship because the only bond between us now could be through letters which Esther would have neither time nor inclination to write. I did have one to say that she had arrived, but marriage had made a different person of Esther; she had grown far from that long-legged untidy-haired girl who used to walk in the grounds of the little school with me and talk about dedicating herself to Art.

I was brought out of the past by the sight of Roc Pendorric's face close to mine, and now there was nothing but sympathy in his eyes. "I've stirred up sad memories."

"I was thinking about my mother and the past."

He nodded and was silent for a few seconds. Then he said: "You don't ever think of going back to her people . . . or your father's people?"

"People?" I murmured.

"Didn't she ever talk to you about her home in England?"

I was suddenly very surprised. "No, she never mentioned it."

"Perhaps the memory was unhappy."

"I never realized it before but neither of them ever talked about . . . before they married. As a matter of fact I think they felt that all that happened before was insignificant."

"It must have been a completely happy marriage."

"It was."

We were silent again. Then he said: "Favel! It's an unusual name."

"No more unusual than yours. I always thought a roc was a legendary bird."

"Fabulous, of immense size and strength, able to lift an elephant . . . if it wanted to."

He spoke rather smugly and I retorted: "I'm sure even you would be incapable of lifting an elephant. Is it a nickname?"

"I've been Roc for as long as I can remember. But it's short for Petroc."

"Still unusual."

"Not in the part of the world I come from. I've had a lot of ancestors who had to put up with it. The original one was a sixth century saint who founded a monastery. I think Roc is a modern version that's all my own. Do you think it suits me?"

"Yes," I answered. "I think it does."

Rather to my embarrassment he leaned forward and kissed the tip of my nose. I stood up hastily. "It really is time I was getting back to the studio," I said.

* * *

Our friendship grew quickly and to me was wholly exciting. I did not realize then how inexperienced I was, and imagined that I was capable of dealing with any situation. I forgot then that my existence had been bounded by school in England, with its regulations and restrictions, our casual unconventional studio on an island, whose main preoccupation was with passing visitors, and my life with my father, who still thought of me as a child. I had imagined myself to be a woman of the world, whereas no one who could lay a true claim to such a description would have fallen in love with the first man who seemed different from anyone else she had met.

But there was a magnetism about Roc Pendorric when he set himself out to charm, and he certainly was determined to charm me.

Roc came to the studio every day. He always took the statuette in his hands and caressed it lovingly.

"I'm determined to have it, you know," he said one day.

"Father will never sell."

"I never give up hope." And as I looked at the strong line of his jaw, the brilliance of his dark eyes, I believed him. He was a man who would take what he wanted from life; and it occurred to me that there would be few to deny him. That was why he was so anxious to possess the statue. He hated to be frustrated.

He bought the bronze Venus then.

"Don't think," he told me, "that this means I've given up trying for the other. It'll be mine yet; you see."

There was an acquisitive gleam in his eyes when he said that and a certain teasing look too. I knew what he meant, of course.

We swam together. We explored the whole island and we usually chose the less well-known places to avoid the crowds.

He hired two Neapolitan boatmen to take us on sea trips and there were wonderful days when we lay back in the boat letting our hands trail in the turquoise and emerald water while Guiseppe and Umberto, watching us with the indulgent looks Latins bestow on lovers, sang arias from Italian opera for our entertainment.

In spite of his dark looks there must have been something essentially English about Roc because Guiseppe and Umberto were immediately aware of his nationality. This ability to decide a person's nationality often surprised me but it never seemed to fail. As for myself there was little difficulty in placing me. My hair was dark blond and there was a platinum-colored streak in it which had been there when I was born; it had the effect of making me look even more fair than I was. My eyes were the shade of water, and borrowed their color from what I was wearing. Sometimes they were green, at others quite blue. I had a short pert nose, a wide mouth and good teeth. I was by no means a beauty, but I had always looked more like a visitor to the island than a native.

During those weeks I was never quite sure of Roc. There were times when I was perfectly happy to enjoy each moment as it came along and not concern myself with the future; but when I was alone—at night, for instance—I wondered what I should do when he went home.

In those early days I knew the beginning of that frustration which later was to bring such fear and terror into my life. His gaiety often seemed to be a cloak for deeper feelings; even during his most tender moments I would imagine I saw speculation in his eyes. He intrigued me in a hundred ways. I knew that given any encouragement I could love him completely, but I was never sure of him, and perhaps that was one of the reasons why every moment I was with him held the maximum excitement.

One day, soon after we met, we climbed to the villa of Tiberius and never had that wonderful view seemed so superb as it did on that day. It was all there for our delight as I had seen it many times before—Capri and Monte Solaro, the Gulf of Salerno from Amalfi to Paestum, the Gulf of Naples from Sorrento to Cape Miseno. I knew it well, and yet because I was sharing it with Roc it had a new magic.

"Have you ever seen anything so enchanting?" I asked.

He seemed to consider. Then he said, "I live in a place which seems to me as beautiful."

"Where?"

"Cornwall. Our bay is as beautiful—more so I think because it changes more often. Don't you get weary of sapphire seas? Now, I've seen ours as blue—or almost; I've seen it green under the beating rain and brown after a storm and pink in the dawn; I've seen it mad with fury, pounding the rocks and sending the spray high, and I've seen it as silky as this sea. This is very beautiful, I grant you, and I don't think Roman Emperors ever honored us in Cornwall with their villas and legends of their dancing boys and girls, but we have a history of our own which is just as enthralling."

"I've never been to Cornwall."

He suddenly turned to me and I was caught in an embrace which made me gasp. He said, with his face pressed against mine, "But you will . . . soon."

I was conscious of the rose red ruins, the greenish statue of the Madonna, the deep blue of the sea, and life seemed suddenly too wonderful to be true.

He had lifted me off my feet and held me above him, laughing at me.

I said primly, "Someone will see us."

"Do you care?"

"Well, I object to being literally swept off my feet."

He released me and to my disappointment he did not say any more about Cornwall. That incident was typical of our relationship.

* * *

I realized that my father was taking a great interest in our friendship. He was always delighted to see Roc, and he would sometimes come to the door of the studio to meet us, after we'd been out on one of our excursions, looking like a conspirator, I thought. He was not a subtle man and it did not take me long to discover that some plan was forming in his mind and that it concerned Roc and me.

Did he think that Roc would propose to me? Was Roc's feeling for me more definite than I dared hope, and had my father noticed this? And suppose I married Roc, what of the studio? How would my father get along without me, because if I married Roc I should have to go away with him?

I felt unsettled. I knew I wanted to marry Roc—but I was not sure about his feelings for me. How could I leave my father? But I had when I was at school, I reminded myself. Yes, and look at the result. Right from the beginning, being in love with Roc was an experience that kept me poised between ecstasy and anxiety.

But Roc had not talked of marriage.

Father often asked him to a meal, invitations Roc always accepted on condition that he should provide the wine. I cooked omelettes, fish, *pasta*, and even roast beef with York-shire pudding; the meals were well cooked because one of the things my mother had taught me was how to cook, and there had always been a certain amount of English dishes served in the studio.

Roc seemed to enjoy those meals thoroughly and would sit long over them talking and drinking. He began to talk a great deal about himself and his home in Cornwall; but he had a way of making Father talk, and he quickly learned about how we lived, the difficulties of making enough money during the tourist season to keep us during the lean months. I noticed that Father never discussed the time before his marriage, and Roc only made one or two attempts to persuade him. Then he gave it up, which was strange, because he was usually per-sistent—but it was characteristic of Roc simply because it was unexpected.

I remember one day coming in and finding them playing cards together. Father had that look on his face which always frightened me—that intent expression which made his eyes glow like blue fire; there was a faint pink color in his cheeks and as I came in he scarcely looked up.

Roc got up from his chair but I could see that he shared my father's feeling for the game. I felt very uneasy as I thought: So he's a gambler too.

"Favel won't want to interrupt the game," said my father.

I looked into Roc's eyes and said coldly: "I hope you aren't playing for high stakes."

"Don't worry your head about that, my dear," said Father.

"He's determined to lure the lire from my pockets," added Roc, his eyes sparkling.

"I'll go and get something to eat," I told them, and went into the kitchen.

I shall have to make him understand Father can't afford to gamble, I told myself.

When we sat over the meal my father was jubilant, so I guessed he had won.

* * *

I spoke to Roc about it the next day at the beach.

"Please don't encourage my father to gamble. He simply can't afford it."

"But he gets so much pleasure from it," he replied.

"Lots of people get pleasure from things that aren't good for them."

He laughed. "You know you're a bit of a martinet."

"Please listen to me. We're not rich enough to risk losing money that has been so hard to come by. We live here very cheaply, but it's not easy. Is that impossible for you to understand?"

"Please don't worry, Favel," he said, putting his hand over mine.

"Then you won't play for money with him any more?"

"Suppose he asks me? Shall I say, I decline the invitation because your strong-minded daughter forbids us?"

"You could do better than that."

He looked pious. "But it wouldn't be true."

I shrugged my shoulders impatiently. "Surely you can find other people to gamble with. Why do you have to choose him?"

He looked thoughtful and said: "I suppose it's because I like the atmosphere of his studio." We were lying on the beach and he reached out and turned me towards him. Looking into my face he went on: "I like the treasures he has there."

It was in moments like this when I believed his feelings matched my own. I was elated and at the same time afraid I should betray too much. So I stood up quickly and walked into the sea; he was close behind me.

"Don't you know, Favel," he said, putting his arm round my bare shoulder, "that I want very much to please you?"

I had to turn and smile at him then. Surely, I thought, the look he gave me was one of love.

We were happy and carefree when we swam, and later, as we lay in the sun on the beach, I felt once more that supreme happiness which is being in love.

* * *

Yet two days later I came in from the market and found them sitting at the card table. The game was finished, but I could see by my father's face that he had lost and by Roc's that he had won.

I felt my cheeks flame and my eyes were hard as I looked into Roc's face. I said nothing but went straight into the kitchen with my basket. I set it down angrily and to my dismay found my eyes full of tears. Tears of fury, I told myself, because he had made a fool of me. He was not to be trusted. This was a clear indication of it; he promised one thing and did another.

I wanted to rush out of the studio, to find some quiet spot away from everyone where I could stay until I was calm enough to face him again.

I heard a voice behind me: "What can I do to help?"

I turned and faced him. I was grateful that the tears had not fallen. They were merely making my eyes look more brilliant, and he should not guess how wretched I was.

I said shortly: "Nothing. I can manage, thank you."

I turned back to the table and then I felt him standing close to me; he had gripped my shoulders and was laughing.

He put his face close to my ear and whispered: "I kept my promise, you know. We didn't play for money."

I shook him off and went to a drawer of the table, which I opened and rummaged in without knowing for what.

"Nonsense," I retorted. "The game wouldn't have meant a thing to either of you if there'd been no stakes. It isn't that you enjoy playing cards. It's win or lose. And of course you both think that you're going to win every time. It seems absurdly childish to me. One of you has to lose."

"But you must understand that I kept my promise."

"Please don't bother to explain. I can trust my eyes, you know."

"We were gambling . . . certainly. You're right when you said it wouldn't interest us if we were not. Who do you think won this time?"

"I have a meal to prepare."

"I won this." He put his hand in his pocket and drew out the statuette.

Then he laughed. "I determined to get it by fair means or foul. Fortunately it turned out to be fair. So you see I kept my promise to you, I had my gamble, and I own this delightful creature."

"Take the knives and forks for me, will you please?" I said.

He slipped the statue into his pocket and grinned at me. "With the greatest pleasure."

*　*　*

The next day he asked me to marry him. At his suggestion we had climbed the steep path to the Grotto of Matromania.

I had always thought it the least exciting of the grottoes and
the Blue, Green, Yellow, and Red, or the Grotto of the Saints,
were all more worth a visit, but Roc said he had not seen it
and wanted me to take him there.

"A very appropriate spot," he commented when we reached
it.

I turned to look at him and he caught my arm and held it
tightly.

"Why?" I asked.

"You know," he replied.

But I was never sure of him—not even at this moment
when he regarded me with so much tenderness.

"Matromania," he murmured.

"I'd heard that this was dedicated to Mithromania known
as Mithras," I said quickly because I was afraid of betraying
my feelings.

"Nonsense," he replied. "This is where Tiberius held his
revels for young men and maidens. I read it in the guide
book. It means matrimony because they married here."

"There seem to be two opinions then."

"Then we'd better give it another reason for its importance. It's the spot where Petroc Pendorric asked Favel
Farington to marry him and where she said . . ."

He turned to me and in that moment I was certain he loved
me as passionately as I loved him.

There was no need for me to answer.

We went back to the studio; he was elated and I was happier than I had ever been before.

* * *

Father was so delighted when we told him the news that it
was almost as though he wished to get rid of me. He refused
to discuss what he would do when I had gone, and I was terribly worried until Roc told me that he would insist on his
accepting an allowance. Why shouldn't he from his own son-
in-law? He'd commission some pictures if that would make it
easier. Perhaps that would be a good idea. "We've lots of bare
wall space at Pendorric," he added.

And for the first time I began to think seriously about the
place which would be my home; but although Roc was always
ready to talk of it in general, he said he wanted me to see it
and judge for myself. If he talked to me too much I might
imagine something entirely different and perhaps be disap-

pointed—though I couldn't believe I could be disappointed in a home I shared with him.

We were very much in love. Roc seemed no longer a stranger. I felt I understood him. There was a streak of mischief in him and he loved to tease me. "Because," he told me once, "you're too serious, too old-fashioned in many ways to be true."

I pondered on that and supposed I was different from girls he had known, because of my upbringing—the intimate family circle, the school which was run on the same lines as it had been twenty or thirty years before. Also, I had felt my responsibilities deeply when my mother had died. I must learn to be more lighthearted, gay, up-to-date, I told myself.

Our wedding was going to be very quiet; there would be a few guests from the English colony, and Roc and I were going to stay at the studio for a week afterwards; then we were to go to England.

I asked him what his family would think of his returning with a bride they had never met.

"I've written and told them we'll soon be home. They're not so surprised as you imagine. One thing they have learned to expect from me is the unexpected," he replied cheerfully. "They're wild with delight. You see they think it's the duty of all Pendorrics to marry, and they believe I've waited long enough."

I wanted to hear more about them. I wanted to be prepared, but he always put me off.

"I'm not very good at describing things," he answered. "You'll be there soon enough."

"But this Pendorric . . . I gather it is something of a mansion."

"It's the family home. I suppose you could call it that."

"And . . . who is the family?"

"My sister, her husband, their twin daughters. You don't have to worry, you know. They won't be in our wing. It's a family custom that all who can, remain at home, and bring their families to live there."

"And it's near the sea."

"Right on the coast. You're going to love it. All Pendorrics do and you'll be one of them very soon."

I think it was about a week before my wedding day that I noticed the change in my father.

I came in quietly one day and found him sitting at the table staring ahead of him and because he had not seen me for a few moments I caught him in repose; he looked suddenly old; and more than that . . . frightened.

"Father," I cried, "what's the matter?"

He started up and he smiled but his heart wasn't in it.

"The matter? Why, nothing's the matter."

"But you were sitting there . . ."

"Why shouldn't I? I've been working on that bust of Tiberius. It tired me."

I accepted his excuse temporarily and forgot about it.

*   *   *

But not for long. My father had never been able to keep things to himself and I began to believe that he was hiding something from me, something which caused him the utmost anxiety.

One early morning, about two days before the wedding, I awoke to find someone moving about in the studio. The illuminated dial of my bedside clock said three o'clock.

I hastily put on a dressing gown, quietly opened the door of my room, and, peeping out, saw a dark shadow seated at the table.

"Father!" I cried.

He started up. "My dear child, I've disturbed you. It's all right. Do go back to bed."

I went to him and made him sit down. I drew up a chair. "Look here," I insisted, "you'd better tell me what's wrong."

He hesitated and then said: "But it's nothing. I couldn't sleep, so I thought it would do me good to come and sit out here for a while."

"But why couldn't you sleep? There's something on your mind, isn't there?"

"I'm perfectly all right."

"It's no use saying that when it obviously isn't true. Are you worried about me . . . about my marrying?"

Again that slight pause. Of course that's it, I thought.

He said: "My dear child, you're very much in love with Roc, aren't you?"

"Yes, Father."

"Favel . . . you're sure, aren't you?"

"Are you worried because we've known each other such a short while?"

He did not answer that, but murmured: "You'll go right away from here . . . to his place in Cornwall . . . to Pendorric."

"But we'll come to see you! And you'll come to stay with us."

"I think," he went on, and it was as though he were talking to himself, "that if something prevented your marriage it would break your heart."

He stood up suddenly. "I'm cold. Let's get back to bed. I'm sorry I disturbed you, Favel."

"Father, we really ought to have a talk. I wish you would tell me everything that's on your mind."

"You go along to bed, Favel. I'm sorry I disturbed you."

He kissed me and we went to our rooms. How often later I was to reproach myself for allowing him to evade me like that. I ought to have insisted on knowing.

* * *

There came the day when Roc and I were married and I was so overwhelmed by new and exciting experiences that I did not give a thought to what was happening to my father. I couldn't think of anyone but myself and Roc during those days.

It was wonderful to be together every hour of the days and nights. We would laugh over trifles; it was really the laughter of happiness, which comes so easily I discovered. Guiseppe and Umberto were delighted with us; their arias were more fervent than they used to be, and after we had left them Roc and I would imitate them, gesticulating wildly, setting our faces into tragic or comic masks, whatever the songs demanded, and because we sang out of tune we laughed the more. He would come into the kitchen when I was cooking, to help me he said; and he would sit on the table getting in my way until with mock exasperation I would attempt to turn him out, which always ended up by my being in his arms.

The memories of those days were to stay with me during the difficult times ahead; they sustained me when I needed to be sustained.

Roc was, as I had known he would be, a passionate and demanding lover; he carried me along with him, but I often felt bemused by the rich experiences which were mine. Yet I was certain then that everything was going to be wonderful. I was content to live in the moment; I had even stopped wondering what my new home would be like; I assured myself that my father would have nothing to worry about. Roc would take care of his future as he would take care of mine.

Then one day I went down to the market alone and came back sooner than I had expected.

The door of the studio was open and I saw them there—my father and my husband. The expression on both their faces shocked me. Roc's was grim; my father's tortured. I had the impression that my father had been saying something to Roc which he did not like, and I could not tell whether Roc was angry or shocked. I imagined my father seemed bewildered.

Then they saw me and Roc said quickly: "Here's Favel."

It was as though they had both drawn masks over their faces.

"Is anything the matter?" I demanded.

"Only that we're hungry," answered Roc, coming over to me and taking my basket from me.

He smiled and putting his arm round me gave me a hug. "It seems a long time since I've seen you."

I looked beyond him to my father; he, too, was smiling, but I thought there was a grayish tinge in his face.

"Father," I insisted, "what is it?"

"You're imagining things, my dear," he assured me.

I could not throw off my uneasiness but I let them persuade me that all was well, because I could not bear that anything should disturb my new and wonderful happiness.

* * *

The sun was brilliant. It had been a busy morning in the studio. My father always went down to swim while I got our midday meal, and on that day I told Roc to go with him.

"Why don't you come too?"

"Because I have the lunch to get. I'll do it more quickly if you two go off."

So they went off together.

Ten minutes later Roc came back. He came into the kitchen and sat on the table. His back was to the window and I noticed the sunlight through the prominent tips of his ears.

"At times," I said, "you look like a satyr."

"That's what I am," he told me.

"Why did you come back so soon?"

"I found I didn't want to be separated from you any longer, so I left your father on the beach and came back alone."

I laughed at him. "You *are* silly! Couldn't you bear to be away from me for another fifteen minutes?"

"Far too long," he said.

I was delighted to have him with me, pretending to help in the kitchen, but when we were ready to eat, my father had not come back.

"I do hope he's not got involved in some long conversation," I said.

"He couldn't. You know how people desert the beach for food and siesta at this time of day."

Five minutes later I began to get really anxious; and with good reason.

That morning my father went into the sea and he did not come back alive.

His body was recovered later that day. They said he must have been overcome by cramp and unable to save himself.

It seemed the only explanation then. My happiness was shattered, but how thankful I was that I had Roc. I did not know how I could have lived through that time if he had not been with me. My great and only consolation was that, although I had lost my father, Roc had come into my life.

It was only later that the terrible doubts began.

2.

ALL THE JOY had gone out of our honeymoon, and I could not rid myself of the fear that I had failed my father in some way.

I remember lying in Roc's arms during the night that followed and crying out: "There was something I could have done. I know it."

Roc tried to comfort me. "But what, my darling? How could you know that he was going to have cramp? It could happen to anybody and, smooth as the sea was, if nobody heard his cry for help, that would be the end."

"He never had cramp before."

"There had to be a first time."

"But Roc . . . there *was* something."

He smoothed my hair back from my face. "Darling, you mustn't upset yourself so. There's nothing we can do now."

He was right. What could we do?

"He would be glad," Roc told me, "that I am here to take care of you."

There was a note of relief in his voice when he said that, which I could not understand, and I felt the first twinges of the fear which I was to come to know very well.

Roc took charge of everything. He said that we must get away from the island as quickly as possible because then I would begin to grow away from my tragedy. He would take me home and in time I should forget.

I left everything to him because I was too unhappy to make arrangements myself. Some of my father's treasures were packed up and sent to Pendorric to await our arrival; the rest were sold. Roc saw the landlord of our studio and arranged to get rid of the lease; and two weeks later we left Capri.

"Now we must try to put that tragedy out of our minds," said Roc as we sailed to the mainland.

I looked at his profile and for one short moment I felt that I was looking at a stranger. I did not know why—except perhaps because I had begun to suspect, since my father's death, that there was a great deal I had to learn about my husband.

We spent two days in Naples and while we were there he

24

told me that he was not in any hurry to get home because I was still so shocked and dazed, and he wanted me to have time to recover before he took me to Pendorric.

"We'll finish our honeymoon, darling," he said.

But my response was listless because I kept thinking of my father, sitting at the studio table in the dark, and wondering what he had on his mind.

"I ought to have found out," I reiterated. "How could I have been so thoughtless? I always knew when something worried him. He found it hard to hide anything from me. And he didn't hide that."

"What do you mean?" demanded Roc almost fiercely.

"I think he was ill. Probably that was why he got this cramp. Roc, what happened on the beach that day? Did he look ill?"

"No. He looked the same as usual."

"Oh Roc, if only you hadn't come back. If only you'd been with him."

"It's no use saying 'if only,' Favel. I wasn't with him. We're going to leave Naples. It's too close. We're going to put all this behind us." He took my hands and drew me to him, kissing me with tenderness and passion. "You're my wife, Favel. Remember that. I'm going to make you forget how he died and remember only that we are together now. He wouldn't have you mourn for him."

* * *

He was right. The shock did become modified as the weeks passed. I taught myself to accept the fact that my father's death was not so very unusual. I must remember that I had a husband to consider now and, as he was so anxious for me to put the tragedy behind me and be happy, I must do my best to please him.

And it was easier as we went farther from the island.

Roc was charming to me during those days; and I felt that he was determined to make me forget all the sadness.

Once he said to me: "We can do no good by brooding, Favel. Let's put it behind us. Let's remember that by a wonderful chance we met and fell in love."

We stayed for two weeks in the South of France and each day, it seemed, took me a step farther away from the tragedy. We hired an Alfa Romeo and Roc took a particular delight in the hairpin bends, laughing at me as I held my breath while he skillfully took the turns. The scenery delighted me, but as

I gazed at terraces of orange stucco villas which seemed to cling to the cliff face, Roc would snap his fingers.

"Wait," he would say, "just wait till you see Pendorric."

It was a joke between us that not all the beauty of the Maritime Alps nor the twists, turns, and truly majestic gorges to be discovered on the Corniche road could compare with his native Cornwall.

Often I would say it for him while we sat under a multicolored umbrella in opulent Cannes or sunned ourselves on the beach of humbler Menton: "But of course this is nothing compared with Cornwall." Then we would laugh together and people passing would smile at us, knowing us for lovers.

At first I thought my gaiety was a little forced. I was so eager to please Roc and there was no doubt that nothing delighted him more than to see me happy. Then I found that I did not have to pretend. I was becoming so deeply in love with my husband that the fact that we were together could overwhelm me and all else seemed of little importance. Roc was eager to wean me from my sorrow; and because he was the sort of man who was determined to have his way he could not fail. I was conscious of his strength, of his dominating nature, and I was glad of it because I would not have wished him to be different.

But I grew suddenly uneasy one night in Nice. We had driven in from Villefranche and, as we did so, noticed the dark clouds which hung over the mountains—a contrast to the sparkling scene. Roc had suggested that we visit the Casino and I, as usual, readily fell in with his suggestion. He took a turn at the tables and I was reminded then of the light in his eyes when he had sat with my father in the studio. There was the same burning excitement that used to alarm me when I saw it in my father's.

He won that night and was elated; but I couldn't hide my concern and when, in our hotel bedroom, I betrayed this he laughed at me.

"Don't worry," he said, "I'd never make the mistake of risking what I couldn't afford to lose."

"You're a gambler," I accused.

He took my face in his hands. "Well, why not?" he demanded. "Life's supposed to be a gamble, isn't it, so perhaps it's the gamblers who come off best."

He was teasing me as he used to before my father's death and, I assured myself, it was only teasing; but that incident seemed to mark a change in our relationship. I was over the first shock; there was no need to treat me with such delicate care. I knew then that Roc would always be a gambler no matter how I tried to persuade him against it, and I experienced once more those faint twinges of apprehension.

*   *   *

I began to think of the future, and there were occasions when I was uneasy. This happened first during the night when I awoke suddenly from a hazy dream in which I knew myself to be in some unspecified danger.

I lay in the darkness, aware of Roc beside me, sleeping deeply, and I thought: What is happening to me? Two months ago I did not know this man. My home was the studio on the island with my father, and now another artist works in the studio and I have no father.

I had a husband. But what did I know of him?—except that I was in love with him. Wasn't that enough? Ours was a deeply passionate relationship and I could at times become so completely absorbed in our need of each other that this seemed all I asked. But that was only a part of marriage. I considered the marriage of my parents and remembered how they had relied on each other and felt that all was well as long as the other was close by.

And here I was waking in the night after a nightmare which hung about me, seeming like a vague warning.

That night I really looked the truth in the eye, which was that I knew very little of the man I had married or of the sort of life to which he was taking me.

I made up my mind that I must have a talk with him and, when we drove into the mountains next day, I decided to do so. The fears of the night had departed and somehow seemed ridiculous by day, yet I told myself it was absurd that I should know so little of his background.

We found a small hotel where we stopped to have lunch.

I was thoughtful as we ate and, when Roc asked the reason, I blurted out: "I want to know more about Pendorric and your family."

"I'm ready for the barrage. Start firing."

"First the place itself. Let me try to see it and then you fill it with the people."

He leaned his elbows on the table and narrowed his eyes as though he were looking at something far away, which he could not see very clearly.

"The house first," he said. "It's about four hundred years

old in some parts. Some of it has been restored. In fact there was a house there in the Dark Ages I believe—so the story goes. . . . We're built on the cliff rock some five hundred yards from the sea; I believe we were much farther from it in the beginning but the sea has a habit of encroaching, you know, and in hundreds of years it advances. We're built of gray Cornish granite calculated to stand against the southwest gales; as a matter of fact over the front archway—one of the oldest parts of the house—there's a motto in Cornish cut into the stone. Translated into English it is: 'When we build we believe we build forever.' I remember my father's lifting me up to read that and telling me that we Pendorrics were as much a part of the house as that old archway and that Pendorrics would never rest in their graves if the time came when the family left the place."

"How wonderful to belong to such a family!"

"You do now."

"But as a kind of outsider . . . as all the people who married into the family must be."

"You'll soon become one of us. It's always been so with Pendorric brides. In a short time they're upholding the family more enthusiastically than those who started life with the name Pendorric."

"Are you a sort of squire of the neighborhood?"

"Squires went out of fashion years ago. We own most of the farms in the district and customs die harder in Cornwall than anywhere else in England. We cling to old traditions and superstitions. I'm sure that a practical young woman like yourself is going to be very impatient with some of the stories you hear; but bear with us—we're the fey Cornish, remember, and you married into us."

"I'm sure I shan't complain. Tell me some more."

"Well, there's the house—a solid rectangle facing north, south, east, and west. Northwards we look over the hills to the farmlands—south we face straight out to sea, and east and west give you magnificent views of a coastline that is one of the most beautiful in England and the most treacherous. When the tide goes out you'll see the rocks like sharks' teeth and you can imagine what happens to boats that find their way onto those. Oh, and I forgot to mention there's one view we don't much like from the east windows. It's known to us in the family as Polhorgan's Folly. A house which looks like a replica of our own. We loathe it. We detest it. We nightly pray that it will be blown into the sea."

"You don't mean that, of course."

"Don't I?" His eyes flashed, but they were laughing at me.

"Of course you don't. You'd be horrified if it were."

"There's actually no fear of it. It has stood there for fifty years—an absolute sham—trying to pretend to those visitors who stare up at it from the beach below that it is Pendorric of glorious fame."

"But who built it?"

He was looking at me and there was something malicious in his gaze which alarmed me faintly because for a second it seemed as though it was directed at me; but then I realized that it was dislike of the owner of Polhorgan's Folly which inspired it.

"A certain Josiah Fleet, better known as Lord Polhorgan. He went there fifty years ago from the Midlands where he had made a fortune from some commodity—I've forgotten what—he liked our coast, he liked our climate, and decided to build himself a mansion. He did and spent a month or so there each year, until eventually he settled in altogether and took his name from the cove below him."

"You certainly don't like him much. Or are you exaggerating?"

Roc shrugged his shoulders. "Perhaps. It's really the natural enmity between the *nouveau* poor and the *nouveau riche*."

"Are we very poor?"

"By the standards of my Lord Polhorgan . . . yes. I suppose what annoys us is that sixty years ago we were the lords of the manor and he was trudging the streets of Birmingham, Leeds, or Manchester—I can never remember which—barefooted. Industry and natural cunning made him a millionaire. Sloth and natural indolence brought us to our genteel poverty, when we wonder from week to week whether we shall have to call in the National Trust to take over our home and show it at half a crown a time to the curious public who want to know how the aristocracy once lived."

"I believe you're bitter."

"And you're critical. You're on the side of industry and natural cunning. Oh, Favel, what a perfect union! You see, you're all that I'm not. You're going to keep me in order marvelously!"

"You're laughing at me again."

He gripped my hand so hard that I winced. "It's my nature, darling, to laugh at everything, and sometimes the more serious I am the more I laugh."

"I don't think you would ever allow anyone to keep you in order."

"Well, you chose me, darling, and if I was what you wanted when you made the choice you'd hardly want to change me, would you?"

"I hope," I said seriously, "that we shan't change, that we shall always be as happy as we have been up till now."

For a moment there was the utmost tenderness in his expression, then he was laughing again.

"I told you," he said, "I've made a very good match."

I was suddenly struck by the thought that perhaps his family, who I imagined loved Pendorric as much as he did, would be disappointed that he had married a girl with no money, but I was touched and very happy because he had married me, who could bring him nothing. I felt my nightmare evaporating and I wondered on what it could possibly have been founded.

"Are you friendly with this Lord Polhorgan?" I asked quickly to hide my emotion.

"Nobody could be friendly with him. We're polite to each other. We don't see much of him. He's a sick man well guarded by a nurse and a staff of servants."

"And his family?"

"He quarreled with them all. And now he lives alone in his glory. There are a hundred rooms at Polhorgan . . . all furnished in the most flamboyant manner. I believe though that dust sheets perpetually cover the flamboyance. You see why we call it the Folly."

"Poor old man!"

"I knew your soft heart would be touched. You may meet him. He'll probably consider that he should receive the new Bride of Pendorric."

"Why do you always refer to me as the Bride of Pendorric . . . as though in capital letters?"

"Oh, it's a saying at Pendorric. There are lots of crazy things like that."

"And your family?"

"Now things are very different at Pendorric. Some of our furniture has been standing where it does at this moment for four hundred years. We've got old Mrs. Penhalligan, who is a daughter of Jesse and Lizzie Pleydell, and the Pleydells have looked after the Pendorrics for generations. There's always a faithful member of that family to see that we're cared for. Old Mrs. Penhalligan is a fine housekeeper, and she mends the counterpanes and curtains which are constantly falling apart. She keeps the servants in order at the same time —as well as ourselves. She's sixty-five but her daughter Maria, who never married, will follow in her footsteps."

"And your sister?"

"My sister's married to Charles Chaston, who worked as an agent when my father traveled a good deal. He manages the home farm with me now. They live in the northern section of the house. We shall have the south. Don't be afraid that you're going to be hemmed in by relations. It isn't a bit like that at Pendorric. You need never see the rest of the family if you don't want to, except at meals. We all eat together—it's an old family custom—and anyway the servant problem makes it a necessity now. You'll be surprised at the family customs we preserve. Really, you'll think you've stepped back a hundred years. I do myself after I've been away for a while."

"And your sister, what is her name?"

"Morwenna. Our parents believed in following the family traditions and giving us Cornish names wherever possible. Hence the Petrocs and Morwennas. The twins are Lowella and Hyson . . . Hyson was my mother's maiden name. Lowella refers to herself as Lo and her sister as Hy. I suspect she has a nickname for all of us. She's an incorrigible creature."

"How old are the twins?"

"Twelve."

"Are they at school?"

"No. They do go from time to time but Lowella has an unfortunate habit of running away and dragging Hyson with her. She always says that they can't be happy anywhere but at Pendorric. We've compromised at the moment by having a governess—a trained schoolmistress. It was difficult getting the permission of the educational authorities . . . but Charles and Morwenna want to keep them at home for a year or so until the child becomes more stable. You'll have to beware of Lowella."

"How?"

"It'll be all right if she likes you. But she gets up to tricks. Hyson is different. She's the quiet one. They look exactly alike but their temperaments are completely different. Thank heaven for that. No household could tolerate two Lowellas."

"What about your parents?"

"They're dead and I remember very little about them. My

mother died when we were five and an aunt looked after us.
She still comes to stay quite often and keeps a suite of
rooms at Pendorric. Our father lived abroad a great deal when
Charles came in. Charles is fifteen years older than Morwenna."

"You said your mother died when *we* were five. Who else
besides you?"

"Didn't I mention that Morwenna and I were twins?"

"No. You said that Lowella and Hyson were."

"Well, twins run in families, you know. Quite obviously
they've started to run in ours."

"Is Morwenna like you?"

"We're not identical like Lowella and Hyson. But people
say they can see a resemblance."

"Roc," I said leaning forward, "you know, I'm beginning to
feel I can't wait to meet this family of yours."

"That's settled it," he replied. "It's time we went home."

*   *   *

So I was, in a measure, prepared for Pendorric.

We had left London after lunch and it was eight o'clock before we got off the train.

Roc had said that he wished we could have motored down
because he wanted to make my crossing of the Tamar something of a ceremony.

However he had arranged that his car should be waiting at
the station so that he could drive me home. Old Toms, the
chauffeur-gardener and man-of-all-work at Pendorric, had
driven it in that morning.

So I found myself sitting beside Roc in his rather shabby
Daimler and feeling a mingling of longing and apprehension,
which seemed natural enough in the circumstances.

I was very anxious to make a good impression. I had suddenly realized what an odd position I was in, for in this new
life to which I was going I knew no one except my husband.

I was in a strange country—for the island had been my
home—and without friends. If Esther McBane had been in
England I should not have felt quite so lonely. But Esther was
far away in Rhodesia now, as deeply absorbed in her new
life as I was becoming in mine. There had been other school
friends, but none as close as Esther, and as we had never exchanged letters after we left school those friendships had
lapsed.

But what foolish thoughts these were! I might not have old friends, but I had a husband.

Roc swung the car out of the station yard and, as we left the town, the quiet of the summer evening closed in about us. We were in a narrow winding lane with banks on either side, which were dotted with wild roses, and there was the sweet smell of honeysuckle in the air.

"Is it far to Pendorric?" I asked.

"Eight miles or so. The sea is ahead of us, the moor's behind us. We'll do some walking on the moors . . . or riding. Can you ride?"

"I'm afraid not."

"I'll teach you. You're going to make this place home, Favel. Some people never can, but I think you will."

"I believe I shall."

We were silent and I studied the landscape avidly. The houses which we passed were little more than cottages, not by any means beautiful—indeed they struck me as rather grim—all made of that gray Cornish stone. I fancied I caught a whiff of the sea as we slowly climbed a steep hill and went forward into wooded country. We were soon descending again on the other side of the hill. "When you see the sea you'll know we're not far from home," Roc told me, and almost immediately we began to climb again.

At the top of the hill he stopped the car and, putting his arm along the back of the seat, pointed towards the sea.

"Can you see the house there, right on the edge of the cliff? That's the Folly. You can't see Pendorric from here because there's a hill in the way; but it's a little to the right."

The Folly looked almost like a medieval castle.

"I wonder he didn't supply a drawbridge and a moat," murmured Roc. "Though heaven knows it would have been difficult to have had a moat up there. Still all the more laudable that he should achieve it."

He started up the car and when he had gone half a mile I caught my first glimpse of Pendorric.

It was so like the other house that I was astonished.

"They look close together from here," said Roc, "but there's a good mile between them on the coast road—of course as the crow flies they're a little nearer—but you can understand the wrath of the Pendorrics, can't you, to find *that* set up where they just can't get it out of their sight."

We had now reached a major road and we sped along this until we came to a turning and began to plunge down one of the steepest hills we had come upon as yet. The banks were covered with the wild flowers which I had noticed before; and stubby fir trees with their resinous scent.

At the bottom of the hill we struck the cliff road, and then I saw the coast in all its glory. The water was quiet on that night and I could hear the gentle swish as it washed against the rocks. The cliffs were covered in grass and bracken and dotted here and there with clumps of pink, red, and white valerian; the sweep of the bay was magnificent. The tide was out and in the evening light I saw those malignant rocks jutting cruelly out of the shallow water.

And there half a mile ahead of us was Pendorric itself, and I caught my breath, for it was awe-inspiring. It towered above the sea a massive rectangle of gray stone, with crenelated towers and an air of impregnability, noble and arrogant as though defying the sea and the weather and any who came against it.

"This is your home, my dear," said Roc and I could hear the pride in his voice.

"It's . . . superb."

"So you're not unhappy? I'm glad you're seeing it for the first time. Otherwise I might have thought you married *it* rather than me."

"I would never marry a house!"

"No, you're too honest . . . too full of common sense . . . in fact too wonderful. That's why I fell in love with you and determined to marry you."

We were roaring uphill again, and now that we were closer the house certainly dominated the landscape. There were lights in some of the windows and I saw the arch leading to the north portico.

"The grounds," Roc explained, "are on the south side. We can approach the house from the south; there are four porticos —north, south, east, and west. But we'll go into the north tonight because Morwenna and Charlie will be waiting for us there. Why, look," he went on, and following his gaze I saw a slight figure in riding breeches and scarlet blouse, black hair flying, running toward us. Roc slowed down the car and she leapt onto the running board. Her face was brown with sun and weather, her eyes were long and black and very like Roc's.

"I wanted to be the first to see the bride!" she shouted.

"And you always get your way," answered Roc. "Favel, this is Lowella, of whom beware."

"Don't listen to him," said the girl. "I expect I'll be your friend."

"Thank you," I said. "I hope you will."

The black eyes studied me curiously. "I said she'd be fair," she went on. "I was certain."

"Well, you're impeding our progress," Roc told her. "Either hop in or get off."

"I'll stay here," she announced. "Drive in."

Roc obeyed and we went slowly towards the house.

"They're all waiting to meet you," Lowella told me. "We're very excited. We've all been trying to guess what you'll be like. In the village they're all waiting to see you too. Every time one of us goes down they say, 'And when will the bride be coming to Pendorric?' "

"I hope they'll be pleased with me."

Lowella looked at her uncle mischievously and I thought again how remarkably like him she was. "Oh, it was time he married," she said. "We were getting worried."

"You see I was right to warn you," put in Roc. "She's the *enfant terrible.*"

"And not such an infant," insisted Lowella. "I'm twelve now, you know."

"You grow more terrible with the years. I tremble to think what you'll be like at twenty."

We had now passed through the gates and I saw the great stone arch looming ahead. Beyond it was a portico guarded on either side by two huge, carved lions, battered by the years but still looking fierce as though warning any to be wary of entering.

And there was a woman—so like Roc that I knew she was his twin sister—and behind her a man, whom I guessed to be her husband and father of the twins.

Morwenna came towards the car. "Roc! So you're here at last. And this is Favel. Welcome to Pendorric, Favel."

I smiled up at her and for those first moments I was glad that she looked so like Roc, because it made me feel that she was not quite a stranger. Her dark hair was thick with a slight natural wave and it grew to a widow's peak which in the half light gave the impression that she was wearing a sixteenth-century cap. She wore a dress of emerald green linen which became her dark hair and eyes and there were gold rings in her ears.

"I'm so glad to meet you at last," I said. "I do hope this isn't a shock to you."

"Nothing my brother does ever shocks us, really, because we're expecting surprises."

"You see I've brought them up in the right way," said Roc lightly. "Oh, and here's Charlie."

My hand was gripped so firmly that I winced. I was hoping Charles Chaston didn't notice it as I looked up into his plump, bronzed face.

"We've all been eagerly waiting to see you, ever since we heard you were coming," he told me.

I saw that Lowella was dancing round us in a circle; with her flying hair, and as she was chanting something to herself which might have been an incantation, she reminded me of a witch.

"Oh Lowella, do stop," cried her mother with a little laugh. "Where's Hyson?"

Lowella lifted her arms in a gesture which implied she had no idea.

"Go and find her. She'll want to say hello to her Aunt Favel."

"We're not calling her aunt," said Lowella. "She's too young. She's just going to be Favel. You'll like that better, won't you, Favel?"

"Yes, it sounds more friendly."

"There you see," said Lowella, and she ran into the house.

Morwenna slipped her arm through mine and Roc came up and took the other as he called: "Where's Toms? Toms! Come and bring in our baggage."

I heard a voice say: "Aye, sir. I be coming."

But before he appeared Morwenna and Roc were leading me through the portico, and with Charles hovering behind we entered the house.

I was in an enormous hall at either end of which was a beautiful curved staircase leading to a gallery. On the paneled walls were swords and shields and at the foot of each staircase a suit of armor.

"This is our wing," Morwenna told me. "It's a most convenient house, really, being built round a quadrangle. It is almost like four houses in one and it was built with the intention of keeping Pendorrics together in the days of large families. I believe years ago the house was crowded. Only a few servants lived in the attics; the rest of them were in the cottages. There are six of them side by side, most picturesque unsanitary . . . until Roc and Charles did something about still draw on them for help; and we only keep Toms and his wife and daughter Hetty, and Mrs. Penhalligan and her daughter Maria living in. A change from the old days. I expect you're hungry."

I told her we had had dinner on the train.

"Then we'll have a snack later. You'll want to see something of the house, but perhaps you'd like to go to your own part first."

I said I should, and as I spoke my eye was caught by a portrait which hung on the wall of the gallery. It was a picture of a fair-haired young woman in a clinging blue gown which showed her shapely shoulders; her hair was piled high above her head and one ringlet hung over her shoulder. She clearly belonged to the late eighteenth century, and I thought that her picture, placed as it was, dominated the gallery and hall.

"How charming!" I said.

"Ah yes, one of the Brides of Pendorric," Morwenna told me.

There it was again—that phrase which I had heard so often.

"She looks beautiful . . . and so happy."

"Yes, she's my great great great . . . one loses count of the greats . . . grandmother," Morwenna said. "She was happy when that was painted, but she died young."

I found it difficult to take my eyes from the picture because there was something so appealing about that young face.

"I thought, Roc," went on Morwenna, "that now you're married you'd want the big suite."

"Thanks," Roc replied. "That's exactly what I did want."

Morwenna turned to me. "The wings of the house are all connected. You don't have to use the separate entrances unless you wish to. So if you come up to the gallery I'll take you through."

"There must be hundreds of rooms."

"Eighty. Twenty in each of the four parts. I think it's much larger than it was in the beginning. A lot of it has been restored but because of that motto over the arch they've been very careful to make it seem that what was originally built has lasted."

We went past the suit of armor and up the stairs to the gallery.

"One thing," said Morwenna, "when you know your own wing you know all the others; you just have to imagine the rooms facing different directions."

She led the way and with Roc's arm still in mine we fol-

lowed. When we reached the gallery we went through a side
door which led to another corridor in which were beautiful
marble figures set in alcoves.

"Not the best time to see the house," commented Morwenna.
"It's neither light nor dark."

"She'll have to wait till the morning to explore," added Roc.

I looked through one of the windows down onto a large
quadrangle in which grew some of the most magnificent
hydrangeas I had ever seen.

I remarked on them and we paused to look down.

"The colors are wonderful in sunlight," Morwenna told me.
"They thrive here. It's because we're never short of rain and
there's hardly ever a frost. Besides, they're well sheltered in
the quadrangle."

It looked a charming place, that quadrangle. There was
a pond, in the center of which was a dark statue which I later
discovered was of Hermes; and there were two magnificent
palm trees growing down there so that it looked rather like
an oasis in a desert. In between the paving stones clumps of
flowering shrubs bloomed and there were several white seats
with gilded decorations.

Then I noticed all the windows which looked down on it
and it occurred to me that it was a pity because one would
never be able to sit there without a feeling of being over-
looked.

Roc explained to me that there were four doors all leading
into it, one from each wing.

We moved along the corridor through another door and
Roc said that we were now in the south wing—our own. We
went up a staircase and Morwenna went ahead of us, and when
she threw open a door we entered a large room with enormous windows facing the sea. The deep-red velvet curtains
had been drawn back and when I saw the seascape stretched
out before me, I gave a cry of pleasure and at once went to
the window. I stood there looking out across the bay; the
cliffs looked stark and menacing in the twilight and I could
just glimpse the rugged outline of the rocks. The smell and
the gentle whispering of the sea seemed to fill the room.

Roc was behind me. "It's what everyone does," he said.
"They never glance at the room; they look at the view."

"The views are just as lovely from the east and west side,"
said Morwenna, "and very much the same."

She turned a switch and the light from a large chandelier
hanging from the center of the ceiling made the room daz-

zlingly bright. I turned from the window and saw the four-poster bed, with the long stool at its foot, the tallboy, the cabinets—all belonging to an earlier generation, a generation of exquisite grace and charm.

"But it's lovely!" I said.

"We flatter ourselves that we have the best of both worlds," Morwenna told me. "We made an old powder closet into a bathroom." She opened a door which led from the bedroom and disclosed a modern bathroom. I looked at it longingly and Roc laughed.

"You have a bath," he said. "I'll go and see what Toms is doing about the baggage. Afterwards we'll have something to eat and perhaps I'll take you for a walk in the moonlight —if there's any to be had."

I said I thought it was an excellent idea, and they left me.

When I was alone I went once more to the windows to gaze out at that magnificent view. I stood for some minutes, my eyes on the horizon, as I watched the intermittent flashes of the lighthouse.

Then I went into the bathroom, where bath salts and talcum powder had all been laid out for me—my sister-in-law's thoughtfulness, I suspected. She was obviously anxious to make me welcome and I felt it had been a very pleasant home-coming.

If only I could have thought of Father at work in his studio I could have been very happy. But I had to start a new life; I must stop fretting. I had to be gay. I owed that to Roc; and he was the type of man who would want his wife to be gay.

I went into the bathroom, ran a bath, and spent about half an hour luxuriating in it. When I came out Roc had not returned but my bags had been put in the room. I unpacked a small one and changed from my suit to a silk dress; and I was doing my hair at the dressing table, which had a three-sided mirror, when there was a knock at the door.

"Come in," I called, and turning saw a young woman and a child. I thought at first that the child was Lowella and I smiled at her. She did not return the smile but regarded me gravely, while the young woman said: "Mrs. Pendorric, I am Rachel Bective, the children's governess. Your husband asked me to show you the way down when you were ready."

"How do you do?" I said, and I was astonished by the change in Lowella.

There was an air of efficiency about Rachel Bective, whom

I guessed to be round about thirty, and I remembered what
Roc had told me about a schoolmistress looking after the
twins' education. Her hair was a sandy color and her brows
and lashes so fair that she looked surprised; her teeth were
sharp and white. I did not warm towards her. She seemed to
me to be obviously summing me up and her manner was calculating and critical.

"This is Hyson," she said; "I believe you met her sister."

"Oh, I see." I smiled at the child. "I thought you were
Lowella."

"I knew you did." She was almost sullen.

"You are so much like her."

"I only *look* like her."

"Are you ready to come down?" asked Rachel Bective.
"There's to be a light supper because I believe you had dinner
on the train."

"Yes, we did, and I'm quite ready."

For the first time since I had come into the house I felt
uncomfortable, and was glad when Rachel Bective led the way
along the corridor and down the staircase.

We came to a gallery and I did not realize that it was not
the same one which I had seen from the north side until I
noticed the picture there and I knew that I had never seen that
before.

It was the picture of a woman in a riding jacket. The
habit was black and she was very fair; she wore a hard black
hat and about it was a band of blue velvet which hung down
forming a snood at the back. She was very beautiful, but her
large blue eyes, which were the same color as the velvet band
and snood, were full of brooding sadness. Moreover the picture had been painted so that it was impossible to escape
those eyes. They followed you wherever you went and even in
that first moment I thought they were trying to convey some
message.

"What a magnificent picture!" I cried.

"It's Barbarina," said Hyson, and for a moment her face
was filled with vitality and she looked exactly as Lowella
had when she had welcomed us.

"What an extraordinary name! And who was she?"

"She was my grandmother," Hyson told me proudly.

"She died . . . tragically, I believe," put in Rachel Bective.

"How dreadful! And she looks so beautiful."

I remembered then that I had seen a picture of another

beautiful woman in the north hall when I had arrived and had heard that she, too, had died young.

Hyson said in a voice which seemed to hold a note of hysteria: "*She* was one of the Brides of Pendorric."

"Well, I suppose she was," I said, "since she married your grandfather."

This Hyson was a strange child; she had seemed so lifeless a moment ago; now she was vital and excited.

"She died twenty-five years ago when my mother and Uncle Roc were five years old."

"How very sad!"

"You'll have to have *your* picture painted, Mrs. Pendorric," said Rachel Bective.

"I hadn't thought of it."

"I'm sure Mr. Pendorric will want it done."

"He hasn't said anything about it."

"It's early days yet. Well, I think we should go. They'll be waiting."

We went along the gallery and through a door and were walking round the corridor facing the quadrangle again. I noticed that Hyson kept taking covert glances at me. I thought she seemed rather a neurotic child, and there was a quality about the governess which I found distinctly disturbing.

* * *

I woke up in the night and for a few seconds wondered where I was. Then I saw the enormous windows, heard the murmuring of the sea, and it sounded like the echo of voices I had heard in my dream.

I could smell the tang of seaweed and the freshness of the ocean. The rhythm of the waves seemed to keep time with Roc's breathing.

I raised myself and, leaning on my elbow, looked at him. There was enough moonlight to show me the contours of his face, which looked as though it had been cut out of stone. He appeared different in repose and, realizing how rarely I saw him thus, again I had that feeling that I was married to a stranger.

I shook off my fancies. I reminded myself that I had sustained a great shock. My thoughts were so often with my father and I wondered again and again what he must have experienced in that dreadful moment when the cramp had overtaken him and he realized that he could not reach land and there was no one at hand to help him. He had come face to face with death and that must have been a moment of intense horror; and what seemed so terrible was that at that moment Roc and I were laughing together in the kitchen of the studio.

If Roc had only stayed with him. . . .

I wished I could stop thinking of my father, sitting in the lonely studio in the darkness, of the anxiety I had seen on his face when I had come upon him and Roc together.

I must have been dreaming about the island and my father for what was disturbing me was the memory of relief I had fancied I saw in Roc's face at the time of the tragedy. It was almost as though he had believed it was the best possible thing that could have happened.

Surely I must have imagined that. But when had I started to imagine it? Was it the hangover from some dream?

I lay down quietly so as not to disturb him, and after a while I slept. But again I was troubled by dreams. I could hear a murmur like background music and it might have been the movement of the waves or Roc's breathing beside me; then I heard the shrill laughter of Lowella, or it might have been Hyson, as she cried out: "Two Brides of Pendorric died young. . . . Now you are a Bride of Pendorric."

I remembered that dream next morning, and what had seemed full of significance in my sleep now seemed the natural result of a day crammed with new experiences.

* * *

The next day the sun was shining brilliantly. I stood at a window watching the light on the water, and it was as though some giant had thrown down a handful of diamonds.

Roc came and stood behind me, putting his hands on my shoulders.

"I can see you are coming under the spell of *that* Pendorric as well as this one."

I turned and smiled at him. He looked so contented that I threw my arms about his neck. He waltzed round the room with me and said: "It is good to have you here at Pendorric. This morning I'm going to take you for a drive and show you off to the locals. You're going to find them very inquisitive. This afternoon I'll have to go into things with old Charles. I've been away a long time—longer than I planned for—and there'll be a little catching up to do. You can go off and explore on your own then, or perhaps Lowella will join you."

I said: "The other child is quite different, isn't she?"

"Hyson?"

"And yet they're so alike I couldn't tell which was which."

"You get to know the slight difference after a while. Perhaps it's in the voices. I'm not sure, but we can usually tell. It's strange, but with identicals you sometimes get two entirely different temperaments. It's as though characteristics have been divided into two neat little piles—one for one, one for the other. However, Rachel takes good care of them."

"Oh . . . the governess."

"That makes her sound rather Victorian, and there's nothing Victorian about Rachel. Actually she's more a friend of the family. She was an old schoolfellow of Morwenna's. Ready?"

We went out of the room and I followed where Roc led, realizing that I must expect to be a little vague as yet about the geography of the house.

We were on the third floor and it seemed that there were linking doors to all wings on all floors. I looked down at the quadrangle as we passed the windows. It was true that it was quite charming in sunlight. I imagined myself sitting under one of the palm trees with a book. It would be the utmost peace. Then I looked up at the windows.

"A pity . . ." I murmured.

"What?" asked Roc.

"That you'd always have the feeling of not being alone down there."

"Oh . . . you mean the windows. They're all corridor windows, not the sort for sitting at."

"I suppose that does make a difference."

I had not noticed that we had come round to the north wing until Roc paused at a door, knocked, and went in.

The twins were sitting at a table, exercise books before them; and with them sat Rachel Bective. She smiled rather lazily when she saw me, reminding me of a tortoise-shell cat who was sleeping pleasantly and is suddenly disturbed.

"Hello, Favel!" cried Lowella leaping up. "*And* Uncle Roc!"

Lowella flung her arms about Roc's neck, lifted her feet from the ground, and was swung round and round.

Rachel Bective looked faintly amused; Hyson's face was expressionless.

"Help!" cried Roc. "Come along, Favel . . . Rachel . . . rescue me."

"Any excuse to stop lessons," murmured Rachel.

Lowella released her uncle. "If I want to find excuses ways can," she said gravely. "That was meant to sa glad I was to see him and the Bride."

"I want you to entertain her this afternoon," said Roc, "while I'll be working. Will you?"

"Of course." Lowella smiled at me. "I've such lots to tell you."

"I'm looking forward to hearing." I included Hyson in my smile but she quickly looked away.

"Now you're here," said Roc, "you must have a look at the old schoolroom. It's a real relic from the past. Generations of Pendorrics sat at that table. My grandfather carved his initials on it and was sternly punished by his governess."

"How was he punished?" Lowella wanted to know.

"Probably with a big stick . . . or made to fast on bread and water and learn pages of *Paradise Lost.*"

"I'd rather the stick," said Lowella.

"You wouldn't. You'd hate that," put in Hyson surprisingly.

"No, I'd love it, because I'd take the stick and start beating whoever was beating me." Lowella's eyes shone at the prospect.

"There you are, Rachel, that's a warning," said Roc.

He had gone to the cupboard and showed me books which must have been there for years; some were exercise books filled with the unformed writing of children; there were several slates and pencil boxes.

"You'll have to have a good look when it's not lesson time, Favel. I believe Rachel's getting a little impatient with us."

He flashed a smile at Rachel, and because I thought I saw intimacy in it I felt a pang of jealousy. Until now it had not occurred to me that the easy manner in which my friendship with Roc had progressed was due to his easy-going friendly nature. Now it occurred to me that he was very friendly with Rachel—and she with him, for if his smile for her was warm, hers was a good deal warmer. I began to wonder then how deep a friendship it was.

I was glad to leave the schoolroom, the exuberant Lowella, the silent Hyson, and Rachel, who was too friendly—towards Roc. There were lots of questions I wanted to ask him about Rachel Bective but I felt that I might betray my jealousy if I did, so I decided to shelve the subject for the time being.

When I was sitting in the car with Roc I felt happy again. He was right when he had suggested that an entirely new life would help me to put the past behind me. So many new impressions were being superimposed on those old ones that they now seemed to belong to another life.

Roc put his hand over mine and I would have said he was a very contented man that morning.

"I can see you've taken to Pendorric like a duck to water."

"It's all so intriguing, so beautiful . . . and the family is interesting."

He grimaced. "We're flattered. I'm going to drive you past the Folly; then you can see what a sham it is."

We drove down the steep road and up again and then we were on a level with Polhorgan. At first glance it appeared to be as old as Pendorric.

"They've deliberately tried to make the stone look old. The gargoyles over the front porch are crumbling artistically."

"There's no sign of life."

"There never is from this side. The master of the house has his apartments on the south side, facing the sea. He owns the beach below and he has magnificent flower gardens laid out on the cliffs. Much grander than ours. He bought the land from my grandfather."

"He has a wonderful view."

"That's as well because he spends most of the time in his room. His heart won't allow him to do otherwise."

We had passed the house and Roc went on: "I'm taking this road which will carry us back to Pendorric because I want you to see our little village. I know you're going to love it."

We had turned back and were going steeply down again to the coast road which led past Pendorric. I gazed at the house in a happy proprietorial way as we passed. In a short time we were roaring up the steep hill to the main road and I could see the sea on our left.

"It's the twists of our coast that make you lose your sense of direction," Roc explained. "This was once an area of terrific volcanic upheaval, which means that the land was flung in all directions. We've been rounding a sort of promontory and we're now coming into the village of Pendorric."

We swooped down again and there it lay—the most enchanting little village I had ever seen. There was the church, its ancient tower about which the ivy clung, clearly of Norman architecture, and it was set in the midst of the graveyard. On one side the stones were dark with age and on the other they were white and new-looking. There was the vicarage, a gray house set in a hollow with its lawn and gardens on an incline. Beyond the church was the row of cottages which Morwenna had mentioned; they had thatched roofs and tiny windows and were all joined together—the whole six of them. I imagined they were of the same period as the church.

Not far from the cottages was a garage with living quarters above it. "It was once the blacksmith's forge," Roc explained. "The Bonds, who lived there, have been blacksmiths for generations. It broke old Jim Bond's heart when there were no longer enough horses in the district to make the smithy worth-while, but they have compromised. The old forge is still in existence and I often pull up here to have the horses shod."

He slowed down and called: "Jim! Hi, Jim!"

A window above was thrown open and a handsome woman appeared there. Her black hair fell loosely about her shoulders and her scarlet blouse seemed too tight for her. She had the look of a gypsy.

"Morning, Mr. Roc," she said.

"Why hello, Dinah."

"Nice to see you back, Mr. Roc."

Roc waved a hand and at that moment a man came out to us.

"Morning, Jim," said Roc.

He was a man in his fifties, an enormous man, just as one would have imagined a blacksmith should look; his sleeves were rolled up to display his brawny muscles. Roc went on: "I've brought my wife along to show her the old forge and get her acquainted with the village."

"I'm glad to see you, m'am," said Jim. "Would 'ee care to come in and have a drop of our old cider?"

I said I should be delighted and we got out of the car and went into the blacksmith's shop, where a strawberry roan was actually being shod. The smell of burning hoof filled the air and the young man who was working at the forge said good morning to us. He seemed to be Jim too.

I was told that he was young Jim, the son of old Jim, and that there had been Jim Bonds at the forge for as long as anyone could remember.

"And us reckons there always will be," said old Jim. "Though . . . times change." He looked a little sad.

"You never know when your luck will turn," Roc told him.

Old Jim went to a corner and came out with glasses on a tray. He filled the glasses from a great barrel with a tap at the side, which stood in a corner of the shop.

"The Bonds have always been noted for their cider," Roc explained.

"Oh yes, m'dear," said old Jim. "Me Granny used to keep a live toad in the barrel and 'twas said that hers was a cider as had to be tasted to be believed. Now don't 'ee look scared like. We don't use the old toad now. 'Tis just the juice of good old Cornish apples and the way we Bonds have with 'em."

"It's as potent as ever," said Roc.

"It's very good," I commented.

"Sometimes a bit too much for the foreigners," said old Jim, looking at me as though he hoped I was teetering on the verge of intoxication.

The younger man went on stolidly with his work and hardly looked at us.

Then a door opened and the woman who had looked from the window came in. Her black eyes were sparkling and she swayed her hips as she walked; she was wearing a short full skirt and her shapely legs were bare and brown; her feet, slightly grubby, were in scuffed sandals.

I noticed that all three men were intensely aware of her the moment she came in. Old Jim scowled at her and didn't seem very pleased to see her; young Jim couldn't take his eyes from her; but it was Roc's expression which was not easy to construe. I could see immediately the effect she had on the others, but not on Roc. It was my husband whom I could not understand.

She herself studied me intently, taking in each detail of my appearance. I felt she was a little scornful of my clean linen dress, as she smoothed her hands over her hips and smiled at Roc. It was a familiar and, I thought, even intimate gaze. I was a little ashamed of myself then. Was I overjealous because I had a very attractive husband? I must stop myself wondering what his relationship had been with every young woman he had known before he met me. "This is Dinah, young Mrs. Bond," Roc was explaining to me.

"How do you do?" I said.

She smiled. "I do very well," she answered, "and I'm terrible glad to see Mr. Roc has brought a bride to Pendorric."

"Thank you," said Roc. He drained his glass. "We have a lot to do this morning," he added.

"Can I fill up your car, sir?" asked old Mr. Bond.

"We're all right for a bit, Jim," said Roc, and I had a feeling that he was anxious to get away.

I felt a little dizzy—it was the cider, I told myself—and I was rather glad to get out into the fresh air.

The old man and Dinah stood watching as we drove away. There was a slow smile on Dinah's face.

"Dinah rather broke up the happy party," I said.

"The old fellow hates her, I'm afraid. Life doesn't go smoothly at the old forge since Dinah came to live there."

"She's very attractive."

"That seems to be the majority opinion—including Dinah's. I hope it works out, but I fancy young Jim doesn't have too good a life between the old man and the young woman. Old Jim would have liked to see him marry one of the Pascoe girls from the cottages; they'd have had a little Jim by now. But young Jim—always a docile lad till he fell in love with Dinah—married her and that has not made for peace at the old forge. She's half gypsy and used to live in a caravan in the woods about a mile away."

"Is she a good and faithful wife?"

Roc laughed. "Did she give you the impression that she was?"

"Far from it."

Roc nodded. "Dinah wouldn't pretend to be what she isn't."

He pulled up the car before a gate and a voice called to us: "Why, Mr. Pendorric, how nice to see you back."

A plump rosy-cheeked woman who had a basket full of roses on her arm and cutters in her hand came to the gate and leaned over.

"This is Mrs. Dark," said Roc. "Our vicar's wife."

"So nice of you to call so quickly. We've been so eager to meet Mrs. Pendorric."

We got out of the car and Mrs. Dark opened the gate and took us into a garden which consisted of a lawn bounded by flower beds and enclosed by hedges of macrocarpous.

"The vicar will be very pleased to see you. He's in the study working on his sermon. I hope you'll have some coffee."

We told her we had just had cider at the forge. "And," added Roc, "I'd like to show my wife the old church. Please don't disturb your husband."

"He'd be so sorry if he missed you." She turned to me. "We're so pleased to have you with us, Mrs. Pendorric, and we do hope you're going to enjoy living here and will be with us quite a lot. It's always so pleasant when the big house takes an interest in village things."

"Favel is already enormously interested in Pendorric affairs," said Roc. "She's looking forward to seeing the church."

"I'll go and tell Peter you're here."

We walked through the garden with her and, passing through a hedge, were on the lawn that sloped down to the vicarage. Opposite the house was the church and we went towards it while Mrs. Dark hurried across the lawn to the house.

"We don't seem to be able to escape people this morning," said Roc, taking my arm. "They're all determined to have a look at you. I wanted to show you the church on my own, but Peter Dark will be on our trail soon."

I was conscious of the quietness about us as we passed the yews, which had grown cumbersome with age, and crossed a part of the old graveyard and went into the church.

I immediately felt that I had stepped back in time. There was a thirteenth-century church looking little different, I imagined, from what it had in the days when it had been built. The light filtered through the stained-glass windows onto the altar with its beautiful embroidered cloth and exquisite carving. On the wall, carved in stone, were the names of the vicars from the year 1280.

"They were all local people," Roc explained, "until the Darks came. They come from the Midlands somewhere and they seem to know far more about the place than any of us. Dark is an expert on old Cornish customs. He's collecting them and writing a book on them."

His voice sounded hollow and, as I looked up at him, I was not thinking of the Darks nor the church, but of the expression I had seen in Rachel Bective's eyes that morning and later in those of Dinah Bond.

He was extremely attractive; I had known that the moment I set eyes on him. I had fallen deeply in love with him when I knew little about him. I knew little more now and I was more deeply in love than ever. I was so happy with him except when the doubts came. I was wondering now whether I had married a philanderer who was a perfect lover because he was so experienced; and it was not turning out to be such a happy morning as I had imagined it would.

"Anything wrong?" asked Roc.

"Should there be?"

He took me by the shoulders and held me against him so that I couldn't see his eyes. "I've got you . . . here in Pendorric. How could anything be wrong with that?"

I was startled by the sound of a footstep and breaking away

I saw that a man in clerical clothes had come into the church.

"Hello, Vicar," said Roc easily.

"Susan told me you were here." He advanced towards us, a pleasant-mannered man with a happy alert expression which suggested he found his life one of absorbing interest. He took my hand. "Welcome to Pendorric, Mrs. Pendorric. We're so pleased to have you with us. What do you think of the church? Isn't it fascinating?"

"It is indeed."

"I'm having a wonderful time going through the records. It's always been an ambition of mine to have a living in Cornwall. It's the most intriguing of all the counties . . . don't you think, Mrs. Pendorric?"

"I can well believe it might be."

"So individual. I always say to Susan that as soon as you cross the Tamar you notice the difference. It's like entering a different world . . . far away from prosaic England. Here in Cornwall one feels anything might happen. It's a fey country. It's due to the old superstitions and customs. There are still people here who really do leave bread and milk on their doorsteps for the Little People. And they swear it's disappeared by morning."

"I warned you," said Roc, "that our vicar is enthusiastic about the customs of the place."

"I'm afraid I am. Mrs. Pendorric, are you interested?"

"I hadn't thought much about it. But I believe I could be."

"Good. We must have a talk some time." We started to walk around the church and he went on: "These are the Pendorric pews. Set apart from the rest, you see . . . at the side of the pulpit. I believe in the old days they used to be filled by the family and the retainers. Things have changed considerably."

He pointed to one of the most beautiful of the stained-glass windows. "That was put in in 1792 in memory of Lowella Pendorric. I think the coloring of the glass is the most exquisite I've ever seen."

"You've seen her picture in the north hall," Roc reminded me.

"Oh yes . . . didn't she die young?"

"Yes," said the vicar, "in childbirth with her first child. She was only eighteen. They call her the First Bride . . ."

"The first! But there must have been other brides. I understood there had been Pendorrics for centuries."

The vicar stared blankly at the window. "The sayings become attached and the origins are often steeped in legend. This is a memorial to another Pendorric. A great hero. A friend and supporter of Jonathan Trelawny who is himself buried at Pelynt, not so very far from here. The Trelawny, you know, who defied James II and of whom we sing:

> "And shall Trelawny die?
> Here's twenty thousand Cornishmen will know
> the reason why."

He went on to point out other features of the church and, after renewing his wife's invitation to coffee, he left us, but not before saying that he looked forward to meeting me soon and that if I wanted any information about ancient Cornwall he would be pleased to give it to me.

I thought his kind face was a little anxious as he laid his hand on my arm and said: "It doesn't do to take much notice of these old stories, Mrs. Pendorric. They're interesting just as curiosities, that's all."

He left us outside the church and Roc gave a little sigh. "He can become rather trying when he gets onto his favorite hobby. I began to think we were in for one of his longer lectures and we'd never get rid of him." He looked at his watch. "Now we'll have to hurry. But just a quick look round the old graveyard. Some of the inscriptions are amusing."

We picked our way between the gravestones; some were so old that the words which had been engraved upon them were obliterated altogether; others leaned at grotesque angles.

We stopped before one which must have been more sheltered from the winds and weather than most, for although the date on it was 1779 the words were clearly visible.

Roc began to read them aloud:

> "When you, my friends, behold
> Where now I lie,
> Remember 'tis appointed
> For all men once to die.
> For I myself in prime of life
> The Lord took me away.
> And none that's on the Earth can tell
> How long they in't may stay."

He turned to me, smiling: "Cheerful!" he said. "Your turn.

When Morwenna and I were children we used to come here and read them to each other, taking turns."

I paused before another stone, slightly less ancient, the date being 1842.

>   *"Though some of you perhaps may think*
>   *From dangers to be free.*
>   *Yet in a moment may be sent*
>   *Into the grave like me."*

I stopped and said: "The theme is similar."

"What do you expect here among the dead? It's appropriate enough."

"I'd rather find one that didn't harp so much on death."

"Not so easy," said Roc. "But follow me." He led the way through the long grass and eventually stopped and began to read:

>   *"Tho I was both deaf and dumb*
>   *Much pleasure did I take*
>   *With my finger and my thumb*
>   *All my wants to relate."*

We smiled. "That's more cheerful," I agreed. "I'm so glad he was able to find pleasure through his misfortune."

I turned to look at a stone nearby and as I did so I tripped over the edge of a curb which was hidden in the long grass and I went sprawling headlong over a grave.

Roc picked me up. "All right, darling? Not hurt?"

"I'm all right, thanks." I looked ruefully at my stocking. "A run. That seems to be all the damage."

"Sure?" The anxiety in his eyes made me feel very happy and I forgot my earlier vague misgivings. I assured him that I was all right and he said: "Now some of our neighbors would say that was an omen."

"What sort of an omen?"

"I couldn't tell you. But falling over a grave! I'm sure they'd see something very significant in that. *And* on your first visit to the churchyard, too."

"Life must be very difficult for some people," I mused. "If they're continually seeing omens it doesn't give them much chance of exercising their own free will."

"And you believe in being the master of your fate and captain of your soul, and the fault not being in your stars and so on."

"Yes, I think I do. And you, Roc?"

He took my hand suddenly and kissed it. "As usual you and I are in unison." He looked about him and said: "And that's the family vault over there."

"I must see that."

I made my way to it, more cautiously this time, Roc following. It was an ornate mausoleum of iron and gilt, with three steps leading down to the door.

"Locked away there are numerous dead Pendorrics," said Roc.

I turned away. "I've thought enough about death for one bright summer's morning," I told him.

He put his arms round me and kissed me. Then he released me and went down the three steps to examine the door. I stood back, where he had left me, and saw that on one of the gilded spikes of the railings a wreath of laurels had been put.

I went towards it and looked at it more closely. There was a card attached to it and on it was written:

For Barbarina.

I did not mention the wreath to Roc when he came up to me. He did not seem to have noticed it.

I felt a strong desire to get away from this place of death; away to the sun and the sea.

*　　*　　*

Lunch was a pleasant meal served in one of the small rooms leading off the north hall. I felt that during it I became better acquainted with Morwenna and Charles. The twins and Rachel Bective ate with us. Lowella was garrulous; Hyson said scarcely a word; and Rachel behaved as though she were indeed a friend of the family. She reproved Lowella for overexuberance, and seemed determined to be friendly with me. I wondered whether I had made a hasty judgment when I had decided I did not like her.

After lunch Roc and Charles went off together and I went to my room to get a book. I had decided that I would do what I had wanted to ever since I had seen it—sit under one of the palm trees in the quadrangle.

I took my book and found my way out. It was delightfully cool under the tree and, as I sat gloating on the beauty of the place, it occurred to me there was a look of a Spanish patio about it. The hydrangeas were pink, blue, and white, and multicolored masses of delightful blooms; the lavender scented the air about the water over which bronze Hermes was poised; I saw the flash of gold as the fish swam to and fro.

I tried to read but I found it difficult to concentrate because of those windows which would not allow me to feel alone. I looked up at them. Who would want to peer out at me? I asked myself. And if someone did what would it matter? I knew I was being absurd.

I went back to my book and, as I sat reading there, I heard a movement close behind me, and I was startled when a pair of hands was placed over my eyes and quite unable to repress a gasp as I said rather more sharply than I intended: "Who is it?"

As I touched the hands, which were not very large, I heard a low chuckle and a voice said: "You have to guess."

"Lowella."

The child danced before me. "I can stand on my head," she announced. "I bet you can't."

She proved her words; her long thin legs in navy-blue shorts waving perilously near the pond.

"All right," I told her, "you've proved it."

She turned a somersault and landed on her feet, then stood smiling at me, her face pink with the effort.

"How did you guess Lowella?" she asked.

"I couldn't think of anyone else."

"It might have been Hyson."

"I was certain it was Lowella."

"Hyson doesn't do things like that, does she?"

"I think Hyson's a little shy."

She turned another somersault.

"Are you afraid?" she asked suddenly.

"Afraid of what?"

"Being one of the Brides."

"What brides?"

"The Brides of Pendorric, of course."

She stood very still, her eyes narrowed, as she surveyed me. "You don't know, do you?" she said.

"That's why I'm asking you to tell me."

She came towards me and, putting her hands on my knees, she looked searchingly into my face; she was so close that I could see the long dark eyes which slightly resembled Roc's, and the clear unblemished skin. I was aware again of another quality that reminded me of Roc. I thought I sensed a certain mischief in her look but I was not sure.

"Will you tell me?" I asked.

For an instant she looked over her shoulder and up at the windows, and I went on: "Why did you ask me if I was afraid?"

"Because you're one of the Brides, of course. My Granny was one. Her picture's in the south hall."

"Barbarina," I said.

"Yes. Granny Barbarina. She's dead. You see, she was one of the Brides too."

"This is all very mysterious to me. I don't know why she should die simply because she was a bride."

"There was another Bride too. She's in the north hall. She was called Lowella and she used to haunt Pendorric until Granny Barbarina died. Then she rested in her grave."

"Oh, I see, it's a ghost story."

"In a way, but it's a live person's story too."

"I'd like to hear it."

Again she turned to look at me and I wondered whether she had been warned not to tell me.

"All right." She spoke in a whisper. "When Lowella in the south hall was a bride there was a great banquet to celebrate her wedding. Her father was very rich and lived in North Cornwall and he and her mother and all her sisters and brothers and cousins and aunts came to dance at a ball here at Pendorric. There were violins on the dais and they were all eating and dancing when the woman came into the hall. She had a little girl with her; it was her little girl, you see, and she said it was Petroc Pendorric's too. Not Roc's . . . because this was years and years ago. It was another Pendorric with that name . . . only they didn't call him Roc. This Petroc Pendorric was Lowella's bridegroom, you see, and the woman with the little girl thought he ought to have been hers. This woman lived wild in the woods with her mother, and the mother was a witch so that makes it a curse that works. She cursed Pendorric and the Bride and all the fun stopped then."

"And how long ago did this happen?" I asked.

"Nearly two hundred years."

"It's a long time."

"But it's a story that goes on and on. It doesn't have an ending, you see. It's not only Lowella's story and Barbarina's story . . . it's yours too."

"How could that be?"

"You haven't heard what the curse was. The Bride was to die in the prime of her life and she wouldn't rest in her grave until another Bride had gone to her death . . . in the prime of *her* life, of course."

I smiled. I was astonished that I could feel so relieved. That ominous phrase the Brides of Pendorric was now explained. It was only this old legend which, because we were in Cornwall, where superstitions prevailed, had lived on and provided the old house with a ghost.

"You don't seem very worried. I would if I were you."

"You haven't finished the story. What happened to that bride?"

"She died having her son exactly a year after her wedding day. She was eighteen years old, which you must admit is very young to die."

"I expect a great many women died in childbirth. Particularly in those days."

"Yes, but they said she used to haunt the place waiting for a bride to take her place."

"To do the haunting, you mean?"

"You're like Uncle Roc. He always laughs at it. I don't laugh though. I know better."

"So you believe in this haunting business."

She nodded. "I've got the second sight. That's why I'm telling you you won't always laugh."

She leaped away from me and turned another somersault, her long thin legs swaying before me. I had the impression that she was rather pleased because I was going to be shocked out of my skepticism.

She came to stand before me again and with a virtuous expression said: "I thought you ought to know. You see, the Bride Lowella used to haunt Pendorric till my Granny Barbarina died. Then she rested in her grave because she'd lured another bride to take her place and do the haunting. My Granny Barbarina's been doing it for twenty-five years. I reckon she's tired. She'd want to rest in her tomb wouldn't she? You can bet your life she's looking out for another bride to do the job."

"I see what you mean," I said lightly. "I'm the bride."

"You're laughing, aren't you?" She stepped back and turned another somersault. "But you'll see."

Her face seen from upside down looked jaunty, as her long dark ponytail trailed on the grass.

"I'm sure you've never seen the ghost of your grandmother—have you?"

She did not answer but regarded me stolidly for a few seconds; then she turned a rapid somersault and did a few more handsprings on the grass, going farther and farther away from me until she reached the north door. She went through this and I was alone.

I returned to my book but I found that I kept looking up at the windows. I had been right when I had thought so many windows would be disconcerting; they really were like the eyes of the house.

It's all this talk of ghosts, I thought. Well, I had been warned of the superstitions of the Cornish, and I suspected that Lowella had mischievously tried to frighten me.

The north door opened with a crash and I saw the brown face, the dark ponytail, the light blue blouse, and dark blue shorts.

"Hello! Uncle Roc said I was to look after you in case you were lonely."

"Well, you've been doing that after your fashion," I told her.

"I couldn't find you. I went up to your room and you weren't there. I hunted everywhere and then I thought of the quad. So I came here. What would you like to do?"

"But you were here a little while ago."

She looked at me blankly.

"You told me the story of the brides," I reminded her.

She clapped her hands over her mouth. "She *didn't*, did she?"

"You're not . . . Hyson, are you?"

"Of course not. I'm Lowella."

"But she said . . ." Had she said she was Lowella? I was not sure.

"Did Hy pretend she was me?" The child began to laugh.

"You are Lowella, aren't you?" I persisted. "You really are."

She licked a finger and held it out and said: "See my finger's wet?"

She wiped it.

"See my finger's dry?"

She drew it across her throat.

"Cut my throat if I tell a lie."

She looked so earnest that I believed her.

"But why did she pretend she was you?"

Lowella's brows puckered, then she said: "I think she doesn't like being the quiet one. So when I'm not there she thinks she'll be me. People who don't know us much can't tell the difference. Would you like to come to the stables and see our ponies?"

I said I would; I felt that I wanted to escape from the quadrangle as I had from the graveyard that morning.

*   *   *

Dinner that night was a comfortable meal. The twins did not join us and there were the five of us. Morwenna said that when I was ready she'd show me the house and explain how it was run.

"Roc thinks that just at first, until you've settled in, you would like things to go on as they are." Morwenna smiled at her brother affectionately. "But it's to be as you want. He's very insistent on that."

"And don't think," put in Roc, returning his sister's look, "that Wenna will mind in the least whatever you want to do in the house. Now if you should want to root up her magnolia tree or turn the rose garden into a rockery that would be quite another matter."

Morwenna smiled at me. "I've never been much of a housekeeper. Who cares? It's not really necessary. Mrs. Penhalligan's a treasure. I do love the garden but of course if you want anything changed . . ."

"So," cried Roc, "the battle of the trees is about to begin."

"Don't take any notice of him," Morwenna said. "He loves to tease us. But then I expect you've discovered that by now."

I said I had and that I knew nothing of gardening and had always lived in a tiny studio which was as different from a mansion as any place could be.

I felt very happy to hear this banter between Roc and his sister because the affection which lay beneath it was very obvious. I was certain that Roc was anxious that Morwenna should not feel put out because he had brought a wife into the midst of their household, which could easily bring a lot of change. I loved him for his consideration of his sister; and when they asked me questions about Capri and were very careful not to mention my father, I guessed that Roc had warned them of my grief.

How considerate he was of us all; I loved him all the more because he never made a show of his care for us, but hid it under that teasing manner.

Morwenna and Charles were clearly trying to make me feel at home, because they were kindly and so fond of Roc. I was less certain of Rachel. She seemed absorbed in impressing on the servants that she was an honored member of the family; she was a little on the defensive I thought, and, when her face was in repose, I fancied I caught a bitterness in her expression.

We sat in one of the small drawing rooms drinking coffee which was served to us by Mrs. Penhalligan while Charles and Roc talked estate business, and Morwenna and Rachel, one on either side of me, launched into a description of local affairs. I found it all very interesting, particularly after the brief glimpse I had had that morning of the little village. Morwenna said she would drive me into Plymouth when I wanted to shop because it would be better for me to have someone who knew the shops the first time I went.

I thanked her, and Rachel said that if by any chance Morwenna wasn't available I could count on her.

"That's nice of you," I replied.

"Only too pleased to do all I can for Roc's bride," she murmured.

Bride! Bride! I thought impatiently. Why not wife, which would have sounded so much more natural? I think it was from that moment that the eeriness of the house seemed to close in on me and I was conscious of the darkness outside.

We went to bed early and when Roc and I were walking along the corridor on our way to our rooms on the south side, I looked out of the window to the quadrangle and remembered my conversations with the twins that afternoon.

Roc stood close to me as I looked down.

"You like the quadrangle garden, don't you?"

"Apart from the eyelike windows which are watching all the time."

He laughed. "You mentioned that before. Don't worry. We're all too busy to peep."

As we went along to our bedroom Roc said: "Something's on your mind, darling."

"Oh . . . it's nothing really."

"There is something then."

I tried to laugh lightly, but I was aware of the silence of that great house and I could not stop thinking of all the tragedies and comedies which must have taken place within those walls over the hundreds of years they had been standing. I could not feel indifference to the past, which in such a place seemed so much closer than it possibly could in my father's studio.

I blurted out what had happened that afternoon.

"Oh, those terrible twins!" he groaned.

"This story about the Brides of Pendorric . . ."

"Such stories abound in Cornwall. You could probably go to a dozen places and hear a similar story. These people are not cold-blooded Anglo-Saxons, you know. They're Celtic—a different race from the phlegmatic English. I know of course that they may have haunted houses in Huntingdon, Hereford, and Oxfordshire—but they're merely houses. According to the Cornish, the whole of Cornwall is haunted. If it's not the piskies it's the knackers from the mines. There are the Little People in their scarlet jackets and sugar-loaf hats. There are footlings who are born feet first, which is supposed to be a sign of their magical powers. There are pillar families—those inheriting power from fishermen ancestors who rendered some service to a mermaid; there are witches, white and black. So of course there are a few common ghosts."

"I gather Pendorric has that kind."

"No big house in Cornwall could possibly be without at least one. It's a status symbol. I'll bet Lord Polhorgan would give a thousand or two for a ghost. But the Cornish won't have it. He's not one of us, so he's going to be denied the privilege of being haunted."

I felt comforted, though I scorned myself for needing reassurance; but that child this afternoon had really unnerved me, chiefly because I had believed I was talking to Lowella. I thought Hyson a very strange little person indeed and I did not like the almost gloating pleasure in my uneasiness which I had noticed.

"About the story," I said. "After all, it concerns the Brides of Pendorric of whom I am one."

"It was very unfortunate that Lowella Pendorric died exactly a year to the day after her wedding. That probably gave rise to the whole thing. She brought the heir into the world and departed. A common enough occurrence in those days, but you have to remember that here in Cornwall people are always looking for something on which to hang a legend."

"And she was supposed to haunt the place after that?"

He nodded. "Brides came and went and they must have forgotten the legend although they'd tell you now that Lowella Pendorric continued to walk by night. Then my mother died when Morwenna and I were five years old. She was only twenty-five."

"How did she die?"

"That's just what revived the legend, I imagine. She fell from the north gallery into the hall, when the balustrade gave way. The wood was worm-eaten and it was very frail. The shock, and the fall combined, killed her. It was an unfortunate accident and because the picture of Lowella hangs in the gallery, the story soon got round that it was Lowella's influence that caused her to fall. Lowella was tired of haunting the house, they said, so she decided Barbarina should take her place. I am certain that the part about having to haunt the house until another bride took her place started at that time. You'll hear now that the ghost of Pendorric is my mother, Barbarina. Rather a young ghost for such an old house, but you see we haunt in relays."

"I see," I said slowly.

He put his hands on my shoulders and laughed; I laughed with him.

Everything seemed comfortingly normal that night.

* * *

The woman in the riding jacket and blue-banded hat had begun to haunt my thoughts and I found myself drawn toward the spot where her picture hung, whenever I was alone in that part of the house. I was not anxious that anyone should guess how much the picture attracted me, because I thought it would appear that I was affected by this ridiculous legend.

It was so realistic that the eyes seemed to flicker as you watched them, the lips as though they were about to speak. I wondered what her feelings had been when she felt the balustrade giving way beneath her weight; I wondered if she had felt an unhealthy interest in that other bride . . . as I was beginning to feel in her.

No, I told myself. I was merely interested in the painting and I was certainly not going to allow the legend to bother me.

All the same, I couldn't resist going to look at the picture.

Roc found me there two mornings later. He put his arm through mine and said he had come to take me for a drive.

"We don't take after her, do we?" he said. "Morwenna and I are both dark as Spaniards. You mustn't feel morbid about her. She's only a picture, you know."

He drove me out to the moor that morning; and I was fascinated by that stretch of wild country with its tors and boulders so strangely shaped that they looked like grotesque parodies of human beings.

I thought that Roc was trying to make me understand

Cornwall, because he knew that I had been upset by the legend and he wanted to make me laugh at it.

We drove for miles, through Callington and St. Cleer, little towns with gray granite façades, and out onto the moor again. He showed me the Trethevy Quoit, a neolithic tomb made of blocks of stone; he pointed out the burial grounds of men who had lived before history was recorded; he wanted me to know that a country which could offer so much proof of its past must necessarily be one of legend.

He stopped the car high on the moor and in the distance I could see that fantastic formation of rock known as the Cheesewring.

He put his arm round me and said: "One day I'll take you farther west and show you the Merry Maidens. Nineteen stones in a circle which you will be asked to believe were once nineteen girls who, deciding to defy tradition and go dancing in a sacred place, were turned to stone; and indeed the stones lean this way and that as if they had been caught and petrified in the midst of a dance." His eyes were very tender as he turned to me. "You'll get used to us in time," he went on. "Everywhere you look in this place there's some legend. You don't take them seriously."

I knew then that he was worried about me and I told him not to be because I had always prided myself on my common sense.

"I know," he said. "But your father's death was a greater shock than you realize. I'm going to take extra special care of you."

"Then," I replied, "I shall begin to feel very precious indeed, because I fancy you have been taking rather a lot of care of me ever since that awful day."

"Well, remember I do happen to be your husband."

I turned to him then and said almost fiercely, "It's something I couldn't possibly forget for a minute . . . even if I wanted to."

He turned my face up to his and his kiss was tender.

"And you don't want to?"

I threw myself against him, and as I clung to him, his grip on me tightened. It was as though we were both trying to make each other understand the immense depth of the love between us.

It was the comfort I needed.

Roc could always emerge from an emotional scene with more ease than I could, and in a short time he was his old teasing self. He began to tell me stories of Cornish legends, some so fantastic that I accused him of inventing them.

Then we both started inventing stories about the places we passed, trying to cap each other's absurdities. It all seemed tremendous fun, although anyone listening to us would have thought we were crazy.

As we drove back in these high spirits I marveled at the way in which Roc could always comfort and delight me.

* * *

During the next few days I spent a great deal of time in Roc's company. He would take me with him when he went on his rounds of the farms and I was welcomed everywhere, usually with a glass of some homemade wine or cider; I was even expected to eat a Cornish pasty as they came hot from the oven.

The people were warm and friendly once I had overcome a certain initial suspicion which they felt towards 'foreigners' from the other side of the Tamar. I was English; they were Cornish; therefore to them I was a foreigner.

"Once a foreigner, always a foreigner," Roc told me. "But of course marriage makes a difference. When you've produced a little Cornish man or woman you'll be accepted. Otherwise it would take all of fifty years."

Morwenna and I drove into Plymouth one afternoon and stopped and had tea near the Hoe.

"Charles and I are very pleased Roc's married," she told me. "We wanted to see him happily settled."

"You're very fond of him, aren't you?"

"Well, he is my brother, and my twin at that. And Roc's a rather special person. I expect you'll agree with that."

As I agreed so wholeheartedly I felt my affection for Morwenna increasing.

"You can always rely on Roc," went on Morwenna, and as she stirred her tea thoughtfully, her eyes were vague as though she were looking back over the past.

"Were you very surprised when he wrote and said he was married?"

"Just at first, perhaps. But he's always done the unexpected. Charles and I were beginning to be afraid he'd never settle down, so when we heard, we were really delighted."

"Even though he'd married someone who was a stranger to you."

Morwenna laughed. "That state of affairs didn't last long, did it? You're one of us now."

That was a very pleasant jaunt because I was always so happy to talk about Roc and to see how much he was loved by those people who had known him all his life.

Morwenna and I called on the Darks at the vicarage and I had an interesting afternoon listening to the stories the vicar had to tell of Cornish superstitions.

"I think they're so sure that certain things are going to happen that they make them happen," he told me.

We also talked of the people who lived on the Pendorric estate and I learned of some of the benefits which had come to them since Roc had been in control. I glowed with pride as I listened.

It was at the vicarage that I met Dr. Andrew Clement, a man in his late twenties or early thirties. He was tall, fair, and friendly and we liked each other from the start.

He told me that he, too, was what was known as a foreigner, having come from Kent and been in Cornwall some eighteen months.

"I come past Pendorric several times a week," he told me, "when I visit your neighbor, Lord Polhorgan."

"He's seriously ill, isn't he?"

"Not so much seriously ill as in danger of becoming so. He has angina and threatening coronary thrombosis. We have to watch him very carefully. He has a nurse living there all the time. Have you met her yet?"

"No, I haven't."

"She does occasionally come to Pendorric," said Morwenna. "You'll meet her sooner or later."

That was a very pleasant afternoon and as Morwenna and I drove back the conversation turned to the twins.

"Rachel seems to be very efficient," I said.

"Very."

"I suppose you're lucky to get her. A person with her qualifications must be rather difficult to come by nowadays."

"She's here . . . temporarily. The twins will have to go to school in a year or so. They can't be at home like this forever."

Was it my imagination or had Morwenna's manner changed when I mentioned Rachel?

There was a short silence between us and I reproved myself because I suspected I was becoming oversensitive. I was beginning to look for things which didn't exist, and I wondered whether I had changed since coming to Cornwall.

I wanted to go on talking about Rachel because I was eager to know more about her. I wanted to find out what the relationship between her and Roc had been—if in fact there had been anything unusual in their relationship.

But Morwenna had dismissed the subject. She began to talk animatedly about the Darks and the changes they had made at the vicarage.

*   *   *

That afternoon I went to the quadrangle. I was drawn there somewhat unwillingly, for I would rather have taken a book into the garden that was on the south side and that led down to the beach.

There I could have sat in one of the sheltered arbors among the hydrangeas, the Buddleias, and the sweet-smelling lavender, the house behind me, the sea before me. It would have been very pleasant.

Yet because of that faint revulsion I had experienced in the quadrangle—mainly on account of the windows which looked down on it—I was aware of a compulsion to go there. I was not the sort of person who enjoyed feeling even vaguely afraid, and I was sure that by facing whatever disconcerted me, I should more quickly overcome it.

I sat under the palm tree with my book and tried to concentrate, but once more I found myself continually glancing up at the windows.

I had not been there very long when the twins came out of the north door.

When I saw them together I had no difficulty in distinguishing them. Lowella was so vital; Hyson so subdued. I began to wonder then whether it really had been Hyson who had warned me to beware of Barbarina, or whether it had been a mischievous trick of Lowella's to try to frighten me and then pretend that it was Hyson who had done it.

"Hello," called Lowella.

They came and sat on the grass and gazed at me.

"Are we disturbing you?" asked Lowella politely.

"I wasn't very deep in my book."

"You like it here?" went on Lowella.

"It's very peaceful."

"You're shut right in. You've got Pendorric all around you. Hy likes it here too. Don't you, Hy?"

Hyson nodded.

"Well," went on Lowella, "what do you think of *us?*"

"I hadn't given the matter a great deal of thought."

"I didn't mean the two of us. I mean all of us. What do you think of Pendorric and Uncle Roc, Mummy, Daddy, and Becky Sharp?"

"Becky Sharp?"

"Old Bective, of course."

"Why do you call her that?"

"Hy said she was like a Becky Sharp she read about in a book. Hy's always reading."

I looked at Hyson, who nodded gravely.

"She told me about Becky Sharp and I said, 'That's Rachel.' So I called her Becky Sharp. I give people names. I'm Lo. She's Hy. Wasn't it clever of Mummy and Daddy to give us names like that. Though I'm not sure that I like being Lo. I'd rather be Hy . . . only in my name I mean. I'd rather be myself than old Hy. She's always sitting about and thinking."

"Not a bad occupation." I smiled at Hyson, who continued to regard me gravely.

"I've got names for everybody . . . my own secret names . . . and Becky Sharp is one of them."

"Have you got one for me?"

"You! Well, you're the Bride, aren't you? You couldn't be anything else."

"Does Miss Bective like the name you've given her?" I asked.

"She doesn't know. It's a secret. But you see, she was at school with Mummy and she was always coming here and Hy said, 'One day she'll come to stay because she never wants to go away.' "

"Has she said so?"

"Of course not. As if she would. It's all secret. Other people never know what Becky Sharp is up to. But she wants to stay. We thought she was going to marry Uncle Roc."

Hyson came and put her hands on my knees; she looked into my face and said: "It was what she wanted. I don't suppose she likes it much because you did."

"You're not supposed to say that, Hy," Lowella warned.

"I'll say it if I want to."

"You can't. You mustn't."

Hyson was suddenly fierce. "I can and I will."

Lowella chanted: "You can't. You can't." And began to run round the pond. Hyson went in pursuit of her. I watched them running about the quadrangle until Lowella disappeared through the north door. Hyson made as though to follow her, hesitated, and, turning, stood looking at me for a few moments. Then she came back.

"Lowella's really very childish," she told me. She knelt at my feet and looked at me, and feeling a little embarrassed by her scrutiny I said: "You never talk very much when she's there. Why not?"

She shrugged her shoulders. "I never talk unless I have something to say," she murmured primly.

Now it seemed she had nothing to say for she continued to kneel at my feet in a silence which went on for several minutes, then she rose suddenly and stood looking up at the windows.

She lifted her hand and waved, and following her gaze, I saw that the curtain at one of the windows was slightly pulled back and someone was standing about a foot from the window looking down. I could just make out a vague figure in a black hat with a band of blue about it.

"Who's that?" I asked sharply.

She rose to her feet and said slowly: "That was Granny."

Then she smiled at me and walked sedately to the north door and I was alone in the quadrangle. I looked up at the window. There was no one there and the curtain had fallen into place.

"Barbarina," I murmured, and I felt as though eyes were watching me, and I did not want to stay in the courtyard any longer.

This was ridiculous, I told myself. It was a trick. Of course, Lowella had gone in and they had decided to amuse themselves at my expense.

But it had not been a child I had seen at the window. It had been a tall woman.

I hurried into the house through the south door and I paused before the picture of Barbarina. I fancied that the eyes were mocking me.

This is absurd, I said as I mounted the staircase. I was a normal, uncomplicated person who did not believe in ghosts.

Or had I changed? Was I still so self-sufficient since I had experienced emotions which had only been names to me before I met Roc Pendorric? Love, jealousy—and now fear?

3.

I WENT straight up to my room, and as I opened the door I gasped, for a woman was sitting in an armchair with her back to the light. After my experience in the courtyard I must really have been unnerved, because it seemed several seconds before I recognized Morwenna.

"I'm afraid I startled you," she said. "I'm so sorry. I came up to look for you . . . and sat down for a moment."

"It was silly of me, but I didn't expect to see anyone here."

"I came up because Deborah has arrived. I want you to meet her."

"Who, did you say?"

"Deborah Hyson. She's my mother's sister. She spends a lot of time here. She has been away and only got back this afternoon. I think she's come back on your account. She can't bear things to be happening in the family and not take part in them."

"Could I have seen her at one of the windows not long ago?"

"Very likely. Was it the west side?"

"Yes, I think it was."

"Then I expect it was. Deborah has her rooms there."

"She was looking down on the quadrangle and Hyson waved to her, then ran off without explaining."

"Hyson's very fond of her, and she of Hyson. I'm glad, because Lowella is usually so much more popular. Are you coming down now? We're having tea in the winter parlor, and Deborah's very anxious to meet you."

"Let's go then."

We went down to the little room on the first floor of the north wing, where a tall woman rose to greet me; I was almost certain that she was the one I had seen at the window.

She was not wearing the hat now, but her abundant white hair was in a style which might have been fashionable thirty years or so ago; and I noticed too that there was an old-fashioned look about her clothes. Her eyes were very blue and her frilly crepe de chine blouse matched them perfectly. She was very tall and slender in her black tailored suit.

68

She took both my hands and looked earnestly into my face.

"My dear," she said, "how glad I am that you have come!" I was astonished by the fervor of her greeting; and I could only conjecture that, like most of the family, she was delighted to see Roc married, and therefore was prepared to accept me as a blessing. "As soon as I heard the news I came."

"That's very kind of you."

She smiled almost wistfully while her eyes remained on me.

"Come and sit beside me," she said. "We'll have lots to talk about. Morwenna dear, is that tea coming soon?"

"Almost at once," Morwenna replied.

We sat side by side and she went on: "You must call me Deborah, dear. The children do. Oh, by the children I mean Petroc and Morwenna. The twins call me Granny. They always have. I don't mind in the least."

"You don't look like a Granny!"

She smiled. "I expect I do to the twins. They think anyone of twenty somewhat aged, and after that of course quite ancient. I'm rather glad they do though. They hadn't a Granny. I supplied the need."

Mrs. Penhalligan brought in the tea and Morwenna poured it.

"Charles and Roc won't be in for an hour or so," she told Deborah.

"I'll see them at dinner. Oh, here *are* the twins."

The door had burst open and Lowella rushed in followed sedately by Hyson.

" 'Lo, Granny," said Lowella, and walking to Deborah's chair was embraced and kissed. Hyson followed; and I noticed that the hug she received was even more affectionate. There was no doubt that these two were very fond of each other.

Lowella went to the tea trolley to see what there was for tea, while Hyson stood leaning against Deborah's chair.

"I must say it is pleasant to be back," said Deborah, "though I miss the moor." She explained to me: "I have a house on Dartmoor. I was brought up there and now that my parents are dead it belongs to me. You must come out and see it one day."

"I'll come with you," said Lowella.

"Dear Lowella!" murmured Deborah. "She never likes to be left out of anything. And you'll come too Hyson, won't you?"

"Yes, Granny."

"That's a good girl. I hope you're looking after your Aunt Favel, and making her feel at home."

"We don't call her Aunt. She's just Favel and of *course* we've been looking after her," said Lowella. "Uncle Roc told us we had to."

"And Hyson?"

"Yes, Granny, I've been showing her what she ought to see and telling her what she ought to know."

Deborah smiled and began gently pulling Hyson's ponytail in a caressing way.

She smiled at me. "I must show you pictures of the children. I have lots of them in my rooms."

"On the walls," cried Lowella, "and in albums with writing underneath. It says 'Petroc aged six.' 'Morwenna in the Quadrangle aged eight.' And there are lots of Granny Barbarina and Granny Deborah when they were little girls—only they're in Devon."

Deborah leaned towards me. "There's usually a person like myself in all families—the one who did not marry but could be called in to look after the children. She keeps all the pictures and knows the dates of birthdays."

"Granny Deborah never forgets," Lowella told me.

"Did I see you when I was in the quadrangle?" I could not prevent myself asking, for foolish as it was, I had to satisfy myself on this point.

"Yes. I had only just arrived. I hadn't told Morwenna or Roc that I was coming today. I peeped out and saw you and Hyson. I didn't know you'd seen me or I should have opened the window and spoken to you."

"Hyson waved and I looked up and saw you. I was astonished when she said you were her Granny."

"And didn't she explain? Oh Hyson, my dear child!" She went on caressing the ponytail.

"I told her it was my Granny, and it was." Hyson defended herself.

"You're eating very little," Morwenna scolded Deborah and me. "Do try these splits. Maria will be hurt if we send too many back."

"I always say this Cornish cream isn't as good as ours in Devonshire," said Deborah.

Morwenna laughed. "That's sheer prejudice. It's exactly the same."

Deborah asked me about my life in Capri and how Roc and I had met.

"How delightful!" she cried when I had answered her questions. "A lightning romance! I think it's charming, don't you, Morwenna?"

"We're all very pleased, of course . . . particularly now that we know Favel."

"And we were longing for the new Bride of Pendorric," said Hyson quietly.

Everyone laughed and conversation was general while we finished tea.

When the meal was over, Hyson asked if she could help her Granny unpack. Deborah was very pleased and said of course she could. She added: "And I don't suppose Favel has seen my rooms, has she? We'll invite her to come with us, shall we, Hyson?"

I thought Hyson rather grudgingly agreed, but I accepted quickly because I was anxious to know more of this new member of the household.

The three of us went off together and soon were in the west corridor passing that very window at which Deborah had appeared and so startled me.

She opened the door of a room which had windows very like those in Roc's and my bedroom and which gave a superb view of the coastline stretching out towards the west and Land's End. My eyes went immediately to the bed—a four-poster like ours—because on the rose-colored counterpane lay the black hat with the blue band. It was not really like the one in the picture but the coloring was similar. I felt rather foolish as well as relieved, because it was comforting to solve the mystery of the apparition so quickly, but at the same time it was disconcerting to remember how shaken I had been at the sight of it.

I saw then that a part of one of the walls was covered with photographs of all sizes and types, some being studio portraits, others snapshots.

Deborah laughed and followed my gaze. "I have always hoarded pictures of the family. It's the same in Devonshire, isn't it, Hyson?"

"Yes, but they're all pictures of you before . . . these are after."

"Yes, of course. Time seems rather divided like that . . . before Barby's marriage . . . and after."

"Barbarina," I murmured involuntarily.

"Yes, Barbarina. She was Barby to me, and I was Deb. No one else ever called us by those versions of our names. Barbarina was the name of an ancestress of ours. It's unusual, isn't it. Until Barbarina's marriage she and I were always together." The blue eyes clouded momentarily and I guessed that there had been great devotion between the sisters. "Oh well," she went on, "it's all so long ago. Sometimes I find it hard to believe that she is dead . . . and in her grave . . ."

"But . . ." began Hyson.

Deborah laid her hand on the child's head and went on: "When she . . . died, I came to live here and I brought up Petroc and Morwenna. I tried to take her place, but can anyone take the place of a mother?"

"They're very fond of you, I'm sure."

"I think they are. Do let me show you the photographs. I think some of them are very charming. You'll want to see your husband in the various stages of his development, I expect. It's always rather fun, don't you think, to see people as they were years and years ago."

I smiled at the mischievous-eyed boy in the open shirt and cricket flannels; and the picture of him standing side by side with Morwenna—Morwenna smiling coyly at the camera, Roc scowling at it. There was a picture of them as babies; they lay side by side and a beautiful woman was bending over them.

"Barbarina and her twins," murmured Deborah.

"How beautiful she is!"

"Yes." There was a note of infinite sadness in her voice. So she still mourns her sister, I thought; and there came into my mind the memory of the family vault with the laurel hanging on the spike. I guessed who had put that there.

I turned my attention to a picture of a man and a woman; I had no difficulty in recognizing Barbarina, and the man who was with her was so like Roc that I guessed he was Barbarina's husband.

There it was, the almost challenging smile, the face of a man who knew how to get the best out of life, the reckless gambler, the indefinable charm. I noticed that the ears were slightly tilted at the corners. It was a handsome face, made even more attractive by that streak of mischief . . . wickedness . . . or whatever it was that I had sensed in Roc.

"Roc's parents," I said.

"Taken a year before the tragedy," Deborah told me.

"It is very sad. He looks so fond of her. He must have been heartbroken."

Deborah smiled grimly, but she did not speak.

"Aren't you going to show Favel the albums?" Hyson asked.

"Not now, dear. I've my settling in to do, and stories of the past can be a little boring, I'm afraid, to those who haven't lived them."

"I'm certainly not bored. I'm very eager to learn all I can about the family."

"Of course . . . now that you are one of us. And I shall enjoy showing you the albums at another time."

It was a kind of dismissal and I said that I, too, had things to do and would see her later. She came towards me and, taking my hands, smiled at me affectionately.

"I can't tell you how pleased I am that you are here," she told me earnestly; and there could be no doubting her sincerity.

"Everyone has been so charming to me at Pendorric," I told her. "No bride could have been more enthusiastically welcomed, and considering how sudden our marriage had been and that my coming must have been rather a shock to the family, I'm very grateful to everybody."

"Of course we welcome you, my dear."

Hyson said earnestly: "We've been waiting for her for years . . . haven't we, Granny?"

Deborah laughed, and gently pulled Hyson's ear. "You take in everything, child," she said. And to me: "We're delighted that Roc's married. The Pendorrics usually marry young."

The door opened and a little woman came into the room. She was dressed in black, which was not becoming to her sallow skin; her hair was what is known as iron gray and must have been almost black once; her dark bushy brows met over small, worried eyes; she had a long thin nose and thin lips.

She was about to speak, but seeing me hesitated. Deborah said: "This is my dear Carrie who was our nurse and has never left me. Now she looks after me . . . completely, and I just don't know what I should do without her. Carrie, this is the new Mrs. Pendorric."

The worried-looking eyes were fixed on me. "Oh," she murmured, "the new Mrs. Pendorric, eh."

Deborah smiled at me. "You'll get to know Carrie very quickly. She'll do anything for you, I'm sure. She's a wonder with her needle. She makes most of my things as she always did."

"I made for the two of them," said Carrie with pride. "And

I used to say there was no one better dressed in the whole of Devonshire than Miss Barbarina and Miss Deborah."

I noticed then the slight burr in her speech and the tenderness in her voice when she spoke of those two.

"Carrie, there's some unpacking to do."

Carrie's expression changed and she looked almost disgruntled.

"Carrie hates leaving her beloved moor!" said Deborah with a laugh. "It takes her quite a time to settle down on this side of the Tamar."

"I wish we'd never crossed the Tamar," Carrie muttered.

Deborah smiled at me and, putting her arm through mine, walked into the corridor with me.

"We have to humor Carrie," she whispered. "She's a privileged servant. She's getting on now and her mind wanders a little." She withdrew her arm. "It'll be fun showing you the pictures some time, Favel," she went on. "I can't tell you how pleased I am that you're here."

I left her, feeling grateful for several reasons; not only was she affectionate and eager to be friends, but she had made me feel myself again now that I was sure it was a person of living flesh and blood who had looked down on me from the window.

* * *

The mail at Pendorric was brought up to our bedrooms with early morning tea; and it was a few days later when Roc, looking through his, came to a letter which made him laugh aloud.

"It's come," he called to me in the bathroom. "I knew it would."

"What?" I asked, coming out wrapped in a bath towel.

"Lord Polhorgan requests the pleasure of Mr. and Mrs. Pendorric's company on Wednesday at three-thirty."

"Wednesday. That's tomorrow. Are we going?"

"Of course. I'm so eager for you to see the Folly."

I thought very little more about Lord Polhorgan's invitation because I was far more interested in Pendorric; and I could not feel the almost malicious delight the family seemed to take in deriding the Folly and its master. As I said to Roc, if the man from Manchester, Leeds, or Birmingham wanted to build a house on the cliffs, why shouldn't he? And if he wanted it to look like a medieval castle, again why shouldn't he? The Pendorrics had apparently been glad to sell him the land. It was not for them to tell him how he must use it.

As Roc and I set out that Wednesday afternoon he seemed to be enjoying some secret joke.

"I can't wait to see what you think of the setup," he told me.

To my unpracticed eye the house looked as old as Pendorric. "Do you know," I said to Roc, as we approached the stone unicorns which did the same service as our battered lions, "I shouldn't know that this wasn't a genuine antique if you hadn't told me."

"Ah, you wait till you've had a chance to examine it."

We pulled the bell in the great portico and heard it clanging through the hall.

A dignified manservant opened the door and, bowing his head, said solemnly: "Good afternoon, sir. Good afternoon, madam. His lordship is waiting for you, so I'll take you up immediately."

It took quite a long time to reach the room where our host was waiting for us; and I noticed that although the furniture was antique the carpets and curtains were expensively modern.

We were finally led to a large room with windows overlooking the beautifully laid-out cliff garden which ran down to the sea; and resting on a chaise longue was the old man.

"My lord," the manservant announced, "Mr. and Mrs. Pendorric."

"Ah! Bring them in, Dawson. Bring them in."

He turned his head, and the intentness of those gray eyes was rather disturbing, particularly as they were directed towards me.

"Good of you to come," he said rather brusquely, as though he didn't mean this. "You'll have to forgive my not rising."

"Please don't," I said quickly; and I went to his chaise longue and took his hand.

He had a high color with a faint purplish tinge, and I noticed how the veins stood out on his long thin hands.

"Sit down, Mrs. Pendorric," he said, still in the same brusque manner. "Give your wife a chair, Pendorric. And put it near me . . . that's right, facing the light."

I had to suppress a slight resentment that I was being put under a shrewd scrutiny, and I experienced a certain nervousness which I hadn't expected I should.

"Tell me, how do you like Cornwall, Mrs. Pendorric?"

He spoke sharply, jerkily, as though he were barking orders on a barrack square.

"I'm enchanted," I said.

"And it compares favorably with that island place of yours?"

"Oh yes."

"All I see of it now is this view." He nodded towards the window.

"I can't imagine you'd find a more beautiful one anywhere."

He looked from me to Roc; and I was aware that my husband's expression had become rather sardonic. He didn't like the old man, that much was clear; and I felt annoyed with him because I was afraid he made it obvious.

Our host was frowning towards the door. "Late with tea," he said. He must give his servants a difficult time, I thought, for even if he had asked for tea to be served immediately we arrived it was not very late; we had not been in the room more than three or four minutes.

Then the door opened and a tea wagon was wheeled in. It was overladen with cakes of all descriptions besides bread and butter and splits, with bowls of clotted cream and jam.

"Ah," Lord Polhorgan grunted, "at last! Where's Nurse Grey?"

"Here I am." A woman came into the room. She was so beautiful that for a moment I was startled. The blue in her striped dress matched her eyes, her starched apron was snowy white, and her cap, set almost jauntily on her masses of golden hair, called attention to its beauty. I had never seen a nurse's uniform worn so becomingly; then I realized that this woman would look dazzling whatever she wore, simply because she was so very beautiful.

"Good afternoon, Mr. Pendorric," she said.

Roc had risen to his feet as she entered and I could not see his face as he looked at her. He said: "Good afternoon, Nurse." Then he turned. "Favel, this is Nurse Grey, who looks after Lord Polhorgan."

"I'm so glad to meet you." She had a wide mouth and perfectly shaped teeth.

"What about giving Mrs. Pendorric some tea?" growled Lord Polhorgan.

"Of course," said Nurse Grey. "It's all here, I see. Now Mrs. Pendorric, you'd like to sit near Lord Polhorgan. I'll put this little table here for you."

I thanked her and she went to the tea wagon and began to pour out while Roc brought over a plate of splits and cream and jam, which he set on the table.

"I don't need a nurse all the time," Lord Polhorgan told me.

"But I may need one at any moment. That's why she's here. Quite an efficient woman."

"I am sure she is."

"Easy job. Gets a lot of free time. Beautiful surroundings."

"Ideal," I murmured, wondering how Nurse Grey liked being referred to in the third person. I glanced at her. She was smiling at Roc.

I handed Lord Polhorgan the splits, and I noticed that he moved slowly and was rather breathless as he took one.

"Shall I spread the jam and cream for you?" I asked.

"H'm!" he barked, which meant assent. "Thanks!" he added when I had done it. "Good of you. Now help yourself."

Nurse Grey asked if I preferred China or Indian and I was given delicious Mandarin Pekoe with lemon.

She then sat down near Roc. I very much wanted to hear what they were saying, but Lord Polhorgan demanded my attention by firing questions at me. He appeared to be very interested in the way we had lived on the island, and I promised to show him some of my father's work, which had been sent to Pendorric.

"Good," he said. He made me talk about my childhood and in a short time I was living it all again.

"You're not happy," said Lord Polhorgan suddenly, and I blurted out the story of my father's death to which he listened gravely, and then said: "You were very fond of him. Was your mother fond of him too?"

I told him something of their life together then, how they had lived for each other, how ill she had become, and how they had made me aware that they wanted to live every hour to the full because they knew that the time would come when they could not be together; and as I did so I marveled that I could talk so intimately to such a gruff old man on such short acquaintance.

He laid his veined hand on my arm. "Is that how it is with you?" he said sharply; and he looked towards Roc, who was laughing with Nurse Grey.

I hesitated just a second too long.

"Marry in haste . . ." he added. "Seem to have heard that said somewhere."

I flushed. "I'm very happy at Pendorric," I retorted.

"You rush into things," he said. "Bad habit. I never rushed. Made decisions, yes . . . and sometimes quick ones, but always gave them adequate thought. You coming to see me again?"

"If you ask me."

"Then you are asked now."

"Thank you."

"You won't want to though."

"Yes I shall."

He shook his head. "You'll make excuses. Too busy. Another engagement. What would a young woman like you want with visiting a sick old man?"

"But I'd love to come."

"You've got a kind heart. But kindness doesn't always go very deep. Don't want to hurt the old man . . . go now and then. But a bore. What a nuisance!"

"It will be nothing of the sort. You're so interested in things. And I'm attracted by this house."

"Pretty vulgar, eh? The old man of the people who wanted to build up a bit of background. Doesn't go down well with the aristocrats, I can tell you."

"Why shouldn't people build backgrounds if they want them?"

"Listen, young woman. There's no reason why anyone shouldn't build anything. You get your just deserts in this world. I wanted to make money and I made it. I wanted to to have a family mansion . . well, I've got it. In this world you say, I want this and I want that. And if you've got any guts you go and get it. You get what you pay for, and if it doesn't turn out as you planned, well then you have to look for where you went wrong, because, you can depend on it, you've gone wrong somewhere."

"I expect you're right."

"I'd like you to come again even if you are bored. Perhaps you'd be less bored after a while . . . when we got to know each other."

"I haven't started to be bored yet."

He clenched and unclenched his hand, frowning at it. "I'm an old man . . . incapacitated by illness . . . brought on, they tell me, by the life I've led." He patted his chest. "I've put a big strain on this, it seems, and now I've got to pay for it. All right, I say, life's a matter of settling bills and drawing dividends. I'm ready."

"I can see you have a philosophy."

"Play chess?"

"My mother taught me."

"Your mother, eh?"

"She also taught me reading, writing, and arithmetic, before I came to school in England."

"I reckon you were the apple of her eye."

"I was her only child."

"Yes," he said soberly. "Well, if you played a game of chess with me now and then, you wouldn't be so bored with the old man's efforts at conversation. When will you come?"

I considered. "The day after tomorrow," I said.

"Good. Teatime?"

"Yes, but I mustn't eat so many of these splits or I shall put on too much weight."

He looked at me and his eyes were suddenly soft. "You're as slight as a sylph," he said.

Nurse Grey came over with plates of cakes, but we did not seem in the mood for eating any more.

I noticed that Nurse Grey's eyes had grown more luminous and that there was a faint pink color in her cheeks. I wondered uneasily whether Roc had had anything to do with that, and I was reminded of Rachel Bective and Dinah Bond, the young blacksmith's wife.

The conversation became general, and after an hour we left.

Roc was clearly amused as we walked home.

"Another conquest for you," he commented. "The old fellow certainly took to you. I've never known him so gracious before."

"Poor old man, I don't think people try to understand him."

"They don't need to," retorted Roc. "He's as easy to read as an A.B.C. He's the typical self-made man—a character off the shelf. There are some people who mould themselves on old clichés. They decide the sort of person they're going to be and start playing the part; after a while they're so good at it that it becomes second nature. That's why there are so many stock characters in the world." He grinned at me. "You don't believe me, do you? Well, look at Lord P. Started selling newspapers . . . perhaps not newspapers, but some such job. It's the pattern that matters, not the detail. Never goes in for any fun, piles up the little capital to start with and, by the time he's thirty, industry and skill have turned it into a big capital and he's on the way to becoming a millionaire. That's all very well, but he can't be *himself* . . . he has to be one of the band of self-made men. He clings to his rough manners.

'I came up from nothing and I'm proud of it!' Doesn't go in for the ordinary graces of conventional living. 'Why should I change myself? I'm perfect as I am.' Oh, I don't have to *try* to understand Lord P. If he were made of glass I shouldn't be able to see through him more clearly."

"You don't forgive him for building his house."

Roc shrugged his shoulders. "Perhaps not. It's fake and I hate fakes. Suppose all the self-made men made up their minds to build along our coast? What a sight! No, I'm against these pseudo-antiques; and to have put one on our doorstep is an imposition. Polhorgan's Folly is an outsider here on our coast with houses like Pendorric, Mount Mellyn, Mount Widden, Cotehele and the like . . . just as its master is . . . with his Midland manners calling himself Lord Polhorgan. As though Tre, Pol, and Pen did not belong to Cornishmen."

"How vehement you are!" I said, and trying to speak lightly added: "And if *I* made a conquest, what of you?"

He was smiling as he turned to me. "Thea, you mean?"

"You call her that?"

"That's her name, my dear. Althea Grey—Thea to her friends."

"Of whom you are one."

"Of course, and so will you be. As for my conquest," he went on, "that's one of long standing. She has been here eighteen months, you know."

Then he put his arm about me and began to sing:

> *"Wherever you hear Tre Pol and Pen*
> *. You'll know that you're with Cornishmen."*

He smiled at me and continued:

> *"Alas, I have to add a rider . . .*
> *One can't ignore the rich outsider."*

"I think," I said, "that you prefer the nurse to the invalid." I saw the teasing light in his eyes.

"With you it's exactly the reverse," he commented. "That's why it was such a successful visit. I took care of the nurse while you devoted yourself to your host."

* * *

Two days later, as we had arranged, I went to play chess with Lord Polhorgan. I came back and told Roc rather defiantly that I liked the old man even more than on the first occasion; which seemed to amuse him very much. Nurse Grey was not present, and I poured out the tea. The old man was delighted when he beat me, then he looked at me shrewdly and said: "Sure you're not humoring the old man—letting him win, eh?" I replied that I had done my best to beat him, and that satisfied him. Before I left I had promised to call again in a day or so in order to give him a return match.

I was settling into life at Pendorric. I did a little gardening with Morwenna, and it was pleasant to chat with her while we worked.

"It's a useful hobby," she said, "because we haven't the gardeners we once had. In my father's day there were four of them; now it's Bill Pascoe from the cottages three afternoons a week, with Toms working when he gets a chance. Both Roc and I were always fond of growing things."

"Roc doesn't do much in the gardens now," I put in.

"Well, there's the farm to take up his time. He and Charles work hard on that." She sat back on her heels and smiled at the fork in her hands. "I'm so pleased they get on well together—but then of course they're two wonderful people. I've often thought how lucky I am . . ."

"I know what you mean," I answered soberly. "We're both lucky."

Charles was very friendly to me in a quiet and unassuming way and I liked his chubby charm. When Roc took me round the farm for the first time I was immediately aware of the respect Charles had for Roc's judgment, and that made me like him all the more.

I even liked Rachel Bective a little better than I had in the beginning and reproached myself for a too hasty judgment because I had fancied I detected something rather sly in her sandy looks.

On one occasion we went for a walk together and she volunteered a little information about herself, telling me how she had met Morwenna when they had been at school together and had come to spend a summer holiday at Pendorric. From then she had been there often. She had to earn her living and had taken up teaching, so she had agreed to take a leave of absence from her school for a year to supervise the twins' education because she knew what a trial they were to their mother.

The twins themselves had a habit of coming upon me at unexpected moments, and seemed to take a special pleasure in leaping out on me and startling me.

Lowella addressed me as Bride, which at first I thought amusing but later was not so sure; Hyson had a habit of fixing her silent gaze on me whenever she was in my company, which I also found disconcerting.

Deborah was as determined as the others to make me feel at home; she told me that she felt like a mother towards me because Roc had been like her own son.

I was sitting in the quadrangle one afternoon when I suddenly had the eerie feeling that I was being watched. I shook off this feeling which was always ready to worry me when I was in the quadrangle, but it persisted and, when I looked up at the window on the west side where I had seen Deborah on the day she arrived, I almost expected to see her there.

I stared for a few seconds at those curtained windows; then I turned and looked at the east side. I was certain then that I saw a movement.

I waved and continued to look, but there was no response. Ten minutes later Deborah joined me in the quadrangle.

"How you love this spot!" she said, and she pulled up one of the white and gilded chairs to sit close to me.

"My feelings for the place are a little mixed," I told her frankly. "I am immensely attracted, and yet I never feel exactly comfortable here."

"Why ever not?"

I looked over my shoulder. "It's the windows, I think."

"I often say it's a pity that it is only corridor windows which look down on the quadrangle. It would make such a lovely view and a change from the great vistas of sea from south, west, and east, and country from the north."

"It's the windows themselves. They take away privacy."

She laughed. "I believe you're rather a fanciful person after all."

"Oh no, I'm not really. Were you on the east side a little while ago?"

She shook her head.

"I'm sure someone was looking down."

"I shouldn't think so, dear, not from the east side. Those rooms are rarely used now. The furniture's covered in dust sheets . . . except in her rooms."

"Her rooms?"

"Barbarina's. She always liked the east side. She didn't mind Polhorgan in the least, like the others did. *They* couldn't

bear to look at it. She had her music room there. She said
it was ideal because she could practice there to her heart's
content without disturbing anyone."

"Perhaps it was one of the twins I saw up there."

"That may be so. The servants don't go there very much.
Carrie looks after Barbarina's room. She gets rather angry if
anyone else attempts to. But you should see them. You ought
to see all over the house. You are, after all, its new mistress."

"I would love to see Barbarina's rooms."

"We could go now."

I rose eagerly and she took my arm as we walked across
the quadrangle to the east door. She seemed excited at the
prospect of taking me on a tour of that part of the house.

The door closed behind us and as we walked along a short
corridor which led into the hall I was conscious of silence. I
told myself that it had something to do with my mood, for
naturally if there was no one in this wing why should the
silence surprise me?

"The servants say this is now the haunted part of the house,"
Deborah told me.

"And Barbarina is the ghost?" I asked.

"You know the story then? Lowella Pendorric was supposed to have haunted the house until Barbarina took her
place. A typical Cornish situation, my dear. I'm glad I was
born on the other side of the Tamar. I shouldn't want to be
perpetually ingratiating myself with piskies and ghosties and
things that go bump in the night."

I looked about the hall, which was an exact replica of the
others in its proportions. There were the steel weapons on
the walls, the pewter utensils on the refectory table, the
suits of armor at the foot of the staircases. The pictures in
the gallery were different, of course, and I gazed casually at
them as we mounted the stairs.

We reached the corridor and I glanced through the windows at the quadrangle, wondering at which one I had seen
a movement.

"Barby's rooms were on the second floor," Deborah told
me. "I used to come and stay when she married. You see we
had scarcely been separated all our lives and Barby didn't see
why we ever should be. This became a second home to me.
I was here as much as I was in Devonshire."

We had mounted to the second floor and Deborah opened
several of the doors to show me rooms shrouded in dust

sheets. They looked ghostly, as all such rooms do in large and silent houses.

Deborah smiled at me and I guessed she was reading my thoughts and perhaps trying to prove to me that I was not as immune from Cornish superstition as I should like her to believe.

"Now," she said; and threw open a door. "This is the music room."

There were no dust sheets here. The huge windows gave me a view of the coast with Polhorgan rising majestically on the cliff top; but it was not the view I looked at this time, but at the room, and I think what struck me most was that it had the look of a room which was being lived in There was a dais at one end of it and on this was a stand with a piece of music opened on it. Beside the stand, on a chair, was a violin, looking as though it had just been placed there; the case lay open on a nearby table.

Deborah nodded. "A silly habit. But some people find comfort from it. At first none of us could bear to move anything. Carrie dusts and puts things down exactly where they were. Carrie feels really fierce about it and it's more for her sake than anything else that we leave it as it is. I can't tell you how devoted she was to Barbarina."

"And to you too."

Deborah smiled. "To me too. But Barbarina was her favorite."

"You were identical twins?"

"Yes. Like Lowella and Hyson. When we were young some people found difficulty in telling us apart, but as we grew older all that passed. She was gay and amusing; I was rather stolid and slow-witted. There's more to looks than features, isn't there. It's beginning to show in Hyson and Lowella. It's only when they're asleep that they seem so much alike. As I was saying, Barby was everybody's favorite, and because she was as she was . . . I seemed more dull and less interesting than I should if she had not always been with me."

"Did you resent it?"

"Resent it! I adored Barbarina with the rest. In fact she hadn't a more devoted admirer. When she was praised I was happy because in a way it seemed as though I were being praised. It's sometimes like that with twins; they can share each other's triumphs and disasters more fully than ordinary people do."

"And did she feel the same about you?"

"Absolutely. I wish you could have known Barbarina. She was a wonderful person. She was all that I should have liked to be myself; and because she looked so like me and was my twin sister, when we were little I was quite happy that it should be so."

"It must have a blow to you when she married."

"We didn't let that part us more than we could help. I had to be in Devonshire for a good part of the time because our father needed me to look after him. Our mother had died when we were fifteen and he had never really got over the shock. But whenever I could I would be at Pendorric. She was very glad to see me. In fact, I don't know what she would have done . . " She hesitated and I had the impression that she was on the verge of confiding in me. Then she shrugged her shoulders and seemed to change her mind.

But here in Barbarina's music room I was conscious of a great desire to learn more about her. I was—although I wouldn't admit it at this stage—becoming more and more absorbed in the story of this woman who had been my immediate predecessor as a Pendorric Bride.

"Was it a happy marriage?" I asked.

Deborah turned away from me and went to the window; I was embarrassed, realizing that I had asked an awkward question, so I went to her and, laying my hand gently on her arm, said: "I'm sorry. I'm being too inquisitive."

She turned to me and I noticed how brilliant her eyes had become. She shook her head and smiled. "Of course not, and naturally you're interested. After all, you're one of us now, aren't you? There's no reason why we should try to keep family secrets from you. Come and sit down and I will tell you about it."

We sat in the window looking along the coast towards Rame Head and Plymouth. The headland jutted out darkly in the gray water and one could imagine it was a supine giantess who lay there. The tide was out and the tops of the jagged rocks were visible. I gazed at Polhorgan whose gray walls were the color of the sea today.

"There's a distant family connection between the Hysons and the Pendorrics," said Deborah. "Cousins, many times removed. So from our childhood we knew Petroc and his family. I don't mean your Roc, of course, but his father, who was Barbarina's Petroc. When he was a boy he used to stay with us. He was a year older than we were."

"He was like Roc, wasn't he?

"So like him that sometimes when I see Roc now I get a little shock and for the moment I think he's Petroc come back."

"In looks you mean."

"Oh . . . in many ways. The voice . . . the gestures . . . his ways . . . everything. There's a very strong resemblance that runs through most of the Pendorric men. I used to hear stories of Petroc's father—another Petroc—and all that I heard could have applied to his son. Barbarina fell in love with him when she was about seven. She remained in that state until she died."

"She must have been happy when she married him."

"A feverish sort of ecstasy. It used to frighten me. She cared for him so much."

"And he for her?"

Deborah smiled a little wistfully. "Petroc liked women in general too much to care very deeply for one in particular. That's what I always felt and so I saw how it would be. I warned Barbarina, but she wouldn't listen of course."

There was silence and after a while she went on. "We used to ride on Dartmoor. Our place is on the moor, you know. You must come and see it. The view is wonderful . . . if you like that kind of view. You can step from our garden right onto the moor. Once we all went riding together and they lost me. The mist came up as it does on the moor and however well you think you know the place you can easily be hopelessly lost. You are apt to wander round and round in circles. It was really rather frightening. I found my way back but they didn't come home until next day. They'd sheltered in some hut they'd discovered and Petroc had had the foresight to load up with chocolate. Sometimes I think he arranged the whole thing."

"Why? I mean, if she was in love with him, couldn't he have been with her . . . more comfortably?"

Again that silence. Then she sighed and said: "He was in love with some local girl whom he'd promised to marry. She was a farmer's daughter. But the family wanted this marriage with the Hysons because our father was well-off and money was badly needed at Pendorric. Barbarina was very unhappy She'd heard that Petroc was going to marry this girl, and she knew he must be very much in love with her because Pendorric meant a great deal to him, and it was possible that if he couldn't bring some money into the family something would have to be done about it. So she knew he must have been deeply in love with the girl to contemplate marrying

someone who couldn't bring a penny into the place. He was
fond of Barbarina. It wouldn't have been any hardship to
marry her . . . if he hadn't been so besottedly in love with this
other woman. Petroc was the sort of man who would get
along with any woman . . . like . . . well, you know the type."

I nodded uneasily.

"Were the Pendorrics very poor then?"

"Not exactly, but the great change had set in. Things
weren't what they had been for their sort of people. The house
needed expensive renovations. And Petroc had gambled
rather rashly in the hope of recuperating the family fortunes."

"So he was a gambler."

She nodded. "As his father was."

"And what happened after that night on the moor?"

"I think Petroc had made up his mind that he would have
to marry Barbarina. Pendorric was important, so he would
fall in with the wishes of his family and Barbarina's. But he
couldn't tell Barbarina that . . . bluntly. So they got lost on
the moors and Barbarina was seduced and . . . that made it
all easy."

"She told you this?"

"My dear Favel, Barbarina didn't have to *tell* me things.
We were as close as two people can be. Don't forget that
during the months of our gestation we had been as one. I knew
exactly what had happened and why."

"And after that she married him and she was happy."

"What do you expect? Petroc couldn't be faithful. It
wasn't in his nature to be, any more than it had been in his
father's. He took up with the farmer's daughter again. It was a
notorious scandal. But she wasn't the only one. Like his father
he couldn't resist a woman nor a chance to gamble. Women
couldn't resist them either. I thought that, when Roc and
Morwenna were born, she would cease to fret for him, and
for a while she did. I hoped that she would have more children and make them her life."

"And you were disappointed?"

"Barbarina was a good mother, don't mistake me; but she
wasn't one of those women who can ignore her husband's infidelities and become completely absorbed in her children.
Petroc meant too much to her for that."

"So she was very unhappy?"

"You can imagine it, can't you. A sensitive woman . . . in
a place like this . . . and an unfaithful husband who didn't

make a secret of his infidelities; there was nothing secret
about Petroc. He never tried to pretend he was other than
he was—a reckless gambler and a philanderer. He seemed to
take up the attitude: it's a family characteristic, so there's
nothing I can do about it."

"Poor Barbarina," I murmured.

"I used to come down as often as I could, and then when
my father died I almost lived here. It was through me that
she became interested in her music again. I believe that in
other circumstances she might have been a concert violinist.
She was really very good. But she had never practiced enough.
However she found great pleasure in it, particularly towards
the end. In fact she was very gifted. I remember when we
were at school . . . we must have been about fourteen then . . .
she was in the school play. It was *Hamlet* and she was
Ophelia, a part which suited her absolutely I was the ghost.
That was about the limit of my capabilities. I believe I was a
very poor one. But Barbarina was the hit of the show."

"I can imagine that .   from her picture, I mean. Particularly the one in the gallery."

"Oh, that's Barbarina as she really was. Sometimes when I
look at it I almost imagine she will step out of the frame and
speak to me."

"Yes, there's a touch of reality about it. The artist must
have been a very good one."

"It was painted about a year before her death. She took
great pleasure in riding. In fact I sometimes felt it was a
feverish sort of pleasure she was taking in things . . . her
music . . . riding, and so on. She was lovely in that particular
ensemble, and that was why she was painted in it. It was
sad that she—like Ophelia—should have died before her
time. I wish you could have heard her sing that song from the
play. She had a strange voice . . . a little off key, which
suited the song and Ophelia. I remember at the school show
how silent the audience was when she came on the stage in a
flowing gown of white and flowers in her hair and in her
hands. I can't sing; but it's that one that goes something like
this:

> "*How should I your true love know*
> *   From another one?*
> *   By his cockle hat and staff*
> *   And his sandal shoon.*

He is dead and gone, lady,
  He is dead and gone;
  At his head a grass-green turf,
  At his heels a stone."

She quoted the words in a low monotone; then she flashed her smile at me. "I wish I could make you hear it as she sang it. There was something about it that made one shiver. Afterwards it became one of her favorite songs and there was a verse which she didn't sing at the school play but she used to sing that later.

"Then up he rose, and donn'd his clothes
  And dupp'd the chamber-door;
  Let in the maid, that out a maid
  Never departed more."

"There would be an odd little smile about her lips as she sang that, and I always felt it had something to do with that night on the moor."

"Poor woman! I'm afraid she wasn't very happy."

Deborah clenched her fists as though in sudden anger. "And she was meant to be happy. I never knew anyone so capable of being happy. If Petroc had been all that she hoped he would be . . . if . . . but what is the good? When is life ever what you hope it will be; and in any case it is all so long ago."

"I heard about it; the balustrade was faulty and she fell to the hall."

"It was unfortunate that it happened in the gallery where Lowella Pendorric hung. That really gave rise to all the talk."

"It must have revived the legend."

"Oh, it didn't take all that reviving. The people round about had always said that Pendorric was haunted by Lowella Pendorric, the bride of long ago."

"And now they say that Barbarina has taken her place."

Deborah laughed; then she looked over her shoulder. "Although I've always laughed at such talk, sometimes when I'm in this house I feel a little more inclined to accept it."

"It's the atmosphere of old houses. The furniture is often standing in exactly the same place it was in hundreds of years ago. You can't help thinking that this house looked almost exactly the same to that Lowella whom they call the First Bride."

"I only wish that Barbarina *would* come back!" said Deb-

orah vehemently. "I can't tell you what I'd give to see her
again." She stood up. "Let's go for a walk. We're getting morbid sitting here in Barbarina's room. We'll have to get mack-
intoshes. Look at those clouds. The wind's in the southwest
and that means rain's not far off."

I said I should enjoy that, and we left the east wing together. She came with me to my room while I put on my
outdoor things; then I went with her to hers; and when we
were ready she led me around to the north wing and we
paused on the gallery before the picture of Lowella Pendorric.

"This is where she fell," explained Deborah. "Look, you
can see where the balustrade has been mended. It should have
been noticed long before the accident. Actually the place is
riddled with worm. It's inevitable and it'll cost a fortune to
put it right."

I looked up into Lowella Pendorric's painted face and I
thought exultantly: But Roc is not really like his father and
his grandfather, and the gambling, philandering Pendorrics.
If he had been in his father's place he would have married
the farmer's daughter, as he married me, for what had I to
bring him? In ten minutes we were strolling along the cliff
path, the warm sea-scented wind caressing our faces.

* * *

I had no wish to lead an idle life. On the island there had
always been so much to do. I had been my father's housekeeper
as well as his saleswoman. I pointed out to Roc that I wanted
to do something.

"You might go down to the kitchens and have a little
chat with Mrs. Penhalligan. She'd appreciate it. After all,
you're the mistress of the house."

"I will," I agreed, "because Morwenna won't mind in the
least if I did make suggestions."

He put his arm around me and hugged me. "Aren't you the
mistress of the house, anyway?"

"Roc," I told him, "I'm so happy. I wouldn't have thought
it possible so soon after . . ."

Roc's kiss prevented me from going on with that.

"Didn't I tell you? And talking of having something to do
. . . as Mrs. Pendorric you should take an interest in village
activities, you know. It's expected, as I guess you've gathered
from the Darks. I tell you, Favel, in a few weeks' time you'll

not be complaining of having too little to do, but too much."

"I think I'll call on the Darks. This afternoon, by the way, I've promised to have tea with Lord Polhorgan."

"What, again? You really do like that old man."

"Yes," I said almost defiantly, "I do."

"Then enjoy yourself."

"I believe I shall."

Roc studied me, smiling as he did so. "You certainly seem to hit it off."

"I feel that he's really rather a lonely old man and he seems sort of paternal."

Roc's smile faded and he nodded slowly. "You're still grieving," he said.

"It's so hard to forget, Roc. Oh, I'm so happy here. I love it all; the family are so kind to me and you . . ."

He was laughing. "And I'm kind to you too? What did you expect? A wife-beater?"

Then he put his arms about me and held me close to him. "Listen, Favel," he said, "I want you to be happy. It's what I want more than anything. I understand what you feel about the old man. He's paternal. That's what you said; and in a way he makes up for something you miss. He's lonely. You can bet your life he's missed a lot. So you like each other. It's understandable."

"I wish you liked him more, Roc."

"Don't take any notice of what I've said. It was mostly said jokingly. When you get to know me better you'll understand what a joker I am."

"Don't you think I know you well then?"

"Not as well as you will twenty years hence, darling. We'll go on learning about each other; that's what makes it all so exciting. It's like a voyage of discovery."

He spoke lightly, but I went on thinking of what he said; and I was still remembering those words when I passed under the great archway on my way out that afternoon, until I heard footsteps behind me and, turning, saw Rachel Bective, a twin walking sedately on either side of her.

"Hello," called Rachel, "going for a walk?"

"I'm going to tea at Polhorgan."

They caught up with me and we walked along together.

"Hope you're prepared," warned Rachel. "It's going to rain."

"I've brought my mack."

"The wind's blowing in from the southwest, and once it

starts to rain here you begin to wonder whether it's ever going to stop."

Hyson came to the other side of me so that I was in between her and Rachel; Lowella skipped on ahead.

"Do you go round by the cliff path to Polhorgan?" asked Rachel. "It's at least five minutes shorter."

"I've always kept to this road."

"We'll show you the short cut if you like."

"Don't let me take you out of your way."

"But we're only going for a walk."

"Well, thanks—if it really won't."

"Lowella," Rachel called. "We're going down Smugglers' Lane to show your Aunt Favel the short cut to Polhorgan."

Lowella wheeled sharply around. "Good. It'll be lovely and squelchy down Smugglers' Lane."

"It won't. There hasn't been that much rain."

We turned aside from the road and took a steep narrow path on either side of which the hedges had run so wild that sometimes we had to go in single file.

Lowella found a broken-off branch and went ahead of us, beating the overgrown hedges and shouting: "Beware the awful avalanche. Beware the pine tree's withered branch. Excelsior!"

"Oh Lowella, do be quiet," begged Rachel.

"Of course if you don't want me to lead you to safety, say so."

"Hyson reads to her when they're in bed at night," Rachel told me, "and she goes on repeating what appeals to her."

"You like reading, don't you?" I said to Hyson.

She merely nodded. Then she said: "Lowella's such a child. As if this is anything like the awful avalanche!"

The path ended abruptly and we stepped onto what looked like a ledge. Beneath us—a long way beneath us—was the sea, and beside us, towering above, rose the shaley face of the cliff, with here and there a bush of gorse or bracken clinging to the brown earth.

"It's perfectly safe," said Rachel Bective. "Unless of course you have a phobia about heights."

I told her I hadn't and added that we were several feet lower than we had been on the coast road.

"Yes, but that's a proper road. This is just a path, and a little farther on it gets even narrower. There's a notice saying use it at your own risk, but that's for visitors. Local people all use it."

Lowella went on ahead, pretending to pick her way. "Wouldn't it be super if we had a rope attaching us all," she cried. "Then if the Bride fell over the cliff, we'd haul her up."

"That's kind of you, but I don't intend to fall."

"She's still the youth who bore mid snow and ice the banner with the strange device," murmured Hyson.

"Excelsior!" cried Lowella. "Isn't it a smashing word!" She ran on, shouting it.

Rachel looked at me and shrugged her shoulders.

In a few seconds I saw what they meant about the path's narrowing; for some two yards it was little more than a shelf; we walked rather gingerly in single file, then we rounded a part of the cliff which projected over the water, and as we did so I saw that we were almost at Polhorgan.

"It's certainly a short cut," I said. "Thanks for showing me."

"Shall we go back the same way?" Rachel asked the twins.

Lowella turned and was already on her way back. I heard her shouting "Excelsior" as I went on to Polhorgan.

Lord Polhorgan was delighted to see me. I fancied the manservant treated me with rather special deference, and it occurred to me that it must be rare for his master to become so friendly in such a short space of time.

When I went into his room, Nurse Grey was with him, reading to him from the *Financial Times*.

"Please don't let me interrupt," I said. "I must be early. I'll go and have a walk in the garden. I've always wanted to explore it."

Lord Polhorgan looked at his watch. "You are punctual," he said, and waved a hand at Nurse Grey, who promptly folded the paper and rose. "Never could abide people who have no respect for time. Unpunctuality is a vice. Glad to see you, Mrs. Pendorric. And I'd like to show you the garden, but I can't manage it these days. Too steep for me to walk; too steep for me to be wheeled."

"I'll enjoy it from the window today," I answered.

"Nurse Grey must show you one day."

"I'd be delighted to," said Althea Grey.

"Tell them to bring in the tea. And Nurse, there's no need for you to stay. Mrs. Pendorric will do the honors, I'm sure."

Nurse Grey bowed her head and murmured: "I'll hurry on the tea then."

Lord Polhorgan nodded and the nurse went out, leaving us together.

"Tea first," he said, "and we'll have our chess after. Sit down and talk to me for a while. You're settling in here now. Liking it?"

"Very much."

"All well at Pendorric?" He shot a quick glance at me from under his shaggy brows.

"Yes." I went on impulsively: "Did you expect it to be otherwise?"

He evaded the question. "It's never easy settling in to a new life. Must have been very gay—that island of yours. Find it quiet here?"

"I like this quiet."

"Better than the island?"

"When my mother was alive I was completely happy. I didn't think there was anything in the world but happiness. I was sad when I went away to school, but after a while I was used to that and being back was more fun than ever."

He gave me a look of approval. "You're a sensible young woman. I'm glad. Can't stand the other sort."

"Nurse Grey seems a sensible young woman."

"H'm. Too sensible perhaps."

"Can one be too sensible?"

"Sometimes I wonder why she stays here. I don't think it's out of love for her patient. I'm what's known as an old curmudgeon, Mrs. Pendorric."

I laughed. "You can't be such a bad one, since you admit it."

"Can't I! You forget, when a man's made money he's invariably surrounded by people who are anxious to relieve him of it . . . or some of it."

"And you think Nurse Grey . . ."

He looked at me shrewdly. "Handsome young woman . . fond of gaiety. Not so much to be had here."

"But she seems contented."

"Ay, she does and all." He nodded shrewdly. "Often wonder why. Perhaps she thinks she won't be forgotten . . . when the great day comes."

I must have shown my embarrassment, for he said quickly: "A fine host I am. Why, you'll be making excuses not to come and see me if I don't watch out. Shouldn't like that . . . shouldn't like it at all."

"I wouldn't make excuses to you. You're forthright and say what you mean, so I would try to do the same."

"We're alike in that," he said and chuckled.

The tea arrived and I poured. This had become a habit which was a further indication of the rate at which our friendship had developed. He seemed to take pleasure in watching me.

While I was serving tea I saw Althea Grey walking through the gardens down to the beach. She had changed her uniform for brown jeans and a blouse the color of delphiniums, which was a perfect foil for her fair hair, and I guessed her eyes matched the blouse. She looked back suddenly and, seeing me, waved; I waved back.

"It's Nurse Grey," I explained to my host. "She's off duty for a few hours I suppose."

He nodded. "Was she on her way down to the beach?"

"Yes."

"Polhorgan Cove belongs to me by rights but I was soon led to understand that the natives wouldn't think very kindly of me if I made it a private beach. There's a gate and hedges shutting off the garden; but you go through the gate right onto the beach."

"It's rather like Pendorric."

"The same arrangement. Pendorrics own their beach and I own mine, but I don't think half the people who scramble over the rocks at low tide know that."

"If the beaches were fenced off it would mean people couldn't walk along for very far; they'd have to keep coming up and making a detour."

"Always believed that what was mine was mine and I had a right to say what was to be done with it. I was very unpopular when I first came, I can tell you. I've grown mellow. You learn as you get older. Sometimes if you stand out for your rights you lose what might mean more to you."

He was momentarily sad and I fancied that he looked a little more tired than when I had last seen him.

"Yes, I think there's a lot in that," I said.

"There you were, with your mother and father in that island . . . perfectly happy, and I don't suppose you owned the house you lived in, let alone the ground all around and a private beach."

"It's true. We were very poor and very happy."

He frowned and I wondered if I had been tactless. He

went on rather brusquely: "Nurse Grey goes down to the beach a great deal. Do you use yours much?"

"Not so far. But I shall, of course. I've hardly settled in yet."

"I'm taking up too much of your time."

"But I like coming and I enjoy playing chess."

He was silent for a while and then again he led me back to the subject of my life on the island.

I was surprised that he could be such a good listener, but while I talked he remained attentive and fired so many questions at me in his rather brusque manner that I went on talking about myself.

When the tea had been cleared away I drew up the exquisite little table on which we played; it was a dainty piece, of French origin, with inlaid ivory and tortoise-shell squares; I put out the ivory chessmen, which were as beautiful as the table, and the game began.

When we had been playing for about fifteen minutes, to my surprise I had him at a disadvantage. I was delightedly pursuing my strategy when, looking up, I saw that he was in considerable discomfort.

"Sorry," he muttered. "Please forgive me." He was groping in his pocket.

"You've lost something?"

"A little silver box. I always keep it near me."

I stood up and, looking about me, saw a small silver box on the floor at his feet. I picked it up and gave it to him. His relief was apparent as he quickly opened it and took a small white tablet from it. This he placed under his tongue. For some seconds he sat back gripping his chair.

I was alarmed because I knew that he was ill, and I got up, going to the bell to call the manservant, but seeing what I was about to do, Lord Polhorgan shook his head. I stood uncertainly. "Better in a minute," he muttered.

"But you're ill. Shouldn't I . . .?"

He continued to shake his head while I stood helplessly by. In about five minutes he began to look a little better and it was as though a tension had been eased.

He drew a deep breath and murmured: "Better now. I'm sorry."

"Please don't be so sorry. Just tell me what I can do."

"Just sit down . . . quietly. In a few minutes I'll be all right."

I obeyed, watching him anxiously. The gilded French clock over the ornate fireplace ticked loudly, and apart from that there was silence in the room. From faraway I could hear the gentle swishing of the waves against the rocks.

A few more minutes passed and he gave a deep sigh. Then he smiled at me. "I'm sorry that happened while you were here. Mislaid my tablets. Don't usually stir without them. They must have dropped out of my pocket."

"Please don't apologize. I'm the one who is sorry. I'm afraid I didn't know what to do."

"There's nothing much anyone can do. If I'd had my box I'd have slipped a tablet into my mouth while you were busy over the game and you wouldn't have noticed anything. As it was . . . I delayed a little too long."

"I'm glad I found them."

"You look sad. Shouldn't, you know. I'm an old man. And one of the disadvantages of being old is that one is too old to deal with the disadvantages. But I've had my day. Besides, there's a lot of life in me yet. Don't like mislaying my tablets though. Could be dangerous."

"What wonderful tablets they must be!"

"Not always effective. They are ninety-nine times out of a hundred though. T.N.T. Expand the veins and arteries."

"And if they're not?"

"Then it's a dose of morphia."

"I'm terribly sorry."

He patted my hand. "The old engine's creaking," he said. "I need decarbonizing. Pity I can't ask you to run me into old Jim Bond's and have it done, eh?"

"Shouldn't you rest now?"

"Don't you worry. I'll phone my doctor and ask him to come in and see me. Haven't been feeling so well this last day or so."

"Shouldn't we phone at once?"

"Nurse Grey will do it when she comes in. Can't imagine how those tablets came to be on the floor."

"Perhaps there's a hole in your pocket."

He felt, and shook his head.

"You know, I think you ought to rest. Shall I go now? Or better still, telephone the doctor?"

"All right then. His number's in the little book by the telephone. Dr. Clement."

I went at once to the book and dialed the number. I was fortunate, for Dr. Clement happened to be in. I told him that I was speaking from Polhorgan and that Lord Polhorgan wanted him to look in soon.

"Right," said Dr. Clement. "I'll be along."

I replaced the receiver and went back to the table. "Can I do anything for you?" I asked.

"Yes, sit down and finish the game. I'm afraid I let you get the better of me. I was thinking about my silver box. Just to show you how quickly I can recover we'll continue the game and I'll beat you yet."

I kept taking uneasy glances at him as we played, which made him chuckle, and before we had finished the game, Dr. Clement arrived.

I rose to go but Lord Polhorgan wouldn't hear of it.

"I'm all right now," he said. "I only let Mrs. Pendorric call you because she was anxious about me. Tell her there's nothing to be done for me. The trouble was, Doctor, I'd mislaid my T.N.T.s and it was some minutes before Mrs. Pendorric found them."

"You should always keep them within reach," said Dr. Clement.

"I know. I know. Can't think what happened. Must have pulled them out of my pocket. Have some tea. Perhaps Mrs. Pendorric would ring for Dawson. That's cold by now."

The doctor declined the tea and I said I really should go. I was certain that he would want to be alone with his patient.

"The game's unfinished," protested Lord Polhorgan.

"We can finish it next time."

"I've frightened you away," said Dr. Clement almost wistfully.

I was determined to go, and I left. As I came through the portico I glanced at my watch and saw that I was half an hour earlier than I had intended to be, so instead of making my way to the road, or the path which led to the short cut Rachel and the twins had shown me that afternoon, I thought I would like to go down to the beach by way of the cliff garden and scramble over the rocks to Pendorric Cove, and through our own garden up to the house.

The tide was out so it would be possible. I walked around to the side of the house and saw one of the Polhorgan gardeners emerging from a greenhouse. I asked him how I could get to the beach from the garden and he offered to show me the way.

He led me along a path bounded on each side by a box hedge; at the end of this path was a small gate, and passing through this I was in the cliff garden. It was a wonderful sight, for in this semitropical climate plants grew in profusion.

There was a palm tree in a sheltered alcove, which reminded me of those in the quadrangle; and the hydrangea blooms were even bigger than those at Pendorric; they flaunted their brilliant blues and pinks, whites and multicolors. There seemed to be hundreds of fuchsias with larger flowers than I had seen before; and great white Arum lilies which filled the air with their slightly funereal scent.

The path I had taken wound in zigzag fashion towards the sea to eliminate the strain of walking down such a steep slope; first I faced east, then west, then turned again as I went past borders of flowers whose names I did not know, past seats which had been set under arches and in alcoves the trellis work of which was ablaze with Paul's Scarlet, American Pillar, and Golden Dawn roses.

I thought that if the sun were shining and the sea blue it would be almost too dazzling. But today was a gray day and the cry of the gulls seemed melancholy as they swooped and soared.

I came at length to the little gate which opened onto the beach and, as I stood in Polhorgan Cove, I looked back at that wonderful garden set out on the cliff side to the stone walls of Polhorgan's Folly looming above.

Not such a folly, I thought. A lovely house in a lovely spot.

The tide was well out. I knew that at high tide it came up almost as far as the gates of Pendorric garden and I imagined those of Polhorgan too. It was only when the tide was really out that one could walk along the beach. Even as far as I could see the place was deserted. Ahead of me the rocks jutted out almost to the water, shutting me in the little bay which was known as Polhorgan Cove. I guessed it would take me longer to reach Pendorric this way than by the road so I started westward immediately. It was not easy rounding the jagged rocks; there were so many to be climbed, and interesting little pools to be leaped over. I came to a large rock which actually did jut into the sea. It was rather difficult getting over that one, but I managed it; and then I saw our own beach, our garden, far less grand than that of Polhorgan, but perhaps as beautiful in its wild state.

I leaped onto the soft sand and as I did so I heard the sound of laughter.

Then I saw them. She was half lying on the sand, her face propped up by her hands, and he was stretched out beside her, leaning on one elbow. He looked as dark as he had when I had first seen him sitting in the studio with my father.

They were talking animatedly, and I thought uneasily; they wouldn't have expected to see me here suddenly.

I wanted them to know quickly that I was close-by. Perhaps I was afraid that if I did not make my presence known I might hear or see something which I did not want to. I called out: "Hello."

Roc sprang to his feet and for a few seconds stared at me; then he came running towards me, taking both my hands in his.

"Look who's here! I thought you were still at the Folly."

"I hope I didn't startle you."

He put his arm round me and laughed. "In the most pleasant way," he said.

We walked over to Althea Grey, who remained where she was on the sand. Her blue eyes, fixed on me, seemed shrewd and alert.

"Is everything all right at Polhorgan?" she asked.

I told her what had happened, and she got up.

"I'd better get back," she said.

"Come up to Pendorric," said Roc, "and I'll drive you there."

She looked up the steep garden to the gray walls of Pendorric and shook her head. "I don't think it would be any quicker. I'll go over the rocks." She turned to me. "I've done it so often, I'm becoming like a mountain goat. See you later," she added, and started to hurry across the sand.

"You look shaken," said Roc. "I believe the old man often has those attacks. He's been having them for years. Pity it happened when you were alone with him."

We opened the gate and started the climb through the garden to the house.

"What made you come the beach way?" asked Roc.

"I don't know. Perhaps because it was a way I hadn't been before and as I was leaving a little early I thought I'd try it. Is Althea Grey a friend of . . . the family?"

"Not of the family."

"Only of you?"

"You know what a friendly type I am!"

He caught me to him and hugged me. Questions were on my lips but I hesitated. I didn't want him to think I was going to be foolishly jealous every time he spoke to another woman. I had to remember I had married a Pendorric and they were noted for their gallantries.

"Do you often meet on the beach?"

"This is a small place. One is always running up against neighbors."

"I wonder why she preferred our beach to Polhorgan."

"Ah, from Pendorric beach you can look up at real antiquity; from Polhorgan you only get the fake."

"It's a very beautiful fake."

"I believe you're getting very fond of his lordship." He regarded me ironically: "Ought I to be jealous?"

I laughed, but I felt almost as uneasy as I had when I had come into the cove and seen them lying there together. Was he trying to turn the tables, as guilty people often did? Was he saying: You spend your afternoon with Lord Polhorgan, so why shouldn't I spend mine with his nurse?

It was an incongruous suggestion, but he went on: "I should be very jealous, so you mustn't provoke me."

"I hope you will remember to do unto others as you would they should do unto you."

"But you would never be jealous without reason. You're far too sensible."

"Yet I suppose it would be more reasonable to be jealous of a beautiful young woman than a sick old man."

"Often in these matters there are other factors to be considered besides personal charms."

"Such as?"

"You don't find millionaires lurking on every rock and patch of sand."

"What a hideous suggestion!"

"Isn't it? And I'm a beast to mention such mundane matters as money; but then, as you once said, I am a satyr, which is a form of beast, I suppose. Actually I fancied you were not very pleased to come upon Thea and me together and I wanted to tell you how ridiculous you were to be . . . not very pleased."

"You're not hinting that you'd rather I didn't visit Lord Polhorgan?"

"Good heavens, no! I'm delighted that you do. Poor old man, he's only just beginning to realize that his millions can't buy him all he wants. He's getting more pleasure out of having a beautiful young woman to pour his tea and hover over his ivory chessmen than he's had for years. And all without paying out a penny! It's a revelation to him. It reminds me of Little Lord Fauntleroy, the terror of my youth because I was forced to read of his adventures by a well-meaning nurse. I found him particularly nauseating—perhaps because he was the opposite of myself. I could never see myself in plum-colored velvet with my golden curls falling over my lace collar, going to soften the hard heart of dear old Lord Somebody, Fauntleroy, I believe . . . old Fauntleroy. That was one thing I could never do—bring warring relations together by my childish charm."

"Stop it, Roc. Do you really object to my visits to Polhorgan?"

He picked one of the Mrs. Simkins pinks that grew in rather untidy clumps, filling the air with their delicious scent, and gravely put it into the buttonhole of my short linen jacket.

"I've been talking a lot of nonsense because I'm garrulous by nature. Darling, I want you to feel absolutely free. As for visiting Lord Polhorgan, don't for heaven's sake stop. I'm glad you're able to give him so much pleasure. I know he ruined our east view with his monstrosity, but he's an old man and he's sick. Go as often as he asks you."

He leaned forward to smell the pink; then he kissed my lips. He took my hand and we climbed to the house.

As usual he had the power to make me accept what he wanted to; it was only when I was alone that I asked myself: Does he want me to visit Lord Polhorgan so that Althea Grey is free to be with him?

* * *

I went down to the kitchen one morning to find Mrs. Penhalligan at the table kneading dough, and there was the delicious smell of baking bread in the air.

The kitchens at Pendorric were enormous and, in spite of electric cookers, refrigerators, and other recently installed modern equipment, looked as though they belonged to another age. There were several rooms—a bakehouse, a buttery, a washhouse, and another room called the dairy, which had a floor of blue tiles and had once been a storeroom for milk, butter, eggs, and such. Across the ceiling were great oak beams supplied with hooks on which joints of meat, hams, sides of bacon, and Christmas puddings had once hung.

The kitchen itself, though large, was a cozy room with its red tiled floor and dressers, its refectory table at which generations of servants had had their meals, and the wooden one scrubbed white, at which, on this occasion, Mrs. Penhalligan was working. Through an open door I could see Maria preparing vegetables in the washhouse.

Mrs. Penhalligan bridled with pleasure when she saw me.

I said: "Good morning, Mrs. Penhalligan. I thought it was about time I paid a visit to the kitchens."

"It's good to see you, m'am," she answered.

"Is that bread baking? It smells delicious."

She looked very pleased. "We've always baked our own bread at Pendorric. There's nothing like the homebaked, I always say. I bake for Father at the same time. It's always been understood."

"How is your father?"

"Oh, fair to middling, m'am. Don't get no younger, but he be wonderful for his age. He'll be ninety next Candlemas."

"Ninety! That's a great age."

"And there bain't much wrong with him . . . 'cept of course his great affliction."

"Oh?"

"You didn't know, m'am, and I reckon none as yet thought fit to tell you. Father went blind . . . oh—it'll be nigh on thirty years ago. No. I bain't telling you the truth. It'll be twenty-eight years. It started . . . twenty-eight years come harvest time."

"I'm very sorry."

"Oh, don't 'ee be. Father bain't sorry for himself. He's happy enough . . . with his pipe and all he wants to eat. He likes to sit at the door on sunny days and it 'ud astonish you, m'am, how good his hearing is. Sort of makes up for not having his sight, so it seems."

"I expect I'll see him sometime."

"He'd be real pleased if you stopped and had a little chat with him. He's always asking about Mr. Roc's new bride."

"I'll look for him."

"You can't make no mistake. It's the second of the cottages down Pendorric Village. Lives all alone there. Independent since mother went. But Maria and me, we're always in and out. And we pop over with a plate of hot something for his dinner regular as clockwork. He don't pay no rent, and he's got his bit of pension. Father's all right. He'd be wonderful . . . if he had his sight."

I was glad Mrs. Penhalligan was the loquacious type because I had been wondering what I should say to her.

"I've been hearing about how your family have been at Pendorric for generations."

"Oh yes . . . always Pleydells at Pendorric. But then father and mother didn't have no son. I was their only daughter.

Then I married Penhalligan, who was gardener here till he died. And we only had one too . . . my Maria. She'll be working here till the end . . . and then that'll be the end of the Pleydells at Pendorric."

"What a pity!"

"All things has to come to an end, m'am. And did you want to give me some orders or something?"

"Not really. I thought I'd like to see how things were worked down here."

"Right and proper that you should, m'am. You be the mistress. Miss Morwenna, she was never one to take much interest. Now Miss Bective . . ." Mrs. Penhalligan's face hardened, "she was up another street. When she first come here, it was, 'Mrs. Penhalligan, we'll have this and we'll have that.' But I know my place if some don't, and I take orders from the mistress of the house and none other."

"I expect she was trying to be helpful."

"Helpful! I don't need help in my kitchen, m'am . . . no more than I've got. My Maria's been well trained and I'm not doing too bad with Hetty Toms."

"Everything is very well organized, I'm sure."

"And so should be . . . the years I've been at it. I was in the kitchen when the other Mrs. Pendorric first come here."

I felt excited as I always did at the mention of Barbarina. "Was she interested in the kitchen?"

"She were like yourself, m'am. Interested, I'd say, but not one to want to change things. I remember the day she came into my kitchen, her lovely face all glowing with health; she'd come in from a ride and she was in her riding clothes . . . breeches and coat like a man's. But there was nothing of the man about her. There was a little blue flower in her buttonhole and she had one of them riding hats on with a band of yellow 'round it. She always wore them . . . like in the picture in the south hall, only she's in blue there."

"Yes, I know the picture well."

"A lovely lady, and it was a pleasure to serve her. It was terrible when— But my tongue runs away with me. Maria always says so and she's right."

"It's pleasant to have a chat though. That's really what I came down for."

Mrs. Penhalligan's face shone with pleasure as her nimble fingers went on kneading the bread.

"She was like that too . . . always ready for a chat, particularly in the beginning. Afterwards she was . . ."

I waited and Mrs. Penhalligan frowned down at her dough. "She was less friendly later?" I prompted.

"Oh, not less friendly. Just sad, I think; and sometimes she wouldn't seem to see you. Reckon she was thinking of other things, poor lady."

"Of her troubles?"

"She had those. She was very fond of him, you see . . ." She seemed to recall to whom she was talking and stopped. "I suppose, m'am, you have a preference for the wholemeal bread. I bake some white . . . but more wholemeal. Father, he likes white . . . done in the old-fashioned coberg style. Father's one to have what he wants. Though I must say now though that his mind wanders a bit. It's not being able to see, I think. That must make a difference."

I said I personally preferred wholemeal, and that I thought the bread she made was the best I had ever tasted.

Nothing could have delighted her more; she was my ally from that moment. She relaxed too; she had concluded that, although I was the mistress of the house, I was fond of gossip.

"I'll certainly look out for your father when I next pass the cottages," I told her.

"I'll tell him. He'll be that pleased. You must be prepared though for him to wander a bit. He's close to ninety and he gets a bit muddled. He's had it on his mind a bit lately. I reckon it's because there's a new bride here at Pendorric."

"Had what on his mind?" I asked.

"Well, m'am, you'll have heard of course how Mr. Roc's and Miss Morwenna's mother died."

"Yes, I have heard."

"Well, Father was there when it happened. It preyed on his mind a bit for a time. Then he seemed to forget like . . . but things are likely to bring it back, which is all natural. And when he heard there was a new bride at Pendorric, you see . . ."

"Yes, I see. He was there, you say."

"He were there. In the hall when she, poor soul, did crash from the gallery. He weren't completely blind then neither . . . but almost he were. He couldn't see clear enough, but he knew her were up there and it was him that gave the alarm. That's why it preyed on his mind like. That's why he remembers now and then, though it be twenty-five years since it happened."

"Does he believe . . . the story about the ghost?"

Mrs. Penhalligan looked surprised. "Father knows there be

such things. I don't rightly know what he thinks about Mrs. Pendorric's fall. He don't talk much. He just sits brooding. Can't get him to talk much about it. Might be better if we could."

"I shall certainly look out for him when I pass the cottage, Mrs. Penhalligan."

"You'll see him . . . puffing away at his old pipe. He'll be that pleased. Maria'll just be taking the first batch out of the oven. I still use the old cloam oven for bread. Can't be beat. Would you like to come and see it, m'am?"

I said I would; and as I went through the kitchens to the bake-house and returned the greeting of Maria and Hetty Toms, I was not thinking of them or the golden brown loaves fresh from the oven; I kept seeing that beautiful young woman crashing from the gallery, the smiling painted face of Lowella Pendorric behind her; and in the hall, an almost sightless man, peering towards the falling figure, trying so hard to see what was happening.

* * *

After my talk with Mrs. Penhalligan I felt that I was truly mistress of the house. The faithful housekeeper, daughter of the Pleydells, who had served the family for generations, had accepted me. My sister-in-law had no great desire to manage the house, and I felt delighted to have something to do.

I wanted to know every inch and corner of Pendorric. I was beginning to love it, and to understand that a house which had stood for hundreds of years must necessarily have a stronger appeal than one which had stood only a few years.

I told Roc how I felt and he was delighted.

"What did I tell you?" he cried. "The brides of Pendorric fall fiercely in love with the place."

"It must be because they're so happy to have become Pendorrics."

The remark delighted him. He put his arm about me and I felt suddenly secure . . . safe.

"There are lots of things I want to ask you about the place," I told him. "Is it true that wood worm is slowly destroying parts of it?"

"The little beasts are the enemies of the stately homes of England, darling. They're almost as destructive as the Inland Revenue."

"That's another thing: You did seem rather sorry because you weren't so rich as Lord Polhorgan. Do you really think it'll be necessary to hand over Pendorric to the National Trust?"

Roc took my face in his hands and kissed me lightly.

"Don't worry, sweetheart. We'll manage to keep the wolf from the ancestral home."

"So we aren't living beyond our means?"

He laughed lightheartedly. "I always knew I'd married a businesswoman. Listen, darling; when I've talked over this with Charles I'm going to show you how things work here. I'm going to make use of you, you see. I'm going to show you all the inner workings of an estate like ours. Then you'll see what it's all about."

"Oh Roc dear, I'll love that."

"I thought you would. But first I've got to make up for my long absence from home. Then I've got to prepare old Charlie. He's a bit old-fashioned. Keep the women out of business and all that. He doesn't realize the sort of woman I've found for myself. You see, Morwenna's never been the least bit interested in anything except the gardens."

"Do persuade him soon."

"Trust me." He was serious suddenly. "I want us to be . . . together in everything. Understand?"

I nodded. "No secrets," I added.

He held me tightly for a moment. "Quite close . . . forever and ever until death do us part."

"Oh, Roc, don't talk of death."

"Only as something in the dim and distant future, my love. But you're happy now."

"Wonderfully happy."

"That's how I want you to stay. So no worries about the house. Don't I have you to help me? Then there's Charles. He'd die rather than see the old place go. Not that it goes completely if you hand over to the National Trust. But you can't tell me your home's the same if you're going to have people wandering round from two till six-thirty every afternoon except Wednesdays."

I felt completely happy after that talk; never had the tragedy of my father's death seemed so far behind me. My life was here at Pendorric; it was true I was a newcomer, but everyone accepted me as a member of the family and Roc had given me the comfort that only he could give.

Soon afterwards I decided I would make a tour of all the

rooms and see if I could detect anything that was in need of urgent repair. I was sure it was something that should be done, for Charles was interested in the farm, Morwenna in the garden, and Roc had the entire estate to manage.

I would begin with the east wing because that was the one which was unoccupied; and after luncheon one day I went down to the quadrangle, sat by the pond for a few minutes, and then entered the house by way of the east door.

As soon as that door closed behind me I began to think of Barbarina, who had loved this part of the house, and I longed to see her music room again.

I went straight to that floor, and as I mounted the stairs a sudden impulse came to me to turn back, but I quickly thrust this aside for I was not going to feel afraid every time I came to this part of the house simply because of an old legend.

When I reached the door of the music room, I quickly turned the handle and went in.

Everything was as it had been when I had last seen it: the violin lying across the chair, the music on the stand.

I shut the door behind me, reminding myself that I had come here for a practical purpose. Where, I wondered, would wood worm most likely be found? In the woodwork about the windows? In the oak beams across the ceiling? In the floor perhaps, or the doors? If it did exist the sooner it was dealt with the better.

My eyes kept straying to the music stand, and I was picturing her there, her eyes bright with inspiration, faint color in her cheeks. I knew exactly what she looked like, and I wondered what her thoughts had been the last time she had stood there, her violin in her slim hands with their tapering fingers.

"Barbarina!" The name was spoken in a whisper.

I felt a prickly sensation in my spine. I was not alone in this room.

"Barbarina! Are you there, Barbarina?"

A movement behind me made me spin around hastily. My eyes went to the door and I saw that the handle was slowly being turned.

My hands had involuntarily placed themselves across my heart which was beating painfully as the door was slowly opened.

"Carrie!" I cried reproachfully. "You startled me."

The little eyes beneath those heavy brows glinted as she looked at me.

"So it's Mr. Roc's bride," she said. "I thought for the moment . . ."

"You thought I was somebody else?"

She nodded slowly and looked about the room as though she were seeking something.

I went on because I wanted to know what was in her mind: "You said: 'Barbarina.' "

Again she nodded without speaking.

"She's dead, Carrie."

"She don't rest," was the low reply.

"So you believe that she haunts the house . . . haunts these rooms?"

"I know when she's getting ready to walk. There's a kind of stirring." She came close to me and looked into my face. "I can feel it now."

"Well, I can't." Then I was afraid that I had spoken rather sharply and I remembered that she had been nurse to Barbarina and Deborah and had loved them dearly. When loved ones died, often those who had lost them made themselves believe that they could come back. I could see the devotion shining in Carrie's eyes, and I knew that when she had heard me in the music room she had really hoped it was Barbarina.

"You will," said Carrie.

I smiled disbelievingly. "I must get on," I said. "I'm rather busy."

I walked out of the music room, but I didn't want to stay any longer in the east wing. I went back to the quadrangle and sat there; and every now and then I would find myself looking up involuntarily at those windows.

* * *

When I next called on Lord Polhorgan, Dr. Clement was there. He had tea with us and I found his company pleasant, as I was sure our host did.

I was very pleased to see that Lord Polhorgan had recovered from his recent attack and I was surprised that he could appear as well as he did.

We talked about the village and I discovered that Dr. Clement, like the Reverend Peter Dark, was very interested in the customs of the place.

He lived on the outskirts of Pendorric village in a house which he had taken over from the doctor who had retired on his arrival.

"It's called Tremethick, which is apt, because in Cornish it means the doctor's house. You must come and meet my sister some time."

I said I should be delighted to; and he talked of his sister Mabell, who was interested in pottery and made quite a number of the little pots and ash trays which were for sale in some of the shops in the towns along the coast. She was something of an artist, too, and not only supplied pottery but her pictures 'on sale or return' to the shops.

"It keeps her busy—that and the house."

She had turned the old stables into a workshop and had her oven there.

"She'll never make a fortune out of her pottery," our host commented. "Too much mass production against her."

"Not a fortune, but a lot of pleasure," retorted the doctor. "And it pleases her that there's a small profit in it."

There was no chess that day and, when I got up to go, the doctor said he had his car outside and would drive me home.

I told him that there was no need, but he insisted that he went past Pendorric, so I accepted.

As we drove along he asked if I always made the journey from Pendorric to Polhorgan by the top road, and I said that there were three ways of getting there: by that road, Smugglers' Lane and the short cut, and by way of the beach and the gardens.

"If I'm in a hurry," I told him, "I take the short cut."

"Oh yes," he said, "you can save quite five minutes that way. Once there was a road here with houses on either side. I found an old map the other day. It gives you some idea how the sea is gradually encroaching on the land. It couldn't have been more than a hundred and fifty years old. Why not come along now and meet Mabell? She'd be delighted to see you, and I'd run you back."

I looked at my watch and, thinking that Roc might already be home, said that I didn't really think I had time.

He dropped me at Pendorric. I thanked him and he gave me a friendly wave as his car roared away.

I turned to the house. There was no one in sight, and I stood for a while under the arch and looked up at the inscription in Cornish.

It was a gray day; there had been no sun lately; nor would there be, Roc had told me, until the wind changed. It was now blowing straight in from the southwest—soft and balmy, the sort of wind that made one's skin glow.

The gulls seemed even more mournful than usual today,

but that may have been because of the grayness of the sea and the leaden sky.

I walked around the house to the south side and stood for a moment looking down on the garden, but even the colors of the flowers seemed subdued.

I went into the house and as soon as I entered the hall my eyes fixed themselves on the portrait of Barbarina. I was afraid they were making a habit of doing that. The eyes in the picture followed me as I passed the suits of armor and started to go up the stairs. I went up to the gallery and stood right beneath the portrait looking up at it, and as Barbarina's eyes looked straight into mine, I could almost imagine the lips curved into a smile—a warm, inviting smile.

I was really being rather silly, I told myself.

The hall was gloomy today because it was so gray outside. If the sun were shining through those big mullioned windows it would seem quite different.

Was Roc home? I wondered. There was a great deal to be done on the farm and about the estate, and that work was still very much in arrears, because he had been abroad so long.

I walked along the gallery to the corridor. Several of the windows were open and I could never seem to resist looking down at the quadrangle. And as I stood there I could distinctly hear the music of a violin.

I threw up the window and leaned out. Yes, there was no doubt about it; and one of the windows on the east side was open. Was the sound coming from the east wing?

It might well be. I was sure it was. My eyes went to the second floor. If someone were playing in the music room could I hear from across the corridor and the quadrangle?

I was ashamed of feeling so frightened. I was not going to be taken in by my foolish imagination. I reminded myself of the day Carrie had come into the music room while I was there, and how scared I had been because she went creeping around calling Barbarina; as soon as I had seen that it was Carrie, I had ceased to be scared; I was not the least bit taken in by her talk of "stirring."

I began to walk resolutely round the corridor to the east wing. As I went in I heard the violin again. I hurried up the stairs to the music room.

There was no sound of the violin now. I threw open the door. The violin lay on the chair; the music was on the stand.

There was no one in the room and I felt the stillness of the house close about me.

Then suddenly I heard the shriek of a gull outside the window.

It seemed to be laughing at me.

* * *

Because I was not anxious to stay in the house I decided to go for a walk in the direction of the home farm, hoping to meet Roc.

As I walked I reasoned with myself: Someone in the house plays the violin, and you presumed it came from the east wing because you had seen the violin there. If you really are disturbed about it, the simplest thing is to find out who in the house plays the violin and casually mention that you heard it being played.

Out of doors everything seemed so much more rational than it did in the house. As I climbed onto the road and walked across the fields in a northerly direction I was quickly recovering my good spirits. I had not walked this way before and I was delighted to explore fresh ground. The countryside seemed restful after the rugged coast views and I was charmed by the greenish gold of the freshly mown fields and the scarlet of the poppies growing here and there. I particularly noticed the occasional tree, slightly bent by the southwest gales, but taller than those stunted and distorted ones which survived along the coast. I could smell the fragrance of meadow-sweet growing on the banks, mingling with the harebells and scabious.

And while I was contemplating all this I heard the sound of a car and to my delight saw it was Roc's.

He pulled up and put his head out of the window.

"This a pleasant surprise."

"I've never walked this way. I thought I'd come and meet you."

"Get in," he commanded.

When he hugged me I felt secure again and very glad I had come.

"I got back from Polhorgan to find no one around, so I decided I wouldn't stay in."

Roc started the car. "And how was the old man today?"

"He seemed to have quite recovered."

"I believe that's how it is with his complaint. Poor old fellow, it must be a trial for him, yet he's cheerful enough . . . about his health."

"I think he's very brave."

Roc gave me a quick look. "Relations still remain friendly?"

"Of course."

"Not everyone gets along with him so well. I'm glad you do."

"I'm still surprised that you should be when you so obviously don't like him."

"The lady of the manor has always gone round visiting the sick. It's an old custom. You've started well."

"Surely the custom was to visit the sickly poor and take them soup and blankets."

Roc burst out laughing. "Imagine your arriving at Polhorgan with a bowl of soup and a red flannel blanket, and handing them to Dawson for the deserving millionaire!"

"This is quite a different sort of visiting anyway."

"Is it? He wants company; they wanted comforts. Same thing, but in a different form. No, really, darling, I'm delighted that you're able to bring sunshine into the old man's life. You've brought such lots into mine, I can spare him a little. What do you talk about all the time? Does he tell you about his wicked family who deserted him?"

"He hasn't mentioned his family."

"He will. He's waiting for the opportunity."

"By the way," I said, "I heard someone playing the violin this afternoon. Who would it have been?"

"The violin?" Roc screwed up his eyes as though puzzled. "Where?"

"I wasn't sure where. I thought it was in the east wing."

"Hardly anyone goes there except old Carrie. Can't believe she's turned virtuoso. In our youth, Morwenna and I had a few lessons. They soon discovered, in my case at least, that it was no use trying to cultivate stony ground. Morwenna wasn't bad. But she dropped all that when she married Charles. Charles is tone deaf—wouldn't know a Beethoven concerto from 'God Save the Queen'; and Morwenna is the devoted wife. Everything that Charles thinks, she thinks; you could take her as a model, darling."

"So you're the only two who could play the violin?"

"Wait a minute. Rachel gave the twins lessons at one time, I believe. Lowella takes after me and is about as talented in that direction as a bull calf. Hyson now . . . she's different. I think Hyson was quite good at it."

"It could have been Hyson or Rachel I heard playing."

"You seem very interested. Not thinking of taking it up yourself? Or are you a secret genius? There's a lot I don't know about you, Favel, even though you are my wife."

As we came onto the coast road we met Rachel, and Roc slowed down the car for her to get in.

"I've been looking for the twins," she told us. "They went shrimping this afternoon, down at Tregallic Cove."

"I hope you took advantage of your respite," Roc said.

"I did. I went for a long walk as far as Gorman's Bay. I had tea there and planned to pick them up on the way back. I expect they've already gone home."

"Favel thought she heard you playing the violin this afternoon."

I turned and looked at Rachel. Her expression seemed faintly scornful, her sandy eyes more sly than usual.

"You'd hardly have heard me on the road from Gorman's Bay."

"It must have been Hyson then."

Rachel shrugged her shoulders. "I don't think Hyson will qualify for the concert platform, and I'd be surprised if she deserted shrimps for music."

As we were going to the house the twins arrived, with their shrimping nets and a pail in which Lowella carried their catch.

Rachel said: "By the way, Hyson, you didn't come back and play your violin this afternoon?"

Hyson looked bewildered. "Whatever for?" she said.

"Your Aunt Favel thought she heard you."

"Oh," said Hyson thoughtfully. "She didn't hear *me* playing it."

She turned away abruptly, and I was sure it was because she didn't want me to see that Rachel's remark had excited her.

* * *

The next day it rained without stopping and continued through the night.

"There's nothing unusual about that," Roc told me. "It's another old Cornish custom. You'll begin to understand why ours is the greenest grass in this green and pleasant land."

The soft southwest wind was blowing and everything one touched seemed damp.

The following day the rain was less constant, though the lowering sky promised more to come. The sea was muddy brown about the shore and farther out it was a dull grayish green.

Roc was going off to the farm and as I had decided that I

would go along to Polhorgan to complete that unfinished
game of chess, he drove me there on his way.

Lord Polhorgan was delighted to see me; we had tea as
usual and played our game of chess, which he won.

He liked to have an inquest after it was over, and point
out where I had given him the game. It put him in a good
humor and I enjoyed it because after all the purpose of my
visits was to give him pleasure.

As I was leaving Dr. Clement called. He was getting out
of his car, as I came out by the unicorns, and looked
disappointed.

"Just leaving?" he said.

"Yes, I've stayed rather longer than I meant to."

"Mabell is very much looking forward to meeting you."

"Tell her I'm also looking forward to it."

"I'll get her to telephone you."

"Please do. How ill is Lord Polhorgan?"

Dr. Clement looked serious. "One can never be sure with
a patient in his condition. He can become seriously ill very
quickly."

"I'm glad Nurse Grey is always at hand."

"It's rather essential that he should have someone in attendance. Mind you . . ."

He did not continue and I guessed he was about to offer a
criticism of Althea Grey and changed his mind.

I smiled. "Well, I'll have to hurry. Good-by."

"Good-by."

He went into the house and I made my way towards the
coast road. Then I changed my mind and decided to use the
short cut.

I had not gone far when I realized I'd been rather foolish
to come, for the path was a mass of reddish brown mud and I
guessed Smugglers' Lane would be even worse. I stood still
wondering whether to turn back, but as I should have to plow
through mud to do so, I decided it couldn't be much worse if
I went on. My shoes were filthy by now in any case.

I had not quite reached the narrow ledge when I heard
Roc's voice.

"Favel! Stop where you are. Don't move till I get to you."

I turned sharply and saw him coming towards me.

"What's wrong?"

He didn't answer but coming close he put out an arm and
held me tightly against him for some seconds. Then he said:
"This path is dangerous after a heavy rain. Look! Can you

see the cracks in the ground? Part of the cliff has collapsed. It's unsafe even here."

He took my arm and drew me back the way I had come, carefully picking his steps.

When we reached the beginning of the cliff path he stopped and sighed deeply. "I was thoroughly scared," he said. "It suddenly occurred to me. I came hurrying over to Polhorgan and they told me you'd just left. Look back. Can you see where the cliff side has crumbled? Look at that heap of shale and uprooted bracken halfway down the slope."

I saw it and shuddered.

"The narrow part is absolutely unsafe," went on Roc. "I'm surprised you didn't see the notice. Come to think of it I didn't see it myself."

"It always says THIS PATH USED AT OWN RISK. But I thought that was for visitors who aren't used to the cliffs."

"After heavy rain they take that away and put up another notice: PATH UNSAFE. Can't understand why it wasn't done." He was frowning and then he gave a sudden cry. "Good Lord," he said, "I wonder who did this?" He stooped and picked up a board which was lying face down. There were two muddy prongs attached to it which clearly had recently been embedded in the ground. "I don't see how it could have fallen. Thank heaven I came."

"I was going very carefully."

"You might have managed but . . . oh, my God . . . the risk."

He held me close to him and I was deeply touched because I knew he was anxious that I should not see how frightened he was. He stuck the notice board into the ground and said gruffly:

"The car's not far off. Come on! Let's get home."

*   *   *

When we drove up to the portico Morwenna was busy forking plantains from the stretch of lawn.

Roc slammed the car door and shouted: "Someone must have uprooted the danger board on the cliff path. I just stopped Favel going along it in time."

Morwenna stood up looking startled. "Who on earth . . . ?" she began.

"Some kids, I expect. It ought to be reported. It suddenly occurred to me that she might go that way . . . and she did."

"I've often been over it when the danger board's been up."

"There was a bad landslide," Roc said shortly. He turned to me. "The path shouldn't be used until they've done something about it. I'm going to speak to Admiral Weston—the chairman of the local council."

Charles had come around by the side of the house; I noticed that his boots were muddy.

"Anything wrong?"

Roc repeated the story of what he seemed to regard as my narrow escape.

"Visitors," grumbled Charles. "I bet it's visitors."

"All's well that ends well," said Morwenna, drawing off her gardening gloves. "I've had enough for today. I could do with a drink. What about you, Favel? I expect Roc could do with one, and Charles never says no."

We went into the house to a little parlor leading off the hall. Morwenna took drinks from a cabinet and, while she was serving them, Rachel Bective came in with Hyson. They were wearing slippers, and Morwenna's look of approval called my attention to them. I guessed they had changed at the back door where the gum boots and house shoes were kept ready for occasions like this.

The subject of the notice board was brought up again and Rachel Bective did not look at me as she said: "That could have been dangerous. It was a good thing you remembered, Roc." Hyson was staring at her slippers and I fancied I saw a slight smile curve her lips.

"Where's Lowella?" asked Morwenna.

Neither Rachel nor Hyson had any idea.

It was five or ten minutes later when Lowella joined us and she was immediately followed by Deborah. Lowella told us that she had been swimming; and Deborah had obviously just got up from her usual afternoon nap; she still looked sleepy and no one mentioned the notice-board incident after that, but I could see that several of them hadn't forgotten it. Roc still looked worried; Rachel Bective almost rueful; and Hyson secretive as though she knew something which she was determined not to tell.

I half wondered whether Hyson had removed the board. She knew where I had gone and that I'd probably come home by the short cut. She might even have watched me. But what reason could she possibly have for doing it? There might be more than a streak of mischief in her nature. But, I decided, Roc had made a great deal out of something not very important, simply because of his love for me.

I felt rather cozily content, until the following day, when the doubts began.

*   *   *

The weather had completely changed by next morning. The sky was a guileless blue and the sea sparkled so brilliantly that it was almost too dazzling to contemplate. It was like a sheet of silk, with scarcely a ripple in it. Roc took me with him to the forge, where one of his horses was being shod that morning. I was offered another glass of cider from the barrel in the corner; and while young Jim shod the horse, Dinah came into the forge to give me the benefit of her bold lustrous stare; I guessed that she was wondering about my relationship with Roc and that made me suspect that he and she had been on intimate terms at some time, and that she was trying to convey this to me.

"Maybe," she said, "I'll tell Mrs. Pendorric's fortune one day."

Old Jim murmured that he doubted whether Mrs. Pendorric would be interested in such nonsense.

She ignored him. "I'm good with the cards but it's your own hand and the crystal that's best. I could tell you a fine fortune, Mrs. Pendorric."

She smiled, throwing back her dark head so that the gold-colored rings in her ears danced.

"One day perhaps . . ." I murmured.

"Don't make it too long. Delay's dangerous."

When we left the forge and passed the row of cottages I saw an old man sitting at the door of one of them.

"Morning, Jesse," called Roc.

"Morning, sir."

"We must speak to Jesse Pleydell," Roc whispered.

The gnarled hands were grasping the bony knees and they were trembling. I wondered why; then I saw how very old he was and thought this was the reason.

"Be that your lady as is with you, sir?" he asked gently.

"It is, Jesse; she's come to make your acquaintance."

"How do you do," I said. "Your daughter was talking to me about you."

"She be a good girl, my Bessie . . . and Maria, she be good too. Don't know what I'd do without 'em . . . now I be so old and infirm like. 'Tis a pleasure to think of her . . . up at the House."

"We wish that you could be there too, Jesse," said Roc, and

the gentleness of his voice delighted me and made me feel as happy as I had before Dinah Bond had put misgivings into my mind.

"Ay, sir, that's where my place be. But since my eyes was took from me, it's little use I be to God or man."

"Nonsense, we're all proud of you, Jesse. You've only got to live another twenty years and you'll make Pendorric famous."

"Always one for a joke, Master Roc . . . like his father. Now he were one for a joke till . . ." His hands began to pluck at the cloth of his trousers nervously.

"Like father, like son," said Roc. "Well, we must be moving on."

On impulse I stepped closer to the old man and laid a hand on his shoulder. He was very still and a smile touched his lips.

"I'll come and see you again," I said.

He nodded and his hands began to tremble again as they sought his bony kneecaps and rested there.

" 'Tis like old times . . ." he murmured. "Like old times, with a new bride up to Pendorric. I wish *you* all the best of luck, m'dear."

When we were out of earshot I said: "Mrs. Penhalligan told me he was in the hall at the time of your mother's accident."

"She told you that, did she?" He was frowning. "How they do go on about things that are past and over." He glanced at me and, perhaps because I looked surprised at his mild annoyance, he went on: "I suppose so little happens in their lives that they remember every little thing that's out of the ordinary routine."

"I should certainly hope someone's untimely death would be very much out of routine."

He laughed and put his arm through mine. "Remember that when you feel tempted to go scrambling over dangerous paths," he said.

Then we came to the Darks' house and the Reverend Peter invited us in; he was so eager to show us pictures he had taken of the Helston Furry dancers the preceding May.

That afternoon I went to the quadrangle, not to sit, for, in spite of the warm sun of the morning, the seats had not yet dried out after the rain. Hyson followed me there and gravely walked round at my side. The hydrangeas looked fresher than ever and their colors more brilliant.

Hyson said suddenly: "Did you feel frightened when Uncle Roc rescued you on the cliff path?"

"No. It didn't occur to me that there was any danger until he pointed it out."

"You probably would have got through all right. It was just that there *might* have been an accident."

"It was a good thing I was stopped from going on then, wasn't it?"

Hyson nodded. "It was meant," she said, in a small hollow voice.

I looked at her sharply.

"Perhaps," she went on, "it was just a warning. Perhaps . . ."

She was staring at one of the windows on the east side as she had before. I looked up; there was no one there. She saw my glance and smiled faintly.

"Good-by," she said; and went into the house through the north door.

I felt irritated. I had an idea that the child wanted to make an impression on me. What was she suggesting? That certain matters which were obscure to ordinary people were revealed to her? Really it was rather silly of her. But she was only a child. I must remember that; and it was rather sad if she were jealous of her sister.

Then quite suddenly I heard the voice and for a moment I had no idea from where it was coming. It floated down to me, a strange voice singing slightly out of tune. I heard the words distinctly.

> *"He is dead and gone, lady,*
> *He is dead and gone;*
> *At his head a grass-green turf,*
> *At his feet a stone."*

I looked up at the windows on the east side. Several of them were open.

Then I went resolutely through the east door and up the stairs to the gallery.

"Hyson," I called. "Are you there, Hyson?"

There was no answer; and I realized how very cool it seemed in the house after coming in from the sunshine. I was angry, telling myself that someone was trying to tease me. I was more angry than I should have been; and there, in that silent part of the house, I understood that I was so angry because I was beginning to be frightened.

4.

SOMEONE WAS AMUSING himself—or herself—at my expense.

I had heard the playing of a violin; I had heard the singing. Why should I be the one singled out to hear these things? I was sure it was because of the legend and because I was the new Bride. Had my practical attitude, my determination not to be affected by stories of ghosts and hauntings, irritated someone? Was my skepticism a challenge? That seemed the most likely. Someone who believed in the ghost of Pendorric was determined to make me change my tune.

I wondered to whom I could talk about this subject, which was beginning to take up too much of my thoughts.

If I mentioned it to Roc, he would laugh and tell me I was coming under the spell of Pendorric as all the brides did. Morwenna was always friendly but somehow remote; as for Charles, I saw less of him than of anyone in the household and I couldn't imagine myself chatting cozily with him. The twins? Impossible. Lowella was too much of a scatterbrain and I could never be sure what Hyson was thinking. Indeed, if someone was trying to scare me I rather suspected it might be Hyson, for, after all, there was an element of childishness in the method.

I had never liked Rachel Bective and it occurred to me that she might have sensed my dislike, returned it, and was trying to make me uncomfortable in my new home.

There seemed only one person in whom I could confide and that was Deborah. She was more affectionate than Morwenna, more inclined to share confidences; and I felt that, being a Devonshire woman, she was practical and looked on superstition much as I myself did.

There was an opportunity to talk to her when I went to her room to look at her albums, and we sat in the window seat of her sitting room with the books across our knees while she explained the pictures to me. They had been arranged with care, in chronological order, with a caption beneath each; and most of the early ones were of Barbarina and her husband.

121

There were several of Barbarina and Deborah herself and I couldn't distinguish which was which.

"That's because we're in repose," explained Deborah. "She was much more animated than I; she had all the charm. But you don't see that in a snapshot."

There were many of Roc and Morwenna; and I found it absorbingly interesting to study his little face and discover there a hint of traits which were his today.

Then I turned a page and there were no more pictures.

"That last one was taken a week before Barbarina died," Deborah told me. "After that I didn't use this book. This was what I thought of as Barbarina's Book. It couldn't go on after she had gone." She picked up another album and opened it. I looked at pictures of an older Roc and Morwenna. "After a while," went on Deborah, "life started to go on in a new pattern, and I took my pictures again."

I turned a page and stopped, for I was looking at what I thought was a group consisting of Roc, Morwenna, and Barbarina.

"This one doesn't belong in this book."

Deborah smiled. "Oh yes, it does. That isn't Barbarina. She died six months before that was taken."

"So it's you. But you look so exactly like her."

"Yes . . . when she was no longer there to be compared with me people thought I was more like her than I had been before. But that was because she wasn't there, of course." She turned the page as though she couldn't bear to look at it. "Oh, and here's Morwenna and Charles. He's very young there. He came to Pendorric when he was eighteen or so. Petroc's idea was to train him so that he could take over, and that was what he did. See how Morwenna gazes up at him. He was a god to her." She laughed. "It was rather amusing to see the effect he had on her. Every sentence she uttered began with 'Charles says . . .' or 'Charles does . . .' She adored him from the moment he came to Pendorric, and she's gone on doing so ever since."

"They're very happy, aren't they?"

"Sometimes I used to think that there was too much devotion there. I remember one occasion when he went down to market and was involved in a smash-up. It was only a minor affair, and he was in hospital for less than a week, but Morwenna was . . . stricken. And I thought then: 'You're not living a life of your own, my dear. You're living Charles's life. That's well enough if Charles goes on living and loving you. But what if he doesn't?' I think she'd die of a broken heart."

"Charles seems quite devoted to her."

"Charles would always be a faithful husband, but there are other things in his life than his marriage. He's devoted to the Church, you know. Peter Dark often says he doesn't know what he'd do without him. Charles's father was a parson, and he was very strictly brought up. He's deeply religious. In fact I wonder he didn't take holy orders. I think cultivating the land is a sort of religion with him. As a matter of fact he has moulded Morwenna to his ways. There was a time when she was as ready for mischief as her brother. I've never known her to go against Charles in any way . . . except perhaps one thing."

I waited expectantly and Deborah hesitated as though wondering whether to go on.

"I meant . . . her friendship with Rachel Bective."

"Oh, doesn't Charles like Rachel?"

"I don't think he has any strong feelings of dislike, but at one time Morwenna used to bring her home from school for every holiday. I asked if she hadn't another friend who might come, or whether Rachel hadn't a home of her own to go to, and I remember how stubborn Morwenna was. 'She *must* come here,' she said. 'She wants to come and she hates going to her own home.' Charles didn't actually say he disapproved of her, but he never took the two of them riding or with him when he went round the farms, as he took Morwenna when she was alone. I thought that would be enough to make her stop inviting Rachel. But it wasn't."

"And now she's living here!"

"Only until the children go away to school again. And then I expect she'll find some excuse to stay, although perhaps now you're mistress of the house . . ."

Deborah sighed and I knew what she meant. Unprivileged Rachel had come from a poor home to Pendorric, had loved what she had seen and longed to make it her own. Had she believed that *she* might be the new bride of Pendorric? Roc had evidently been friendly with her, and I could understand how easy it was to fall in love with him. Was Rachel in love with Roc? Or had she been at some time? Yes, I decided in that moment, Rachel Bective might have a very good reason for resenting me.

I said slowly: "Do you remember telling me about Barbarina's playing Ophelia and singing a song from the play?"

Deborah was very still for a few seconds and I was aware that she did not look at me. She nodded.

"I thought I heard someone singing that song in the east wing. I wondered who it could be."

The silence seemed to go on for a long time, but perhaps it was only for a few seconds. Then Deborah said: "I suppose anyone might sing that song."

"Yes, I suppose so."

Deborah turned to get one of the albums which I had not yet seen; she sat beside me explaining the pictures. She evidently did not appear to think it strange that I should have heard someone singing the song.

* * *

A few days later, in response to an invitation, I called at the doctor's house. It was a charming place—early nineteenth century—surrounded by a garden in which were beehives. Mabell Clement was a very busy person, tall and fair like her brother, and she wore her hair in a thick plait which hung halfway down her back—at least that was how it was when I first met her; on later occasions I saw it made into a knot in the nape of her neck that was always threatening to escape restriction; she wore smocks sometimes, caught in at the waist by girdles, with raffia sandals, amber beads, and swinging earrings.

She was determined that everyone should recognize her as an artist, and this seemed to be her one foible, for she appeared to be good-natured, easygoing, and a good hostess. She was very proud of her brother; and he was affectionately tolerant towards her. I imagine that meals were served at odd times in that household for Mabell admitted that, when the urge to paint or pot or look after her garden came to her, she simply had to obey it.

I was shown over Tremethick itself, the pottery shed, and what was called the studio, and I had an interesting afternoon.

Dr. Clement said that he would drive me back to Pendorric, but half an hour before I was due to leave a call came through from one of his patients and he had to go off immediately.

Thus I walked back to Pendorric alone.

As I came into the village there was no sign of anyone. It was one of those still afternoons, very hot and sultry; I passed the row of cottages, and looked for Jesse Pleydell, but he was not at his door today. I wondered whether to call on him as I had promised to do, but decided against it. I wanted to find out from Mrs. Penhalligan or Maria what tobacco he smoked and take some along for him when I went.

The churchyard lay on my right. It looked cool and somehow inviting. I hesitated and then slipped through the lych gate. I have always been attracted by graveyards, particularly deserted ones. There seems to me to be a sense of utter peace within them, and I liked to think of all those people, lying beneath the gray stones, who had once lived and suffered and now were at peace.

I walked among the tombstones and read some of the inscriptions as Roc had, not very long ago; and eventually I saw ahead of me the Pendorric vault.

Irresistibly attracted, I went to it. I wanted to see if the laurel wreath was still there.

It had gone but in its place was a small wreath of roses, and as I went closer I recognized the Paul's Scarlets that grew in the garden. There was no note on the flowers but I was sure they were there in memory of Barbarina. It occurred to me then that Carrie was the one who put them there.

I heard a rustle in the grass behind me and, turning sharply, saw Dinah Bond picking her way towards me. She looked even more vital here among the dead than she did in the old blacksmith's shop; she held herself erect and swung her hips as she walked, in a manner which was both graceful and provocative.

"Hello there, Mrs. Pendorric," she called jauntily.

"Hello," I answered.

"It be quiet in here . . . peaceful like."

"I thought the village looked peaceful today."

"But too hot to move about much. There's thunder in the air. Can't you feel it? All still and waiting like . . . for the storm to break."

"I expect you're right."

She smiled at me insolently and, what was worse, with something which I felt might have been compassion.

"Having a look at the family vault? I often do. I bet 'ee haven't been inside, Mrs. Pendorric."

"No."

She laughed. "Time enough for that, I reckon you think. It's cold as death inside . . . and all the coffins laid out on shelves. Sometimes I come and look at it . . . like this afternoon . . . just for the pleasure of knowing I'm outside and not locked in—like Morwenna once was."

"Morwenna! Locked in! How did that happen?"

"It's years ago. I was only a kid then . . . about six, I think. When are you going to let me tell your fortune?"

"Sometime I expect."

"No time like the present."

"Why are you so anxious?"

"I'm just taken that way."

"I haven't any silver to cross your palm with."

"That! It's just a way to get the money. I wouldn't do it for money . . . not for you, Mrs. Pendorric. Now I'm married to Jim Bond, I don't do it professional like. That went out when I gave up my gypsy ways."

"Tell me about the time Morwenna was locked in the vault and who did it."

She didn't answer, but sat down on the edge of a grave-stone and, resting her chin in her hands, stared broodingly at the vault.

"The key of the vault was always kept in a cupboard in Mr. Petroc's study. It was a big key. She'd come down for the holidays."

"Who?"

"Rachel Bective."

"How old was she then?"

"I'd say about as old as those twins are now . . . perhaps a year or so younger. I was always trailing them. I think it was the color of her hair. Mine was that black and hers was ginger color. I wanted to keep looking at it. Not that I liked it, mind, I liked Morwenna though. 'Miss Morwenna' we were told to call her. I never did though and she didn't mind.

"She was like Roc . . . they never minded things like that. But *she* did . . . that ginger one. She'd say to me: 'You'll call me Miss Rachel or I'll know the reason why.' Miss Rachel! Who did she think she was?"

"Tell me how Morwenna came to be in the vault."

"I was always in the churchyard. I used to come here to play among the tombstones; and one day I saw them together and I hid and listened to them talking. After that I just wanted to watch them and listen to them some more, so I was often where they were, when they didn't know it. I knew they'd be at the vault because I'd heard about it the day before when they were in the graveyard, reading the inscrip-tions. Morwenna told Rachel that's what she used to do with her brother, and that made Rachel want to do it, for she did always want to do everything they did. She wanted to be one of them and she couldn't . . . she couldn't ever be . . . no more than she can now. Oh, she be educated, I do know . . . but I'd be as good as her if I'd had the schooling."

"What has she done to you, that you hate her so much?"

" 'Tain't what she's done to me. Her wouldn't deign to give much thought to the likes of I, Mrs. Pendorric. It's what she'd do to others."

"You were telling me."

"So I were." She held her hands in front of her, as though she were reading her own fortune. Then she went on: "I heard 'em talking. She wanted Morwenna to get this key so that they could have a look at the vault, and Morwenna didn't want to. You see, it was in her father's study. He was away at the time . . . he were often away after the accident . . . and she said to Morwenna: 'You'll be sorry if you don't.' I was up in a tree and they couldn't see me, but I knew that Morwenna would get the key because she would really be sorry if she didn't. Then I heard they were coming there next afternoon, so I were there too."

"So Morwenna did get the key."

Dinah nodded. "I was here in the graveyard next day when they come, and they had the key. Rachel Bective opened the door of the vault and they went in, though Morwenna didn't want to much, but Rachel was saying: 'You've got to. You'll be sorry if you don't,' and Morwenna was saying: 'I can't. Not again.' Then all of a sudden Rachel laughed and ran out of the vault, slamming the door after her. Then she locked it and Morwenna was shut in."

"It must have been a horrible experience. I hope she didn't stay there long."

Dinah shook her head. "No. There's a little grating in the vault and Rachel was soon at that. She kept calling out: 'I won't let you out till you say you'll ask me for Christmas. I'll go back and I'll tell them I don't know where you are. Nobody'll think you're in here because I'll take the key back and put it where it belongs . . . and it'll be weeks before they find you, then you'll be a skeleton like the bride in the Mistletoe Bough.' So Morwenna said she would do what she wanted and Rachel opened the door. I never forgot that, and I don't never pass this spot without thinking on it and how poor Morwenna had to say she would do what it was Rachel wanted, and how pleased Rachel looked in her sly way."

"She was only a child, I suppose, and she must have longed to come to Pendorric for holidays."

"And you reckon that excuses her . . . doing a thing like that!"

"It was a childish trick . . ."

"Oh, no 'tweren't. She'd have left her there if Morwenna hadn't given way."

"I'm sure she wouldn't."

Dinah looked at me scornfully. "I'm beginning to read your fortune, Mrs. Pendorric, without so much as a look at your hand. You're one of them that says: 'Oh no, it bain't that way . . .' just when you don't want it to be. Your sort has to beware."

"You're quite wrong. I assure you I face facts when I know they're there to be faced."

"Ay, but it's knowing they're there that's important, don't 'ee think, Mrs. Pendorric? I'll tell 'ee this: There's people that don't change much all through their lives. You can't tell 'tis so till you've proved like . . . but it don't do no harm to be on your guard. Oh, I do know a lot about Pendorrics . . . living close you might say, all of me born natural life."

"I expect there's always been a great deal of gossip about the family."

"There was at the time and though I was yet to be born, they were still talking of it when I were a little 'un. My mother was a sharp one. Nothing much she missed. I remember hearing her talk of Louisa Sellick, the one he were sweet on before he married Mrs. Barbarina."

"Louisa Sellick?" I repeated, for I had never heard that name mentioned before.

"Oh, 'tis an old story and all happened long ago. Ain't no sense in reviving it like . . . 'cept of course, you be the next Bride."

I went over to Dinah and, looking down at her, said earnestly: "I sometimes get the impression that you're trying to warn me about something."

She threw back her hair and laughed up at me. "That's because I want to tell your fortune. They say 'The gypsy warned me,' don't 'em. 'Tis a kind of joke."

"What do you know of Louisa Sellick?"

"Only what my mother told me. Sometimes I've been out that way . . . where she do live now, and I've seen her. But that was after he were dead like . . . so it weren't the same. They say he used to go out to visit her and that Barbarina

Pendorric killed herself because she couldn't endure it no more . . . him liking Louisa better than her. She'd thought when she first married that it was all over; that were when Louisa went out to live on the moor."

"And is Louisa still living there?"

Dinah nodded. "Well, least she were when I were last that way. 'Tis Bedivere House—a sizable place. He bought it for her. 'Twas their love nest, you might say. And when he rode out on his business he'd land up at Bedivere. Perhaps there'd be mist on the moors or he was too busy to get back to Pendorric . . . see what I mean? But it was found out that she were there . . . and then things happened."

"Do you often go out that way?"

"Not now. I got a home of me own now, remember. I married Jim Bond, didn't I? I sleep on a goose feather bed and there's four walls all around me. But when I go out that way . . . Dozmary Pool and Jamaica Inn way . . . I see the house and I look for Louisa. She ain't so young and pretty now . . . but we none of us stay that way forever, do us?"

I remembered suddenly that, listening to Dinah's conversation, I had stayed out longer than I had intended to. I looked at my watch.

"I'd no idea it was so late," I said.

She smiled lazily. "You'd better get back, Mrs. Pendorric. Time don't matter to me, but I know it does to the likes of you. Some folks rush about like they thought they hadn't got much time left. Perhaps they're right. Who's to say?"

She was smiling her mocking, enigmatic smile.

"Good-by," I said, and started to pick my way through the gravestones to the lych gate.

* * *

My interest in Barbarina grew as each day passed. I went often to that room of hers and thought about her. I wondered if she had been of a passionate and jealous nature. She must have been terribly unhappy if, as Dinah had suggested, her husband had paid periodic visits to that woman on the moor.

I had heard no more violin playing, or singing in that strange, off-key voice. Whoever had been responsible for that had evidently decided to give it a rest, and I was only faintly disconcerted because I had failed to discover who was playing the part of the ghostly musician. But I did want to know more of Barbarina.

Deborah was always willing to talk about her, and in fact

obviously delighted in doing so. She was gradually building up
the picture of her sister in my mind; sometimes she would
even describe the dresses they had worn for certain parties,
and so vividly did she talk that it was as though Barbarina
materialized before my eyes.

Since my talk with Dinah the picture had become even
clearer and I knew that one day my curiosity would be too
much for me and I should have to go out on the moor to see
if I could catch a glimpse of Louisa Sellick for myself.

I had not made any excursions alone by car so far, and I
couldn't very well ask Roc to take me there, or Morwenna.
I had an uneasy feeling that I'd do better to leave the past
alone and yet, because I could not suppress a feeling that I
ought to know, I seemed unable to stop. Dinah's veiled warn-
ings didn't help me to leave the subject alone, either.

There were three small cars in the garage besides Roc's
Daimler and Charles's Land Rover; Morwenna used one of
them and I had been told that the others were for general use.

I had often said that I wanted to go into Plymouth to do
some shopping and, although I didn't exactly say I was going
there on this occasion, I let Morwenna think so.

Roc had gone off on estate business that morning and I
hadn't even told him I was going out, which, after all, did
occur to me on the spur of the moment.

I had paused by the picture of Barbarina in the gallery and
looked up into those sadly brooding eyes, wondering, when
she had discovered that her husband was visiting that house
on the moor, whether she had confronted him with her discovery. "I should if I ever found that Roc was involved in
such an affair," I said to myself; and I remembered the sly
looks of Rachel, the bold ones of Dinah Bond, and the beauty
of Nurse Grey.

I was not the sort to suffer in silence. If I had a shred of
evidence that Roc was being unfaithful to *me*, I should
confront him with it and insist on the truth.

What had Barbarina done?

Was I identifying myself with Barbarina and reading things
from her life into mine so that our stories were beginning to
seem similar?

In any case my interest in her was becoming a little
morbid.

Although this thought occurred to me it did not prevent
my wanting to see the house where my father-in-law had installed her rival, but I did try to tell myself that it was really

the moor that fascinated me, and it was the ideal morning for a drive.

I set out about half past ten and, branching off the road to Plymouth, I was on the moor in a very short time.

It was a glorious morning. A fresh breeze ruffled the rough grass and I felt a sense of adventure as I looked ahead at the folds of moor and drove for miles without seeing any person or building.

Eventually I slowed down before a signpost and saw that I was only a few miles from Dozmary Pool.

I drove on. I could see the hills, with Brown Willy towering above them, and Rough Tor in the distance. This was a very lonely spot and, looking about me, I saw several mounds which earlier Roc had pointed out to me as the burial grounds of ancient Britons.

It was here that King Arthur was reputed to have fought his last battle. If it were really so, I thought, it would have looked exactly as it looked today.

And suddenly I saw the Pool; it was not large and I guessed that at its widest part it could not have been more than a quarter of a mile across. I stopped the car and getting out walked to the water's edge. There was no sound but the murmur of the wind in the rough grass.

I thought of the legend as I remembered it and as I supposed thousands of visitors to this place must have done: Of Bedivere standing at the edge of the water with the dying Arthur's sword in his hand, debating whether or not to throw it, as commanded, into the middle of the mere.

Finally he had done so and an arm had appeared from the center of the Pool and grasped the sword Excalibur.

I smiled and turned away.

Bedivere, I murmured. Bedivere House. It must be fairly near; Dinah had said so.

I got back into the car and drove slowly for half a mile, and then found a narrow road which I decided to explore.

I had not gone very far when a boy came out of a narrow lane and started to walk in the direction I was going. Drawing up beside him I saw that he was about fourteen; he smiled and right from the first moment I knew there was something familiar in that smile.

"Are you lost?" he asked.

"Not exactly. I'm just wandering round. I've come from Dozmary Pool."

He grinned. "Well, this is a second-class road. It doesn't

lead anywhere much except to Bedivere House . . . and then back onto the main road. Only it gets a bit rougher. Your best plan, if you want to get onto the main road, is to turn back."

"Thank you," I said. "But I'll go on for a bit and look at Bedivere House. What's it like?"

"Oh, you can't miss it. It's the gray house with the green shutters."

"Sounds interesting . . . especially with a name like that."

"Oh, I don't know," he said with a grin. "I live there, you see."

He had his back to the light, and then I noticed that the tips of his rather prominent ears were faintly pink and pointed.

He had stepped back. "Good-by," he said.

"Good-by."

As I started off a woman came into sight. She was tall and slim and she had a mass of white curly hair.

"Ennis," she called. "Oh, there you are."

She glanced at me as I passed and as I rounded the bend I saw the house at once. The boy had been right; there was no mistaking it. There were the green shutters. It was more than a cottage—a house of some seven or eight rooms, I imagined. There was a green gate opening onto a lawn with a flower border; and a glass-walled and -roofed porch before the front door. Inside it were plants, which looked like tomatoes; and both the doors of the glass porch and the house itself were open.

I drove a little way past, then got out of the car and, shading my eyes, looked around me at the view.

I was aware of the woman and the boy coming back; they were arm in arm; and together they went into Bedivere House.

I was certain then that I had seen Louisa Sellick; but I did wonder who the boy could be. Ennis. I believed there was a Cornish saint of that name; there was no doubt of whom he reminded me. Of some of the portraits I had seen at Pendorric —and, of course, of Roc.

* * *

I was changing for dinner when I next saw Roc, and still thinking of the boy to whom I had spoken near Dozmary. By now my imagination had made the resemblance between him and Roc more startling.

Roc must have looked exactly like that at thirteen or

fourteen, I told myself. I could picture him playing in the graveyard with Rachel and Morwenna; riding his horse out to Jim Bond's when it cast a shoe; swimming, boating . . .

I was already dressed, when he came into our room, and was sitting at the window watching the waves below us.

"Hello," he called. "Had a good day?"

"Yes, Roc. And you?"

I stood up and found myself staring at the tips of his ears. Surely only Pendorrics had such ears.

"Very good."

"I took the Morris onto the moors," I told him.

"I wish I'd been with you."

"So do I."

He picked me up and swung me off my feet.

"It's good to have you to come home to," he said. "I've talked to Charlie about your looking into estate affairs with me. We'd be partners then. What do you say?"

"I'm so glad, Roc."

"You were the brains behind that studio," he said. "We need brains in Pendorric."

I had a sudden vision of my father at work in the studio, and, as whenever I thought of him I must think also of his death, I knew that a shadow passed across my face.

Roc went on quickly: "We need brains, now that the days of the *grands seigneurs* are over. It's the farm workers who get the best end of the stick these days. They've got their unions to look after them. I've never heard of a union to protect the interests of the poor landowner. Rents must not be put up; repairs must be done. You see how we could use a businesswoman like you!"

"Oh Roc, I'm going to love it."

He kissed me. "Good. You're in business."

"Roc, you're not worried, are you?"

"I'm not the worrying type . . . otherwise . . ."

"Otherwise you would be?"

"Oh, darling, what's the good of worrying? If we can't afford to go on in the old way, we've got to adjust ourselves to the new. Temper the wind to the shorn lamb, or is it the other way round? My God, we're shorn all right . . . fleeced in fact. Left, right, and center."

I had put my arms about his neck and my fingers almost involuntarily caught his ears—a habit they had. He was smiling and I was vividly reminded of the boy I had seen that afternoon.

"Roc," I said, "I saw a pair of ears exactly like yours today."

He burst out laughing. Then he looked grave. "I thought they were unique. You've always told me so."

"They're Pendorric ears." I touched them with my forefinger. "And they match your eyes. They give you that satyr's look."

"For which I have to be truly thankful, because it was that which made you fall in love with me."

"He had the same sort of eyes . . . now I come to think of it."

"Tell me where you found this paragon?"

"It was on the moor near Dozmary Pool. I asked him the way and he told me he lived at a place called Bedivere House and his name was Ennis."

There was just a short pause, but during it I fancied—or did I think this afterward?—that Roc's expression had become a little guarded.

"What a lot of information he gave! After all you only asked the way, didn't you?"

"It was all very naturally given. But the likeness was really astonishing. I wonder if he's related to you."

"There's Pendorric blood all over the Duchy," said Roc. "You see we were a roistering riotous band. Not that we were the only ones. The old days were very different from these. In those days it was 'God bless the squire and his relations and make us mind our proper stations'; it was touching the forelock and thinking themselves lucky to have a place in the stables, the kitchen or the gardens. It was the *droit de seigneur*. Now of course it's 'We're as good as you' and crippling taxation. Ah, the good old days have gone forever. And talking of the rights of the squire . . . well, there's your answer. You walk round this countryside and you'll discover traces of Pendorric in half of the natives. It was the order of things."

"You sound regretful. I believe you're sighing for the old days."

He put his hand on my shoulder and smiled at me. Did I fancy that there was a hint of relief in his face, as though he had come up to a dangerous corner and had rounded it satisfactorily?

"Since I met and married Favel Farington," he replied, "I ask nothing more of life."

And although he was smiling, I couldn't doubt that he

meant what he said; and, as usual, he had the power to disperse all my doubts and fears with a look, a word, and a smile.

*   *   *

Roc kept his promise and the next day took me with him to his study and, as much as he could in a short time, explained certain matters about the estate. It didn't take me long to grasp the fact that, although we were by no means verging on bankruptcy, we were in a way fighting a losing battle against the times.

Roc smiled at me ruefully. "It's like the tide slowly but surely creeping in. The end of the old way is not exactly imminent, but it's creeping towards us. Mind you, we've hung on longer than most. I'd be sorry if we fell to the National Trust in my time."

"You think it's certain to happen, Roc?"

"Nothing in life is certain, darling. Suppose I were to win a hundred thousand . . . I reckon that would put us on our feet for a few generations."

"You're not thinking of gambling?" I asked in alarm.

He put his arm about me. "Don't worry," he said. "I never risk what I can't afford to lose."

"You told me that before."

"It's only one of the many things I've told you before. How much I love you, for one thing."

"The conversation is wandering from the point," I said with a laugh.

"That's right," he retorted. "I know you're going to be a good businesswoman. You'll keep me on the straight path, won't you? Things have been in a far worse state than they are now, I can assure you; and we've pulled through. Why, in my father's day . . ."

"What happened then?"

"We were in much greater difficulties. Fortunately my mother brought enough to put us on our feet again."

I stared at the open book before me and instead of the columns of figures saw that sad sweet face under the blue-banded hat. There seemed no escape from Barbarina.

Roc, who was standing behind my chair, stooped suddenly and kissed the top of my head. "Don't let it worry you. Something will turn up, you'll see. It always does for me. Did I ever tell you I was born lucky?"

Strangely enough that was a very happy day for me and the fact that the finances at Pendorric were not as sound as they should have been gave me a feeling of deep comfort.

I had begun to think that Roc was too much like his father and that my story was turning out to be too similar to that of Barbarina.

But this was the difference: Barbarina had been married for her money when Roc's father was in love with Louisa Sellick. Roc, needing money for Pendorric, as his father had, had met me, a penniless girl, and had married her.

Oh no, my story was very different from that of Barbarina.

Mrs. Penhalligan was making Cornish pasties when I went down to the kitchen.

She looked up, flushed and bright-eyed, when I entered; her pink cotton sleeves were rolled up above the elbow, her short fat fingers busy.

One of the twins was sitting under the table eating a pasty.

"Good afternoon, Mrs. Pendorric," said Mrs. Penhalligan.

"Good afternoon, Mrs. Penhalligan."

Mrs. Penhalligan went on rolling her pastry. "Don't do to let it hang about too long, m'am," she murmured apologetically. "The secret be to make it and pop it into the oven as quick as you can. This be for Father. He's terrible particular about his pasty and he do want one regular each night. So when I bake I do four or five for him. I keep them in a tin . . . they be all nice and fresh that way, though the best is them as is eaten straight from the oven."

"I've come to ask what tobacco your father smokes. I thought I'd go along to see him when I have the time and take him something to smoke."

A head popped up over the side of the table. "Beware the Ides of March," said a voice low with prophecy.

"Oh give over, Miss Lowella, do," said Mrs. Penhalligan. "She's been under my feet all day. Looking through the window . . . popping up here and there with her talk of beware of this and that. Reckon she belongs to be in Bodmin Asylum."

Lowella smiled and went into the bakehouse.

"I don't know," grumbled Mrs. Penhalligan. "That Miss Bective, she's supposed to be looking after they two. Well, where be she to, half the time, I'm wondering."

"You were going to tell me what tobacco."

"That I were, and right good it is of you, m'am. 'Tis Three Nuns . . . the Empire, you do know. His one extravagance.

But then it's only the two ounces a week he smokes and Maria and me like him to have his little treat."

"I'll remember."

Lowella had come back; she was holding a small pasty in her hand.

"Someone won't be wanting her supper like as not," commented Mrs. Penhalligan.

Lowella regarded us both solemnly before crawling under the table.

"He'll be that pleased," went on Mrs. Penhalligan. "I reckon he'll be sitting out this afternoon. It'll make his day."

"I'll be getting along," I told her.

As I made for the door Lowella darted out from under the table and reached it before me.

"I say, Bride," she said, "I'll come with you if you like . . . to see old Jesse, I mean."

"Don't bother," I replied. "I know the way."

She shrugged her shoulders and went back into the kitchen, presumably to sit under the table and finish her pasty and now and then pop up to tell Mrs. Penhalligan or Maria or Hetty to beware the Ides of March.

* * *

Not far from the cottages was a house which had been turned into a general store. It was small, overcrowded, and run by a Mrs. Robinson, who had come to Pendorric for a holiday twenty years before, realized that the nearest shop was two miles away, and had bought the house and made it into a shop. She sold, among other things, the brands of tobacco smoked by her neighbors, and kept stocks in readiness for them. So I had no difficulty in getting what I wanted.

As I came out of the shop I saw that the twins were waiting for me.

I was not pleased, for I had wanted to be alone with the old man, but there was nothing I could do but accept their company as graciously as possible.

They fell into step beside me without a word, as though we had arranged to meet.

"Where's Miss Bective?" I asked.

The twins exchanged glances as though each was waiting for the other to speak.

It was Lowella who answered. "She's gone off in the little Morris. She said we were to pick her six different wild flowers. It's botany."

"How many have you found so far?"

"We haven't looked yet. My dear Bride, how long do you think it's going to take *us* to find six different wild flowers? Becky won't say much if we find 'em anyway. She'd never say we were undisciplined, would she, because if she did they'd say we ought to go to school, and if we went to school there wouldn't be any excuse for Becky to be at Pendorric."

"Don't you think you ought to obey her instructions? After all she is your governess."

"You oughtn't to be worrying about *us*," said Hyson.

Lowella leaped on ahead and ran up the bank to pick a wild rose. She stuck it in her hair and danced before us singing: "Beware . . . beware . . . beware the Ides of March."

Hyson said: "Lowella is quite childish sometimes. She goes on repeating things."

"She seems to like warning people," I commented. "I remember, 'Beware the awful avalanche!' "

"I like Ides better," called Lowella. "You can't have avalanches in Cornwall but you can have Ides anywhere. Pity they're in March and this is July."

"She doesn't *know* anything," put in Hyson scornfully. She went on to quote:

> *March, July, October, May,*
> *The Ides fall on the fifteenth day.*

Lowella had paused. "But what *are* Ides?"

"Just a date, stupid. Instead of saying the fifteenth, the Romans said the Ides."

"Only a date," wailed Lowella. "It sounds marvelous. I thought it was something like witches . . . or ghosts. Fancy having to beware of a *date*."

"If something was going to happen on a certain date, if it were prophesied to happen . . . that would be more frightening or as frightening as witches or ghosts."

"Yes," said Lowella slowly, "I suppose it would."

We had reached the row of cottages and old Jesse was seated at his door. I went over to him and said: "Good afternoon. I'm Mrs. Pendorric."

I noticed that his hands, resting on his knees, started to shake. " 'Tis good of 'ee, m'am," he said.

"I've brought you some tobacco. I found out from Mrs. Penhalligan what brand you smoke."

His trembling hands closed over the tin and he smiled.

"Why, 'twas thoughtful of 'ee, m'am. I mind how kind *she* always were . . ."

Hyson had gone into the cottage and brought out a stool which she set beside the old man's chair. She nodded to me to sit down while she squatted on the other side of him. Lowella had disappeared.

"Your daughter has been baking pasties this morning," I told him.

"A wonderful cook, my Bessie. Don't rightly know what I'd do without her. I've got a lot to be thankful for. Mr. Roc—he's been good to me. Is the little 'un here?"

"Yes, I'm here," Hyson answered.

He nodded and turned to me. "I hope you find this place to your liking, m'am."

"I'm delighted with it."

" 'Tis a long time since we've had a new bride at Pendorric."

"There was my mother," said Hyson, "and before that my Granny Barbarina."

"A sweet lady, she were. I remember the day she come."

"Tell us, Jesse," urged Hyson. "The new bride wants to hear about it."

"Well, we'd seen her many a time. 'Twasn't like her coming from nowheres. I remember her as a little 'un, her and her sister. Used to visit us . . . and master and mistress used to visit them. Hyson their name was. Such pretty names. Miss Barbarina and Miss Deborah."

"I was named after them," put in Hyson.

"So you were pleased when she became Mrs. Pendorric," I said.

"I reckon I were, Mrs. Pendorric. We didn't rightly know what would happen. We knew something of how it were and there was talk of giving up Pendorric. Pendorric as it were in the old days, that be. Us didn't know what would happen to we like. There was talk of Mr. Petroc marrying that Sellick girl and then . . ."

"But he didn't," Hyson said. "He married my Granny Barbarina."

"I remember the wedding. 'Twas a wonderful summer's day. It was there in the church. The Reverend Trewin were parson then. Oh, it were a grand wedding. And Miss Barbarina was a picture with Miss Deborah her maid of honor, and Mr. Petroc looking that handsome . . . and it was so right and proper that it should be."

"What about the other girl?" I asked.

"Oh, that were reckoned to be done with. She'd gone away . . . and all was merry . . ."

"Merry as a marriage bell," murmured Hyson.

"A wonderful mistress she were. Kind and good . . . and gentle like. She used to ride a lot and play the violin. Often I've been working on the quadrangle gardens and heard her."

I was aware of Hyson, looking at me intently. Hyson, I thought, was it you who tried to scare me? And if so, why?

"Then she had a way of singing to herself. I remember once coming home I heard her singing in the graveyard. It sounded so queer and yet beautiful and like something not quite natural. I went in and saw her. She'd been putting flowers on the grave of little Ellen Pascoe from the cottages. Little Ellen had died of the meningitis and it was her way of saying she was thinking of 'un. We thought a terrible lot of her here in the cottages."

"You remember her very well," I said softly.

"It seems only yesterday she were talking to me, as you be now. I was working then. Right up to the time she died I was working. But she knew I couldn't go on. I told her what was happening to me and she did comfort me. She said: 'Never be feared, Jesse. I'll see that you be all right.' And every time she saw me she'd ask after me. And I was getting blind, Mrs. Pendorric. I can't even see you now. But you remind me of her in a way. You've got a kindness which was hers. Then you be happy. I can tell that. So were she . . . at first. But it changed for her, poor gentle lady. Then she weren't happy no more. My tongue be running away with me, I fear. Bessie says I be alone so much that when people come to see me I've got so much to make up for."

"I'm glad you want to talk," I said. "It's very interesting."

"She's the new bride, so she naturally wants to hear about the other one," said Hyson.

"Aye," went on the old man. "You're happy . . . as she were when she first come. 'Twas only after, poor body . . . I wish you all happiness, Mrs. Pendorric. I wish for you to stay as you be now forevermore."

I thanked him and asked him about his cottage; he told me that if I cared to look over it, he would be pleased. It was kept clean and tidy by his daughter and granddaughter. He rose and, taking a stick from the side of his chair, led the way into the cottage. The door opened straight into the living room; it was certainly clean and tidy. There was his armchair, with his pipe rack and ash tray on a table beside it with a small transistor radio. There was a framed photograph on the wall, of Jesse standing, his hand resting on the shoulder of a woman sitting, whom I presumed to be his wife; they were both looking into the camera as though they were only engaged in the unpleasant duty for the sake of posterity. There were photographs of Mrs. Penhalligan at her wedding.

Leading from this sitting room was a kitchen with a door which opened into a garden. This, like the cottage, was trim and well kept; with wallflowers and cabbage roses bordering a small lawn, a water barrel leaned against the wall to catch the rain.

There were two rooms upstairs, he told me; and he managed the stairs well enough. There was nothing wrong with him except his affliction and the fact that his memory was not what it had been.

He settled in his armchair and bade me be seated while he told me about his meeting and marriage to Lizzie, and how she had been under-housemaid up at Pendorric in the days when he had worked in the gardens there.

This went on for some time and during it Hyson, presumably becoming bored, slipped away.

The old man said suddenly: "The child has gone?"

"Yes," I told him. "I expect she's gone to find her sister. They're supposed to be collecting flowers for a botany lesson."

"The little one . . . she questions and cross-questions . . ."

"She's a strange child."

He nodded. "She wants to know about it. It's on her mind. 'Taint good, I reckon. Her's young. 'T'as nought to do with her."

"I think the story has caught her imagination. It's because it's a ghost story."

"Mrs. Pendorric." He almost whispered my name, and I went closer to him.

"Yes, Jesse?"

"There's something I don't talk of no more. I told Mr. Petroc and he said, 'Don't talk of it, Jesse. 'Tis better not.' So I didn't talk. But I want to tell you, Mrs. Pendorric."

"Why do you want to tell me, Jesse?"

"I don't know . . . but you be the next bride, see . . . and there's something tells me 'tis right and proper you should know."

"Tell me then."

"My eyes was bad and getting worse. Days was when I

couldn't make out shapes and such like. I'd think I saw someone and when I come close I'd find it to be a piece of furniture. That bad they'd got to be. But the more bad they got the more I seemed to hear, and sometimes I knew summat without seeing or hearing. They say 'tis the compensation of the blind, Mrs. Pendorric."

"Yes, Jesse, I am sure there are compensations."

"That day I come into the hall, Mrs. Pendorric. And she were in the gallery. I knew who 'twas because I heard her speak. Low like she spoke . . . and then 'twas as though there were two shadows up there . . . I don't rightly know . . . and 'tis a long time to look back. But I believe, Mrs. Pendorric, that there were two on 'em up on that gallery a minute or two afore Mrs. Pendorric fell."

"And you didn't make this known before?"

"Mr. Pendorric said for me not to. You see, the picture were there . . . the picture of that other bride and they did say she'd haunted the place for more than a hundred years trying to lure a bride to take her place. There were two on 'em up there. I swear it, Mrs. Pendorric . . . but Mr. Petroc he didn't want it said. I'd always obeyed the master, as my father had and his father afore him, so I said nothing . . . but I tell *you* this, Mrs. Pendorric."

"It's so long ago. It's best forgotten, Jesse."

"So I thought, Mrs. Pendorric. And have thought these twenty-five years. But you being here . . . and reminding me of her . . . in a way . . . and you being so good and friendly to me like, well, I thought I should tell 'ee. 'Tis a warning like. And there's a feeling in here . . ." He tapped his chest. "There's a feeling that I shouldn't keep 'ee in the dark."

I couldn't see why he should feel this, but I thanked him for his concern and changed the subject, which wasn't difficult, for now that he had told me he seemed more relaxed, as though he had done his duty. He talked of the cottage and the old days when his Lizzie had been alive; and after a time, I left.

I did not see the twins as I walked back to Pendorric.

* * *

The next day Nurse Grey telephoned me.

"Oh, Mrs. Pendorric," she said. "Lord Polhorgan has asked me to ring. He was wondering if you could come over this afternoon. He rather wants to see you."

I hesitated and said that I thought I could manage it, and asked how he was.

"Not quite so well. He had an attack during the night. He's resting today, but he says that he hoped you would be able to come, if not today, tomorrow."

I set out that afternoon, wondering whether to pick some flowers from the garden to take to him; but as he had so many more than we had that seemed rather unnecessary.

When I arrived he was in his usual chair, not dressed, but wearing a Paisley silk dressing gown and slippers. He seemed delighted to see me.

"Good of you to come so promptly," he said. "I was afraid you wouldn't be able to manage it."

"I'm sorry you haven't been so well."

"It's all ups and downs, my dear. I'll get over this little bout as I have others. They're bringing in the tea. Will you pour, as usual?"

I did so and noticed that he ate very little, and seemed rather more silent than usual, yet in a way expectant.

And as soon as the tea was cleared away he told me what, he said, he had been longing to ever since we had first met.

"Favel . . ." he began, and it was the first time he had used my Christian name, "come and sit near me. I'm afraid what I have to say is going to be a great shock to you. I told you when we first met that I was an old curmudgeon, didn't I?"

I nodded.

"An impossible person. In my young days I thought of nothing but making money. It was the only thing of importance to me. Even when I married my chief thought was to have sons . . . sons to whom I would leave my fortune . . . sons who would carry on my business and add new fortunes to the one I made. I had a successful business life but I was not so successful in my domestic affairs. My wife left me for another man—one of my own employees. He wasn't a success. I couldn't understand why she could leave a luxurious home for him . . . but she did. I divorced her and I got custody of our daughter, which was something she hadn't bargained for. The child was six years old at the time. Twelve years later *she* left me."

"Doesn't it distress you to talk of the past?"

"It's a distressing subject but I want you to understand. My daughter left me because I was trying to arrange a marriage for her. I wanted her to marry Petroc Pendorric, who was then a widower. His wife had died accidentally and I thought there was a good opportunity of joining up the families. I was an outsider here, and I thought that if mine was linked with one of the oldest Cornish families I should be so no longer. Pendorric needed money. I had it. It seemed to me ideal, but *she* didn't agree."

There was silence during which he looked at me helplessly, and for the first time since I had known him he seemed at a loss for words.

"There are often such disagreements in families," I said.

"My wife went . . . my daughter went. You'd think I'd learned my lesson, wouldn't you? Flattered myself that in the world of commerce I'd learned all the lessons as they came along. So I had . . . but this was something I was pretty backward in. Favel, I don't know how to explain. Open that drawer. There's something in there that will tell you what I'm trying to."

I went to the drawer and, opening it, took out a photograph in a silver frame. As I stared at it I heard his voice, hoarse as I had never heard it before, with the depth of his emotion. "Come here to me, my child."

I came to him and he no longer seemed the same man to me. Sitting there in that very luxurious room he had become more frail, more pitiable; and at the same time infinitely closer to me.

I acted on impulse and, going to him, I took his frail body in my arms and held him against me as though he were a child and I were assuring him that he could rely on me to protect him.

"Favel . . ." he whispered.

I drew back and looked at him. His eyes were wet, so I took the silk handkerchief from the pocket of his dressing gown and wiped them.

"Why didn't you tell me before . . . Grandfather?" I asked.

He laughed suddenly and his stern features were relaxed as I had never seen them before. "Afraid to," he said. "Lost wife and daughter. Was making a bid for the granddaughter."

It had been such a shock to me that I was still feeling all this was unreal. My thoughts were muddled. It did not occur to me in that moment to ask myself the explanation of that extraordinary coincidence which had allowed me to marry a man who came into my life by chance and turned out to be a neighbor of my grandfather. That was to come later.

"Well," he asked, "what do you think of your old grandfather?"

"I don't know yet what to think. I'm so bewildered."

"I'll tell you what I think of my granddaughter then. If I could have chosen just how I wanted her to be, she wouldn't have been different in one detail. Do you know, Favel, you're so like your mother that when you've been sitting there playing chess with me, I've often found my mind slipping back . . . and I'd be thinking she'd never gone away. You've got the same fair hair though she didn't have that white streak in it; and your eyes are the same color . . . sometimes blue, sometimes green. And you're like her in your ways . . . the kindest heart and the impetuosity. Rushing in before you've had time to consider. I often wondered how that marriage of hers would work out. Used to tell myself it couldn't last, but it seems it did. And she chose a Cornish name for you. That shows, doesn't it, that she didn't think of the past always with regret."

"But why was I never told? She never spoke of the past, and you . . ."

"She never told you? Nor did your father? You'd have thought they'd have mentioned it now and then. And you never asked, Favel. How was that?"

I looked back to those sunlit days of my childhood. "I think that they felt all that had happened before their marriage was unimportant. That's how it strikes me now. Their lives were so . . . entwined. They lived for each other. Perhaps they knew she hadn't long to live. I suppose that sort of thing makes a difference. As for myself, I never thought of things being other than they were. That was why, when she died, everything changed so much for us."

"And you were fond of your father too?" he said wistfully. I nodded.

"He came down here to paint one summer. Rented a little place a mile or so away along the coast . . . little more than a shack. When she told me she was going to marry him I thought it was a joke at first. Soon I learned it wasn't. She could be obstinate . . . I told her she was a fool. Never stopped to think. Told her I wouldn't leave her a penny if she married this man. Told her he was after her money anyway. So they just went away one day and I never heard from her again."

He was thinking of all the years that had been lost to him. Here he sat in the midst of his opulence—the loneliest old man I had ever met. And it need never have been.

Now he had learned that he was the one who had been

foolish—not my mother and father. And pitiably he was reaching out to me to give him, for the short time left to him, the affection which more than twenty years ago he had rashly thrown away.

I turned to him impulsively and said: "Grandfather, I'm glad I came home to you."

"My dear child," he murmured. "My dearest child." Then he went on: "Tell me about her. Did she suffer much?"

I shook my head. "There were several months when she knew and we knew ... They were terrible months, particularly for my father, but it wasn't really long—though it seemed so."

"I could have paid for the best attention for her," he said angrily.

"Grandfather," I replied, "it's over. It doesn't do any good to reproach yourself ... or them ... or anyone. You've got to put that behind you. I'm here now. Your own granddaughter. I shall see you more often now. I shan't feel like waiting for a reasonable period before calling again. You're my very own grandfather and it's wonderful that my home is so close to yours ..." I stopped, picturing myself coming into the studio and seeing Roc there with my father. "It seems so strange that Roc should have come to my father's studio ... and that we should have married," I said slowly. "I mean, it seems too lucky to be true."

My grandfather smiled. "It wasn't just a matter of chance, my dear. Your mother never wrote to me. I had no idea where she was or what was happening to her. I had told her that if she married her artist I wanted nothing to do with her, and she took me at my word. But ... your father wrote. It was a month or so before Roc went abroad. He told me that your mother was dead and that they had a daughter: Favel. He asked me if I would like to see you, and he gave me the address of that studio place of yours."

"I see," I said. "I wonder why Father wrote."

"I had my suspicions. I thought he was after something. People often say that men in my position are *comfortably* off. Having money isn't always comfortable, I can tell you. You're constantly watching in case you're going to lose something; you're forever on the alert for ways of increasing what you have; and you're always suspecting that people are seeking your acquaintance because they want a little of what you've got. No. I'd say I'm *un*comfortably off. In any case I was wary of your father. I said: He wants to borrow something.

Lilith wouldn't let him write when she was alive—too proud. But now she's dead he's after something. I put his letter on one side and didn't answer it. But the thought of my granddaughter kept bothering me. I wondered what she was like . . . how old she was. Your father hadn't said. And I wanted to know more about her."

He paused and looked at me reflectively, and I said: "So you asked Roc to . . . spy out the land?"

He nodded. "I knew he was going to Italy, so I asked him to do me this favor. I couldn't go myself. I wanted him to find out what this studio place was like and what my granddaughter was like. My plan was that when he came back, providing I liked what he told me, I'd invite my granddaughter to Polhorgan . . . her father, too, perhaps, if she wouldn't come without him."

"So that was why Roc came to the studio."

"That was it. But you're impetuous like your mother. You fell in love with him. So instead of his bringing back a report to me, he brought you back as his bride."

"So Roc was carrying out your wishes," I said.

"He knew."

"But he didn't give me a hint . . . in fact he never has."

"Well, you see, I'd asked him not to. I didn't want you to come over to see your grandfather. I wanted us to meet as strangers. I wanted to know what you thought of me and I wanted to know what I thought of you. But the minute I saw you—you were so like your mother—I felt she'd come back to me. My dear child, I can't tell you what a difference this has made to me."

I touched his hand, but I was thinking of Roc . . . Roc as he had come into the studio, Roc lying on the beach talking about Pendorric, about the Folly and the man who lived in it, who, he knew all the time, was my grandfather.

"So Roc was carrying out your wishes," I said.

"He did even more than I asked. He brought you home."

"I can understand his not telling me *that* in the beginning, but later . . ."

"I told him that I wanted to break the news to you myself."

I was silent. Then I said: "You wanted my mother to marry Roc's father."

"Ah, that was in the days when I thought I could manage people's lives better than they could themselves. I know different now."

"So I've pleased you . . . by marrying a Pendorric."

"Had you wanted to marry a fisherman, granddaughter, I'd have made no objection. I learn my lessons . . . in time. All the lonely years need not have happened if I'd not tried to interfere. Fancy, if I'd raised no objections to their marrying, I'd have had them with me all those years. She might never have died. I shouldn't have had to wait till my granddaughter was a married woman before I knew her."

"Grandfather," I insisted, "you wanted my mother to marry a Pendorric. Are you glad I've married Roc?"

He was silent for a few moments; then he said: "Because you're in love with him . . . yes. I shouldn't have wanted it otherwise."

"But you spoke of linking the families. My mother left home because you wanted her to marry Roc's father."

"That was years ago. I suspect those Pendorrics wanted not so much my daughter as my money, and your father wanted her for herself . . . must have done, because she knew me well enough to understand that when I said there'd be nothing for her if she ran away, I meant it."

I was silent and he lay back in his chair and closed his eyes, though he had taken my hand and kept it in his. I could see how the veins stood out at his temples and that he was more flushed than usual. Such excitement was not good for him, I was sure.

My grandfather! I thought, watching him. So I had a relative after all. My eyes went round the room at the paintings on the wall. They were all of the old school. Grandfather would not buy modern paintings, which he loathed, but all the same he would have an eye for a bargain. I guessed that the pictures in this room alone were worth a fortune.

Then I thought of the studio and my mother who had bargained so fiercely over my father's work; and it seemed to me that life was indeed ironical.

I was glad that I had a grandfather. I liked him from the moment we met; but I wished—oh, how I wished that he were not such a rich man. I remembered what he had said about being *un*comfortably off.

Although it was less than an hour since I had discovered I was the granddaughter of a millionaire, I understood very well what he meant.

I sat with him for an hour after that; we talked of the past and the future. I told him incidents from those early days which I had not thought of telling before, because I now understood how vitally interested he was in every seemingly insignificant detail. And he told me that Polhorgan was now my home and that I must treat it thus.

I walked back to Pendorric in a state of bewilderment, and when I was midway between the two houses I looked from one to the other.

My homes, I murmured. And my pride in them was spoilt by an uneasy suspicion which was beginning to grow within me.

* * *

I was relieved, when I went up to our bedroom, to find that Roc had come in.

"Roc," I called; and as he turned to look at me, he said: "So he's told you?"

"How did you guess?"

"My darling, you look just like a woman who has been told that she is the granddaughter of a millionaire."

"And you knew all the time!"

He nodded, smiling.

"It seems extraordinary that you could keep such a secret."

He was laughing, as he took me by the shoulders. "It's women who can't keep secrets, you know."

He put his arm round me and held me against him; but I withdrew myself because I wanted to look into his face.

"I want to think about it all . . . as it happened," I said. "You came to the studio, looking for me. You were going to report on me to my grandfather."

"Yes. I was going to take some pictures of you to show him. I was determined to do the job thoroughly."

"You did it very thoroughly indeed."

"I'm glad that you approve of my methods."

"And my father . . ." I said. "He knew too."

"Of course he knew. He'd lived near Pendorric. That was how he first met your mother."

"Father knew . . . and didn't tell me."

"I'd explained to him my promise of secrecy."

"I can't understand. It was so unlike him to have secrets from me."

"This was a very important matter. I reckon he wanted you to please your grandfather. It's understandable."

I looked at him sharply; he was smiling complacently.

"How I wish . . ." I began.

"What do you wish?"

"That you hadn't known."

"Why? What difference does it make?"

I was silent. I felt I was going too far. I was almost on the point of asking Roc whether he had married me on account of my grandfather's money, when I didn't even know that I was his heiress. But everything was changed. When I had thought of Barbarina I had continually told myself that our positions were so different because she had been married for her money. The simple fact was that now I was beginning to wonder whether I too had been.

"What's on your mind?" persisted Roc.

"It's the shock," I replied evasively. "When you think you haven't any family and you suddenly find yourself confronted by a grandfather . . . it's a little bewildering. It takes time to adjust yourself."

"You're a little aloof, you're weighing me up. I don't much like it." He was looking at me intently, very seriously.

"Why?"

"I'm afraid of being weighed in the balance and found wanting."

"Why should you be afraid?"

"Because you're hiding something from me . . . or trying to."

"You are the one who hides things successfully."

"Only one thing—and I had made a promise not to tell." He laughed suddenly and, seizing me, lifted me and held me up so that I had to look down on him. "Listen," he said, "and get this clear. I married you because I fell in love with you. It would have been the same if you were the granddaughter of old Bill the Beachcomber. Understand me?"

I put out my hands and touched his ears; he lowered me until my face was on a level with his. Then he kissed me; and as usual, while I was with him, I forgot my fears.

*   *   *

Now that the news was out, the whole of Pendorric village was agog with it. I knew that I only had to appear for the subject to be discussed. People looked at me as though they had discovered something different about me. In the first place I had come out of the blue as the Bride of Pendorric; and now it turned out that I was the granddaughter of old Lord Polhorgan. Many of them could remember my mother's running away with the painter; and it seemed a fitting romantic sequel that I should return as a bride.

Mrs. Robinson at the general store whispered to me that my story was good enough for television; Dinah Bond told me, when I met her one day in the village, that she knew there was something dramatic in my hand and she would have told me if only I'd let her; Morwenna and Charles appeared to be delighted; Lowella was vociferous, squealing her delight, and went about singing something about "when Grandpappa asked Grandmamma for the second minuet," which appeared to be quite irrelevant; Hyson regarded me with silent interest as though this new development was not entirely unexpected.

For several days everyone talked of it, but I guessed that it would turn out to be a nine days' wonder.

There were two conversations which stood out in my mind. One I had with Rachel Bective, the other I overheard.

I had gone down to Pendorric beach to swim one afternoon and as I came out of the water I saw Rachel emerge from the gardens and step onto the beach.

I looked about for the twins, but she was alone.

She came over and said: "What's the sea like today?"

"Quite warm," I answered, and lay down on the shingle.

She sat down beside me, and started playing idly with the pebbles.

"What a surprise it must have been for you!" she said. "Had you no idea?"

"None at all."

"Well, it's not everyone who gets presented with a grandfather at your time of life. And a millionaire peer at that!"

I thought her expression a trifle unpleasant and I half rose, preparing to go up through the gardens.

"Roc knew of course," she went on. Then she laughed. "He must have been tickled to death."

"You think it's an amusing situation when families are broken up?"

"I think it's amusing that Roc should go out to find you and bring you back—his bride. No wonder he has been looking so smug."

"What do you mean?"

Her greenish eyes under the sandy brows glinted a little; her mouth was straight and grim. I thought: She is either very hurt or very angry; and suddenly I wasn't so annoyed with her as I had been a few minutes before.

She seemed to take a grip of herself: "Roc always liked to know what other people didn't. He'd think it great fun having a secret like that, and the rest of us being in the dark. Besides . . ." I waited for her to go on, but she shrugged her shoulders. Then she gave a harsh laugh which seemed to hold a note of bitterness. "Some people have all the luck," she said. "Mrs. Pendorric *and* granddaughter of Lord Polhorgan, who already dotes on her."

"I'm going up to the house," I said. "It's not so warm as I thought."

She nodded and as I crunched my way over the shingle she sat looking out at the sea; and I could imagine the expression on her face, for she had betrayed the fact that she was jealous of me. Jealous because I was the granddaughter of a rich man? Or jealous because I was Roc's wife? Or both.

The second conversation took place the following day and I heard the end of it unwittingly. I was in the quadrangle gardens and one of the windows on the ground floor of the north wing was wide open, so the voice came floating through to me and I had caught the gist of the conversation before I could get out of earshot.

It was Charles and Morwenna who were speaking, and at first I did not realize they were talking of me.

"I thought he was looking pleased with himself." That was Charles.

"I've never known him so contented."

"She's a pleasant creature."

"She has everything."

"Well, it won't be before it's needed, I can tell you. I've had some anxious moments wondering what the outcome could possibly be. Of course we're taking things for granted."

"Not a bit of it. That type never leaves much outside the family. After all, she's his granddaughter and he can't last much longer . . ."

I got up and walked across to the south door, my cheeks flaming.

As I entered the house my eyes went at once to the picture of Barbarina. I stood looking up at it. I could almost fancy the expression had changed; that a pitying look was in those blue eyes, that she was saying to me: "I understand. Who could understand better than one to whom it has all happened before?"

*　　*　　*

My grandfather wanted the whole neighborhood to know how delighted he was to welcome his granddaughter home. He told me that it was years since there had been any entertaining at Polhorgan and he proposed to give a ball to which he would invite all the local gentry.

"You are not nearly well enough," I told him; but he assured me that he would come to no harm. He put his hand over mine. "Don't try to dissuade me. It'll give me the greatest pleasure. The ball will be for you and your husband. I want you to arrange it all; I want it to be a setting for you, my dear. Please say you will."

He looked so pleased at the prospect that I could only agree, and when I told Roc and Morwenna about it they were amused and, I could see, delighted. I had ceased to be angry with Morwenna and Charles, telling myself that loving this old house as they obviously did, it was only natural that they should be pleased because a member of the family might very possibly come into a great deal of money.

"Just fancy," said Morwenna, "Polhorgan is going to throw off its dust sheets."

The twins were delighted. When she was told that balls were not for twelve-year-olds, Lowella boldly called on my grandfather and asked for an invitation for herself and her sister. Such conduct, which he called initiative, delighted him and he immediately wrote to Morwenna asking her to allow the twins to attend.

Lowella was wild with excitement when she heard this: Hyson's eyes gleamed with secret pleasure. Lowella went about the house quoting in an ominous voice:

"There was a sound of revelry by night . . ."

Morwenna helped arrange the list of invitations for, as a Pendorric, she knew everyone in the neighborhood.

They will all want to come and see Lord Polhorgan's granddaughter, she told me. Roc, who was present, put in: "Nonsense. It's Mrs. Pendorric they want to see, for she's a far more important person than his lordship's granddaughter."

"They must think it all very extraordinary," I suggested.

"Nine days' wonder, darling," Roc assured me. "You know there are a lot of skeletons locked away in cupboards in these parts."

"It's true enough," Morwenna assured me.

Deborah was as excited as the twins at the prospect of the ball and invited me to her room to see some material which Carrie was going to make up for her. There was a choice of two colors and she wanted me to help her decide.

Laid out on a table were two rolls of crepe de chine—one delicate mauve, the other pale pink.

I was fingering the stuff. "One hardly ever sees it now," I commented.

"We've had it a few years, haven't we, Carrie," said Deborah.

I had not noticed Carrie come silently into the room; she carried a tape measure about her neck, and a pair of scissors and a pin cushion were attached to her belt.

"I found it in Plymouth," she said. "I was afraid there wouldn't be enough for the two of you."

Deborah looked at me, smiling gently; then she laid her hand on Carrie's shoulder. "Carrie's a wonder with her needle. I'm sure she'll make me something worthy of the ball."

"You remember the dresses I made for the engagement party?" whispered Carrie, her eyes ecstatic. "Empire style. You had the pink then; she had the mauve."

"Yes, we decided we had to be different then."

"Before that it was always the same. What one had the other had."

"I've brought Mrs. Pendorric up to help me decide which color," said Deborah.

"Mauve was her color. She wore it a lot . . . after . . ."

"Perhaps I'd better decide on the pink," murmured Deborah.

She took me into her sitting room and as we sat together looking over the sea she said: "I rather dread Carrie's making new things for me. It always brings it home to her. You see, in Devon she used to make everything in twos. She can't forget."

When I left Deborah I ran into Rachel Bective. She gave me a grudging smile and looked almost wistful.

"Everyone's talking about the ball your grandfather's giving," she said. "I feel like Cinderella. Still, I suppose the governess can't expect to be invited."

"What nonsense," I retorted. "Of course you're invited."

The smile which lighted her face made her almost pretty.

"Oh," she muttered in an embarrassed way, "thank you. I . . . I'm honored."

As she turned and left me I thought: Her trouble is this complex about being employed here. If only she could forget that, she'd be so much happier and I should like her so much better.

*   *   *

During the next few days I spent a great deal of time at Polhorgan. My grandfather was anxious that I should make a thorough tour of the house, and this I did in the company of Dawson and his wife, who were very respectful to me now that they knew I was their master's granddaughter.

Polhorgan was not built in the same mould as Pendorric. This was one large house whereas ours at Pendorric was like four smaller ones. At Polhorgan there was an immense hall which was to serve as the ballroom, and Dawson and his wife had uncovered the furniture so that I could see it in all its glory.

It was a magnificently proportioned room with its high vaulted ceiling and paneled walls; and there was a dais at one end which would be ideal for our orchestra. Dawson suggested that some of the exotic plants should be brought in from the greenhouses and that I might like to talk to Trehay, the head gardener, about what I should like.

Leading from this hall were several rooms which would serve as supper rooms. I could see that Mrs. Dawson was a most efficient woman and delighted at the prospect of being able to show what a skillful housekeeper she was.

She showed me the kitchens which were models of modernity.

"All this, madam," sighed Mrs. Dawson, "and no one to use it for! I could have cooked for his lordship with one little stove, for all he eats. Although the nurse wants a bit of waiting on, I do assure you!"

Mrs. Dawson's lips tightened at the mention of Nurse Grey, and I began to wonder whether the nurse was generally unpopular in the household.

It was while she was showing me round that Althea Grey herself appeared. She was looking as attractive as ever in her uniform, and she gave me a pleasant smile. I was struck afresh by the perfection of her features and I remembered uneasily the occasion when I had found her on the beach with Roc.

"So you're showing Mrs. Pendorric the house," she said.

"Well, it looks like it, Nurse." Mrs. Dawson's voice was tart.

"If you like I'll take over. I expect you have work to do."

"As housekeeper I reckon it to be my duty to show Mrs. Pendorric the house, Nurse."

Nurse Grey smiled at me and shrugged her shoulders;

but as though defying Mrs. Dawson to challenge her right to be there, she remained with us.

Mrs. Dawson was put out and behaved as though she were unaware of the nurse's presence. I wondered what Althea Grey had done to make herself so disliked.

We walked up a beautiful staircase and inspected the rooms on the first floor of the mansion with their enormous windows and those superb views to which I had become accustomed at Pendorric.

Mrs. Dawson uncovered some of the furniture and showed me beautiful pieces, mostly antique, which I guessed must be worth a great deal.

"Jeweled in every hole," murmured Althea Grey, her lovely blue eyes laughing.

The obvious hostility between them made me a little uncomfortable.

"I hear we're to have about sixty guests, Mrs. Pendorric," said Althea Grey. "It's a good thing we have a sizable ballroom, otherwise we should be treading on each other's toes."

"Well, Nurse," put in Mrs. Dawson with a twitch of her nose, "that shouldn't worry you, should it?"

"Oh, but it will. I hate having my toes trodden on." She laughed. "Oh, you're thinking that as I'm merely Lord Polhorgan's nurse, I shan't be there. But you're wrong, Mrs. Dawson. Of course I shall be there. I couldn't let him go without me in attendance, could I?"

She was smiling at me as though inviting me to join in her victory over Mrs. Dawson, who looked extremely put out; and I supposed this was the usual tug of war between one servant who thought herself in a higher position than another. That must be the reason for the animosity.

"Of course not," I said hastily; and Mrs. Dawson's face was grim.

"I reckon, madam," she said, "that Nurse Grey could show you the upper rooms."

I thanked her and assured her that I should be pleased if she stayed with us, but she muttered something about having things to see to, and left us.

Althea Grey grinned when we were alone. "She'd make life a trial if I'd let her. Jealous old witch."

"You think she's jealous of you?"

"They always are, you know. I've come up against this sort of thing before . . . nursing in private houses. They don't

like it because they have to wait on us. They're anxious all
the time to tell us that they're as good as we are."

"It must be awkward for you."

"I don't let it bother me. I can manage the Mrs. Dawson
characters, I can tell you."

In spite of her delicate beauty I was sure she could.

We had come to my grandfather's room and when I went
in with her, he gave me his warm and welcoming smile and I
felt my spirits rising when I realized what a difference my
coming had made to him.

Nurse Grey ordered tea and the three of us had it together.
Conversation was all about the ball, and before she left us
Nurse Grey warned my grandfather that he was becoming
far too excited.

"You have your pills handy?" she said.

For answer he took the little silver box from his pocket and
showed her.

"That's good."

She smiled at me and left us together.

*   *   *

I had had a busy morning and after lunch, because the
sun was shining and it was a long time since I had been in
the quadrangle, I went there and sat in my favorite spot under
the palm tree.

I had not been there more than five minutes when the
north door opened and a twin came out.

I was always a little ashamed of my inability to distinguish
which was which when they were not together, and tried
to discover without exposing my ignorance.

She came and stood before me. "Hello. How you like this
place! But you haven't been here lately, have you?"

"I've been too busy."

She regarded me solemnly. "I know. It is a busy business . . . suddenly finding you're Lord Polhorgan's granddaughter." She stood on one foot and hopped a few paces
nearer. "Just fancy! You might have been here always . . .
if your mother and father hadn't gone away. Then we should
always have known you."

"That could easily have happened," I admitted.

"But it was more exciting the other way. There wouldn't
have been this ball perhaps . . . if you'd always been here.
There wouldn't be any sense in giving a fatted calf sort of
ball if you'd never been away, would there?"

"Would you say this was like the prodigal's return?"

She nodded vigorously. "You're rich now, aren't you; and you must have been poor, though perhaps you didn't eat the husks that the swine did eat."

I was sure it was Lowella now. She had started to hop all round my seat, and when she was immediately behind me she stood close, breathing down my neck. "Everybody wasn't pleased when *he* came home, were they? There was the brother who'd stayed at home. He didn't see why the fatted calf should be killed for the brother who'd run away when he wanted to."

"Don't worry. I haven't got a brother who'll be jealous of my having a welcome."

"There doesn't have to be a *brother*. A parable's different, isn't it. It doesn't always mean exactly what it says. You have to work it out . . . Becky says so. Carrie's waiting for me to try on my dress for the ball."

"She's making it for you, is she?"

"Yes, it's gold color. She's making two . . . exactly alike. It'll be fun. They won't know which is Hy and which is Lo."

"You'd better go if Carrie wants to fit your dress, hadn't you?"

"You come with me and see it. It's very pretty."

She started to hop towards the west door and I rose and followed her into the house, unsure again whether I had been speaking to Hyson or Lowella.

She started to hum as we went up the stairs, and the song she hummed was the tune that I had heard in that strange, off-key voice which had startled me so. This humming was quite different though, rather monotonous and tuneless.

"What's that you're singing?" I asked.

She stopped, turned slowly, and looked down on me, for she was standing several stairs above me. I knew then that she was Hyson.

"It's Ophelia's song in Hamlet."

"Did you learn it at school?"

She shook her head.

"Did Miss Bective teach it to you?" I was becoming too anxious, I realized; and she guessed it and found it amusing.

Again she shook her head. She was waiting mischievously for the next question.

I merely continued: "It's a haunting tune," and started up the stairs.

She ran on ahead of me until she came to the door of Carrie's sewing room.

Carrie was seated at an old-fashioned sewing machine and I saw that she was working on a gold-colored dress.

There were two dressmaker's dummies in the room; one a child's and the other an adult's. On the smaller one was another gold-colored dress; on the larger a mauve evening dress.

"Ah, there you are, Miss Hyson," said Carrie. "I've been waiting for you. Come here, do. That neck don't please me."

"Here's Mrs. Pendorric, too," said Hyson. "She wanted to see the dresses so I brought her up."

I went over to the dummy on which the other gold-colored dress had been arranged.

"It's lovely," I said. "This is Lowella's of course."

"I fitted it on Miss Hyson," mumbled Carrie. "Miss Lowella can't stand still for more than a second or two."

"It's true," said Hyson primly. "Her mind flitters and flutters like a butterfly. She can't concentrate on anything for any length of time. Becky says it's deplorable."

"Come here then," said Carrie, snipping a cotton and withdrawing the dress from the machine.

Hyson stood meekly while Carrie slipped off her dress and put on the gold-colored silk.

"It's delightful," I said.

"The neck's wrong." Carrie was breathing heavily as she purred and clicked over the neck of the dress. I went over to the mauve dress and examined it. It was beautifully made, but like all Deborah's clothes it had that slightly old-world look. The rows of flounces in the long skirt would have been fashionable many years ago, so would the lace fichu at the neck. It was like a charming period piece.

"I thought you were going to make up the pink," I said.

"Ur," grunted Carrie, her mouth full of pins.

"I suppose Deborah changed her mind, but when I was here, I thought she said she would have the pink."

Hyson nodded at me vigorously and inclined her head towards a dress hanging behind the door. I looked and saw an exact replica of the dress, this time in pink.

I stared in astonishment.

"Carrie made two, didn't you, Carrie?" said Hyson. "She made two gold dresses . . . one for me, one for Lowella, and she made two like that—one pink and one mauve—because ever since they left Devon they never had the same color. It was different after they left Devon, wasn't it, Carrie?"

Hyson was regarding me almost triumphantly and I felt impatient with her.

"What on earth are you talking about?" I demanded.

Hyson became engrossed in the tips of her shoes and would not answer me.

"Carrie," I insisted, "I suppose Miss Deborah has had the two dresses made up. Perhaps it's as well if you've had the material for a long time . . . which I believe you said you had."

"The pink's for Miss Deborah," said Carrie. "I like her in pink."

"And the mauve . . . ?"

Hyson darted away from Carrie and ran to me; she laid a hand on my arm and smiled up at me.

"The pink was made for Granny Deborah," she whispered, "and the mauve for Granny Barbarina."

Carrie was smiling at the mauve dress as though she saw more than a dress; she said quietly: "Mauve were your color, my dear; and I always say there weren't two prettier maidens in Devonshire than my Miss Deborah and Miss Barbarina."

I was suddenly impatient with the stuffy sewing room. I said: "I've things to do," and went out.

*   *   *

But when I had shut the door I asked myself what motive lay behind Hyson's strange behavior. I could understand that Carrie's mind wandered a little; she was old; and she had clearly been devoted to Barbarina. Deborah had said that she had never recovered from the shock of her death. But where did Hyson come into this? Could it be that for some reason she resented my coming to Pendorric? That talk about the fatted calf—what had been the meaning behind that?

I looked over my shoulder and restrained the impulse to go back into the room. Instead I went along the corridor until I came to the door of Deborah's sitting room.

I hesitated for a moment, then I knocked.

"Come in," said Deborah.

She was seated at a table reading.

"My dear, what a pleasant surprise. Why, is anything wrong?"

"Oh no . . . nothing. I'm just a little puzzled, that's all."

"Come and sit down and tell me what's puzzling you."

"Hyson's a queer child, isn't she? I'm afraid I don't understand her."

She shrugged her shoulders. "It's not always easy to understand what goes on in the mind of a child."

"But Hyson is so very strange. Lowella is quite different."

"It's the case of the extrovert and introvert. They are twins of entirely different character. Tell me what Hyson's been doing to upset you."

I told her about the dress I had seen on the stand in Carrie's sewing room.

Deborah sighed. "I know," she said. "She'd done it before I could stop her. I'd decided on the pink and the pattern; then I found that she was making up not only the pink but the mauve."

"Does she really think that Barbarina is still alive?"

"Not all the time. There are occasions when she's as lucid as you or I. And at others she thinks she is back in the past. It doesn't matter. The dresses are exactly alike so that I can wear either of them. I never scold her."

"But, what about Hyson?" I said. "Does Carrie talk to her?"

"Hyson understands perfectly the state of affairs. I've explained to her. But I've told her that she must never hurt Carrie's feelings. Hyson's a good child. She does her best. You look disapproving, my dear."

"I think it's a little . . . unhealthy," I said.

"Oh, it does no harm, and it makes Carrie happy. While she can believe that Barbarina is still with us she's contented. It's when she faces up to what really happened that she is depressed and sad. It's easier in Devonshire. There of course she is often under the impression that Barbarina is in Cornwall, and that we shall shortly be visiting her. Here it's not so easy because she thinks Barbarina should be here."

I was silent and she laid her hand over mine.

"My dear," she went on softly, "you're young and bursting with sound common sense. It's difficult for you to understand the vagaries of people whose minds are not quite as normal as your own. Don't let Carrie upset you. She's been like this for so long. I couldn't bear to make her unhappy . . . that's why I humor her. So I let her say: Miss Deborah shall go to the ball in the pink dress and Miss Barbarina in the mauve. It's of little consequence. And talking of dresses, tell me, what are you going to wear?"

I told her that it was a green and gold dress which I had bought in Paris during my honeymoon. I had so far had no chance to wear it and the ball seemed the ideal occasion.

"I'm sure you'll look wonderful, my dear, quite wonderful; and your grandfather and your husband will be so proud of you. Oh Favel, what a fortunate woman you are to find a husband and a grandfather all in a few months!"

"Yes," I said slowly, "it's certainly very strange."

She laughed merrily. "You see, strange things are beginning to happen to *you* since you came to Pendorric."

* * *

It was arranged that Roc and I should go to Polhorgan half an hour before the guests were due to arrive, so that we should be there, with Lord Polhorgan, to receive them.

I bathed and dressed in good time and was rather pleased with my appearance when I put on my dress. It was a sheath of green silk chiffon billowing out from the knees into a frothy skirt; there was a narrow gold belt at the waist and a gold tracing showed through the chiffon from the satin underskirt.

I had piled my hair high on my head, and I was delighted with the Parisian effect.

Roc came in while I was standing before the mirror and, taking my hands, held me at arms' length to examine me.

"I haven't a doubt who'll be the belle of the ball," he said. "And what could be more apt?" He drew me to him and kissed me as lightly as though I were a porcelain figure which he feared might break under rough handling.

"You'd better dress," I warned. "Remember we have to be early."

"First I want to give you this," he said, and took a case from his pocket.

I opened it and saw a glittering necklace of emeralds and diamonds.

"Known—rather grandiosely—as the Pendorric Emeralds," he told me. "Worn at her wedding by her whom they call the First Bride."

"They're exquisite, Roc."

"I had them in mind when I suggested you should buy that dress. I don't pretend to know anything about clothes, but being green it did seem they'd match."

"So I'm to wear them tonight?"

"Of course." He took them from the case and fastened them about my neck. I had looked *soignée* before, but now I was regal. The emeralds did that for me.

"Why didn't you tell me that you were giving me these?"

"But in all the best scenes the jewels are clasped about the lady's neck at the precise psychological moment!"

"You have an eye for drama. Oh Roc, they're quite lovely. I shall be afraid of losing them."

"Why should you? There's a safety chain. Pendorric brides have been wearing them for nearly two hundred years and not lost them. Why should this bride?"

"Thank you, Roc."

He lifted his shoulders and surveyed me sardonically. "Don't thank me, darling. Thank that other Petroc who married Lowella. He bought them for her. They're your heritage anyway. It'll be nice to show that opulent grandfather of yours that you've a husband who can give you something worth having."

"You've given me so much that's worth having. I don't want to disparage the necklace but . . ."

"I know, darling. Kind hearts are more than emeralds. A sentiment with which I am in complete agreement. But it's getting late, so we'll develop that line of thought later."

"Yes, you'd better hurry."

He went into the bathroom and I looked at my watch. We should be leaving in fifteen minutes. Knowing his tendency to talk while dressing and feeling this would delay him, I went out of the room into the corridor and stood at the window looking down at the quadrangle. I was thinking about my grandfather and all that had happened to me in the last weeks, and it seemed to me that my life, which until then had run along expected lines, had suddenly become dramatic. I did not think I should be very surprised at whatever happened to me next.

Still, I was happy. I was more deeply in love with my husband every day; I was growing fonder of my grandfather, and I found great pleasure in being the one who could bring such happiness into his life. I knew that he had changed a great deal since I had come; and, since he had revealed his relationship to me, even more. He often reminded me of a boy in his enthusiasm for simple things, and I understood that this was because he had never had time to be really young.

Some impulse made me lift my eyes from the pond and the palms. That feeling which came to me often when I was in the quadrangle was strong at that moment. I had never analyzed it, but it was a feeling of eerie discomfort, a notion that I was being watched intently and not casually or in a friendly way.

My eyes went at once to the east windows . . . to that floor on which Barbarina had had her music room.

There was a movement there. Someone was standing at the corridor window—not close, but a little way back. Now the figure came nearer. I could not see the face but I knew it was a woman because she was wearing a mauve dress.

It was the one I had seen on the dressmaker's dummy; the dress which Carrie had made for Barbarina.

"Barbarina . . ." I whispered.

For a few seconds I saw the dress clearly, for a pale hand had drawn back the curtains. I could not see the face though . . . then the curtain fell back into place.

I stood staring at the window.

Of course, I said to myself, it was Deborah. She has decided to wear the mauve dress after all. That's the answer. But why did she not wave to me or let me see her?

It had been all over in a few seconds, hadn't it? She couldn't have seen me.

Roc came out of the room, shouting that he was ready.

I was about to tell him what I had seen, but somehow it had become unimportant. When I saw Deborah at the ball in the mauve dress I should be satisfied.

*　　*　　*

The ballroom at Polhorgan was magnificent. Trehay, eager to show off his more exotic blooms, had made a wonderful show, but it was the hydrangeas, indigenous to Cornwall, that, in my opinion, were the most dazzling.

My grandfather was already in the ballroom in his wheel chair, with Althea Grey beside him, looking startlingly beautiful in her egg-shell blue off-the-shoulder dress, with a white camellia adorning it. Her hand was resting on my grandfather's chair in a proprietorial way.

"You look more like your mother than ever," said my grandfather brusquely; and I knew he was moved as I stooped and kissed him.

"It's going to be wonderful," I replied. "I'm so looking forward to meeting all your friends."

My grandfather laughed. "Not *my* friends. Few of them have ever been here before. They've come to meet Mrs. Pendorric—and that's a fact. What do you think of the ballroom?

"Quite magnificent."

"Have you got anything like this at Pendorric, Roc?"

"I'm afraid we don't run to such glory. Our halls are tiny in comparison."

"Like that paneling? I had that specially brought here from the Midlands. Some old mansion that was broken up. Used to say to myself: 'One day that'll be mine.' Well, so it was in a way."

"There's a lesson in it," said Roc. "Take what you want and pay for it."

"I paid for it all right."

"Lord Polhorgan," said Althea, "you mustn't get over-excited. If you do I shall have to insist on your going back to your room."

"You see how I'm treated?" said my grandfather. "I might be a schoolboy. In fact I'm sure at times Nurse Grey thinks I am."

"I'm here to look after you," she reminded him. "Have you your T.N.T.s?"

He put his hand in his pocket and held up the silver box.

"Good. Keep them handy."

"I shall be keeping my eye on him too," I said.

"How fortunate you are, sir," Roc murmured. "The two most beautiful women at the ball to watch over you!"

My grandfather put his hand over mine and smiled at me. "Aye," he agreed, "I'm lucky."

"That sounds like the first of the guests," said Althea.

It was. Dawson, spectacular in black livery with gold frogs and buttons, was announcing the first arrivals.

*   *   *

I felt very proud standing there between my grandfather and my husband as I greeted the guests. My grandfather was cold and formal; Roc quite the opposite. I was, naturally, the center of a great deal of interest; I guessed that many of these people wanted to see what sort of woman Roc Pendorric had married. The fact that I was Lord Polhorgan's granddaughter meant that they were aware of our romantic meeting, for they all knew my mother had run away from home and had not communicated with her father again. It made a good story and naturally there had been a certain amount of gossip about it.

Roc was told that he was lucky, and now and then I sensed the underlying significance of that remark. Polhorgan was an imposing structure, but a great many of these people possessed houses as grand. The difference was that they had been in their families for hundreds of years, while my grandfather had earned the money to build his. Moreover, it was unlikely that any of these people could match the opulence of the furnishings they now saw. It was well known that my grandfather was either a millionaire or something near it.

So when they told Roc he was lucky, I presumed my grandfather's wealth had something to do with it.

However, I was beginning to enjoy myself. The music had started and the guests were still arriving. They were not all young; indeed there were some very old people present, for the invitations had been issued to whole families. It was going to be a very mixed ball.

The party from Pendorric had arrived, and the twins came ahead, arm in arm, looking exactly alike in their gold-colored dresses; behind them Charles and Morwenna, and then . . . Deborah.

Deborah was wearing the pink dress that Carrie had made for her, and looking as though she had stepped out of a twenty-five-year-old magazine.

But pink! Then who had been wearing the mauve?

I forced myself to smile at them; but I could not stop thinking of the vision I had seen at the window. Who could it have been?

Deborah had taken my hands. "You look lovely, dear. Is everything all right?"

"Why yes . . . I think so."

"I thought you looked a little startled when you saw me."

"Oh no . . . not really."

"It *was* something. You must tell me later. I'd better pass on now."

More guests were approaching and Roc was introducing me. I took the outstretched hands, still thinking of the vision I had seen in the mauve dress.

*   *   *

I danced with Roc and with many others that night. I was aware of my grandfather's eyes, which never seemed to leave me.

I think I was a successful hostess.

I was grateful to Deborah, who was determined to put me at my ease since I had shown her that I was disturbed.

She took the first opportunity of talking to me.

Roc was dancing with Althea Grey and I was standing by my grandfather's chair when she came up.

"While you have a moment, Favel," she said, "I'd like to chat. Tell me, why were you startled when you saw me?"

I hesitated, then I replied: "I thought I'd seen you earlier in the evening at the east window—before we left Pendorric . . . in the mauve dress."

There was silence for a few seconds and I went on: "I was dressed and waiting for Roc when I looked out of the window and saw someone in the mauve dress."

"And you didn't recognize who it was?"

"I couldn't see a face. I only saw the dress and that someone was wearing it."

"Whatever did you think?"

"I thought you'd decided to wear it."

"And when I came in the pink surely you didn't think you'd seen . . . Barbarina?"

"Oh no, I didn't think that really. But I wondered who . . ."

She touched my hand. "Of course you wouldn't think it. You're too sensible." She paused and said: "There's a simple explanation. I had a choice of two dresses. Why shouldn't I try on the mauve and finally decide on the pink?"

"So it *was* you."

She did not answer; she was staring dreamily at the dancers. I realized that I didn't believe what she was hinting. She had not said that she had tried on the mauve dress; she had put it differently. "Why shouldn't I try on the mauve . . . ?" It was as though she did not want to tell a lie but at the same time was trying to set my mind at rest.

That was just a fleeting thought which came into my head as I looked at her kind, gentle face.

Almost immediately I said to myself: Of course, Deborah tried on the mauve first. It was natural. And moreover it was the only explanation.

But why should she go to the east wing to do it? Because Carrie would have put the dress there, was the obvious answer.

I dismissed the matter from my mind. Deborah saw this and seemed contented.

* * *

Grandfather said that I must not remain at his side as he liked to see me among the dancers. I told him I was rather anxious about him, as he looked more flushed than usual.

"I'm enjoying it," he said. "I should have liked to have done more of this in the past. Perhaps we will now, eh, now you've come home? Where's your husband?"

He was dancing with Nurse Grey and I pointed him out. They were the most striking couple in the room, I thought; she with her fair looks, he so dark.

"He ought to be dancing with you," said my grandfather.

"He did suggest it, but I told him I wanted to talk to you."

"Now that won't do. Ah, here's the doctor. Nice to see you unprofessionally, Dr. Clement."

Andrew Clement smiled at me. "It was good of you and Mrs. Pendorric to ask me."

"Why don't you ask my granddaughter to dance? Don't want her glued to the old man's chair all the evening."

Andrew Clement smiled at me and we went on to the floor together.

"Do you think this is too much excitement for my grand-father?" I asked.

"I wouldn't say he was too excited. No, I think it's doing him good. I'll tell you something, Mrs. Pendorric; he's been much better since you've been here."

"Has he?"

"Oh yes, you've given him a real interest in life. There were times when I was afraid he'd die of melancholia . . . sitting in that room day after day, staring out at the sea. Now he's no longer lonely. I think he's changed a great deal; he's got something to live for, and you know he's a man of immense energy. He's always gone all out for what he wants, and managed to get it. Well, now he wants to live."

"That's excellent news."

"Oh yes, he's told me how delighted he is with you. He wanted me to witness his signature on some important docu-ments the other day, and I said to Nurse Grey afterwards that I hadn't found him so well for a very long time. She said it was all thanks to that granddaughter of his on whom he doted."

"I can't tell you how happy I am if I can be of help to him. Is your sister here tonight?"

"Oh, yes, though ballroom dancing isn't much in her line. Now if it were folk dancing . . ."

He laughed and at that moment he was tapped on the shoulder by a dark, handsome young man. Andrew Clement pretended to scowl and said: "Oh, is it that sort of dance?"

"Afraid so," said the young man. "I'm claiming Mrs. Pendorric."

As I danced with this young man he told me he was John Poldree and that he lived a few miles inland.

"I'm home for a bit," he went on. "Actually I'm studying law in London."

"I'm so glad you were home for the ball," I told him.

"Yes, it's good fun. All very exciting too—your turning out to be Lord Polhorgan's granddaughter."

"Most people seem to think so."

"Your grandfather has a striking-looking nurse, Mrs. Pendorric."

"Yes, she's certainly very beautiful."

"Who is she? I've seen her somewhere before."

"Her name is Althea Grey."

He shook his head. "Can't recall the name. The face is familiar though. Seem to connect her with some law case or other . . . I thought I had a good memory for such things but it seems I'm not so good as I thought."

"I should think if you'd met her you'd remember her."

"Yes. That's why I was so sure. Well, it'll come back I expect."

"Why don't you ask her?"

"As a matter of fact I did. She absolutely froze me. She was certain she had never met *me* before."

There was a tap on his shoulder, and there was Roc waiting to claim me.

I was very happy dancing with my husband. His eyes were amused and I could see that he was enjoying himself.

"It's fun," he said, "but I don't see half enough of the hostess. I expect she has her duties though."

"The same thing applies to you."

"Well, haven't you seen me performing? I've had my eyes on every wallflower."

"I've seen you on several occasions dancing with Althea Grey. Was she wilting for lack of attention?"

"At things of this sort people like Althea and Rachel could be at a disadvantage. The nurse and the governess! There's a certain amount of snobbery still in existence, you know."

"So that's why you've been looking after Althea. What about poor Rachel?"

"I'd better keep my eye on her too."

"Then," I said lightly, "as you're going to be so busily engaged elsewhere I'd better make the most of the time that belongs to me."

He squeezed my hand. "Have you forgotten," he asked, his lips touching my ear, "that the rest of our lives belong together?"

*　*　*

Supper was very gay. We had arranged that it should be served in three of the larger rooms which adjoined the hall; they all faced south and the great French windows opened onto terraces which looked over the gardens to the sea. There was plenty of moonlight and the view was enchanting.

Trehay's flower scheme was as beautiful in the supper rooms as it was in the ballroom; and no effort had been spared to achieve the utmost luxury. On the overladen table were fish, pies, meats, and delicacies of all description. Dawson and his under-servants in their smart livery took charge of the bar while Mrs. Dawson looked after the food.

I shared a table with my grandfather, John Poldree and his brother, Deborah and the twins.

Lowella was as silent as Hyson on this occasion; she seemed to be quite overawed and when I whispered to her that she was unusually subdued, Hyson answered that they had made a vow not to call attention to themselves, in case someone should remember that they weren't really old enough to go to balls, and tell Rachel to take them home.

They had escaped Rachel, they told me, and their parents; and so would I please not call attention to them in case Granny Deborah noticed?

I promised.

While we were talking together, some of the guests strolled out onto the terraces and I saw Roc and Althea Grey walk by the window.

They stood for a while looking out over the sea, and seemed to be talking earnestly, and the sight of them threw a small shadow over my enjoyment.

It was midnight when several of the guests started to leave, and finally only the Pendorric party remained.

Althea Grey hovered while we said good-by and congratulated each other on the success of the evening. Then she wheeled my grandfather's chair to the lift, which he had had installed some years before when he had first been aware of his illness, and he went up to his bedroom while we went out to our cars.

It was half past one by the time we reached Pendorric, and as we drove under the old archway to the north portico, Mrs. Penhalligan opened the front door.

"Oh, Mrs. Penhalligan," I said, "you shouldn't have stayed up."

"Well, madam," she said, "I thought you'd like a little refreshment before settling down for the night. I've got some soup for you."

"Soup! On a hot summer's night!" cried Roc.

"Soup! Soup! Glorious soup!" sang Lowella.

"One of the old customs," Morwenna whispered to me. "We can't escape them if we want to."

We went into the north hall and Mrs. Penhalligan led the way into the small winter parlor, where soup plates had been set out; and at the sight of them Lowella danced round the room chanting: "There was a sound of revelry by night."

"Oh Lowella, please," sighed Morwenna. "Aren't you tired? It's after one."

"I'm not in the least tired," insisted Lowella indignantly. "Oh, isn't this a wonderful ball!"

"The ball's over," Roc reminded her.

"It's not . . . not till we're all in our beds. There's soup to be had before that's over."

"You'd better let them sleep late tomorrow, Rachel," said their mother.

Mrs. Penhalligan came in with a tureen of soup and began ladling it out into the plates.

"It was always like this in the old days," said Roc. "We used to hide in the gallery and watch them come in; do you remember, Morwenna?"

Morwenna nodded.

"Who?" asked Hyson.

"Our parents, of course. We couldn't have been more than . . ."

"Five," said Hyson. "You'd have to be, wouldn't you, Uncle Roc? You couldn't have been more, could you?"

"What memories these children have!" murmured Roc lightly. "Have you been coaching them, Aunt Deborah?"

"What soup's this?" asked Lowella.

"Taste it and see," Roc told her.

She obeyed and rolled her eyes ecstatically.

We all agreed that it was not such a bad custom after all, and that although we should not have thought of hot soup on a summer's night there was something reviving about it, and it was pleasant to sit back and talk about the evening.

When we had finished the soup no one seemed in a hurry to go to bed, while the twins sat back in their seats, desperately trying to keep awake, looking like daffodils which had been left too long out of water.

"It's time they were in bed," said Charles.

"Oh Daddy," wailed Lowella, "don't be so old-fashioned!"

"If you're not tired," Roc pointed out, "others might be. Aunt Deborah looks half asleep and so do you, Morwenna."

"I know," said Morwenna, "but it's so comfortable sitting here and it's been such a pleasant evening I don't want it to end. So go on talking, all of you."

"Yes, do, quick," cried Lowella; and everyone laughed and seemed suddenly wide awake. "Go on, Uncle Roc."

"This reminds me of Christmas," said Roc obligingly, and Lowella smiled at him with loving gratitude and affection.

"When," went on Roc, "we sit round the fire, longing for our beds and too lazy to go to them."

"Telling ghost stories," said Charles.

"Tell some now," pleaded Lowella. "Do, please. Daddy. Uncle Roc."

Hyson sat forward, suddenly alert.

"Most unseasonable," commented Roc. "You'll have to wait a few months yet, Lo."

"I can't. I can't. I want a ghost story . . . *now!*"

"It certainly is time you were in bed," commented Morwenna.

Lowella regarded me with solemn eyes. "It'll be the Bride's first Christmas with us," she announced. "She'll love Christmas at Pendorric, won't she? I remember last Christmas we sang songs as well as telling ghost stories. Real Christmas songs. I'll tell you the one I like best."

" 'The Mistletoe Bough,' " said Hyson.

"You'd like that, Bride, because it's all about another bride."

"I expect your Aunt Favel knows it," said Morwenna. "Everyone does."

"No," I told them, "I've never heard it. You see, Christmas on the island wasn't quite like an English Christmas."

"Fancy! She's never heard of 'The Mistletoe Bough.' " Lowella looked shocked.

"Think what she's missed," mocked Roc.

"I'm going to be the one to tell her," declared Lowella.

"Listen, Bride! This other bride played hide and seek in a place . . ."

"Minster Lovel," supplied Hyson.

"Well, the place doesn't matter two hoots, silly."

"Lowella," Morwenna admonished; but Lowella was rushing on.

"They were playing hide and seek and this bride got into the old oak chest, the lock clicked and fastened her down forever."

"And they didn't open the chest until twenty years later," put in Hyson. "Then they found her . . . nothing but a skeleton."

"Her wedding dress and orange blossom were all right though," added Lowella cheerfully.

"I'm sure," said Roc ironically, "that must have been a comfort."

"You shouldn't laugh, Uncle Roc. It's sad, really."

"A spring lock lay in ambush there," she sang. "And fastened her down forever."

"And the moral of that," Roc put in, grinning at me, "is, don't go hiding in oak chests if you're a bride."

"Ugh!" shivered Morwenna. "I'm not keen on that story. It's morbid."

"That's why it appeals to your daughters, Wenna," Roc told her.

Charles said: "Look. I'm going up. The twins ought to have been in bed hours ago."

Deborah yawned. "I must say I find it hard to keep awake."

"I've an idea," cried Lowella. "Let's all sing Christmas songs for a bit. Everyone has to sing a different one."

"I've a better idea," said her father. "Bed."

Rachel stood up. "Come along," she said to the twins. "It must be nearly two."

Lowella looked disgusted with us because we all rose; but no one took any notice of her and we said good night and went upstairs.

* * *

The next day I went over to Polhorgan to see how my grandfather was after all the excitement.

Mrs. Dawson met me in the hall and I congratulated her on all that she and her husband had done to make the ball a success.

"Well, madam," she said, bridling, "it's a pleasure to be

appreciated, I must say. Not that Dawson and I want *thanks*. It was our duty and we did it."

"You did it admirably," I told her.

Dawson came into the hall at that moment and when Mrs. Dawson told him what I had said, he was as pleased as his wife.

I asked how my grandfather was that morning.

"Very contented, madam, but sleeping. A little tired after all the excitement, I think."

"I won't disturb him for a while," I said. "I'll go into the garden."

"I'm sending up his coffee in half an hour, madam," Mrs. Dawson told me.

"Very well, then I'll wait till then."

Dawson followed me into the garden; there was something conspiratorial about his manner, I thought; and when I paused by one of the greenhouses he was still beside me.

"Everyone in the house is glad, madam, that you've come home," he told me. "With one exception, that is."

I turned to look at him in astonishment, and he did not meet my eyes. I had the impression that he was determined to be the good and faithful servant, dealing with a delicate situation because this was something I ought to know.

"Thank you, Dawson," I said. "Who is the exception?"

"The nurse."

"Oh?"

He stuck out his lower lip and shook his head. "She had other notions."

"Dawson, you don't like Nurse Grey, do you?"

"There's nobody in this house that likes her, madam . . . except the young men. She being that sort. There's some that don't look beyond a pretty face."

I thought again that probably Nurse Grey gave orders in the kitchens, which they did not like. It was not an unusual situation. And now that they knew I was Lord Polhorgan's granddaughter, they regarded me as the mistress of the house. This was the Dawsons' way of telling me I was accepted as such.

"Mrs. Dawson and I have always felt ourselves to be in a privileged position, madam. We have been with his lordship for a very long time."

"But of course you *are*," I assured him.

"We were here, begging your pardon, when Miss Lilith was at home."

"So you knew my mother?"

"A lovely young lady and, if you'll forgive the liberty, madam, you're very like her."

"Thank you."

"That's why . . . Mrs. Dawson and I . . . made up our minds that we could talk to you, madam."

"Please say everything that's in your mind, Dawson."

"Well, we're uneasy, madam. There was a time when we thought she would try to marry him. There was no doubt that was what she was after. Mrs. Dawson and I had made up our minds that the minute that was decided on we should be looking for another position."

"Miss Grey . . . marry my grandfather!"

"Such things have happened, madam. Rich old gentlemen do marry young nurses now and then. They get a feeling they can't do without them and the nurses have their eyes on the money, you see."

"I'm sure my grandfather would never be married for his money. He's far too shrewd."

"That was what we said. She would never achieve that, and she didn't. But Mrs. Dawson and I reckon it wasn't for want of trying." He came closer to me and whispered: "The truth is, madam, we reckon she's what you might call . . . an adventuress."

"I see."

"There's something more. Our married daughter came to see us not long ago . . . it was just before you came home, madam. Well, she happened to see Nurse Grey and she said she was sure she'd seen her picture in the paper somewhere. Only she didn't think the name was Grey."

"Why was her picture in the paper?"

"It was some case or other. Maureen couldn't remember what. But she thought it was something very bad."

"People get mixed up about these things. Perhaps she'd won a beauty competition or something like that."

"Oh no, it wasn't that or Maureen would have remembered. It was something to do with the courts. And it was Nurse something. But Maureen didn't think it was Grey. It was just the face. She has got the sort of face, madam, that once seen is never forgotten."

"Did you ask her?"

"Oh no, madam, it wasn't the sort of thing we could ask. She would be offended and, unless we'd got proof, she could deny it, couldn't she? No, there's nothing we can put a finger on. And now you've come home it doesn't seem the same. His lordship's not so likely to get caught—that's how Mrs. Dawson and I see it, madam. But we're keeping our eyes open."

"Oh . . . it's Mrs. Pendorric."

I turned sharply to see Althea Grey smiling at me, and I flushed rather guiltily, feeling at a disadvantage to have been discovered discussing her with the butler. I wondered if she had overheard anything. Voices carried in the open air.

"*You* don't look as if you've been up half the night," she went on. "And I'm sure you must have been. What an evening! Lord Polhorgan was absolutely delighted with the way everything went off."

Dawson slipped away and I was left alone with her. Her hair, piled high beneath the snowy cap, was beautiful; but I wondered what it was that made her face so distinctive. Was it the thick brows, several shades darker than her hair; the eyes of that lovely deep blue shade that is almost violet and doesn't need to take its color from anything because it is always a more vivid blue than anything else could possibly be? The straight nose was almost Egyptian and seemed odd with such Anglo-Saxon fairness. The wide mouth was slightly mocking now. I felt sure that even if she had not overheard our conversation, she knew that Dawson had been speaking of her derogatively.

It was a face of mystery, I decided, a face that concealed secrets; the face of a woman of the world, a woman who had lived perhaps recklessly and had no desire for the past to prejudice the present, or future?

I remembered that the young man with whom I had danced had mentioned something from the past too. So Dawson's suspicions were very likely not without some foundation.

I felt wary of this woman as I walked with her towards the house.

"Lord Polhorgan was hoping you'd come this morning. I told him you most certainly would."

"I was wondering how he felt after last night."

"It did him a world of good. He enjoyed feting his beautiful granddaughter."

I felt that she was secretly laughing at me, and I was glad when I was with my grandfather and she had left us alone together.

* * *

It was a week later that there was a call in the night.

The telephone beside our bed rang and I was answering it before Roc had opened his eyes.

"This is Nurse Grey. Could you come over at once? Lord Polhorgan is very ill, and asking for you."

I leaped out of bed.

"What on earth's happened?" asked Roc.

When I told him he made me slip on some clothes and, doing the same himself, said: "We'll drive over right away."

"What's the time?" I asked Roc, as we drove the short distance between Pendorric and Polhorgan.

"Just after one."

"He must be bad for her to ring us," I said.

Roc put his hand over mine, as though to reassure me that whatever was waiting for me, he would be there to share it.

As we drove up to the portico the door opened and Dawson let us in.

"He's very bad, I'm afraid, madam."

"I'll go straight up."

I ran up the stairs, Roc at my heels. Roc waited outside the bedroom while I went in.

Althea Grey came towards me. "Thank God you've come," she said. "He's been asking for you. I phoned as soon as I knew."

I went to my bed, where my grandfather lay back on his pillows; he was quite exhausted and I could see that he was finding it difficult to get his breath.

"Grandfather," I said.

His lips formed the name Favel; but he did not say it.

I knelt by the bed and took his hand in mine; I kissed it, feeling desolate. I had found him such a short time ago. Was I to lose him so soon?

"I'm here, Grandfather. I came as soon as I heard you wanted me."

I knew by the slight movement of his head that he understood.

Althea Grey was at my side. She whispered: "He's not in pain. I've given him morphia. He'll be feeling the effect of it now. Dr. Clement will be here at any moment."

I turned to look at her and I saw from her expression that his condition was very grave. Then I saw Roc standing some little way from the bed. Althea Grey moved back to where he was and I turned my attention to my grandfather.

"Favel." It was a whisper. His fingers moved in mine, and

I knew that he was trying to say something to me so I brought my face nearer to his.

"Are you there . . . Favel?"

"Yes, Grandfather," I whispered.

"It's . . . good-by, Favel."

"*No.*"

He smiled. "Such a short time . . . but it was a happy time . . . the happiest time . . . Favel, you must be . . ."

His face puckered and I bent nearer to him.

"Don't talk, Grandfather. It's too much of an effort."

His brows puckered into a frown. "Favel . . . must be . . . careful . . . it'll be yours now. Make sure . . ."

I guessed what he was trying to tell me. Even when he was fighting for his breath he was preoccupied with his money.

"It's different . . ." he went on, "when you have it . . . can't be sure . . . can never be sure . . . Favel . . . take care . . ."

"Grandfather, please don't worry about me. Don't think about anything but getting better. You will get better. You *must* . . ."

He shook his head. "Couldn't find . . ." he began; but his battle for breath was too much for him; his eyes were closing. "Tired," he murmured. "So tired. Favel . . . stay . . . be careful . . . it's different with money. Perhaps I was wrong . . . but I wanted . . . be careful . . . I wish I could stay awhile to . . . look after you, Favel."

His lips were moving now but no sound came. He lay back on his pillows, his face looking shrunken and gray.

He was very near the end by the time Dr. Clement arrived.

* * *

We sat in the room where I had played so many games of chess with him—Dr. Clement, Roc, Nurse Grey, and myself.

Dr. Clement was saying: "It's not entirely unexpected. It could have happened at any time. Did he ring the bell?"

"No. Or I should have heard him. My room is next to his. The bell is always by his bed for him to ring if he wanted anything in the night. It was Dawson who went in. He said he was locking up when he saw Lord Polhorgan's light on. He found him gasping and in great pain. He called me and I saw that it was necessary to give him morphia, which I did."

Dr. Clement rose and went to the door.

"Dawson," he called. "Are you there, Dawson?"

Dawson came into the room.

"I've heard that you came in and found Lord Polhorgan in distress."

"Yes, sir. He'd snapped on the light and seeing it I looked in to make sure he was all right. I saw he was trying to ask for something, but I didn't know what for a while. Then I found out it was his pills. I couldn't find them then so I called Nurse and came back with her. That was when she gave him the morphia."

"So it seems as though this attack developed into a major one because he had no chance of holding it off."

"I'd always impressed on him the need to have his pills at hand," said Althea Grey.

Dawson was looking at her scornfully. "I found them after, sir. After his lordship had had the morphia, that was. The box was lying on the floor. It had come open and the pills was scattered, sir. The bell was on the floor also."

"He must have knocked them over when he reached for the pills," said Althea Grey.

I looked at Roc, who was staring straight ahead of him.

"A sad business," murmured Dr. Clement. "I think I ought to give you a sedative, Mrs. Pendorric. You're looking all in."

"I'll take her home," said Roc. "There's no point in waiting here now. We can do nothing till the morning."

Dr. Clement smiled at me sadly. "There was nothing we could do to prevent it," he told me.

"If he had had his pills," I said, "that might have prevented it."

"It might have."

"What an unfortunate accident . . ." I began; and my eyes met Dawson's and I saw that his were gleaming with speculation.

"It couldn't be helped," Roc was saying. "It's easy to see how it happened . . . reaching out . . . in a hurry . . . knocking over the box and the bell."

I shivered and Roc put his arm through mine.

I wanted to get out of that room; there was something in Dawson's expression which frightened me; there was something too in the calm, beautiful features of Althea Grey.

I felt as though I were outside looking in on all that had happened since Roc and I came into this house. I saw myself leaning over my dying grandfather; I heard his voice warning me of some danger which he sensed ahead of me. Roc and Althea were standing together in that room of death. What words did they exchange while my grandfather told me to take care? What had been the expressions in their eyes as they looked at each other?

Dawson had done this with his hatred of the nurse, with his groundless suspicions. But did I really know that they were groundless?

I felt the cool night air on my face and Roc's tender voice beside me.

"Come on, darling, you're quite worn out. Clement's right. It has been a terrible shock to you."

* * *

Those were sad weeks which followed, for only when I had lost him did I realize how fond I had become of my grandfather. I missed him deeply; not only his company, I began to understand; not only the complacent joy I had felt because I had brought so much pleasure into his lonely life; but he had given me a sense of security, and that I had lost. I had subconsciously felt that he was there—a powerful man of the world to whom I could go if I were in trouble. My own flesh and blood. I could have trusted him to do anything in his power to help me . . . should I have needed his help.

It seemed strange that I should have felt this need. I had a husband who could surely give me any protection I wanted; but it was the loss of my grandfather which brought home to me the true relationship between myself and my husband. To have lost him would have been complete desolation; he could amuse and delight me, too, but the truth remained that I was not sure of him; I did not know him. Yet, in spite of this uncertainty I loved him infinitely, and my entire happiness depended on him. I was wretched because I must be suspicious of his relationship with Althea Grey, Rachel Bective, and even Dinah Bond. And I had begun to feel— since I had discovered that I had a grandfather—that he was someone who had for me a deep and uncomplicated affection. Now I had lost him.

I was his heir and there were many visits from his solicitor. When I heard the extent of the fortune he had left I felt dizzy at the prospect of my riches. There were several bequests. The Dawsons had been left a comfortable pension; there was a thousand pounds for the nurse who was employed by him at the time of his death; all the servants had been remembered and rewarded according to their length of service; he had left a sizable sum to be used for the benefit of orphans—he himself had been an orphan—and I was very touched that he had remembered this charity. Death duties, I was informed, would swallow up a large proportion, but I should still have a considerable fortune.

Polhorgan itself was mine with all its contents; and this in itself was worth a great deal.

My grandfather's death seemed to have changed my whole life. I was so much poorer in affection, so much richer in worldly goods; and I was beginning to be afraid that this last fact colored people's attitude towards me.

I fancied people like the Darks and Dr. Clement were not quite so friendly; that the people in the village whispered about me when I had passed. I had become not merely Mrs. Pendorric, but the rich Mrs. Pendorric. But it was in Pendorric itself that I felt the change most and this was indeed disturbing. I felt that Morwenna and Charles were secretly delighted, and that the twins watched me a little furtively as though they had overheard gossip which had made them see me in a different light.

Deborah was more outspoken than the others. She said: "Barbarina was an heiress, but nothing of course to be compared with yourself."

I hated this kind of talk. I wished that my grandfather had not been such a rich man. I wished that he had left his money elsewhere, for I was realizing now that one of the facts which had made me so happy at Pendorric was that, although the old house and estate needed money, Roc had married a girl without a penny. I could no longer say to myself: "He could only have married me for love."

It was with my grandfather's money that the canker had touched our relationship.

It was some weeks after my grandfather's death that I had an interview with his solicitor and he brought home to me the advisability of making a will.

So I did so and, with the exception of one or two legacies, I left the residue of my fortune to Roc.

* * *

September had come. The evenings were short and the mornings misty; but the afternoons were as warm as they had been in July.

It was two months since my grandfather's death and I was

still mourning him. I had done nothing about Polhorgan, and the Dawsons and all the servants remained there; Althea Grey had decided to have a long holiday before looking for a new post and had taken a little cottage about a mile from Pendorric, which, during the months of June, July, and August, was let to holiday makers.

I knew I should have to do something about Polhorgan and an idea had come to me. It was to turn the house into a home for orphans—such as my grandfather must have been—the deprived and unwanted ones.

When I mentioned this to Roc, he was startled.

"What an undertaking!" he said.

"Somehow I think it would have appealed to my grandfather because he was an orphan himself."

Roc walked away from me—we were in our bedroom—and going to the window stared out at the sea.

"Well, Roc, you don't like the idea?"

"Darling, it's not the sort of project you can rush into."

"No, of course not. I'm just thinking about it."

"Things aren't what they used to be, remember. There'd be all sorts of bureaucratic regulations to be got over . . . and have you thought of the cost of running a place like that?"

"I haven't thought about anything very much. It was just a faint idea. I'm brooding on it though."

"We'll have to do a lot of brooding," he said.

I had a notion that he was not impressed with the idea, and I shelved it for the time being, but I was determined not to give it up easily.

I often called on Jesse Pleydell, who always seemed delighted to see me apart from the tobacco I took him. Mrs. Penhalligan said I kept him supplied and he was grateful, though it was my visits that meant as much to him as the tobacco.

I shall never forget that September day because it brought the begining of the real terror which came into my life, and it was at this time that I began to understand how the pleasant picture had changed piece by piece until I was confronted with the cruelest of suspicions and horror.

The day began normally enough. In the morning I went down to Mrs. Robinson's and bought the tobacco. Knowing that I was going, Deborah asked me to buy some hairpins for her, and Morwenna asked me to bring some bass she needed for tying up plants. I met Rachel and the twins as I was setting out; they were going on a nature ramble so they all three walked with me as far as the shop. When I came back I met Roc and Charles going off to the home farm together.

But I didn't leave for the cottages until after tea, and when I arrived Jesse was sitting at his door, catching the last of the sun.

I sat beside him for a while and, because I thought it was getting a little chilly, I went inside with him and he made me a cup of tea. It was something he enjoyed doing and I knew better than to offer to help. While we sat drinking the thick brew, Jesse talked of the old days and how the Pendorric gardens had looked in his time.

"Ah, madam, you should have been here forty years ago . . . that was the time. I had four men working under me all the time, and the flowers in the cliff garden was a picture . . . a real picture."

He would go on and on in this strain and, because he enjoyed it, I encouraged him to do so. I learned a good deal about life at Pendorric forty or fifty years ago when Jesse was in his prime. It was a more leisurely life, but even so the beginning of change had set in.

"Now when I were a boy things were different."

That would have been about eighty years ago. Very different indeed, I thought.

"There was no talk then of not being able to keep up like," mused Jesse. "There was no thought that things 'ud ever be different from what they always had been. Polhorgan House wasn't here then . . . nor thought of, and all Polhorgan meant to us was the little old cove down there."

I listened dreamily, staying rather longer than I had intended, and it was six o'clock when I rose to go.

It was always gloomy in the cottages on account of the small, latticed windows, so I hadn't noticed how dark it had grown. The sea mist had been lurking in the air all day, but now it had thickened. It was warm and sea-scented and not by any means unpleasant; it hung in patches and in some spots was really thick. It was especially so near the church; and as I paused at the lych gate to look at the gravestones with the mist swirling about them, thinking how strangely picturesque everything was, I heard it; it seemed to be coming from inside the graveyard—singing in that strange, high voice, which was slightly out of tune.

> *"How should I your true love know*
> *From another one?*

*By his cockle hat and staff
And his sandal shoon."*

My heart began to beat fast; my hand on the lych gate trembled. I looked about me but I seemed to be alone with the mist.

Someone was in there singing, and I had to find out who, so I opened the lych gate and went into the graveyard. I was determined to know who it was who sang in that strange voice, and because I was sure that it was someone from the house, instinctively I made my way to the Pendorric vault. I was almost certain now that it must be Carrie. She brought wreaths for her beloved Barbarina and she would have heard her sing that song; what more natural than that hearing it often she had learned it by heart?

It must be Carrie.

As I reached the Pendorric vault, I drew up short in astonishment because the door was open. I had never seen it open before and was under the impression that it would never be opened except when it was prepared to receive those who had died.

I went closer and as I did so I heard the voice again.

*"He is dead and gone, lady,
He is dead and gone;
At his head a grass-green turf,
At his heels a stone."*

And it appeared to be coming from *inside* the vault.

I went down the stone steps. "Who's there?" I called. "Carrie. Are you in there?"

My voice sounded strange at the entrance of that dark vault.

"Carrie," I called. "Carrie." I put my head inside and saw that four or five stone steps led down. I descended, calling: "Carrie! Carrie! Are you there?"

There was silence. Because of the light from the open door I could see the ledges with the coffins on them; I could smell the dampness of the earth. Then suddenly I was in darkness and for a few seconds I was so shocked and bewildered that I could not move. I could not even cry out in protest. It took me several seconds to understand that the door had closed on me and I was shut in the vault . . .

I gave a gasp of horror.

"Who's there?" I cried. "Who shut the door?"

Then I tried to find the steps, but my eyes were not yet adjusted to the darkness, and, groping, I stumbled and found myself sprawling up the cold stone stairs.

Frantically I picked myself up. I could make out the shape of the steps now, and I mounted them. I pushed the door but it was firmly shut and I could not move it.

For some moments, I'm afraid, I was hysterical. I hammered on the door with my fists. "Let me out of here," I screamed. "Let me out of here."

My voice sounded hollow and I knew that it would not be heard outside.

I lay against the door, trying to think. Someone had lured me into this dreadful place, someone who wanted to be rid of me. How long could I live here? But I should be missed. Roc would miss me. He would come to look for me.

"Roc!" I called. "Oh . . . Roc . . . come quickly."

I covered my face with my hands. I did not want to look about me. I was suddenly afraid of what I might see, shut in this vault with the Pendorric dead. How long before I became one of them?

Then I thought I heard a movement near me. I listened. Was that the sound of breathing?

The horror was deepening. I did not believe in ghosts, I tried to tell myself. But it is easy to say that when you are above ground in some sunny spot, some well-lighted room. Very different, buried alive . . . among the dead!

I had never known real fear until that moment. I was clammy with sweat, my hair was probably standing on end. I did not know because there was no room in my mind for anything but fear, the knowledge that I was locked in with the dead.

But I was not alone. I knew it. Some breathing, living thing was in this tomb with me.

I had covered my face with my hands because I did not want to see it. I dared not see.

Then a cold hand touched mine. I screamed, and I heard myself cry: "Barbarina!" because in that moment I *believed* the legend of Pendorric. I believed that Barbarina had lured me to my tomb so that I could haunt Pendorric and she might rest in peace.

"Favel!" It was a sharp whisper and the one who said it was as frightened as I was.

"Hyson!"

"Yes, Favel. It's Hyson."

Floods of relief! I was not alone. There was someone to share this horrible place with me. I felt ashamed of myself, but I couldn't help it. I had never been so glad to hear a human voice in the whole of my life.

"Hyson . . . what are you doing here?"

She had come up the stairs and snuggled close beside me.

"It's . . . frightening . . . with the door shut," she said.

"Did you do this, Hyson?"

"Do it . . . do what?"

"Lock me in."

"But I'm locked in with you."

"How did you come to be in here?"

"I knew something was going to happen."

"What? How?"

"I knew. I came to meet you . . . to see if you were all right."

"What do you mean? How could you know?"

"I do know things. Then I heard the singing . . . and the door was open . . . so I came in."

"Before I did?"

"Only a moment before. I was hiding down at the bottom of the steps when you came in."

"I don't understand what it means."

"It means Barbarina's lured you in. She didn't know I was here too."

"Barbarina's *dead*."

"She can't rest, till you take her place."

I was recovering my calm. It was amazing what the presence of one small human being could do.

"That's nonsense, Hyson," I said. "Barbarina is dead and this story of her haunting the place is just an old legend."

"She's waiting for a new bride to die."

"I don't intend to die."

"We'll both die," said Hyson, almost unconcernedly; and I thought: She knows nothing of death; she has never seen death. She has looked at the television and seen people drop to the ground. Bang! You're dead. In a child's mind death is quick and neat, without suffering. One forgot that she was only a child posing as a seer.

"That's absurd," I said. "We shan't. There must be a certain amount of air coming into this place. They'll miss us and there'll be search parties to find us."

"Why should they think of looking in the vault?"

"They'll look everywhere."

"They'll never look in the vault."

I was silent for a while. I was trying to think who could have done this, who had been waiting for me to leave Jesse Pleydell's cottage and lure me to the vault with singing like some cruel siren of the sea.

Someone who wanted me out of the way had done this. Someone who had waited for me to enter the vault, descend the stone steps, and then glided out from some hiding place and locked the door on me.

I was recovering rapidly from my fear and realizing that I was not afraid of human scheming; I felt myself equal to deal with that. As soon as I could rid myself of the notion that I was being lured to death by someone who was dead, I felt my natural resilience returning. I was ready to match my wits with those of another human being. I could fight the living.

I said: "Someone locked the door. Who could it be?"

"It was Barbarina," whispered Hyson.

"That's not reasonable. Barbarina's dead."

"She's in here, Favel . . . in her coffin. It's on the ledge with my grandfather's beside it. She couldn't rest and she wants to . . . that's why she's locked you in here."

"Who opened the door?"

"Barbarina."

"Who locked the door?"

"Barbarina."

"Hyson, you're getting hysterical."

"Am I?"

"You mustn't. We've got to think of how we can get out of here."

"We never shall. Why did she lock me in too? It's like Meddlesome Matty. Granny was always warning me. I shouldn't have come."

"You mean that then I should have been the only victim." My voice was grim. I was ashamed of myself. It was a terrible experience for the child; and yet it was doing me such a lot of good not to be alone.

"We shall stay here," said Hyson, "forever. It'll be like 'The Mistletoe Bough.' When they next open the vault there'll only be our bones, for we shall be skeletons."

"What nonsense!"

"Do you remember the night of the ball? We all talked about it."

I was silent with a new horror because the idea flashed into my mind that on that night when we had sat drinking soup after the ball, one member of our party may have thought of the vault as a good substitute for the old oak chest.

I shivered. Could there be any other explanation than that someone wanted *me* out of the way?

I gripped Hyson's shoulder. "Listen," I said. "We've got to find a way out of this place. Perhaps the door isn't really locked. Who could have locked it anyway?"

"Bar . . ."

"Oh, nonsense." I stood up cautiously. "Hyson," I said, "we must see what we can do."

"She won't let us."

"Give me your hand and we'll see what it's like here."

"We know. It's all dead people in coffins."

"I wish I had a torch. Let's try the door again. It may have got jammed."

We stood on the top step and beat against it. It did not budge.

"I wonder how long we've been in here," I said.

"An hour."

"I don't think five minutes. Time goes slowly on occasions like this. But they'll miss us at dinner. They'll start searching for us in the house and then they'll be out, searching for us. I want to look around. There might be a grating somewhere. We might shout through that."

"There'll be nobody in the churchyard to hear us."

"There might be. And if they come looking . . ."

I dragged her to her feet and she cowered close to me. Then together, keeping close, we cautiously descended the steps.

Hyson was shivering. "It's so cold," she said.

I put my arm round her and we stepped gingerly forward into the darkness. I could see vague shapes about me and I knew these to be the coffins of dead Pendorrics.

Then suddenly I saw a faint light and feeling my way towards it discovered that it was a grating at the side of the vault. I peered through it and fancied I saw the side of a narrow trench. I knew then that a certain amount of air was coming into the vault and I felt my spirits rising. I put my face close to the grating and shouted: "Help! We're in the vault. Help!"

My voice sounded muffled as though it were thrown back at me, and I realized that however loudly I shouted I should not be heard unless someone were standing very close to the vault.

Nevertheless I went on shouting until I was hoarse, while Hyson stood shivering beside me.

"Let's try the door again," I said. And we made our way slowly back to the steps. Once again we forced our weights against it and still it remained fast shut. Hyson was sobbing and bitterly cold, so I took off my coat and wrapped it round us both. We sat side by side on that top step, our arms about each other. I tried to comfort her and tell her that we should soon be rescued, that this was quite different from the old oak chest. We had seen the grating, hadn't we? That meant that air was coming in. All we had to do was wait for them to come and find us. Perhaps we should hear their voices. Then we would shout together.

Eventually she stopped trembling and I think she slept.

I could not sleep although I felt exhausted, bitterly cold, stiff and cramped; and I sat there holding the body of the child against me, peering into the darkness, asking myself over and over again: Who has done this?

* * *

There was no means of knowing the time for I could not see my watch. Hyson stirred and whimpered; I held her closer and whispered assurances to her, while I tried to think of a plan to escape from this place.

I pictured the family coming down to dinner. How upset they would be! Where was Favel? Roc would want to know. He would be a little anxious at first and then frantic with worry. They would already have been searching for us for hours.

Hyson had awakened suddenly: "Favel . . . where are we?"

"It's all right. I'm here. We're together . . ."

"We're in that place. Are we still alive, Favel?"

"That's one thing I'm sure of."

"We're not . . . just ghosts then?"

I pressed her hand. "There are no such things," I told her.

"Favel, you *dare* say that . . . down here . . . among them."

"If they existed they would surely make us aware of them, just to prove me wrong, wouldn't they?"

I could feel the child holding her breath as she peered into the darkness.

After a while she said: "Have we been here all night?"

"I don't know, Hyson."

"Will it be dark like this all the time?"

"There might be a little light through the grating when the day comes. Shall we go and look?"

We were so stiff and cramped that we could not move our limbs for some seconds.

"Listen," said Hyson fearfully, "I heard something."

I listened with her; but I could hear nothing.

I felt my way cautiously down the steps holding Hyson's hand as we went.

"There," she whispered, "I heard it again."

She clung to me and I put my arm about her.

"If only we had a lighter or a match," I murmured as we picked our way to where I thought the grating had been, but there was no light coming from the wall, so I guessed it was still dark outside. Then I saw a sudden flash of light; I heard a voice call: "Favel! Hyson!"

The light had shown me the grating and I ran stumbling towards it shouting: "We're here . . . in the vault. Favel and Hyson are here in the vault!

The light came again and stayed. I recognized Deborah's voice. "Favel! Is that you, Favel?"

"Here," I cried. "Here!"

"Oh, Favel . . . thank God. Hyson . . . ?"

"Hyson's here with me. We're locked in the vault."

"Locked in . . ."

"Please get us out . . . quickly."

"I'll be back . . . soon as I can."

The light disappeared and Hyson and I stood still hugging each other.

*   *   *

It seemed hours before the door was opened and Roc came striding down the steps. We ran to him—Hyson and I—and he held us both against him.

"What the . . ." he began. "You gave us a nice fright . . ."

Morwenna was there with Charles, who picked Hyson up in his arms and held her as though she were a baby.

Their torches showed us the damp walls of the vault, the ledges with the coffins; but Hyson and I turned shuddering away and looked towards the door.

"Your hands are like ice," said Roc, chafing them. "We've got the cars by the lych gate. We'll be home in a few minutes."

I lay against him in the car, too numb, too exhausted for speech.

I did manage to ask the time.

"Two o'clock," Roc told me. "We've been searching since soon after eight."

I went straight to bed and Mrs. Penhalligan brought me hot soup. I said I shouldn't be able to sleep; in fact I should be afraid to for fear I should dream I was back in that dreadful place.

But I did sleep—almost immediately; and I was untroubled by dreams.

It was nine o'clock that morning before the sun shining through the windows woke me. Roc was sitting in a chair near the bed watching me, and I felt very happy because I was alive.

* * *

"What happened?" asked Roc.

"I heard someone singing and the door of the vault was open."

"You thought the Pendorrics had left their coffins and were having a little sing-song?"

"I didn't know who it was. I went down the steps and then . . . the door was locked on me."

"What did you do?"

"Hammered on the door; called out. Hyson and I both used all our strength against it. Oh Roc . . . it was horrible."

"Not the most pleasant spot to spend a night, I must say."

"Roc, who could have done it? Who could have locked us in?"

"No one."

"But someone *did*. Why, if Deborah hadn't come there looking for us we'd still be there. Heaven knows how long we should have been there."

"We decided to search every inch of the land for miles around. Deborah and Morwenna did Pendorric village and the Darks joined up with them."

"It was wonderful when we heard Deborah's voice calling us. But it seemed ages before she came back."

"She thought she needed the key, and there's only one I know of—to the vault. It's kept in the cupboard in my study, and the cupboard is locked; so she had to find me first."

"That's why it took so long."

"We didn't waste any time, I can tell you. I couldn't

imagine who could have got at the key and unlocked the vault. The sexton borrowed it some weeks ago. He must have thought he locked it."

"But someone locked us in."

Roc said: "No, darling. The door wasn't locked. I discovered that when I tried to unlock it."

"Not locked! But . . ."

"Wh would have locked you in?"

"That's what I'm wondering."

"No one has a key except me. There had only been one for years. The key was locked in my cupboard. It was hanging on the nail there when I went to get it."

"But Roc, I don't understand how . . ."

"I think it's simple enough. It was a misty evening, wasn't it? You passed the lych gate and went into the churchyard. The door of the vault was open because old Pengelly hadn't locked it when he was there a few weeks ago and the door had blown open."

"It was a very still evening. There was no wind."

"There was a gale the night before. It had probably been open all day and no one had noticed it. Few people go to the old part of the graveyard. Well, you saw it open, and went inside. The door shut on you."

"But if it wasn't locked why didn't it open when we pushed with all our strength?"

"I expect it jammed. Besides, you probably panicked to find yourself shut in. Perhaps if you'd not believed the door was locked you would have discovered it was only jammed."

"I don't believe it."

He looked at me in astonishment. "What on earth's in your mind?"

"I don't quite know . . . but someone locked us in."

"Who?"

"Someone did it."

He smoothed the hair back from my forehead.

"There's only one person who could," he said. "Myself."

"Oh Roc . . . *No!*"

He threw himself down beside me and took me into his arms.

"Let me tell you something, darling," he said. "I'd far rather have you here with me than in that vault with Hyson."

He was laughing; he did not understand that chill of fear which had taken possession of me.

5.

I COULD NOW no longer delude myself. I had to face up to all the fears which I had refused to acknowledge during the last weeks.

Someone had deliberately lured me into the vault and locked me in, for I refused to believe Roc's theory that the door had jammed. In the first moments it was true that I may have panicked; but when I had discovered Hyson and sought to comfort her, I had regained my composure. We had both tried to open that door with all our strength and had failed. And the reason was that it had been locked.

This could only mean one thing. Someone wanted to harm me.

Suppose Deborah had not come by? Suppose she had not heard our call, how long could we have lived in the vault? There was a little air coming in, it was true; but we should have starved to death eventually, because it was a fact that few people came that way, and if they did we should not have heard them unless they had come close to the grating and called us.

It might have been one week . . . two weeks. We should have been dead by then.

Someone was trying to kill me, but in a way which, when my death was discovered, would appear accidental. Who?

It would be the person who would benefit most from my death. Roc?

I couldn't believe that. I was perhaps illogical, as women in love are supposed to be; but I was not going to believe for one moment that Roc would kill me. He wouldn't kill anyone . . . least of all me. He was a gambler, I knew; he might even be unfaithful to me; but he could never in any circumstances commit murder.

If I died, he would be very rich. He had married me, knowing that I was the granddaughter of a millionaire. He needed money for Pendorric, and Roc and I were partners, so that my fortune would make certain that Pendorric remained entirely ours. This was all true; and whether I died or not, Pendorric was safe.

I refused to look beyond that; but I did believe that someone had locked me into the vault in the hope that I should not be discovered until I was dead.

I thought back over everything that had happened and my mind kept returning to the day when Roc had first come to the studio. My father must have known who he was as soon as he heard his name—there could not be many Pendorrics in the world—yet he had not told me. Why? Because my grandfather had not wanted me to know. Roc was to report on me first, take pictures of me. I smiled ruefully. That was typical of my grandfather's arrogance. As for Father, he had probably done everything he did for what he would believe to be my good.

And the day he died? Roc had seemed strange that day. Or had he? He had come back to the studio and left my father to swim alone. And when we knew what had happened, had he seemed . . . relieved, or had I imagined it?

I must stop thinking of Roc in this way, because if I was going to find out who was seeking to harm me I must look elsewhere.

There had been an occasion when I had taken the dangerous cliff path after the rain, and the warning had been removed. I remembered how uneasy I had felt then. But it was Roc who had remembered the path and dashed after me. It was reassuring to remember that. But why should it be reassuring? Because it showed that Roc loved me and wanted to protect me; that he could not possibly have had a hand in this.

But of course I knew he hadn't.

Who then?

My mind went at once to those women in whom, I believed, he had once been interested . . . perhaps still was. One could never be quite sure with Roc. Rachel? Althea? And what of Dinah Bond?

I remembered that she had once told me that Morwenna had been locked in the vault. What of the conversation I had heard between Morwenna and Charles? Oh, but it was natural that they should be pleased because Roc had married an heiress instead of a penniless girl. Why should Morwenna want to be rid of me? What difference could it make to her?

But if I were out of the way my fortune would go to Roc and he would be free to marry . . . Rachel . . . Althea?

Rachel had been there when we had talked about the bride in the oak chest; and if I could believe Dinah Bond, she had, long ago, locked Morwenna in the vault. She had known where to get the key; but there was only one key and Roc had that; it was an enormous key that hung in his cupboard, and the cupboard was kept locked. When they had unlocked the vault they had to find Roc first because he had the only key.

Rachel had known this and she had managed somehow, all those years ago, to get the key from Roc's father's cupboard.

Rachel, I thought. I had never liked her from the moment I had first met her.

I was going to watch Rachel.

* * *

Morwenna said that such an experience was bound to have shocked me, and I ought to take things easily for the next few days. She was going to see that Hyson did.

"I'd rather it had been Lowella who was locked in with you," she told me one day when I came out of the house and saw her working on the flower beds on one of the front lawns. "Hyson's too sensitive as it is."

"It was a horrible experience."

Morwenna straightened up and looked at me. "For both of you. You poor dear! I should have been terrified."

A shadow passed across her face and I guessed she was remembering that occasion, so long ago, when Rachel had locked her in and refused to let her out until she made a promise.

Deborah came out of the house.

"It's a lovely day," she said. "I'm beginning to wonder what my own garden is looking like."

"Getting homesick?" asked Morwenna. She smiled at me. "Deborah's like that. When she's on Dartmoor she thinks of Pendorric, and when she's here she gets homesick for the moor."

"Yes, I love both places so much. They both seem like home to me. I was thinking, Favel, this horrible affair . . . it's been such a shock, and you're not looking so well. Is she, Morwenna?"

"An experience like that is bound to upset anyone. I expect she'll have fully recovered in a day or so."

"I thought of going to the moor for a week or so. Why not come with me, Favel? I'd love to show you the place."

"Oh . . . how kind of you!"

Leave Roc? I was thinking. Leave him to Althea? To Rachel? And how could I rest until I had solved this matter? I must find out who had a grudge against me, who wanted me out of the way. No doubt it would be very restful to spend a week with Deborah, but all the time I should be longing to be back in Pendorric.

"As a matter of fact," I went on, "I've got such lots to do here . . . and there's Roc . . ."

"Don't forget," Morwenna reminded Deborah, "they haven't been married so very long."

Deborah's face fell. "Well, perhaps some other time—but I thought that you needed a little rest and . . ."

"I do appreciate your thinking of it and I shall look forward to coming later on."

"I wish you'd take Hyson," said Morwenna. "This business has upset her more than you think."

"Well, I must take dear Hyson," replied Deborah. "But I did so want to show Favel our old home."

I laid my hand on her arm. "You are kind, and I do hope you'll ask me again soon."

"Of course I shall. I shall positively pester you until you accept. Were you going for a walk?"

"I was just going over to Polhorgan. There are one or two things I have to see Mrs. Dawson about."

"May I walk with you?"

"It would be a great pleasure."

We left Morwenna to her flowers and took the road to Polhorgan. I felt rather guilty about refusing Deborah's invitation and was anxious that she should not think me churlish.

I tried to explain to her.

"Of course, I understand, my dear. You don't want to leave your husband. As a matter of fact I'm sure Roc would protest if you suggested it. But one day perhaps later on you'll come for a weekend when he has to go away. He does sometimes, on business, you know. We'll choose our opportunity. It was just that I thought, after that . . ."

She shivered.

"If it hadn't been for you we might be there still."

"I've never ceased to be thankful that I happened to go into the graveyard. It was just that I was determined to search every square inch. And when I think how chancey it was I shudder. I might have walked right round the vault and you might not have heard me, nor I you."

"I don't like thinking of it . . . even in broad daylight. It's so extraordinary, too, that Roc says the door wasn't locked . . . only jammed. I must say I feel a little foolish about that."

"Well, of course a door *could* get jammed."

"But we were so desperate. We hammered with all our might. It seems incredible. And yet there's only the one key and that was locked in Roc's cupboard."

"So," she went on, "the only one who could have locked you in would have been Roc." She laughed at the ludicrous idea; and I laughed with her.

"There used to be two keys, I remember," she went on. "Roc's father kept one in the cupboard there where Roc keeps it now."

"And who had the other?"

She paused for a few seconds, then she said: "Barbarina."

We were silent after that and scarcely spoke until we said good-by at Polhorgan.

* * *

I had never enjoyed going to Polhorgan since my grandfather's death. The place seemed so empty and useless without him; it had an air of being unlived in, which I always think is so depressing—like a woman whose life has never been fulfilled. Roc often laughed at me for my feelings about houses; as though, he said, they had a personality of their own. Well, at the moment Polhorgan's personality was a negative one. Of course, I thought, if I filled it with orphans who had never seen the sea, had never had any care and attention, what a different house it would be!

Idealistic dreams! I could hear Roc's voice. "Wait until you see how the bureaucrats are going to punish you. This is the Robin Hood State, in which the rich are robbed to help the poor."

I didn't care what difficulties I should encounter, I was going to have my orphans—if fewer than I had first dreamed of.

Mrs. Dawson came out to greet me.

"Good morning, madam. Dawson and I were wondering if you'd come; and as you have, would you be pleased to take a cup of coffee in our sitting room? There's something on our minds . . ."

I said I should be delighted to, and Mrs. Dawson told me she would make the coffee at once and send for Dawson.

Ten minutes later I was in the Dawsons' comfortable sitting room, drinking a cup of Mrs. Dawson's coffee.

Dawson had some difficulty in getting to the point, which I quickly perceived was an elaboration of the suspicions which had occurred to him the night my grandfather died.

"You see, madam, it's not easy to put into words. A man's afraid of saying too much . . . then again he's afraid of not saying enough."

Dawson was the typical butler. Dignified, and self-assured, he was the type of manservant my grandfather would have insisted on having, because he was what Roc would have called a cliché butler in the same way that my grandfather was the cliché self-made man.

"You can be perfectly frank with me, Dawson," I told him. "I'll not repeat anything you say unless you wish me to."

Dawson looked relieved. "I would not wish, madam, to be taken to the courts by the woman in question. Although if it should be true that she had been there before, that could well be counted in my favor."

"You mean Nurse Grey?"

Dawson said that he meant no other. "I am not satisfied, madam, about the nature of his lordship's death; and having talked together, Mrs. Dawson and I have come to the conclusion that it was brought about by a deliberate act."

"You mean because the pills were discovered under the bed?"

"Yes, madam, his lordship had had one or two minor attacks during the day, and Mrs. Dawson and I had noticed that often attacks would follow closely on one another, so it seemed almost certain that he would have another attack some time during the night."

"Wouldn't he call the nurse when he had these attacks during the night?"

"Only if the attack got so bad he needed morphia. Then he'd ring the bell on his side table. But first he'd take his pills. The bell was on the floor too, madam, with the pills."

"Yes, and it looked as though he knocked then over when reaching for the pills."

"That may have been how it was intended to look, madam."

"You are suggesting that Nurse Grey deliberately put the pills and the bell out of his reach?"

"Only within these four walls, madam."

"But why should she wish him dead? She has lost a good job."

"She had a good legacy," put in Mrs. Dawson. "And what's

to prevent her finding another job where she'll get another legacy?"

"But you're not suggesting that she kills off her patients for the sake of the legacies they leave her?"

"It might be so, madam, and I feel impelled to explain my suspicions regarding this young woman, and they are that she is an adventuress who needs to be watched."

"Dawson," I said, "my grandfather is dead and buried. Dr. Clement was satisfied that he died from natural causes."

"Mrs. Dawson and I don't doubt Dr. Clement's word, madam; but what we think is that his lordship was hastened to his death."

"This is a terrible accusation, Dawson."

"I know, madam; and that is why I would not want it to go beyond these four walls; but I thought you should be warned of our suspicions, the young woman still being in the neighborhood."

Mrs. Dawson stared thoughtfully into her coffee cup. "I was talking to Mrs. Greenock," she said, "who owns Cormorant Cottage."

"That's where Nurse Grey is living now, isn't it?"

"Yes, having a little rest between posts, so she says. Well, Mrs. Greenock wasn't very keen on letting to her. She was really after a long let that would go on all through the winter, and Nurse Grey wanted it for what she called an indefinite period. But it seems Mr. Pendorric persuaded Mrs. Greenock to let Nurse Grey have it."

I was beginning to understand why the Dawsons had wanted to talk to me. They were not only underlining their suspicions as to why my grandfather had died when he did, but were telling me that we had an adventuress in our midst, who was none too scrupulous, and was more friendly with my husband than they considered wise.

If they had wanted to make me feel uneasy they had certainly succeeded.

I changed the subject as inconspicuously as I could; we talked about the problems of Polhorgan, and I told them that I wanted them to go on as they were until I made up my mind what to do about the house. I assured them that I had no intention of selling and that I wanted them to remain there and hoped they always would.

They were delighted with me as their new employer. Mrs. Dawson told me so with tears in her eyes and Dawson implied, without sacrificing one part of his dignity, that it was a pleasure to serve me.

But I was very unhappy because I knew that they had spoken as they did out of a genuine concern for my welfare.

*   *   *

That afternoon I went to see the Clements because I wanted to talk to the doctor unprofessionally about my grandfather.

Mabell Clement was emerging triumphant from what she called the pot house when I arrived, her hair half up, half down, and she was dressed in a cotton blouse and bunchy yellow skirt.

"Nice surprise," she declared breezily. "Andrew will be pleased. Come in and I'll make you a cup of tea. It's been one of the most successful days I've had for a long time."

Andrew came to the door of the house to meet me and told me that I'd come at a fortunate time because it was his afternoon off, and his partner, Dr. Lee, was on duty.

Mabell made the tea and, because she couldn't find the cozy, put a woolen balaclava over the pot. There were toasted scones—a little burned—and a cake which had sagged in the middle.

"It tastes rather like a Christmas pudding," Mabell warned.

"I like Christmas pudding," I assured her.

I liked Mabell, too; she was one of the few people who were unimpressed by my sudden wealth.

While we were having tea I told Dr. Clement that I was disturbed about my grandfather's death.

"Could he have lived much longer if he hadn't had that attack?"

"He could have, yes. But we had to expect such attacks and their consequences could be fatal. I was not in the least surprised when I got the call."

"No, but he might have been alive now if he had been able to reach his pills in time."

"Has Dawson been talking to you again?"

"Dawson spoke to you about this, didn't he?" I countered.

"Yes, at the time your grandfather died. He found the pills and the bell on the floor."

"If he had been able to reach his pills . . . or his bell . . ."

"It seemed perfectly clear that he had tried and had knocked them over. In the circumstances a major attack developed and . . . that was the end."

Mabell brought over the cake that was like a Christmas pudding and I took a piece.

"It's over now," she said gently; "it's only disturbing to go over something that's finished."

"Yet, I would like to know."

"Actually I think the Dawsons didn't get on with the nurse," Mabell went on. "Nurses are notoriously bossy; butlers notoriously dignified; housekeepers tend to regard the house as their domain and resent anyone but their employers. I think it was just not very unusual domestic strife: and now the Dawsons see a chance of settling an old score."

"You see," said Andrew, "Dawson could suggest she deliberately put the pills and bell out of reach; she would emphatically deny it. There could be no proof either way."

"She looks like a piece of Dresden china but I reckon she's as sturdy as earthenware," mused Mabell. "It must have been a pleasant job she had with Lord Polhorgan. In any case she seemed to like it. How long had she been with him?"

"More than eighteen months," said Andrew.

"Was she a good nurse?" I asked.

"Quite efficient."

"She seemed . . . hard," I suggested.

"She was a nurse and as such had had some experience of suffering. Nurses . . . doctors . . . you know they can't feel the same as someone like yourself. We see too much of it."

"I know I can trust you two," I said, "so I'll say this: Do you think that she discovered she would get a thousand pounds when my grandfather died and that made her hasten his death?"

There was silence. Mabell took a long amber cigarette holder, opened a silver box, and offered me a cigarette.

"Because," I said slowly, "if she would do a thing like that, it's rather a sobering thought that she's going into other sick rooms, and the lives of other patients will be put into her hands."

Dr. Clement watched me intently. Then he said: "At the moment she's resting. She's taking a holiday before going to a new post, and I think it would be very unwise to talk of this matter beyond this room."

Mabell changed the subject in her blunt way. "I suppose you've quite recovered from that midnight adventure of yours."

"Oh . . . yes."

"An unpleasant experience," commented Andrew.

"I shiver even now when I think of it."

"The door was jammed, wasn't it?"

"I was certain that we were locked in."

"All the rain we've been having might make the door jam," said Andrew.

"Yet . . ."

Mabell thoughtfully knocked the ash from her cigarette. "Who on earth would have locked you in?"

"That's what I've been wondering ever since."

Andrew leaned forward. "So you don't believe the door jammed?"

I hesitated. What impression was I giving them? First I was repeating Dawson's suggestions against Nurse Grey, and now I was hinting that someone had locked me in the vault. They were two intelligent, uninhibited people. They would think I had a persecution mania if I was not careful.

"The general opinion seemed to be that the door had jammed. There was only one key anyway, and that was locked in a cupboard in my husband's study. He brought it down to the vault and it was he who found the door wasn't locked at all."

"Well, thank heaven they did discover you."

"If Deborah hadn't happened to come that way—and it was really purest chance that she did—goodness knows how long we should have been there. Perhaps we should be there now."

"Oh no!" protested Mabell.

"Why not? Such things have been known to happen."

Andrew lifted his shoulders. "It didn't happen."

"In future," Mabell put in, "you must be very careful."

Andrew leaned forward and there was a puzzled expression in his eyes.

"Yes," he repeated, "in future you must be very careful."

Mabell laughed rather nervously and began to talk about a pot she had made which she thought was unusual. When it was fired she wanted my opinion.

I felt that when I was not there they would talk of my affairs. They would say it was surprising that the door of the vault had been jammed and not locked and perhaps that Roc had the only key. They would undoubtedly have heard that Roc had persuaded Mrs. Greenock to let Althea Grey have Cormorant Cottage; and they would ask themselves: What is happening at Pendorric?

My uneasiness was deepening.

*   *   *

I didn't want to talk any more about the disturbed thoughts

which were turning over in my mind; I feared that I had already said too much to the Clements. I wished that I could have talked to Roc of my fears, but I imagined he would laugh at them—besides, he himself was so much involved.

I tried therefore to go on as normally as possible. So exactly a week after my unfortunate adventure I called on Jesse Pleydell again. He greeted me with more than his usual warmth and made it very clear that he was glad I had come. So he, too, had heard the story.

We no longer sat outside his cottage—the afternoon was too chilly. I was in his own armchair, which he insisted on giving up to me while he made me a cup of tea.

He did allow me to pour it out and, when we were sitting opposite each other, he said: "I was worried when I heard 'em talking."

"You mean about . . ."

" 'Twere the last time you did come and see me."

"It was very unfortunate."

He shook his head. "I don't like it much."

"I didn't either."

"You see, it's like as though . . ."

"We decided the sexton left the door open when he was last there, and that it must have been open for some time. Nobody noticed because . . . nobody went near it."

"Oh, I don't know," murmured Jesse.

We were silent for some time, then he said: "Well, me dear, I reckon you should take extra care like. I reckon you should."

"Jesse, what are you thinking?"

"If only these old eyes hadn't been so blind I should have seen who was up there in the gallery with her."

"Jesse, have you any idea who it was?"

Jesse screwed up his face and beat on his knee. "I'm feared I do," he whispered.

"You think it was Lowella Pendorric, who died all those years ago."

"I couldn't see like. But I be feared, for she were the bride, and 'twas said after, that she was marked for death as soon as she was the bride of Pendorric."

"And you think that I . . ."

"I think you have to take care, Mrs. Pendorric. I think you haven't got to go where harm can come to 'ee."

"Perhaps you're right, Jesse," I said, and after a pause: "Your Michaelmas daisies are looking a picture."

"Aye, reckon so. The bees be that busy on 'em. I was always one for Michaelmas daisies, though 'tis sad to see them since it means the end of summer."

I left him and as I came past the cottages and saw the church ahead of me, I stopped at the lych gate and looked into the graveyard.

"Hello, Mrs. Pendorric."

There was Dinah Bond coming towards me. "I heard about 'ee," she said. "Poor Mrs. Pendorric. I reckon you was scared in that place." She was almost laughing at me. "You should have let me read your hand," she went on. "I might have warned you."

"You weren't anywhere around when it happened, I suppose?" I asked.

"Oh no. My Jim had taken me into market with him. We didn't get back till late. Heard about it next morning though. I was sorry because I can guess what it feels like to be in that dark place." She came up to the lych gate and leaned on it. "I've been thinking," she went on, "there's something strange about this. Has it struck you that things seem to be happening twice?"

"What do you mean?"

"Well, Morwenna was shut in the vault, wasn't her? And then you were, with Hyson. Looks as though someone remembered that and thought to try it again."

"Do you think someone locked me in then? The general belief is that the door jammed."

"Who's to say?" She shrugged her shoulders. "Then there was Barbarina being an heiress and marrying a Pendorric, and there was Louisa Sellick who had to go and live near Dozmary because of it. Now there's you—awful rich, so they tell me you be, Mrs. Pendorric—and you're the new Bride while . . ."

"Please go on."

She laughed. "You wouldn't let me read your hand, would you? You didn't believe I was any good. All right, you wouldn't believe what I could tell 'ee. But 'tis all of a piece and so seems as though it was meant, if you get what I mean."

"I'm afraid I don't."

She came through the lych gate and walked past me, smiling as she went.

"You be awful rich, Mrs. Pendorric," she murmured, "but you bain't very bright, I'd say."

She looked over her shoulder at me; then she began to

walk towards the forge, swinging her hips in the provocative way which was second nature to her.

*   *   *

All this did not comfort me. I was longing to have a talk with Roc and tell him what was in my mind, but something warned me not to. It was of course the fact that I was not at all sure where Roc fitted into this.

The house seemed quiet. Deborah had taken Hyson and Carrie with her to Devonshire; and Lowella had refused to do any lessons since her sister was having a holiday. "It wouldn't be fair to Hyson," she explained piously. "I should go so far ahead of her that she'd never catch up."

Morwenna, declaring that this was hardly likely, at the same time gave way, and Lowella, who had become suddenly attached to her father—her affections changed as frequently as the winds—insisted on spending a lot of time at the home farm with him.

I found myself constantly listening for the sound of singing or the playing of a violin, and I became aware that that adventure in the vault had upset me more than I cared to admit. I wanted to get away from the house to think, so I took the car one afternoon and went onto the moor.

In the first place I had no intention of going the way I had before. I merely wanted to be alone to think; and I wanted to do my thinking right away from the house, because I was beginning to suspect that the house had an effect on me, making me more fanciful than I should otherwise have been.

I drew up on a lonely stretch of moor, shut off the engine, and, lighting a cigarette, sat back to brood. I went over every detail of what had happened from the first day I had seen Roc; and whichever way I looked one thought kept hammering in my mind: He knew that I was an heiress when he married me.

Dinah Bond had marveled how events repeated themselves. Barbarina had been married for her money when her husband would have preferred Louisa Sellick. Had I been married for mine when my husband would have preferred . . . ?

It was something I refused to accept. He could never have been such a good actor as to deceive me so utterly. I thought of the passion between us; I thought of the ways in which he had made love to me. Surely that could not have been all lies. I could hear his voice coming back to me: "I'm a gambler, darling, but I never risk losing what I can't do without."

He had never pretended to be a saint. He had never told me that I was the first woman he had ever loved. He had not denied that he was a gambler.

What had happened that day when he went down to swim with my father? What was I thinking now! My father's death had nothing to do with all this. That had been an unfortunate accident.

I threw away my cigarette, started up the car, and drove on for some miles without noticing the direction in which I was going; then suddenly I was aware that I was lost.

The moor looked so much the same whatever road one took. I could only drive on until I came to a signpost.

This I did and when I saw Dozmary on it I discovered I was very eager to have another glimpse of the boy who looked so like Roc. After all, I told myself, Louisa Sellick had played a part in the story of Barbarina, and it seemed as though her story was very closely linked with my own.

When I reached the Pool I left the car and went down to the water's edge; it looked cold and gray and the place was deserted. Leaving the car I started to walk, until I found the road which led to the house.

I started up this, then it occurred to me that if I met the boy again he might recognize me and wonder why I had come back; and as there was another path branching from this one—nothing more than a cart track—I took this and found I was mounting a slight incline.

Now I had a good view of the front of the house, although there were several large clumps of bracken between me and the road in which it stood. I sat down beside one of these clumps and looked at the house, which I could now study at my leisure. I saw a stable and I guessed that the boy had his own horse; there was also a garage and the garden at the front and sides of the house was well kept. I caught a glimpse of greenhouses. It was a comfortable house set in rather unusual surroundings, for it didn't appear to have any neighbors. It must be rather lonely for Louisa Sellick when the boy went away to school, which I supposed he must do. Who was the boy? Her son? But he would be too young. He couldn't be more than thirteen or fourteen; surely Petroc Pendorric had been dead longer than that.

Then who was the boy? That was another of those questions which I didn't want to think too much about. There was beginning to be quite a number of them.

Suddenly the door of the glass-roofed porch opened and someone came out. It was the boy again. I could see the resemblance to Roc even from where I was. He seemed to be talking to someone in the house; then she came out. I think I must have cowered into the bracken for I was suddenly afraid of being recognized, because the woman who had come out of Bedivere House was Rachel Bective.

She and the boy walked towards a car, and I recognized it as the little gray Morris from the Pendorric garages.

She got into it, and the boy stood waving while she drove away.

In a moment of panic it occurred to me that she might pass my car and recognize it. I ran down the cart track and as I came to the main road I was relieved because she had gone in a direction away from where my car was parked.

I walked slowly back and drove thoughtfully home.

Why, I asked myself, was Rachel Bective visiting the boy who was so obviously a Pendorric?

* * *

Deborah, with Hyson and Carrie, returned to Pendorric after a few days. I thought the child looked pale and that the holiday had not done her much good.

"She misses Lowella," Morwenna told me. "They're never completely happy apart although they quarrel almost all the time when they're together."

Deborah smiled sadly. "When you're a twin you understand these things," she said. *"We* do, don't we, Morwenna?"

"Yes, I suppose so," replied Morwenna. "Roc and I were very close always, though we rarely quarreled."

"Roc would never take the trouble to quarrel with anyone," murmured Deborah. She turned to me: "My dear, you're not looking as well as I should like to see you. You should have come with us. My moorland air would have done you the world of good."

"Oh come, it's not as good as our sea air surely," laughed Morwenna.

"It's change that's good for everyone."

"I'm so glad you've come back," I told Deborah. "I've missed you."

She was very pleased. "Come up with me. I've brought you a little present from home."

"For me! How charming of you!"

"It's something I treasure."

"Then I shouldn't take it."

"You must, my dear. What point would there be in giving you something I want to get rid of?"

She slipped her arm through mine and I thought: Perhaps I can ask Deborah. Not outright, of course, but perhaps indirectly. After all, she would know what was happening better than most people.

We went up to her bedroom, where Carrie was unpacking.

"Carrie," cried Deborah, "where's the little gift I brought for Mrs. Pendorric?"

"Here," said Carrie without looking at me.

"Carrie hates leaving her beloved moor," Deborah whispered to me.

She was holding out a small object wrapped in tissue paper. I opened it and, although it was one of the most exquisite things I had ever seen, I was dismayed. For in a frame set with jade and topaz was a delicate miniature of a young girl, her hair falling about her shoulders, her eyes serene.

"Barbarina," I whispered.

Deborah was smiling down at the lovely face. "I know how interested you have always been in her and I thought you'd like to have it."

"It's a beautiful thing. It must be very valuable."

"I'm so glad you like it."

"Is there one of *you*? I would rather have that."

My words evidently pleased her for she looked very beautiful suddenly. "People always wanted to paint Barbarina," she said. "Father invited lots of artists to the house—he was interested in the arts—and they used to say 'We must paint the twins, and we'll begin with Barbarina.' They sometimes did; and when it was my turn, they forgot. I told you, didn't I, that she had something that I lacked. It drew everyone to her—and because I was so like her, I seemed like a pale shadow . . . a carbon copy, you might say, a little blurred, much less attractive."

"Do you know, Deborah," I said, "you always underrate yourself. I'm sure you were every bit as attractive."

"Oh Favel, what a dear child you are! I feel so grateful to Roc for finding you and bringing you to us."

"It's I who should be grateful. Everyone's been so kind to me . . . particularly you."

"I? Boring you with my old photographs and chatter about the past!"

"I've found it immensely interesting. I want to ask you lots of things."

"What's stopping you? Come and sit in the window. Oh, it *is* good to be back. I love the moor, but the sea is more exciting perhaps. It's so unpredictable."

"You must have missed the moor when Roc and Morwenna were young and you were looking after them."

"Sometimes, but when they went away to school I'd go to Devonshire."

"Did they go to Devon for school holidays?"

"Almost always they were at Pendorric. Then of course Morwenna started bringing Rachel for holidays, and it seemed to be a natural thing that she should come to us every time. Morwenna was extraordinarily fond of her for some reason. And she wasn't really a pleasant child. She locked Morwenna in the vault, once. Just for fun! *You* can understand how terrified poor Morwenna was. She had a nightmare soon after it happened and told me about it when I went in to comfort her. But it didn't make any difference to the friendship, and when Roc and Morwenna went to France, Rachel went with them."

"When was that?"

"It was when they were older. They would have been about eighteen then. I always hoped that Morwenna would drop her, but she never did. And at that time the three of them became very friendly."

"When they were about eighteen . . ."

"Yes. Morwenna was anxious to go to France. She wanted to improve her accent; and she said she'd like to go for two months. She had finished at her English boarding school and I was thinking that she might go abroad to school; but she said it would be much better for her to stay in some *pension* where she would learn the language, by mixing with people, more easily than she ever would at school."

"And Morwenna went to France for two months."

"Rachel went with her. So did Roc for a while. I was a bit alarmed at that time. Roc was with them so much and I was beginning to be afraid that he and Rachel . . ."

"You wouldn't have welcomed . . . that?"

"My dear, I expect I'm being rather mean, but somehow I should not have liked to see Rachel mistress of Pendorric. She hasn't the . . . charm. Oh, she's an educated girl but there's something I don't like about her . . . something I don't altogether trust. This is strictly between ourselves, of course; I wouldn't say it to anyone else."

"I think I know what you mean."

"She's too sharp. One gets the idea that she's watching for the main chance all the time. I expect it's my stupid imagination, but I can tell you I had some very deep qualms at that time, because Roc was so anxious to see the girls settled in their *pension* comfortably. And he actually stayed there for a while and went back and forth while they were there. Every time he returned I was terrified that he would announce his intentions. Fortunately it all fell through."

"It was a long time ago," I said.

Deborah nodded.

I was thinking: They were eighteen, and the boy could be about fourteen now. Roc is thirty-two.

I had often felt that Rachel had some hold on the Pendorrics. She gave that impression. She was like a person with a chip on her shoulder and yet at the same time there was a certain truculence about her. It was as though she were continually implying: Treat me as a member of the family or else . . . !

And she visited the boy who was living with Louisa Sellick!

I said: "I suppose at that time their father was dead . . . I mean Roc's and Morwenna's."

"They were about eleven when he died. It was six years after Barbarina . . ."

So the boy was not his, I thought. Oh Roc, why do you keep these secrets from me? There's no need.

My impulse was to talk to Roc at the earliest opportunity, to tell him what I had conjectured.

When I went to my room I put the miniature on the mantelshelf and stood for some minutes looking into the serene eyes depicted there.

Then I decided to wait awhile, to try to find out more about the nature of this web in which I was becoming entangled.

*   *   *

In the midst of this uncertainty Mabell Clement gave a party. When Roc and I drove over, we were both a little subdued; I felt weighed down with thoughts of the boy who lived on the moors, and conjectures as to what part Roc had played in bringing him into the world. I longed to talk to Roc and yet I was afraid to do so. Actually I was afraid to face up to the fact that Roc might not tell me the truth. I was pathetically eager that he should not lie to me, and at the same time, I was desperately trying to keep intact that wonderful happiness which I had known.

As for Roc, he was telling himself that my adventure in the vault had naturally upset me a good deal and that I should need time to recover.

He treated me gently, and reminded me of those days immediately following my father's death.

Mabell, earrings swinging, was a wonderful hostess and there was an informal atmosphere about the party. Several of the local artists were present, for our scenery had made the district an artist's colony; and I was gratified when one of them mentioned my father, and spoke with reverence of his work.

From the other side of the room I heard Roc's laughter and saw that he was the center of a group, mainly women. He seemed to be amusing them, and I wished that I was with them. And how I wished that there were no more doubts and that I could escape from my misgivings into that complete and unadulterated happiness which no one on earth but Roc could give to me.

"Here's someone who wants to meet you." Mabell was at my elbow and with her was a young man. I looked at him for some seconds before I recognized him.

"John Poldree, you remember?" he said.

"Why yes. The ball . . ."

Mabell gave him a little push towards me and then was gone.

"It was a wonderful ball," he went on.

"I'm so glad you enjoyed it."

"And very sad of course that . . ."

I nodded.

"There was something I wanted to tell you, Mrs. Pendorric. Though I don't suppose it matters much now."

"Yes?"

"It's about the nurse."

"Nurse Grey?"

"M'm. Where I'd seen her before."

"And you remember?"

"Yes. It was something in one of the papers. It came back to me. Then I remembered that I was in Genoa at the time and it wasn't all that easy to get English papers. Having fixed the date I went and looked up old copies. She's the one all right. Nurse Althea Stoner Grey. Nurse Stoner Grey, she was called. If I'd heard the double-barreled name I'd have remembered. But I couldn't mistake the face. It's rarely that you find a face as perfect as that one."

"What did you find out?"

"I'm afraid I misjudged her. I'd got it into my head that she'd committed some crime. Hope I didn't give you the wrong impression. All the same it wasn't very pleasant. She was lucky to have a name like Stoner Grey. She could drop the first part and seem like a different person. After all Grey's a fairly common name. Coupled with Stoner, far from it. She lost the case."

"What was the case then?"

"She'd been nursing an old man and he'd left her money; his estranged wife contested the will. It was only a few paragraphs and you know how disjointed these newspaper reports can be."

"When did all this happen?"

"About six years ago."

"I expect she's had a case or two in between that and coming to my grandfather."

"No doubt of it."

"Well, she must have brought good references to my grandfather, I imagine. He was the sort who would make sure of that."

"That wouldn't be difficult for a woman like that. She's got a way of getting round people. You can see that. She's pretty hard boiled, I should think."

"I should think so too."

He laughed. "I wanted to tell you ever since I solved the mystery. I expect she's far away by now."

"No. She's still living fairly near us. She's taking a little holiday and renting a cottage for a time. My grandfather left her a small legacy so she probably feels she can afford to rest."

"Must be a lucrative job—private nursing—providing you have the foresight to choose rich patients."

"Of course, you couldn't be sure that they would conveniently die and leave a legacy."

He lifted his shoulders. "Smart woman, that one. I think she'd be the sort who'd choose with care." He had picked up one of the pieces of pottery which were lying about the studio. "Good this," he said.

And for him the subject was closed; but not for me. I could

not get Nurse Grey out of mind, and when I thought of her
I thought of Roc.

I was very quiet during the drive back to Pendorric.

*   *   *

I noticed a change in Morwenna; there were days when
she gave me the impression that she was walking in her sleep;
and her dreams seemed to be happy ones, for at times her
expression was almost rapturous. She was absent-minded, too,
and I had on one or two occasions spoken to her and received
no answer.

She came up to our room one evening when we were
changing for dinner.

"There's something I want to tell you two."

"We're all ears," Roc told her.

She sat down and did not speak for a few seconds. Roc
looked at me, his eyebrows raised.

"I didn't want to say anything to any of you until I was
absolutely sure."

"The suspense is becoming unbearable," commented Roc
lightly.

"I've told Charles of course and I wanted to tell you two
before it became generally known."

"Are we soon to hear the patter of little feet in the Pendorric nurseries?" asked Roc.

She stood up. "Oh . . . Roc!" she cried, and threw herself
into his arms. He hugged her and then began waltzing round
the room with her. He stopped abruptly with exaggerated concern. "Ah, we have to take great care of you now." He released her and, putting his hand on her shoulder, kissed her
cheek solemnly. "Wenna," he said, reverting to his childhood
name for her, "I'm delighted. It's wonderful. Bless you."

There was real emotion in his voice and I was touched.

"I knew you'd be pleased."

I felt as though I were shut out of their rejoicing; and it
occurred to me how very close they were, because Morwenna
seemed to have forgotten my existence and I knew that, when
she had said she wanted to tell us first, she had meant she had
wanted to tell Roc. Of course, they were twins and how true
it was that the bond between twins was strong!

They suddenly seemed to remember me, and Morwenna
immediately brought me into the picture.

"You'll think we're crazy, Favel."

"No, of course not. I think it's wonderful news. Congratulations!"

She clasped her hands together and murmured: "If only you knew!"

"We'll pray for a boy," said Roc.

"It must be a boy this time . . . it must."

"And what does old Charles say?"

"What do you think! He's rapturous. He's already thinking up names."

"Make sure it's a good old Cornish name, but we don't want any more Petrocs about the place for a while."

Morwenna said to me: "After all these years. It does seem marvelous. You see, we've always wanted a boy . . ."

We all went down to dinner together and after the meal Roc proposed the health of the mother-to-be, and we all became quite hilarious.

Next day I had a talk with Morwenna, who had become more friendly, I thought; I liked her new serenity.

She told me that she was three months pregnant and had started to plan the child's layette; and she was so certain that it was going to be a boy that I was a little afraid for her, because I realized how disappointed she would be if it should be a girl.

"You probably think that I'm behaving like a young girl about to have her first baby," she said with a laugh. "Well, that's how I feel. Charles wanted a boy so much . . . and so do I, and I always felt I was letting him down in some way by not producing one."

"I'm sure he didn't feel that."

"Charles is such a *good* man. He would never show resentment. But I know he longed for a son. I'll have to be careful nothing goes wrong. It did about five years ago. I had a miscarriage and was very ill, and Dr. Elgin, who was here before Andrew Clement, said I shouldn't make any more attempts . . . not for some time in any case. So you see how we feel."

"Well, you must take the greatest care."

"Of course one can take too much care. Some people think you should carry on as normally as possible for as long as possible."

"I'm sure you'll be all right; but suppose it should be a girl?"

Her face fell.

"You'd love it just the same," I assured her. "People always do."

"I should love her, but it wouldn't be the same. I long for a boy, Favel. I can't tell you how I long for a boy."

"What name have you decided to give him?" I asked. "Or haven't you thought of that?"

"Charles is insisting that if it's a boy we call him Ennis. It's a name that's been given to lots of Pendorrics. If you and Roc have a son you'll call him Petroc. That's the custom; the eldest son of the eldest son. But Ennis is as Cornish as Petroc. It's rather charming, don't you think?"

"Ennis," I repeated.

She was smiling and the intensity of her expression disturbed me.

"He's certain to be Ennis," she went on.

I turned to the book of baby patterns which was lying on her lap and expressed more interest in it than I really felt.

* * *

So even Morwenna's news added to my uneasiness. Ennis was a family name; and the boy on the moor had the looks as well as the name; Morwenna had taken Rachel away and Roc had been at hand to help make arrangements; he had visited them during their sojourn abroad, and Deborah had been afraid that Roc was going to marry Rachel.

I thought I was controlling my suspicions but I couldn't hide them from Roc.

One day he announced that he was going to take me out for the day. I mustn't imagine I knew Cornwall just because I had seen our little corner; he was going to take me farther afield.

There was an autumnal mist in the air when we left Pendorric in the Daimler, but Roc assured me that it was only the pride of the morning; the sun would break through before long; and he was right.

We drove onto the moor and then turned northward and stopped at a country hotel for lunch.

It was over the meal that I realized Roc had brought me out to talk seriously.

"Now," he said, filling my glass with Chablis, "let's have it."

"Have what?"

"What's on your mind?"

"On my mind?"

"Darling, innocence, in this case, is unbecoming. You know perfectly well what I mean. You've been looking at me for the last week or so as though you're wondering whether I'm Bluebeard and you're my ninth wife."

"Well, Roc," I replied, "although you're my husband and we've been married quite a few months, I don't always feel I know you very well."

"Am I one of those people who don't improve on acquaintance?"

As usual he caught me up in his mood; and I was already beginning to feel gay and that my suspicions were rather foolish.

"You remain . . . mysterious," I told him.

"And it's time you began to clear up the mysteries, you're thinking?"

"As you're my husband I don't think there should be secrets between us."

He gave me that disarming smile which always touched me deeply. "Nor do I. I know what's disturbing you. You discovered that I haven't lived the life of a monk before my marriage. You're right in that. But you don't want details of every little peccadillo, do you?"

"No," I told him. "Not every one. Only the important ones."

"But when I met you I realized that nothing that had happened to me before was of the slightest significance."

"And you haven't taken up the old way of life since you married me?"

"I can assure you that I have been faithful to you in thought and deed. There! Satisfied?"

"Yes, but . . ."

"So you're not?"

"There are people who seem to regard you in a certain way and I wondered whether they realize that any relationship which existed between you is now . . . merely friendship."

"I know. You're thinking of Althea."

"Well?"

"When she first came to look after your grandfather I thought her the most beautiful woman I had even seen. We became friends. The family was always urging me to marry. Morwenna had been married for years and they all implied that it was my duty to marry, but I had never felt that I wanted to settle down with any woman."

"Until you met Althea Grey?"

"I hadn't actually come to that conclusion. But shall we say the idea occurred to me as a possibility."

"And then my grandfather asked you to come and have a look at me, and you thought I was the better proposition?"

"That sounds a little like your grandfather. There was no question of 'propositions.' I had already decided that I did not want to marry Althea Grey, *before* your grandfather suggested I should come out and look at you. And when I did see you, it happened. Just like that. You were the only one from then on."

"Althea couldn't have been very pleased."

He lifted his shoulders. "It takes two to make a marriage."

"I begin to understand. You must have come very near to being engaged to Althea Grey before you changed your mind. And what about Dinah Bond?"

"What about Dinah? She's assisted in the education of most young men in the district."

"I see. Not serious?"

"Absolutely not."

"And Rachel Bective?"

"Never!" he said almost fiercely. He filled my glass. "Catechism over?" he asked. "Favel, I'm beginning to wonder whether you aren't somewhat jealous."

"I don't think I should be jealous . . . without reason."

"Well, now you know there is no reason."

"Roc . . ." I hesitated, and he urged me to go on. "That boy I saw at Bedivere House . . ."

"Well?"

"He's so like the Pendorrics."

"I know; you told me before. You're imagining that he's the living evidence of *my* sinful past, Favel!"

"Well, I did wonder who he was."

"Do you know, darling, you haven't enough to do. At the weekend I want to go to one of the properties on the north coast. Come with me. We'll be away a couple of nights."

"That will be lovely."

"Something else on your mind?" he asked.

"So many things are not clear. In fact when I go back to the first time I saw you . . . it seems to me that that was when everything began to change."

"Well, obviously things couldn't be the same for either of us after we'd met. We were swept off our feet . . ."

"No, Roc. I didn't mean that. Even my father seemed to change."

He looked grave suddenly; and then he seemed to come to a decision.

"There are certain things you didn't know about your father, Favel."

"Things *I* didn't know?"

"Things he kept from you."

"But he didn't. He always confided in me. We were so close . . . my mother, he and I."

Roc shook his head. "For one thing, my dear, he didn't tell you that he had written to your grandfather."

I had to agree that this was so.

"Why do you think he wrote to your grandfather?"

"Because he thought it was time we met, I suppose."

"Why should he think that was the time when for nineteen years he hadn't considered it necessary? I didn't want to tell you, Favel. In fact, I'd made up my mind not to . . . for years. I was going to wait until you were fifty. A nice cozy grandmother with the little ones playing at your knee. Then it would have seemed too far away to be painful. But I've come 'o the conclusion . . . in the last half hour . . . that there shouldn't be secrets between us."

"I'm certain there shouldn't be. Please tell me what you know about my father."

"He wrote to your grandfather because he was ill."

"Ill? In what way?"

"He had caught your mother's disease through being with her constantly. She wouldn't go away from him, nor he from her; they wanted to pretend that there was nothing wrong. So they stayed together and he was her only nurse until she was so very ill. He told me that if she had gone away she might have lived a little longer. But she didn't want to live like that."

"And he too . . . but I was never told."

"He didn't want you to know. He was very anxious about you. So he wrote to your grandfather telling him of your existence. He hoped that your grandfather would ask you to Cornwall. He himself would have stayed in Capri; and when he became really ill you wouldn't have been there."

"But he could have had attention. He could have gone to a sanatorium."

"That's what I told him. That's what I believed he would do."

"He told you all this . . . and not his own daughter!"

"My darling, the circumstances were unusual. He knew of me, and as soon as I turned up at the studio he knew why I had come. It would have been too much of a coincidence for a Pendorric to arrive only a month or so after he had sent off his letter to Polhorgan. Besides he knew your grandfather's methods. So he guessed at once I had been sent to look round."

"You told him, I suppose."

"I had been asked by Lord Polhorgan not to, but it was impossible to hide it from your father. However, we agreed that we would say nothing to you, and that I should write and tell him what I had seen; then he would presumably write to his granddaughter and invite her to England. That was what your father hoped. But, as you know, we met . . . and that was enough for us."

"And all the time he was so ill . . ."

"He knew that he was on the point of becoming *very* ill. So he was delighted when we said we were going to get married."

"You don't think that he was made a little uneasy by it?"

"Why should he be?"

"You knew that I was the granddaughter of a millionaire."

Roc laughed. "Don't forget he'd had some experience of your grandfather. The fact that you were his granddaughter didn't mean that you would inherit his fortune. He might have taken an acute dislike to you, and me as his son-in-law, in which case you would have been 'cut off with a shilling.' No, your father was delighted. He knew I'd take care of you; and I fancy he was happier to think of you in my care than in your grandfather's."

"I thought he was worried about something . . . just before he died. I thought he was uneasy . . . about *us*. What really happened on the day when you went down to bathe?"

"Favel, I think I know why your father died."

"Why . . . he died?

"He died because he no longer wished to live."

"You mean . . . ?"

"I believe he wanted a quick way out, and found it. We went down to the beach together. It was getting late, you remember. There were few people about; they were all having lunch behind the sun blinds; soon they would be deep in the siesta. When we reached the beach he said to me: 'You know you'd rather be with Favel.' I couldn't deny it. 'Go back,' he said, 'leave me. I would rather go in alone.' Then he looked at me very solemnly and said: 'I'm glad you married her. Take care of her.' "

"You're suggesting that he deliberately swam out to sea and had no intention of coming back?"

Roc nodded. "Looking back, I can see now that he had the look of a man who has written 'The End' to his life. Everything was in order."

I was too filled with emotion to trust myself to speak. I could see it all so clearly; that day when Roc had come back to the kitchen and sat on the table watching me, his legs swinging, the light making the tips of his ears pink. He didn't know then what had happened, because it was only afterwards that one realized the significance of certain words . . . certain actions.

"Favel," said Roc, "let's get out of here. We'll drive out to the moor and we'll stop then and talk and talk. He trusted me to care for you, to comfort you. You must trust me, too, Favel."

*   *   *

When I was with Roc I believed everything he said; it was only when I was alone that the doubts set in.

If only my father had confided in me. I would have cared for him, brought him to England; he could have had the best possible attention. There was no need for him to die so soon.

But had it been like that?

When I was alone I faced the fact that the talk with Roc had not really eased my fears; it had only added to them.

I couldn't help feeling that some clue to the solution of my problem might lie in that house near Dozmary Pool, and I found myself thinking of it continually—and the boy and the woman who lived there. Suppose I called on Louisa Sellick. Why shouldn't I? I could tell her who I was; and that I had heard of her connection with Pendorric. Or could I, considering the nature of that connection?

I had caught a glimpse of her and she had appeared to be a kindly and tolerant woman. Could I go to her and say that I was constantly being compared with Barbarina Pendorric and that I was interested in everyone who had known her?

Scarcely.

And yet the idea that I should go kept worrying me.

Suppose I pretended I had lost my way. No, I didn't want to pretend.

I would go and find a reason when I got there.

I took out the little blue Morris, which I had made a habit of driving and which was now looked upon as mine, and went out to the moor. I knew the way now and was soon passing the pool and taking the second-class road which led to the house.

When I pulled up I was still undecided as to what I should say. What I really wanted to ask was: "Who is the boy who is so like the Pendorrics?" And how could I do that?

While I was looking at the house the door of the glass-roofed porch opened and a woman came out. She was elderly and very plump; she had evidently seen me from a window and had come out to inquire what I wanted.

I got out of the car and said "Good morning" as she approached.

I began: "My name is Pendorric. Mrs. Pendorric."

She caught her breath and her rosy face was immediately a deeper shade of red.

"Oh," she said. "Mrs. Sellick bain't here today."

"I see. You're . . ."

"I'm Polly that does for her."

"You've got a wonderful view here," I said conversationally.

"Us don't notice it much. Been here too long, I reckon."

"So . . . Mrs. Sellick is not at home today."

"She's taking the boy back to school. She'll be away tonight, back tomorrow."

I noticed that the woman was trembling slightly.

"Is anything wrong?" I asked.

She came closer to me and whispered: "You ain't come for to take the boy away, have 'ee?"

I stared at her in astonishment.

"You'd better come in," she said. "We can't talk here."

I followed her over the lawn to the porch, and into a hall; she threw open the door of a cozy sitting room.

"Sit down, Mrs. Pendorric. Mrs. Sellick would want me to give you something, like. Would you have coffee or some of my elderberry wine?"

"Mrs. Sellick didn't know I was coming. Perhaps I shouldn't stay."

"I'd like to be the one to talk to you, Mrs. Pendorric. Mrs. Sellick, she'd be too proud like. She'd say, 'Yes . . . you must do what you wish . . .' and then when you'd gone she'd break her heart. No, I've often thought I'd like the chance to do the talking if this day ever come, and it seems like providence that it has come when her's off with the boy."

"I think there's some misunderstanding . . ."

"There's no misunderstanding, Mrs. Pendorric. You're from Pendorric and 'tis what she's always feared. She's often said: 'I made no conditions then, Polly, and I'll make none now.' She talks to me about everything. I knew her from the first . . . you see. I came with her when she first come to Bedivere. That was when he married. So we've been through a lot together."

"Yes, I see."

"Well, let me get you some coffee."

"I'd rather not. Mrs. Sellick might not be very pleased if she knew I'd come in like this."

"Her's the sweetest, mildest creature I ever saw, and I don't mind telling you I've often thought her too mild. The likes of her gets put upon. But I couldn't bear it to happen, see. Not twice in one lifetime . . . first losing *him* and then the boy. It 'ud be too much. Well, she's had him since he were three weeks old. She were a changed woman when Mr. Roc brought him here."

"Mr. Roc . . . !"

She nodded. "I remember the day well. It was getting dusk. I reckon they'd waited till then. They'd come straight from abroad . . . Mr. Roc was driving the car and the young woman was with him . . . nothing more than a girl, though I didn't see much of her. Wore a hat pulled down over her face . . . didn't want to be seen. She carried the baby in and put him straight into Mrs. Sellick's arms; then she went back to the car and left Mr. Roc to do the talking."

Rachel! I thought.

"You see, she felt guilty like. She'd loved Mr. Roc's father and had thought he was going to marry her. So he would have done, it was said, but the Pendorrics wanted money in the family so he married that Miss Hyson instead. He never gave up Louisa, although there were others, too, but she were the one he really cared for, and when his wife died he begged her to marry him. But she wouldn't—for some reason. She used to think that because his wife had died as she did it wouldn't be right. Then he was away a lot but he came back to see Louisa. No one could be to him what she were. You're a Pendorric yourself now and you've heard tell of all this, so there's no need for me to repeat it. When he died she were heartbroken, and she always longed for a child of his . . . even though 'twould have been born out of wedlock. She took an interest in those twins of his and they were a mischievous pair. They'd heard about their father and this house and they came out once to have a look at Louisa. That was after he was dead; and she brought them in and gave them cakes and tea. And after that they came now and then. She told them that if they were ever in trouble—and they were the kind who might well be . . . of course they've sobered down now, but 'twas different when they were young —she'd help them if it were in her power. Well then she got this letter from Mr. Roc. Here was trouble all right. A baby on the way and would she help?"

"I see."

"Of course she could help. She wanted to help. So she took little Ennis and she's been as a mother to him ever since. It were a turning point like. She began to be happy again when that little boy came into this house. But she never stopped being afeared. You see, he grew up such a beautiful child and he weren't hers. She'd take no money for what she did; she'd make no conditions. So you see, she was always afraid that one day Mr. Roc would come and claim that boy. When she heard he was married she was certain he'd want the boy. . . . She was terrible frit, I can tell 'ee. And I'm telling 'ee all this because I've got to make 'ee *see*."

"Did he come to see the boy?"

"Yes. He comes every now and then. Terrible fond of him he be, and the boy of him."

"I'm glad that he didn't desert him entirely."

"No question of that. But it's puzzling. The Pendorrics were never ones to care much about scandal. There was his father coming to see Louisa. Didn't keep it as dark as some thought he should. But I reckon it was because Mr. Roc was so young. Not much more than eighteen and Louisa advised him not to let it be known . . . for the boy's sake. He's known as Ennis Sellick and thinks Louisa's his aunt." She stopped and looked at me beseechingly. "Please, Mrs. Pendorric, you look kind . . . please understand that he have been here nigh on fourteen years. You can't take him now."

"You mustn't worry about that," I told her. "We have no intention of taking him."

She relaxed and smiled happily. "Why, when you said as who you were . . ."

"I'm sorry I frightened you. As a matter of fact it was very wrong of me to call. My visit was one of curiosity. I'd heard of Mrs. Sellick and wanted to meet her. That was all."

"And you won't take the boy?"

"No, certainly not. It would be too cruel."

"Too cruel," she repeated. "Oh thank 'ee, Mrs. Pendorric. It'll be a weight off our minds. Now won't you let me give you a cup of coffee? Mrs. Sellick wouldn't like you to leave without."

I accepted the invitation. I felt I needed it. While Polly was in the kitchen I was thinking: How can I trust him again? If he could deceive me about the boy, he could about other things. Why hadn't he told me? It would have been so much easier.

Polly returned with the coffee; she was quite happy now; at least my visit had done much to restore her contentment. She told me how she and Louisa had grown to love the moor, and how difficult it was to cultivate the garden, which was so stony.

"Moorland country bain't the most fertile ground, Mrs. Pendorric, I do assure you," she was saying when we heard the sound of a car drawing up outside the house.

"Why, it can't be Mrs. Sellick back already," said Polly, rising and going to the window.

Her next words sent the blood drumming in my ears. "Why 'tis Mr. Pendorric," she said. "Oh dear, I reckon he thought they wasn't going till tomorrow."

I stood up, and my knees were trembling so much that I thought they would give way as I heard Roc's voice. "Polly, I saw the car outside. Who's here?"

"Oh, you've come today, Mr. Pendorric," answered Polly blithely. "Well, Mrs. Sellick thought it 'ud be better to take two days over the driving, seeing it's so far. They'm staying in London and then they'll go on to the school tomorrow. Reckon you thought they wouldn't be leaving till tomorrow."

He was coming through the glass-roofed porch; striding into the sitting room in the manner of someone who well knows the way.

He threw open the door and stared at me. "You!" he said; then his expression darkened. I had never seen him so angry.

We stood staring at each other and I think he felt the same about me as I did about him; that we were both looking at a stranger.

Polly came into the room. "Mrs. Pendorric's been telling me as you won't want to take the boy away . . ."

"*Has* she?" he said; and his eyes took in the used coffee cups.

"I was that relieved. Not that I thought you'd do it, Mr. Roc. It was that pleasant meeting your bride."

"I'm sure it was," Roc answered. "You should have waited, darling, until I drove you over."

His voice sounded quite cold as it had never been before when he spoke to me.

"And you came today unbeknownst to each other, and there's two cars outside. Well, it *is* a day!"

"Yes," echoed Roc almost viciously, "it *is* a day."

"I'll heat up this coffee, Mr. Roc."

"Oh no, thanks, Polly. I came to see the boy before he went to school, but I'm too late. Never mind. I've met my wife instead."

Polly laughed. "I'm sorry Mrs. Sellick didn't warn you, but she doesn't care about telephoning the house, as you know."

"I know," said Roc. He turned to me. "Are we ready to go?"

"Yes," I said. "Good-by, Polly, and thank you for the coffee."

"It's been a pleasure," said Polly.

She stood at the door smiling as we went out to the cars. Roc got into his, I into mine. I drove off and he followed me.

Near that bridge where, it was said, Arthur fought his last fight against Sir Mordred, Roc drove ahead of me and pulled up. I heard the door of his car slam and he came to stand by mine.

"So you lied to me," I said.

"And you saw fit to pry into matters which are no concern of yours."

"Perhaps they are some concern of mine."

"You are quite wrong if you think so."

"Shouldn't I be interested in my husband's son?"

"I would never have believed you'd do anything so petty. I had no idea I'd married a . . . spy."

"And I can't understand why you should have lied; I should have understood."

"How good of you! You are of course extremely tolerant and forgiving, I'm sure."

"Roc!"

He looked at me so coldly that I shrank from him. "There's really nothing more to be said, is there?"

"I think there is. There are things I want to know."

"You'll find out. Your spy system seems excellent."

He went to his car, and drove on towards Pendorric; and I followed him home.

* * *

Back at Pendorric, Roc only spoke to me when necessary. I knew that he was planning his trip to the north coast, but there was now no question of my going with him.

It was impossible to hide from the household that we had quarreled, because neither of us was good enough at hiding our feelings; and I was sure they were all rather curious.

The next few days seemed unbearably long and I had not felt so wretched since the death of my father. Two days after that disastrous visit to Bedivere I went into the quadrangle and sat under the palm tree thinking ruefully that the summer was nearly over, and with it the happiness I had believed was mine.

The sun was shining but I could see the spiders' webs on the bushes, and beautiful as the Michaelmas daisies and chrysanthemums were, they did underline the fact that winter was on the way. But because this was Cornwall, the roses were still blooming; and although the hydrangeas did not flower in such profusion, there were still some to brighten the quadrangle.

One of the twins must have seen me for she came out and began to walk unconcernedly towards the pond, humming as she came.

"Hello," she said. "Mummy says we're not to sit on the seats because they're damp. We'll catch our deaths if we do. So what about you?"

"I don't think it's really damp."

"Everything's damp. You might get pneumonia and die."

I knew this was Hyson, and it occurred to me that since our adventure in the vault her attitude towards me had changed; and perhaps not towards me only; it seemed that she herself had changed.

"It would be one way . . ." she said thoughtfully.

"One way of dying, you mean?"

Her face puckered suddenly. "Don't talk of dying," she said. "I don't like it . . . much."

"You're becoming awfully sensitive, Hyson," I commented.

She looked thoughtfully up at the east windows as though watching for something.

"Are you expecting someone?" I asked.

She did not answer.

After a while she said: "You must have been very glad that I was in the vault with you, Favel."

"It was rather selfish of me, but I was."

She came nearer to me and, putting her hands on my knees,

looked into my face. "I was glad I was there too," she said.

"Why? It wasn't very pleasant and you were horribly scared."

She smiled her odd smile. "Yes, but there were two of us. That made a difference."

She stepped back and put her lips in the position to suggest whistling.

"Can you whistle, Favel?"

"Not very well."

"Nor can I. Lowella can."

She stopped, looking up at the east windows.

"There it is," she said.

It was the sound of the violin.

I stood up and caught Hyson's wrist. "Who is it?" I asked.

"You know, don't you?"

"No, I don't. But I'm going to find out."

"It's Barbarina."

"You know Barbarina's dead."

"Oh Favel, don't go in there. You know what it means . . ."

"Hyson! What do you know? Who is playing the violin? Who locked us in the vault? Do you know that?"

For the moment I thought I saw a madness in the child's eyes, and it was not a pleasant sight. "It's Barbarina," she whispered. "Listen to her playing. She's telling us she's getting tired. She means she won't wait much longer."

I shook her a little because I could see that she was near hysteria. "I'm going to find out who's playing that violin. You come with me. We'll find this person together."

She was unwilling, but I dragged her to the east door. As I opened it I could distinctly hear the sound of a violin.

"Come on," I said, and we started up the stairs. The violin had stopped playing, but we went on to Barbarina's room; I threw open the door. The violin was lying on the chair; the music was still on the stand. The room was just as it had been when I had last seen it.

I looked at Hyson, but she lowered her eyes and was staring at the floor.

I was more frightened than I had ever been, because never before had I felt so utterly alone. First I had had my parents to care for me; then—as I thought—a husband; finally a grandfather.

I had lost them all, for now I could no longer rely on Roc to protect me from the danger which I felt was close.

6.

ROC LEFT for his weekend trip.

Before he went he said to me, when we were in the bedroom together: "I don't like this at all, Favel. We've got to get it sorted out. I wish you hadn't gone snooping. It's all at such an unfortunate time."

He was almost his old self and I immediately swung round to meet him halfway. Eagerly I waited for what he would say next.

"There's a simple explanation to all this," he said. "But I can't tell you yet. Will you wait awhile and trust me?"

"But Roc . . ."

"All right," he said. "You can't. But this isn't going on. I'll think about it while I'm away; but promise me this: You won't think too badly of me, will you? I'm really not quite such a scoundrel as you believe I am."

"Oh Roc," I said, "it's all so unnecessary. There was no need to tell me lies. I just wish you hadn't."

"And you can't trust someone who has once lied, can you?"

He looked at me wistfully and I had the impression that he was trying to charm me as he had so many times before.

"Roc, tell me about it," I pleaded. "Tell me now. Then we can start being happy again."

He hesitated. "Not now, Favel."

"But why not now?"

"It isn't only my affair. I've got to discuss it with someone else."

"Oh, I see."

"But you don't see. Listen, Favel. I love you. And you've got to love me, too. You've got to trust me. Damn it, can't you have a little faith in me?"

I couldn't make myself say yes.

"All right." He put his hands on my shoulders and gave me a swift kiss on the lips with nothing warm or passionate about it. "See you Monday or Tuesday."

Then he was gone, leaving me as baffled and unhappy as before—or almost.

But the fact that he was away did give me an opportunity to think; and several little incidents from the past kept recurring to me. I had been in danger of losing my life on two occasions since coming to Pendorric; which was strange because it was within a very short time, and it was something which had never happened to me before in the whole of my life. I was thinking of that time when someone had removed the danger signal on the cliffs. But then it had been Roc who had *saved* me. At that time I had not known I was Lord Polhorgan's granddaughter. But Roc had, and if I had died then, Roc would have inherited nothing.

A horrible thought came to me. Was it meant to shift suspicion? Was the idea that, when later I had a fatal accident, people would remember how Roc had saved me then? No, that was a hideous thought. I was suggesting that Roc had deliberately locked me in the vault and planned to leave me there!

It was as though my personality had split into two; there was part of me which was determined to defend Roc and prove him innocent, and another equally as determined to prove him guilty.

Who else could have locked the door of the vault? Who else could have come along and unlocked it, and then pretended that it was jammed? Who else had a motive for wanting to be rid of me? On my death Roc would inherit my grandfather's fortune and be free to marry whomsoever he wished. Who would that be? Althea Grey?

Then I thought of what Polly had said that morning in Bedivere House: when Barbarina was dead Roc's father had wanted to marry Louisa.

While I was brooding on these things there was a knock on my door and Morwenna came in. For a moment I felt envious of her radiant happiness.

"Oh hello, Favel. I hoped I'd find you here." She looked at me anxiously. "Roc seems to have gone off in a bit of a huff. Why don't you make it up?"

I was silent and she shrugged her shoulders. "It's unlike him," she went on. "Usually with him it's a big flare up and then everything's as it was before. Yet this thing of yours seems to have been going on for days."

"You mustn't let it bother you," I said.

"Oh, I don't. It'll work itself out, I expect. But an annoying thing has happened. I've had to leave my car at the garage and I was wondering if you were using the Morris this morning."

"Please have it," I said. "I can go to Polhorgan—I've got to go some time, and I don't need a car to go there."

"Are you sure? I want to go into Plymouth. Dr. Clement says I've got to rest every day. He's going to be a bit fussy about me, so I thought I'd do a bit of knitting. It'll be something to do while I put my feet up. I want to get wools and patterns and there's so little to choose from here."

"Do take the Morris and don't worry about me."

She came over to me and, unexpectedly, kissed me. "Things will soon be all right between you and Roc, I know," she said.

When she had gone I left at once for Polhorgan. There was no sense in sitting about and brooding; I went by way of the coast road and tried to stop thinking of Roc's duplicity by planning the orphans' home I might one day have at Polhorgan.

When I arrived, Mr. and Mrs. Dawson came out to greet me, and I could tell by their portentous manner that they had been eagerly looking forward to telling me something.

I was taken to the sitting room and given coffee, and then it came out.

"We wouldn't mention this, madam, but for the fact that Mrs. Penhalligan has been having a word with Mrs. Dawson, and that has somewhat colored our views in the matter. It is a delicate subject, madam, and Mrs. Dawson and I trust that you will understand that it is only in our endeavor to serve you . . ."

I was anxious to cut short the circumlocution so I said: "Oh yes, of course I understand, Dawson."

"Then, madam, I will tell you. I did not care to mention this before because I feared it might reflect on . . . one whom it was not my place to mention. But since Mrs. Penhalligan has spoken to Mrs. Dawson . . ."

"Please tell me all about it, Dawson."

"Well, madam, Dr. Clement was so certain that his lordship died from natural causes and discouraged us from bringing forward what actually happened. There was no inquest, the cause of death being considered natural. But there is a way of hastening death, madam, and Mrs. Dawson and I have long been of the opinion that his lordship was hurried to the grave."

"Yes, I know the bell and the box were on the floor, but

he might very well have knocked them over when he was reaching for them."

"So he might, madam; and who is to say he didn't? One cannot make suppositions in a court of law. But Mrs. Dawson overheard a conversation between his lordship and the nurse on the morning of the night he died."

"Oh? What conversation?"

"His lordship threatened to dismiss her if she continued to see Mr. er . . ." Dawson coughed apologetically. "Mr. Pendorric."

I wanted to protest, but my throat seemed to have closed up and would not let my voice come through. I had had enough. I could not bear any more revelations.

"And it seems, madam, rather coincidental that not many hours later his lordship should be unable to reach his pills. Mrs. Dawson and I do not forget, madam, that a legacy was mentioned in that will for the nurse who was in his lordship's employ at the time of his death . . ."

I was scarcely listening to them. I was thinking: How many lies has he told me? He did admit that he was almost engaged to Althea Grey. Then he had heard of my existence. He had married me as his father had married Barbarina. How much was he influenced by the past? It was as though we were actors in some obscure drama, playing the same parts which had been played before.

Barbarina had been married to bring money into Pendorric when her husband had been in love with Louisa Sellick. Had I been married for the same reason when *my* husband was in love with Althea Grey? Who was the vague shadow sensed by Jesse Pleydell on that day when Barbarina fell to her death? Was it her husband, Petroc Pendorric?

I'm becoming hysterical, I thought. I'm letting my imagination run away with me.

I should never have believed this of Roc before that scene in Bedivere House.

Now my thoughts would not be controlled. Had Althea Grey deliberately removed the pills, hoping to hasten his death? For he had to die, before I could inherit his money; and now . . . I had to die before it was theirs.

I wondered what gossip was going on all around me. Mrs. Penhalligan had talked to Mrs. Dawson. Did they all know then of the trouble between Roc and me? Did they know the reason?

The Dawsons were looking at me with concern and com-

passion. Were they warning me that Roc and Althea Grey
were lovers? Were they suggesting that, since the nurse had
had no compunction in hastening my grandfather to his death,
she and her accomplice might have none in hastening me to
mine?

I said: "It was very unfortunate that my grandfather should
have imagined these things. I think perhaps being such an
invalid he was apt to worry over nonexistent troubles. I have
heard that it is a symptom of the illness he had."

The Dawsons looked at me sorrowfully. Mrs. Dawson
would have continued to speak, but Dawson was too much
of a diplomatist to allow it. He lifted a hand and she was
silent.

On his face was the expression of a man who can be
satisfied that he has done his duty.

*　*　*

When I left Polhorgan I was afraid I should not be able
to keep up my façade of serenity. I was too restless. There
were so many things I wanted to find out and I had to go
into action; one thing I could not endure was inactivity.

I wanted to talk to someone and I believed if Morwenna
had not gone to Plymouth I should have sought her out and
confided everything in her. There was Deborah. I could talk
to her.

I hurried back to the house and went to Deborah's room.
She was not in. Uncertainly I came down to the hall again,
telling myself that it would be easier to think out of doors,
when the hall telephone began to ring.

When I answered it there was a low chuckle at the other
end of the line.

"Ah, I was hoping I'd catch you. This is Althea Grey."

I was startled because she was so much in my thoughts and
I was growing more and more certain that she was playing
a big part in the tangle.

"I was wondering if you'd come and see me before I go."

"Before you go?"

"Yes, I'm leaving very soon. Tomorrow."

"You mean leaving altogether?"

"Come along and I'll tell you all about it. I've been wanting
to have a talk with you for some time. When can you?"

"Why . . . now."

"Suits me." Again there was that low laugh and she rang
off.

I hurried out of the house, out along the coast road; and in due course came to Cormorant Cottage.

It was aptly named; even now the gulls were swooping and soaring about the little cove which lay below, and I saw some cormorants. The cottage itself was perched on a rock which jutted out over the sea; it was small and painted blue and white, and there was a steep path which led up to it. It was the ideal summer cottage.

"Hello!" One of the windows was thrown up. "I've been watching for you. I'll come down."

I started up the path, which was almost overgrown with St. John's Wort, and by the time I reached the door Althea was standing there.

"I'm just packing."

"You're leaving?"

"M'm. Do come in and sit down."

I stepped straight into a room with casement windows which looked onto the sea. It had clearly been furnished for renting, with only the essentials, and everything in drab colors which wouldn't show the dirt.

"Rather a change from Polhorgan," she commented, and held out a cigarette case while she looked at me with what seemed like amusement.

"Nice of you to come and see *me*."

"I might say it was nice of you to ask me."

"I was lucky to catch you in."

"I'd only just come in. Roc's away for a few days."

"Yes, I know."

I raised my eyebrows and again that flicker of amusement crossed her face. "Grape vine," she said. "You can scarcely move in this place without everyone knowing all about it. Did anyone see you come in here?"

"No. Why . . . I don't think so."

"Because if someone did there'd be speculation, you bet."

"I had no idea you were leaving Cornwall so soon."

She shrugged her shoulders. "The season's over. It's lonely. You walk for miles along the cliffs without meeting anyone. You see, you didn't meet anyone coming here from Pendorric. Not my cup of tea. By the way, would you like one?"

"No, thanks."

"Coffee?"

"No, thank you. I can't stay long."

"A pity. We've never had a real cozy chat, have we? And

it's so peaceful here. I've often thought you were rather suspicious of me. I'd like to put that right."

"Suspicious? What do you mean?"

"Now you're playing innocent."

"I should like to know why you asked me here. I thought you had something to tell me."

"I have. And this is the time to tell. You see, I've got another job and I like to tidy everything up before I go." She stretched out her long slim legs and regarded them with satisfaction. "Rich old gentleman going on a world tour needs a nurse in constant attendance. Rich old gentlemen seem to be my speciality."

"Don't rich young ones ever come your way?"

"The trouble with the young is that they don't need nurses." She burst into laughter. "Mrs. Pendorric, you *are* uneasy."

"Uneasy?"

"Well, this is a lonely spot and I don't believe you have a very high opinion of my character. You're beginning to regret coming and are wondering how you can quietly slip away. Yet you came of your own free will, remember. In fact, you jumped at it when I asked you. It wasn't really very wise, was it? You're here and nobody knows you've come. You're rather rash, Mrs. Pendorric. You act on the spur of the moment. Do come and look at my view."

She took my hand and pulled me to my feet. She was strong and I remembered in that moment that Mabell Clement had said she only *looked* as though she were made of Dresden china.

She drew me to the window, holding my arm in a firm grip, while, with her free hand, she threw open the casement window. I looked down at the sheer drop to the sea. A long way below the waves were breaking in the jagged rocks.

"Imagine," she said, her voice close to my ear, "someone falling from this window! Not a chance. It wouldn't do to let this cottage to anyone with sleepwalking tendencies or to someone who was planning a little homicide."

For a few seconds I really believed that she had lured me here to kill me. I thought: She has planned this . . . so that the way will be free to Roc and my grandfather's fortune.

That she read my thoughts was obvious; but what I saw in her face was amusement as she released my arm.

"I think," she said slowly, "that you would be more comfortable sitting down."

"Why did you ask me here?" I demanded.

"That's what I'm going to tell you." She almost pushed me onto the dingy settee and sat in the armchair opposite me.

"Mrs. Pendorric," she said, "you can stop being scared. I only intend to talk. You really shouldn't worry about me, you know. In a few days I shall have gone right away from this place."

"Are you sorry to be going?"

"It's a mistake to be sorry. Once a thing's over it's done with. You were always a little jealous of me, weren't you? There's no need to be. After all, you married him, didn't you? It's true he did think of marrying me once."

"What about you?"

"Certainly. It would have been a good marriage. I don't know whether it would have suited me though; I like adventure. But it's true I'm past thirty now, so perhaps it is time I began to think about settling down."

"You seem to find life . . . amusing."

"Don't you? You should. It's the only way to live it. I've made a decision, Mrs. Pendorric; I'm going to tell you all you came to hear."

She was laughing at me and strangely enough I was ready to believe whatever she told me, for although she seemed tough and extremely worldly, experienced and capable of almost anything, she did seem truthful—largely because she would find it more amusing to tell the truth than lies.

"What were you doing before you came to Polhorgan?" I asked.

"Nursing, of course."

"As Nurse Stoner Grey?"

She shook her head. "In my last case I was Grey. Stoner Grey was before that."

"Why did you drop Stoner?"

"Unpleasant publicity. Not that I minded, but it might not have been easy to get the kind of job I wanted. People have long memories. So you knew about the Stoner Grey incident. Those Dawsons told you, I bet."

"They were a bit vague about it. It was . . . someone else."

She nodded. "If all had gone well I might never have had to take up nursing again. There was nothing wrong with it. The old gentleman made a will in my favor; but they found he was *non compos mentis* . . . and his wife won the case."

"I suppose you persuaded him to make that will."

"Well, what do you think?" She leaned forward. "You're a nice woman, Mrs. Pendorric, and I'm . . . not so nice. You see I didn't have your advantages. No nice millionaire for a grandfather. I wasn't really the sort of girl to marry into Pendorric. I'm an adventuress because I like adventure. It adds a spice to life. I lived the early part of my life in a back street, and I didn't like that much. I was determined to break away . . . I was like your grandfather in my way. I hadn't got the business flair though. I didn't know how to set about earning millions. But it wasn't long before I found out that I was beautiful, and that's one of the best assets a girl can have. I took up nursing and I intended to go into private nursing, which was a way of getting what I wanted. And I saw that I got the right jobs too. That's why I came to look after your grandfather."

"You hoped that *he* would leave you his money?"

"One can always hope. Then there was Roc. Adventuresses always weigh up all the possibilities, you know."

"Roc must have seemed the more hopeful of the two surely . . . when you got to know my grandfather."

She laughed again. "He did. But then he's too shrewd. He saw through me. He liked me, yes. And I liked him. I'd have liked him if he'd been one of the fishermen here. But he always held back; he seemed to be aware of something in me which . . . well, how shall we say? . . . wasn't quite what a gentleman looks for in his wife—not Roc's kind anyway. So we were good friends and then he went away and when he came back he'd married you. He's got a kind heart. He wanted to be friends still, and didn't want me to feel snubbed. That was why he was extra nice to me. But I saw you were getting a little jealous." She laughed. "All clear now?"

"Not quite," I said. "How did my grandfather die?"

She looked at me very intently and seemed more serious than she had during the whole of our interview.

"I have admitted to you that I look out for chances to improve my lot," she said firmly, "but I'm not a murderess. I've always believed that other people's lives mean as much to them as mine does to me. If I can get the better of people . . . all well and good. But I do draw the line at murder." Once again the smile was in her eyes. "So that's why you were so alarmed when you came in! Then I'm doubly glad you came. I want to clear up *that* little point before I go away.

Your grandfather often mislaid his little box. He did so once when you were with him. Don't you remember?"

I did remember. I had left Polhorgan early and found her with Roc on Pendorric beach.

"He dropped the pills; it agitated him that he could not find them when he needed them; and in that agitation he knocked over the bell. That was how he died, Mrs. Pendorric. I'd be ready to swear it. He was, it's true, in rather an agitated state. He was worried about you. He knew that at one time your husband and I had been friendly and he spoke to me about it. It upset him, although I assured him that there was nothing beyond friendship in our relationship. But to worry over imaginary details is a feature of his complaint. But I do assure you that I did nothing intentionally to hasten his death."

"I believe you," I said, because I did.

"I'm glad. I shouldn't have liked you to think me capable of *that*. Most other things . . . yes. But not murder." She yawned and stretched her arms. "Just think, in a month's time I'll be heading for the sun . . . when the mists swirl round Pendorric and the southwest gales batter the walls of Polhorgan. I've got loads of packing to do."

I rose. "Then I'd better go."

She came to the door of the cottage with me, and when I had walked down the path we said good-by. She stood at the door watching me.

* * *

My encounter with Althea Grey had been rather bewildering, for she had been embarrassingly frank. I had believed her while I was sitting with her, but now I wondered whether she had been amusing herself with my gullibility.

Was she really going away? At least she was not with Roc, and there was some measure of comfort in that.

The day seemed to stretch out endlessly before me. I did not want to go back to Pendorric, but there seemed nothing else to do. I thought I would go now and find Deborah and talk to her, not that I was really anxious to confide, even in her.

As I came towards the house Mrs. Penhalligan, who must have seen me approaching, came running out. She was very agitated and could scarcely speak coherently.

"Oh, Mrs. Pendorric, there's been an accident . . ."

My heart missed a beat and then began to gallop to make

up for it. Roc! I thought. I ought to have been with him. . . .

"It's Miss Morwenna, ma'am. She's had an accident in her car. It was the hospital that phoned."

"Morwenna . . ." I breathed.

"Yes, it happened on Ganter Hill. They've taken her to Treganter Hospital."

"She's . . ."

"They say it's very serious. Mr. Chaston's already gone."

"I see."

I felt bewildered. I could not think what I should do for the best.

"The twins . . . ?" I began.

"Miss Bective is with them. She's told them."

Deborah drove up at that moment. She got out of her car and called to us: "Isn't it warm this morning? Hello . . . is anything wrong?"

I said: "There's been an accident. It's Morwenna. She was driving in to Plymouth."

"Is it bad? Is she hurt?"

I nodded. "Charles has gone to Treganter Hospital. It's rather serious, I think."

"Oh, my God," murmured Deborah. "And Hyson . . . and Lowella?"

"They're with Rachel. She'll look after them."

Deborah put her hand over her eyes. "This is terrible." There was a sob in her throat. "At such a time. I wonder how badly hurt she is. It'll be tragic if this has harmed the child."

"Do you think we ought to go to the hospital?"

"Yes," said Deborah. "Let's go at once. Poor Charles! Get in, Favel. It isn't very far."

Mrs. Penhalligan stood watching us as we drove away.

Deborah looked grim and I thought: She loves Morwenna like a mother; and indeed it was natural that she should, for she had brought up Roc and his sister after their mother had died.

"I expect she was thinking of the child," murmured Deborah. "We ought not to have let her drive. She's been so absent-minded lately."

"I could have driven her into Plymouth," I said.

"Or I. Why did she want to go, anyway?"

"For knitting wool and patterns."

"It's so ironical. She's longed for another child and because of it . . ."

I had suddenly remembered and the memory struck me like a blow.

"Deborah," I said slowly, "Morwenna wasn't driving her own car. She was using the little blue Morris, which I usually drive!"

Deborah nodded. "But she's driven it before. Besides she has always been such a good driver."

I was silent. The coincidence did not seem to impress Deborah as it did me. I was almost afraid to examine my thoughts.

I shook them off. I was becoming unnerved. At least, first of all I must wait to hear what had caused the accident.

And if by any chance something in the car had gone wrong, should I be foolish to imagine that it was due to tampering, that someone, believing I should use the car, had done something which made an accident inevitable? I was not such an experienced driver as Morwenna. What would have happened if I had been in the car this morning?

Deborah had laid a hand on mine.

"Favel, we mustn't anticipate trouble, dear. Let us hope and pray that she'll come through."

*   *   *

That was a strange day of brooding horror. Morwenna's life was in danger; I believed mine was too, for I was certain that what had happened to her that day had been part of a plan and no accident, and that someone not very far from me was angry because the wrong person had walked into the trap.

There had been a witness of the accident. It had happened on Ganter Hill—not a very steep hill as Cornish hills go, but rather a long one which sloped gradually into Treganter. One of the local people had seen the car; there was no other involved. Suddenly it had begun to roll about the road, the steering clearly out of control; a glimpse had been caught of the frightened woman at the wheel as the car wobbled down hill and crashed into a tree.

In the late afternoon the hospital rang up, and as a result Charles took the twins to see Morwenna. Deborah and I went with them, at Charles's request. Quite clearly he feared what he would find when we arrived there.

Deborah and I did not go in to see Morwenna because she was very weak and only her immediate family were allowed to see her.

I shall never forget Hyson's face as she came out. It was so pale, and seemed shriveled so that she looked like an old woman. Lowella was crying; but Hyson shed no tears.

Charles told us that Morwenna's condition was still very serious, that he was going to stay at the hospital and wanted us to take the twins home; so I drove, while Deborah sat at the back, a twin on either side of her, her arms about them, holding the sobbing Lowella and the silent Hyson.

When we reached Pendorric, Rachel and Mrs. Penhalligan were waiting to hear the news.

We were all very silent and upset, and Mrs. Penhalligan said we should try to eat something. We went into the winter parlor and when we were there Hyson suddenly cried out: "Her head was all bandaged. She didn't know me. Mummy didn't know me! She's going to die . . . and death's horrible."

Deborah put her arms about the child. "There, my darling, hush. You're frightening Lowella."

Hyson broke free. Her eyes were wild and I could see that she was on the verge of hysteria. "She should be frightened. We all should. Because Mummy's going to die and I . . . I hate it."

"Mummy will get better," Deborah comforted.

Hyson gazed straight before her for a few seconds, and then suddenly her eyes were on mine. She continued to stare at me, and Deborah, noticing this, took the child's head and held it against her breast.

"I'm going to take Hyson up to my room," she said. "She'll stay with me tonight. This has been terrible . . . terrible."

She went out of the room, her arms about Hyson; but Hyson had turned once more to stare at me.

"I hate it . . . I hate it . . ." she cried.

Deborah gently led her away.

*　　*　　*

Roc came home at once, his business uncompleted, and when I saw him I realized again the depth of his affection for his sister. He was stunned by what had happened, and seemed to have forgotten all about our strained relationship.

The next days were spent in going to the hospital, although only Charles and Roc were allowed to see Morwenna. Deborah was wonderful with the twins, and I felt that Hyson needed a good deal of care during those days. I had not guessed how deep was her feeling for her mother.

It was three days after the accident when we heard that

Morwenna would probably recover; but she had lost her baby; and she had not yet been told this.

I remember driving Charles home from the hospital after he had been given that information; he was very upset and talked to me more intimately than he ever had before.

"You see, Favel," he said, "it meant so much to her. I wanted a son, naturally; but she seemed to have a sort of obsession about it. And now there won't be any more children . . . ever. That much they can tell me."

"As long as she recovers . . ." I whispered.

"Yes, as long as she recovers there mustn't be any more regrets."

* * *

When we knew that Morwenna was out of danger Roc went away again. There was nothing he could do at home, he said; either he or Charles had to attend to business, and in the circumstances it was for Charles to remain at Pendorric, close to Treganter.

During the last days I had been so immersed in the tragedy of Morwenna's accident that I had not thought very much about my own position, but as soon as Roc had gone my fears began to return, especially as it seemed firmly established that it was some unusual fault in the steering that had been responsible for the accident; and I knew very well that there had been nothing wrong with the car when I had used it the day before.

I spent a sleepless night after Roc had gone, and the next morning Mabell Clement telephoned me and asked if I would come over and have morning coffee with her. She had sounded rather agitated, and when I arrived at Tremethick Mabell took both my hands in a firm grasp and said: "Thank heaven you've come."

"What's wrong?" I wanted to know.

"I've scarcely slept all night thinking of you. Andrew's very worried. We were talking about you nearly all last night. We don't like it, Favel."

"I don't understand. What don't you like?"

"You know, or perhaps you don't . . . but I assure you he is. I mean Andrew. He's the most level-headed person I've ever known. And he's not satisfied. He thinks this is too much of a coincidence to be ignored."

"You mean . . ."

"Sit down. I've got the coffee made. Andrew will be in at any moment. At least he's going to try to be. But young

Mrs. Pengelly's baby's due, so it's possible he'll be detained. If he is, *I've* got to make you see."

"I've never seen you so agitated, Mabell."

"I don't think I've ever *felt* so agitated. I've never before known anyone who's in danger of being murdered."

I stared at her in horror, because I knew what she meant; and the fact that the thought was in her mind as well as mine gave it substance.

"We've got to be logical, Favel. We've got to look this thing right in the face. It's no use saying 'This sort of thing couldn't happen here . . . or to me.' That's what everybody says. But we know such things do occur. And you happen to be very rich. People envy money more than anything. They're ready to kill for it."

"Yes, I think you're right, Mabell."

"Now listen, Favel. Someone locked you in that vault and intended to keep you there, where your cries wouldn't be heard, and you would have died of fright or starvation or something. That was the plan."

I nodded.

"If Miss Hyson hadn't happened to come that way and hear you call, you might still have been there . . . at least your body might . . . with that of the little girl."

"I think you're right."

"Well, suppose there was an explanation of that. Suppose the door did jam as they said it did . . ."

She paused and I thought: As Roc said it did. Oh Roc . . . not you. That would be more than I could bear.

"Well, I suppose that's possible," she continued. "But what is so strange is that, not so long after, the car which you were expected to be driving should be involved in an accident. When Andrew and I heard what had happened we were quite . . . stunned. You see the same idea had occurred to us both."

I tried to speak steadily. "You think that the . . . person who locked me in the vault, tampered with the car?"

"I think two accidents like that can't be merely chance."

"There was another." I told her about the notice on the cliffs. "Roc happened to remember, and came after me."

I knew what was in her thoughts because her mouth hardened and she said: "It wasn't all that dangerous. It wasn't like the vault . . . and the car."

"Still someone did move the board. It might have been someone who knew I was at Polhorgan. And then of course there's this violin-playing and singing, and the story of the brides."

"As I said, we don't like it. We're very fond of you, Favel—myself and . . . Andrew. I think that someone is trying to harm you and it's someone at Pendorric."

"It's a ghastly thought, and now that Roc's away . . ."

"Oh, so he's away?"

"Yes, he went last weekend on business and he came back when he heard about the accident. He's had to go back now."

Mabell stood up. That hard expression was in her face again, and I knew whom she suspected.

"That nurse has left Cormorant Cottage," she said.

"I knew she was going."

"I wonder where she is now?"

We were silent for a few minutes, then Mabell burst out: "I just don't like the thought of your being at Pendorric."

"But it's my home."

"I think you ought to get away for a bit . . . to sort things out. Why don't you come and stay here for a night or two? We could talk, and you'd feel safe here."

I looked round the room, with the pictures (which Mabell had been unable to sell) on the walls, and examples of her handiwork in evidence over the brick fireplace.

It certainly seemed like a haven. I should feel perfectly at peace here. I should have time to think about what had happened, to talk about it with Mabell and Andrew; but there was no real reason why I should stay with them.

"It would seem so odd," I began.

"Suppose I was going to paint your portrait. Would that give us an excuse?"

"Hardly. People would say I could easily come over for sittings."

"But we hate the thought of your being there. We're afraid of what's going to happen next."

I thought of Roc, going away on business; this time he had not suggested that I should go with him. So why shouldn't I stay with friends?

"Look," said Mabell, "I'll drive you back and you can pack a bag. Just your night things."

She was so determined and I felt so uncertain that I allowed her to get out the car and drive me back to Pendorric.

When we reached the house I said: "I'll have to explain to Mrs. Penhalligan that I shan't be home for a night or so. I'll tell her about the picture . . . only I must say it seems rather strange in the midst of all this trouble."

"Stranger things have been happening," said Mabell firmly.

I went up to my room and put a few things in a bag. The house seemed very quiet. I felt dazed, as I had since I had talked to Mabell. I was certain now that someone was determined to kill me; and that it could happen while I was in Pendorric. The playing of the violin, the singing—they had been the warning signs; someone had tried to unnerve me, to make me believe this story of the woman who was trying to lure me into the tomb to take her place.

But ghosts did not have keys to vaults; they did not tamper with cars.

My bag was packed. I would go down to the kitchen and tell Mrs. Penhalligan. If Morwenna had been here I should have explained to her that I was staying with the Clements for a while. I didn't want to disturb Charles. Of course I could tell Deborah.

I went along to her rooms. She was there reading when I entered, and as she looked at me the serenity faded from her face. She sprang to her feet. "Favel, you're upset."

"Well everything's been so upsetting."

"My dear child." She took my hand and led me to the window seat. "Sit down and tell me about it."

"I've just come to tell you that I'm spending a night or two with the Clements."

She looked surprised. "You mean the doctor and his sister?"

"Yes. Mabell's going to paint my portrait." Even as I said the words I thought how puerile they sounded. She would know that I was making an excuse to leave Pendorric. She had always been so kind to me and I was sure she would understand if I explained to her. It was insulting to her intelligence not to tell her the truth, I felt. So I blurted out: "As a matter of fact, Deborah, I want to get away. If it's only for a day or so I want to get away."

She nodded. "I understand. Things haven't been going quite smoothly between you and Roc and you're upset. And coming on top of all this . . ."

I was silent and relieved when she went on: "It's perfectly understandable. It'll do you good, dear, to get away for a while. I feel the same myself. This anxiety about Morwenna has been . . . terrible. And now we know that she'll be all right we realize how tensed up we've been, and we begin to feel the effects of the shock. So you're going to the Clements."

"Yes. Mabell suggested it. I've just packed a bag."

Deborah frowned. "My dear, I suppose it's wise."

"Wise?"

"Well, it's not as though Mabell's there alone, is it? You see, this is a small place and there's a lot of gossip. Quite absurd of course, but there it is . . . and I've noticed . . . and I expect other people have too . . . that the doctor is rather interested in you."

I felt myself flushing hotly. "Dr. Clement!"

"He's quite young and people are so ready to talk. You might say there's always gossip about Pendorrics, and so there is. The men I mean. It's different with the women. Unfair of course, but that's the way of the world. The women have to be beyond reproach. Because of the children, my dear. This is ridiculous. It's really quite absurd, but so is the gossip and the scandal that goes on in this place. You must please yourself, Favel, but I don't really think that . . . in the circumstances . . . it would be wise for you to go to Tremethick."

I was amazed; then I remembered the eager friendship of the Clements. Andrew Clement had always shown pleasure in my company; Mabell knew this. Was that why she had been so friendly with me?

"I'm sure Mabell Clement would understand if it were put to her," said Deborah. "Let's go to her and bring her in and explain."

We did. Mabell looked surprised when we asked her in, but Deborah put the case very tactfully and, although Mabell quite clearly didn't agree, she made no attempt to persuade me.

"It's this place," said Deborah, waving a hand. "All small places are the same, I suppose. So little happens that people look for drama."

"I shouldn't have said so *little* happens at Pendorric," put in Mabell. "Favel was shut in the vault and Morwenna had a crash that was almost fatal."

"Such happenings give people a taste for more drama," said Deborah. "No, I'm certain it would be wrong. You see, my dears, suppose Favel is going to have her portrait painted, why shouldn't she come over every day?" She turned to me. "Now if you do want to get away, dear, I'll take you to Devon for a weekend. Why not? You've always wanted to see my house. We could leave tomorrow if you liked. How would that be?"

"I'd like that," I said.

Mabell seemed satisfied, although disappointed that I was not going back with her.

"What more natural than that we should get away for a night or two," said Deborah smiling. "Then you'll be back by the time your husband returns."

"It would be a . . . respite," I said.

And Mabell agreed.

* * *

When Mabell had gone, Deborah told Charles what we planned. He thought it was an excellent idea. Rachel Bective was there to look after the twins; and he thought that by the time we returned we should know when Morwenna was leaving the hospital.

"My dear," said Deborah, "I don't see why we shouldn't leave today. Why wait till tomorrow? If you're ready to go, I am."

I was very eager to get away from Pendorric because it was firmly in my mind that the menace which I felt close to me was somewhere in that house.

I collected together the things which I should need and Deborah went off to ask Carrie to do the same for her. Then Deborah brought her car round to the west porch, and Carrie came down with the bags.

As we drove round the side of the house the twins came out of the north door.

They ran up to the car.

"Hello, Granny Deb," said Lowella. "Hello, Bride. We're going to see Mummy this afternoon. Daddy's taking us to the hospital."

"That's wonderful, darling," said Deborah, stopping to smile at them. "Mummy will soon be home."

"Where are you going?" demanded Lowella.

"I'm taking Favel to show her my house."

Hyson had gripped the side of the car. "Let me come with you."

"Not this time, darling. You stay with Miss Bective. We'll be back soon."

"I want to come. I want to be there. I don't want to stay here . . . alone," said Hyson on a shrill note.

"Not this time, dear," said Deborah. "Take your hands

away." She touched them gently. Hyson dropped them and Deborah drove on. I turned and saw Rachel Bective come out of the house; then Hyson started to run after the car.

But Deborah had accelerated. We turned out of the drive.

We crossed the Tamar at Gunnislake, and it seemed to me that as the distance between us and Pendorric grew greater, the higher Deborah's spirits rose. There was no doubt that recent events had depressed her considerably.

She talked a great deal about Morwenna, and what a relief it was to know that she was going to get well.

"When she recovers," she said, "I shall bring her over to the moor. I'm certain it would do her the world of good."

I was beginning to see that she thought her moorland air the cure for all sicknesses, whether of the body or mind.

After passing through Tavistock we were soon on the moor. It reminded me very much of our own Cornish moors, but there was a subtle difference, Deborah told me, and you discovered it when you got to know them well. There was no moor like Dartmoor, she assured me, and insisted that Carrie corroborate this statement—which she readily did.

Carrie was excited too, and I caught their excitement and felt more at ease than I had since my quarrel with Roc.

Laranton Manor House stood alone about a mile from the village of Laranton. It was an impressive building— Queen Anne in style—with massive iron gates at the entrance.

In the grounds was a cottage, and in this, Deborah told me, lived Mr. and Mrs. Hanson and their unmarried son, all of whom worked for her and kept the house in readiness for her return at any time.

She took out a key and opened the front door of the house, about which clematis climbed. It must have been a lovely sight in season.

"Ah, it's good to be home," she cried. "Come along, my dear. Come in and see the old house which will always be home to me."

I met Mrs. Hanson, who expressed no surprise to see her mistress home, and Deborah gave orders in her gentle but competent way.

"Mrs. Hanson, this is my nephew's bride. She's going to stay for a night or two. I want Carrie to get the blue room ready for her."

"The blue room?" repeated Mrs. Hanson.

"Yes, please. I said the blue room. Carrie, put two hot-water bottles in the bed. You know how the first night in a strange bed always seems. And we should like something to eat, Mrs. Hanson. It's a fair journey from Pendorric."

She made me sit down, for I was tired, she was sure.

"I'm going to cosset you," she told me. "Oh, it is fun to have you here. I've always wanted to bring you."

I sat down in a chair near the big window which gave me a view of a neat lawn and flower beds. "Hanson's a good gardener, but it's not so easy to grow things on the moors as it is at Pendorric. The ground here is stony and it can be very cold in winter. Snow's a bit of a rarity at Pendorric; you should see it here in winter. There were times when Barbarina and I were kept in for a whole week—absolutely snowed up."

I looked round the large room with its inglenook and pleasant furniture, and the large bowl of chrysanthemums on a gilt and marble console table.

"I've told Mrs. Hanson always to keep flowers in the house," she told me, following my gaze. "Barbarina used to look after the flowers, until she married. Then I took over. I didn't arrange them as artistically as she did." She lifted her shoulders and smiled. "I'm going to show you your room. They should have it ready very soon. But first I'm hungry. Aren't you? It's our moorland air. Oh, it's good to be home."

"I wonder you spend so much time at Pendorric," I said, "when you so clearly prefer it here."

"Oh, it's because of the family . . . Morwenna, Roc, Hyson and Lowella! Pendorric's their home and if I want to be with them I have to be at Pendorric. I've brought Hyson here quite a lot. Lowella prefers the sea, but Hyson certainly has a taste for the moor."

"She was very eager to come with us this time."

"I know, dear child. But I did feel you needed a thorough rest. And with her mother in the hospital she should be there. When I'm here I feel young again. There's so much to remind me. I can almost imagine that Father is still alive and that at any moment Barbarina will come in through that door."

"Did Barbarina come here often after her marriage?"

"Yes. She felt the same as I do about this place. After all it was home to her. She had spent the greater part of her life here. How I do harp on the past. It's a failing of the aged. Do forgive me, Favel. I want you to be happy here."

"You're very kind."

"My dear, I'm so fond of you."

We were silent for a few moments and I thought that if I

were with Deborah in some small country hotel I could have felt at ease. It was a pity that to escape from Pendorric I had to come to the house where Barbarina had spent the greater part of her life.

Mrs. Hanson came in to tell us that the meal was ready.

"An omelette, madam," she said. "If I'd had more time . . ."

"It'll be delicious, I'm sure," smiled Deborah. "Mrs. Hanson is one of the best cooks in Devon."

The omelette was certainly delicious, and there was apple pie with clotted cream to follow.

"The real Devonshire cream," Deborah told me gleefully. "Now don't you agree it's better than the Cornish?"

I really couldn't tell the difference, so I said it was very good indeed.

"They copied it from us," said Deborah; "but they say we copied it from them!"

We were both growing more lighthearted, and I was sure it was a good thing that Deborah had brought me here; I could see quite clearly now that it would have been most unwise for me to have gone to the Clements'.

When the meal was over we went back to the drawing room for coffee, and when we had finished, Deborah took me up and showed me my room.

It was right at the top of the house, very large and an odd shape. There were two windows, and the ceiling sloped slightly in a way which was charming and told me that we were immediately under the roof. The single bed at the opposite end of the room was partly in an alcove; and there was a desk, wardrobe, bedside table, and dressing table; on the bed was a blue coverlet, and the carpet was blue.

"This is delightful," I said.

"And right at the top of the house. It's so light and airy, isn't it. Come and look out."

We went to one of the windows and because there was a half-moon I could see the moor stretched out beyond the gardens.

"You should see it in daylight," Deborah told me. "Miles and miles of moor. The gorse can be a picture, and the heather too. You can pick out the little streams. They look like flashes of silver in the sunlight."

"I shall enjoy a good walk tomorrow."

She didn't answer. She just gazed, enraptured, at the moor.

She turned to me. "Shall I help you unpack?"

"There's no need. I've brought very little."

"There's plenty of room for your things." She opened the door of the wardrobe.

I took out my things and the two dresses I had brought with me, and she hung them on hangers.

"I'll show you the rest of the house," she said.

* * *

I enjoyed my tour of the house. I saw the nursery, where she told me she and Barbarina had played, the music room, where Barbarina had learned the violin, the big drawing room with its grand piano, and I had peered through the window at the walled garden outside.

"We used to grow lovely peaches on that wall. Our gardener saved all the best for Barbarina."

"Weren't you a little jealous of her?" I asked.

"Jealous of Barbarina . . . never! Why, she and I were . . . close, as only twins can be. I could never really be jealous."

"I think Barbarina was lucky to have you for a sister."

"Yes, she was the lucky one . . . until the end of the course."

"What really happened?" I felt compelled to ask. "It was an accident, wasn't it?"

Her face crumpled suddenly and she turned away.

"It's so long ago," she said almost piteously.

"And you still feel . . ."

She seemed to pull herself together. "There was a suggestion that someone was with her in the gallery at the time."

"Did you believe it?"

"Yes."

"Then who . . . ?"

"It was never said, but lots of people had the idea that it was . . ."

"Her husband?"

"There was scandal about that woman. He was still seeing her. He never gave her up when he married Barbarina. He'd married Barbarina because of the money. He needed money. Houses like Pendorric are great monsters . . . they need continual feeding."

"You think he killed her because he wanted to have Barbarina's fortune and marry Louisa Sellick?"

"It entered the minds of some people."

"Yet he didn't marry her."

"Perhaps he dared not." She smiled at me bravely. "I

don't think we ought to be talking like this. It isn't fair to
. . . Petroc."

"I'm sorry. It's being here in her old home that reminded
me."

"Let's change the subject, shall we? Tell me what you
would like to do while you're here."

"See as much of the country as possible. I intend to be
up early tomorrow. After all I shall be here such a short
time. I want to make the most of it."

"Then I hope you get a good night's sleep. It's not always
easy in a new bed, is it? I'll send Mrs. Hanson up with a
nightcap. What do you like? Horlicks? Milo? Cocoa, or just
plain milk?"

I said I should prefer plain milk.

We sat talking a little while and then she said she would
order the milk and take me up.

We mounted the lovely staircase right to the top of the
house.

"One thing," she told me, "you'll be very quiet up here."

"I'm sure I shall."

"Barbarina always used to say that this was the room
she liked best in the whole of the house. It was her room until
she went to Pendorric."

"Barbarina's room?" I said.

"The most charming of the bedrooms. That's why I gave it
to you."

"It was kind of you."

"You . . . like it, don't you? If you don't I'll give you
another."

"I like it . . ."

She laughed suddenly. "It's Pendorric she's supposed to
haunt. Not the old Manor."

She drew the curtains across the windows and the room
looked even more charming. Then she switched on the lamp
which stood on the hexagonal bedside table.

"There! That should be comfortable. I hope you'll be warm
enough. They should have put two bottles in the bed." She
prodded it. "Yes, they have."

She stood smiling at me. "Good night, dear. Sleep well."
Then she took my face in her hands and kissed it.

"The milk will be coming up. When would you like it . . .
in five or ten minutes?"

"Five, please," I said.

"All right. Good night, dear."

She went out and left me. I undressed and, drawing back the curtains, stood for some seconds looking out over the moor. Peace, I thought. Here I shall be able to think about all the strange things which have been happening to me. I shall be able to make up my mind what I have to do.

There was a knock on my door and I was surprised to see Deborah, who came in carrying a glass of milk on a small tray.

She put this down on the hexagonal table.

"There you are, my dear. I thought I'd bring it myself."

"Thank you."

"You won't let it get cold, will you? Sleep well."

She kissed me and went out.

I sat on the edge of the bed and, picking up the glass, sipped the milk, which was very hot.

I got into bed, but I was not in the least sleepy. I wished that I had brought something to read, but I had left Pendorric in such a hurry that I had forgotten to do so.

I looked around the room to see if I could find a book; then I noticed the drawer of the hexagonal table. Absently I opened it, and lying inside was a book with a leather cover. I took it out and saw written in a round childish hand on the fly leaf: "The diary of Deborah and Barbarina Hyson. This must be the only diary that ever has been written by two people, but of course we are not really two people in the same way that other people are. That is because we are twins: Signed: Deborah Hyson. Barbarina Hyson."

I looked at those two signatures; they might have been written by the same hand.

So Deborah and Barbarina had kept a diary between them.

I was excited by my discovery; then I remembered that I was prying into something private. I shut the book firmly and drank some more milk. But I could not put the diary back into the drawer.

Barbarina had written in it. If I read what she had written I might learn something about her, and she had roused my curiosity from the moment I had heard of her; now of course that curiosity was intense because I had always felt that Barbarina was in some way connected with the things which were happening to me, and as I sat there in that strange bed it occurred to me that my position was not less dangerous because I had left Pendorric for a temporary respite. When I returned, more attempts might be made on my life.

I remembered that strange singing I had heard in the graveyard before I had been locked in the vault. If it were indeed true that someone was planning to murder me, then that someone was going to make it appear that my death was connected with the legend of Barbarina. And there was no doubting the fact that, if the superstitious people who lived round Pendorric were determined that the death of the brides of Pendorric was due to some metaphysical law, they would be less likely to report any strange incident that they might witness.

And as I held that book in my hand, I became convinced that I should be foolish to put aside something which might help me in my need. There might be something in this book, some hint as to how Barbarina had met her death. Had she been in a position similar to mine before that fatal fall? Had she felt, as I was feeling now, that danger was creeping closer and closer, until it eventually caught up with her? If she had felt that, might she not have put it into her diary?

But this was her childhood diary; the one she shared with Deborah. There would scarcely be anything in it about her life at Pendorric.

But I was determined to see, and I opened the book.

It had probably not been intended for a diary in the first place, for there were no printed dates on the pages; but dates had been written in.

The first was September 6. No year was given, and the entry read: "Petroc came today. We think he is the best boy we have ever met. He boasts a bit, but then all boys do. We think he likes us because we are asked to his birthday party at Pendorric."

The next entry was September 12. "Carrie is making our new dresses. She didn't know which of us was which. She is going to put name tabs on our clothes: Barbarina. Deborah. As if we cared. We always wear each other's things, we told her. Barbarina's are Deborah's and Deborah's Barbarina's; but she said we should have our own."

It seemed just a childish account of their lives here in this house on the moor, of the parties they went to. I had no idea who was writing because the first person singular was never used; it was all in the first person plural. I went on reading until I came to a blank page and thought for a moment that was the end; but a few pages on there was more writing, yet it was not the same. It had matured and I presumed that the diary had been forgotten for some time and taken up again. There was more than a change in the hand-writing, for I read:

"August 29. From my window I saw Deborah come back

I was excited because now I could say: That was actually written by Barbarina.

Barbarina seemed to have taken on the diary from that point.

"August 16. Petroc has asked Father and of course Father is delighted. He pretended to be surprised. As if it isn't what they've all wanted for so long! I'm so happy. I'm longing to be at Pendorric. Then I shall escape from Deborah. Fancy wanting to escape from Deborah who up till now has always seemed a part of me. She is in a way a part of me. That was why she had to feel as I do about Petroc. It used to be wonderful before we knew Petroc. There were always two of us to go places, to get ourselves out of trouble . . . silly little troubles, of course, which you think are so important when you're children. But that's all changed now. I want to get away . . . away from Deborah. I can't stand the way she looks at me when I've been with Petroc . . . as though she's trying to read my mind and can't, like she used to . . . as though she hates me. Am I beginning to hate her?"

"September 1. Yesterday Father, Deborah and I arrived at Pendorric for a visit. We're going ahead fast with arrangements for the wedding and I'm so excited. I saw Louisa Sellick today while I was out riding with Petroc. I suppose she's what people would call beautiful. She looks sad. That's because she knows now she has lost Petroc forever. I asked Petroc about her. Perhaps I should have said nothing. But I was never one to stay calm. Deborah was the calm one. Petroc said it was all over. Is it? I wish I'd fallen in love with some of the others. George Fanshawe would have been a good husband and he was very much in love with me. So was Tom Kellerway. But it had to be Petroc. If Tom or George would fall in love with Deborah . . . Why is it they don't? We look so much alike that people can't tell us apart and yet they don't fall in love with Deborah. It's the same as it was when we were young. When we were at parties she'd keep in the background. I never did. She always said: 'People don't want me. I get in on your ticket.' And because she believed it and acted that way, it came to be true. Now Deborah doesn't know I'm going on with our diary I can write exactly what I feel. It's such a relief."

"September 3. Pendorric! What a wonderful old house. I

love it. And Petroc! What is it about him that's different from everyone else in the world! Some magic! He's so gay, but sometimes I'm frightened. He doesn't seem to be entirely with me."

I had come to several blank pages in the book but after that the writing went on.

"July 3. I found this old diary today. It's ages since I wrote in it. The last time was just before I married. I see I've only put the months and days and left out the years. How like me! Still, it doesn't matter. I don't know why I want to write in it again. For comfort, I suppose. Since the twins were born I haven't thought of it. It's only now. I woke up last night and he wasn't there. I thought of that woman, Louisa Sellick. I hate her. There are rumors about her. I suppose he's still seeing her . . . and others. Could anyone be all that attractive and not take advantage of it? If I'd wanted a faithful husband I ought not to have married such an attractive man as Petroc. I notice things. I've seen people at parties talking. They brightly change the subject when I come up. I know they're talking about Petroc and me . . . and some woman. Louisa Sellick probably. The servants look at me . . . pityingly. Mrs. Penhalligan for one . . . even old Jesse. What are they saying? Sometimes I feel I'll go mad if I let things drift like this. When I try to talk to Petroc he'll never be serious. He says: 'Well, of course I love you.' And I snap back: 'And how many others too?' 'Mine's such a loving nature,' he answers. He can never be serious. Life's so amusing to him. I want to shout at him that it's not so amusing to me. When I think of the old days in Father's house I remember how I used to love parties. Everyone made a fuss of me. And Deborah was there . . . she used to be as pleased as I was with my popularity. Once she said: "I enjoy it just as though it were mine.' And I answered: 'It *is* yours, Deb. Don't you remember we always used to say that we weren't two people . . . but one.' In those days that satisfied her."

I had been so excited by what I read that I hadn't noticed what was happening to myself. I had actually yawned several times during the reading and my lids now seemed so heavy that I couldn't keep my eyes open.

If I had been less enthralled I should not have been surprised, but the contents of this diary should surely have kept me wide awake.

I was determined to go on reading.

"August 8. Deborah has been here for the last fortnight.

She seems to come more often now. There is a change in Deb. She's become more *alive*. She laughs more easily. Something has changed her. Other people may not notice . . . but then they don't know her as I do. She borrowed my riding hat the other day—the black one with the band of blue round it. She stood before the looking glass and said: 'I don't believe anyone would know I wasn't you . . . not *anyone.*' And actually she has grown more like me since she became more lively. I know on several occasions the servants called her by my name. It amused her very much. I had an idea that she longed to be in my place. If only she knew. But that's something I wouldn't tell even her. It's too humiliating. No, I couldn't even tell Deborah about all the times when I wake up and find Petroc not with me, how I get up and walk about the room imagining what he's doing. If she knew what I had to suffer she wouldn't want to be in my place. She sees Petroc as so many others see him . . . just about the most fascinating man anyone could meet anywhere. It's different being his wife. Sometimes I hate him."

"August 20. There was another scene yesterday. Petroc says I've got to be calm. He says he doesn't know what'll happen if I don't control myself more. Control myself! When he treats me like this! He says I'm too possessive. He says: 'Don't pry into my life and I won't pry into yours.' What sort of a marriage is this?"

"August 27. He has not been near me for more than a week. Sometimes I think everything is over between us. He can't stand scenes, he says. Of course he can't, because he's in the wrong. He just wants to go on living his own way . . . which is more or less the same as before he was married; but everything must seem all right on the surface. There mustn't be scandal. Petroc hates scandal. The fact is he's lazy. That's why he married me. Pendorric needed money. I had it. It was simple. Marry money and there's no need to worry. Why does he have to be so amusing, so charming on the surface . . . so feckless and cruel underneath? If only I could be as lighthearted as he is! If only I could say 'Oh . . . that's just Petroc. I must take him as I find him.' But I can't. I love him too much. I don't want to share him. Sometimes I think I'll go mad. Petroc thinks so too. That's why he stays away. He hates it when I lose control. Father used to hate it too. But Father was kind and gentle with me. He used to say: 'Barbarina my dear, you must be quiet. Look at Deborah. How calm she is. Be more like your sister,

Barbarina.' And that used to help. I'd remember that Deborah and I were one. She had all the calmness in our nature. I was the volatile one. Father might deplore my wildness; but it was what made me attractive and Deborah a little dull. Deborah ought to comfort me now but even she has changed."

"August 29. From my window I saw Deborah come back from a ride today. She was wearing a hat with a blue band. Not mine this time. She has one exactly like it. As she came round from the stables the children were just going out with their nurse. They called to her. 'Hello, Mummy,' they said. Deborah stooped and kissed first Morwenna, then Roc. The nurse said: 'Morwenna's knee is healing up nicely, Mrs. Pendorric.' Mrs. Pendorric! So the nurse and the children had mistaken her for me. I felt angry. I hated Deborah in that moment and it was like hating myself. I did hate myself. It was some minutes later when I said to myself: 'But why didn't Deborah explain?' But she didn't. She just let them think that she was the children's mother . . . the mistress of the house."

"September 2. If this goes on I think I shall kill myself. I've been thinking about it more and more. A quiet sleep forever and ever. No more Petroc. No more jealousy. Sometimes I long for that. I often remember the Bride story. Some of the servants are sure Lowella Pendorric haunts the place. They won't go in the gallery where she hangs, after dark. This Lowella died after a year of marriage, having a son; she was cursed by her husband's mistress. The Pendorric men haven't changed much. When I think of my life at Pendorric, I'm ready to believe there might be a curse on the women of the house."

"September 3. Petroc says I'm getting more and more hysterical. How can I help that? All I ask is that he should be with me more, should love me as I love him. Surely that's not asking too much. All *he* cares about is that he should miss none of his pleasures, which means women . . . women all the time. Though I believe he's kept on with this Louisa Sellick. So he's faithful to her . . . after his fashion. There's one other thing that he cares about: Pendorric. What a fuss the other day when they discovered wood worm in the gallery. The wood's particularly bad in the balustrade—near Lowella Pendorric's picture—the one who was supposed to have died because of the curse, and haunt the place. That's what's made me think of her so much."

"September 12. Deborah is still with us. She doesn't seem

to want to go back to the moor. She certainly has changed. Sometimes I think she's growing more as I used to be, and I'm becoming more like her. She's inclined to use my things as though they were hers. We did this in the old days but it was different then. She comes into my bedroom and talks. It's odd but I fancy she's trying to get me to talk about Petroc, and when I do she seems to shy away. The other day when we were talking she picked up a jacket of mine—a casual sort of thing in mustard color. 'You hardly wear it,' she said. 'I always liked it.' She slipped it on and as I looked at her I had a strange feeling that I *am* Deborah and that she's so longing to be in my place that she is Barbarina. I felt it was myself I was looking at. Is Petroc right? Is all that I'm suffering driving me crazy? Deborah took off the jacket but when she went out she slung it over her arm and I haven't seen it since."

"September 14. I cry a lot. I'm so wretched. No wonder Petroc hardly ever comes near me. For some weeks he's been sleeping in the dressing room. I try to tell myself it's better that way. Then I don't know whether he's there or not, so I don't have to wonder whom he's with. But of course I do."

"September 20. I can't believe it. I must write it down. I think I'll go mad if I don't. I could bear the others; but not this. I know about Louisa Sellick and I can understand it—and up to a point forgive it. After all he wanted to marry her. It was because of Pendorric that he married me. But this. It's all so unnatural. I hate Deborah now. There isn't room for the two of us in this world. Perhaps there never was. We should have been one person. No wonder she's going about deceiving people . . . not correcting them when they call her Mrs. Pendorric. Petroc and Deborah! It's incredible. But of course it's not. It's inevitable in a way. After all so much of me is Deborah and so much of her me. We are one . . . so why shouldn't we share Petroc as we have shared so many other things? Gradually she's been taking what's mine . . . not only my husband but my personality. The way she laughs now . . . the way she sings. That's not Deborah; it's Barbarina. I go about the house outwardly calm letting the servants think that I don't care. I stand there smiling when they talk to me and pretend to be interested as I did today when old Jesse talked about bringing something into the hall . . . some plant or other. It's getting too cold out of doors or something and he doesn't think the hothouse is quite right for it. Yes, yes, yes, I said, not listening. Poor old Jesse! He's almost blind now. I told him not to worry; we'd see he was all right. And Petroc will, of course. That's one thing about him —he's good to the servants. I'm writing trivialities to prevent myself thinking. Deborah and Petroc—I've seen them together. I know. It's her room he goes to. It leads from the gallery not far from that spot where the picture of Lowella Pendorric hangs. I lay listening last night and heard the door close. Deborah . . . and Petroc. How I hate them . . . both! There shouldn't be two of us. I've tolerated others but I won't tolerate this. But how can I stop it?"

"September 21. I've decided to kill myself. I can't go on. I keep wondering how. Perhaps I'll walk into the sea. They say that after the first moments of struggle, it's an easy death. You don't feel it much. My body would be washed in and Petroc would see it. He'd never forget. I'd haunt him for the rest of his life. It would be his punishment and he deserves to be punished. It would be the legend coming true. The bride of Pendorric would haunt the place, and I, Barbarina, would be that bride. It seems somehow right . . . inevitable. I think it is the only way."

The rest of that page was blank and I thought I had come to the end of the diary. I yawned, I was very tired.

But as I turned the page I came to more writing and what I read startled me so much that I was almost wide awake.

"October 19. They think I am dead. Yet I am here and they don't know it. Petroc doesn't know. It's a good thing that he can't bear to be near me, because he might discover the truth. He's away most of the time. He goes to Louisa Sellick for comfort. Let him. I don't care now. Everything is different. It's . . . exciting. There's no other word for it. I shouldn't write in this book. It's all so dangerous, but I like to go over it again and again. It's funny . . . really funny because it makes me laugh sometimes . . . but only when I'm alone. When I'm with anyone I'm calm . . . terribly calm. I have to be. I feel more alive now than I have for a long time . . . now that they think I'm dead. I must write it down. I'm afraid I'll forget if I don't. I had made up my mind how I would die. I was going to walk into the sea. Perhaps I'd leave a note for Petroc, telling him that he'd driven me to it. Then I'd be sure that I'd haunt him for the rest of his life. It all happened so suddenly. I hadn't planned it that way at all. Then suddenly I saw how it could be done. How a new bride could take the place of Lowella Pendorric, for it was time she rested in her grave, poor thing. Deborah came into my room. She was wearing my mustard-colored jacket, and her eyes were bright; she looked sleek and contented, and I knew, as well as if she'd told me, that he'd been with her the previous night. 'You're looking tired, Barby,' she said. Tired! So would she, had she lain awake as I had. She'd be punished too. She would never forgive herself. I doubted whether she and Petroc would be lovers after I had gone. 'Petroc's really concerned about the gallery,' she said. 'It'll probably mean replacing the whole thing.' How dared she tell me how Petroc felt! How dared she talk in that proprietorial way about Petroc and Pendorric! She used to be so sensitive to my moods; but now her mind was full of Petroc. She picked up a scarf of mine—Petroc himself had bought it for me when we were in Italy—a lovely thing of emerald-colored silk. She put it absently about her neck. The mustard-colored jacket set it off perfectly. Something happened when she took that scarf. It seemed tremendously important. My husband . . . my scarf. I felt I hadn't a life of my own any more. I wonder now why I didn't snatch it away from her, but I didn't. 'Come and look at the gallery,' she said. 'It's really quite dangerous. The workmen will be coming in tomorrow.' I allowed myself to follow her out to the gallery; we stood beneath the picture of Lowella. 'Here,' she said. 'Look, Barby.' Then it happened. It suddenly seemed clear to me. I was going to die because there was no longer any reason to go on living. I had thought of walking into the sea. Deborah was standing close to the worm-eaten rail. It was a long drop down to the hall. I felt Lowella Pendorric was watching us from her canvas, saying: 'A bride must die that I may rest in peace.' It was the old legend and there's a lot of truth in these old legends. That's why they persist. Deborah was, in a sense, a bride of Pendorric. Petroc treated her as such . . . and she was part of me. There were times when I was not sure which of us I was. I'm glad I wrote this down, although it's dangerous. This book must never be seen by anyone. It's safe enough. Only Carrie has ever seen it and she knows what happened as well as I do. When I read it, I can remember it clearly. It's the only way I can come back to what really happened on that day. I can live again that moment when she was standing there, perilously close, and I leaned forward and pushed her with all my might. I can hear her catch her breath in amazement . . . and horror. I can hear her voice, or did I imagine that? But I hear it all the same. 'No, Barbarina!' Then I know of course that I am Barbarina and that it is

Deborah who lies in the Pendorric vault. Then I can laugh and say: How clever I am. They think me dead and I am alive all these years. But it's only when I read this book that I am absolutely sure who I am."

I felt limp with horror.

But there was more to be read and I went on reading.

"October 20. I shouldn't write in the book any more. But I can't resist it. I want to write it down while I remember, because it's fading fast and I am not sure . . . There was someone in the hall. I was frightened. But it was only old Jesse and he couldn't see. I stood in the gallery, looking at the splintered wood. I wouldn't look down onto the hall. I didn't stay long. Old Jesse had run for help. He might not see me but he knew something was wrong. I ran into the nearest room because I had to get out of the gallery before I was seen. It was Deborah's. I threw myself onto her bed and lay there, my heart thundering. I don't know how long I lay there but it seemed like hours. It was a few minutes actually. Voices. Cries of horror. What was happening in the hall? I longed to see but I knew I must stay where I was. After a while there was a knock on the door. I was still lying on the bed when Mrs. Penhalligan came in. She said: 'Miss Hyson, there's been a terrible accident.' I raised myself and stared at her. 'It's the gallery rail. 'Twas worse than we thought. Mrs. Pendorric . . .' I just went on staring at her. She went out and I heard her voice outside the door. 'Miss Hyson, she be terrible shocked, poor dear. 'Tis not to be wondered at . . . they being so close . . . so near like. I for one couldn't tell the one from the other.'

"I went down to the sea and looked at it. It was gray and cold. I couldn't do it. It's easy to talk of dying; but when you face it . . . you're frightened. You're terribly frightened. I'd been so stunned by the news that they'd made me stay in bed until it was all over. I didn't see Petroc unless others were there too. That was as well. He was the one I feared. Surely he would know his own wife. But even so there was something I knew about Petroc. He wasn't the same. The gaiety had gone, the lightheartedness. He blamed himself. The servants were talking. They said it was *meant*. And it happened right under the picture of that other bride. It was no good going against what was meant. Barbarina was meant to die, so that Lowella Pendorric could rest from the haunting. They wouldn't go near the gallery after dark. They believed Barbarina was haunting Pendorric. So she is. She haunted Petroc till the day he died. So the story was true. The Bride of Pendorric had died just as the story said she should and she couldn't rest in her grave.

"I couldn't go. I couldn't leave the children. They call me Aunt Deborah now. I *am* Deborah. I'm calm and serene. Carrie knows though. Sometimes she calls me Miss Barbarina. I'm afraid of Carrie. But she'd never hurt me; she loves me too well. I was always her favorite. I was everybody's favorite. It's different now though. People are different toward me. They call me Deborah and what is happening is that Deborah still lives and it is Barbarina who is dead."

"January 1. I shall not write any more. There is nothing to write. Barbarina is dead. She had a fatal accident. Petroc hardly spoke to me again. I believe he thought that I was jealous of her, and that I did it hoping he'd marry me; he doesn't want to know too much about it in case it's true. I don't care about Petroc any more. I'm devoted to the children. It doesn't matter now that Petroc is never there. I'm not his wife any more; I'm his sister-in-law, taking care of his motherless children. I'm happier than I ever was since my marriage; though sometimes I think of my sister and it's as though she's with me. She comes to me at night when I'm alone and her eyes are mournful and accusing. She can't rest. She haunts me and she haunts Petroc. It's in the legend; and she'll continue to haunt Pendorric until another young bride takes her place; then she will rest forevermore."

"March 20. I have been reading this book. I shall not read it any more. I shall not write in it any more. I shall hide it away. It worries me. Barbarina is dead and I am Deborah; I am calm and serene and I have devoted myself to Roc and Morwenna. Barbarina haunts me; that's because it's in the story that she should . . . until another bride takes her place. But reading this book upsets me. I shall not do it any more."

There was one last entry. It stated simply:

"One day, there'll be a new bride at Pendorric and then Barbarina shall have her rest."

So it was Barbarina who had brought me to this house, who had lured me to the vault, who had sought to kill me.

I did not know what to do. What could I do tonight? I was alone in this house with Barbarina and Carrie, for the Hansons would be in their cottage in the grounds.

I must lock my door. I attempted to get out of bed but my legs seemed unable to move, and even in my agitated state I could not fight the drowsiness which had taken possession of me. A thought came into my head that I was asleep and dreaming; and in that moment the book had slipped from my fingers and falling asleep was like entering a deep dark cave.

* * *

I awoke with a start. For a few seconds I was still in that deep, dark cave of oblivion; then objects started to take shape. Where was I? There was the hexagonal table. I remembered the diary, and then where I was.

I knew, too, that something had awakened me, and the knowledge quickly followed that I was not alone. Someone was in this room.

I had fallen asleep so suddenly that I was lying on my back. I had been aware of the hexagonal table by turning my eyes towards it without moving my head. The heavy sleepiness was still upon me and the deep darkness of the cave was threatening to close about me once more.

I was so tired . . . too tired to be afraid . . . too tired to care that I was not alone in the room.

I'm dreaming, I thought. Of course I'm dreaming. For from out of the shadows came a figure. It was a woman dressed in a blue house coat. As the moonlight touched her face I knew who she was.

My heavy lids were pressing down over my eyes; vaguely I heard her voice.

"This time, there shall be no way out. They will no longer talk of Barbarina's ghost . . . but yours."

I wanted to call out; but some waking instinct warned me not to, and I began to wonder whether after all I was in a dream.

Never before in my life had I been so frightened. Yet never had I been so sleepy, and terror was trying to ward off my sleepiness. What was happening to me? I longed to be in my bedroom at Pendorric with Roc beside me. That was safety. This was danger.

"This is a nightmare," I told myself. "In a moment you will wake up."

She was standing at the foot of my bed looking at me while I watched her through half-closed eyes, waiting for what she would do next.

An impulse came to me to speak to her, but something warned me that I must first find out what she intended to do. This had never happened to me before. I was asleep; yet I was awake. I was terrified; and yet it was as though I stood outside this scene, a watcher in the shadows. I was looking on at the frightened woman in the bed and the other whose purpose was evil.

An idea hit me. I am drugged. The milk was drugged. The milk Deborah brought me. No . . . not *Deborah*. I didn't drink it all. If I had I should now be in a deep, drugged sleep.

She was smiling. Then I saw her hands move in a gesture as though she were sprinkling something over my bed. She went to the window and stooped for a few seconds; and then she stood upright and without giving another glance at my bed, ran from the room.

I was aware of thinking: It is a dream. Then suddenly it seemed I was wide awake. I was looking at a wall of flame. The curtains were on fire. For one second, two seconds, I stared at them, while it was as though I emerged from that black cave to reality.

I smelt petrol and in terrible understanding leaped out of bed and made for the door. I was not a second too soon, for as I did so my bed was aflame.

*   *   *

It is difficult to recall what happened next. I was aware of the blazing bed as I pulled at the door handle and for one hideous second believed that I was locked in this room as I had been locked in the vault. But that was only due to my anxiety to get out quickly. The door was not locked.

I pulled it open and had the sense to shut it behind me. I saw her then. She was running along the corridor, and I went after her shouting: "Fire!" as I did so.

She turned to look at me.

I cried: "Quick! My room's on fire. We must give the alarm."

She looked at me in bewilderment. I knew then that she was completely mad, and for those few dramatic seconds I even forgot the danger we were in.

"You tried to kill me . . . *Barbarina!*" I said.

Horror dawned in her face. I heard her whisper as though to herself! "The diary . . . oh my God, she's read the diary."

I caught her arm. "You've set my room on fire," I said urgently. "It'll spread . . . quickly. Where's Carrie? On this floor? Carrie! Carrie! Come quickly."

Barbarina's lips were moving; she went on muttering to

herself: "It's there . . . in the diary . . . she's seen the diary . . ."

Carrie came into the corridor, wrapping an old dressing gown about her, her hair in a plait tied with a red tape.

"Carrie," I shouted. "My room's on fire. Phone the fire brigade quickly."

"Carrie! Carrie! She . . . *knows* . . ." moaned Barbarina.

I gripped Carrie's arm. "Show me where the phone is. There's no time to lose. We must all get out of the house. Don't you understand?"

Still gripping Carrie I pulled her downstairs. I did not look back, being certain that Barbarina, knowing the intensity of the fire she had started, would follow us.

I never saw Barbarina again. By the time we had phoned for the brigade, the top floor was a mass of flame. All I knew was that Barbarina did not follow us downstairs. I have always believed that, rudely shaken out of her dream world, she had had no thought of anything but the incriminating diary. To her it represented the only way of remembering what had actually happened; and to have lost it would have been to have lost touch with the past. Unbalanced as she was, she had made a futile attempt to save it. I do not like to think what happened to Barbarina when she burst into that room which by then must have been a roaring furnace.

* * *

It was nearly an hour before the fire brigade reached the isolated manor house and by that time it was too late to save it. It was not until we had telephoned for the brigade and the Hansons had arrived that we missed Barbarina. Hanson bravely went up to try to rescue her. We had to prevent Carrie from dashing into the flames to bring out her mistress, for we knew it was hopeless.

Looking back it is hard to remember the sequence of events. But I do remember sitting in the Hansons' cottage drinking tea which Mrs. Hanson brought to me, when suddenly I heard a familiar voice.

"Roc!" I cried and ran to him; we just stood together clinging.

And this was a Roc I had never known before because I had never seen him clearly through the fog of suspicion which surrounded him—strong in his power to protect, weak in his anxiety over my safety, ready to do battle with the powers of darkness for my sake yet terrified for fear some harm should come to me.

7.

IT IS A YEAR since that night and yet the memory of it is with me as vividly as when it happened. Perhaps, if one has come near to violent death, as I did, it is an experience which is never far from the surface of the mind.

I often say to Roc: "If it hadn't been that I was so absorbed in the diary I should have drunk all the milk; I should have been unconscious when Barbarina came into my room and that would have been the end of me." To that Roc answers: "All life is chance. If your father had never come to our coast, you would not have been here at all."

And it is so.

It is difficult to understand everything that went on in Barbarina's mind; I am sure that for much of the time she believed she was Deborah. She could never have played the part so well if she had not; and her character must have changed after Deborah died so that she really did take on the personality of her twin. The more she behaved like Deborah, the more like her she grew, just as Deborah, when Petroc became her lover, began to be like Barbarina. The curse laid on the Brides of Pendorric became an obsession with her. It may have been that she believed Deborah's spirit had actually entered her body, and that she had become Deborah; and because she constantly thought of the sister whom she had sent to her death, she believed she was haunted by her and it was for this reason that she was anxious for another bride to take over the role of ghost at Pendorric.

But how can one follow the tortuous meandering of a sick mind?

My conjectures must have an element of truth in them, though, because there was no doubt that I had been in danger from the moment I had come to Pendorric.

Poor simple-minded Carrie, who had always been dominated by her charges, was easily caught up in this morbid dream life of her mistress; Barbarina and Deborah were one and the same; and Carrie believed it, while she alone knew that the twin who had fallen to her death in the hall at

Pendorric was Deborah. At times she could not understand Barbarina's interpretation of this strange phenomenon; namely that Deborah's mind and soul were now with Barbarina. Carrie could only accept this by telling herself that the two of them were really alive.

It was from Carrie that we gleaned a little understanding of Barbarina's madness; but the years during which she had devoted herself to Barbarina and her crazy conception of life had undermined her own sanity and Roc was anxious that she should not be upset. He sent her away in the care of an old nanny of his who had a cottage on the Devon coast and there she is now.

It was not so easy with Hyson, for Barbarina had tried to draw the child into her orbit. She saw in Lowella and Hyson a repetition of herself and Deborah; and because for most of the time she believed she *was* Deborah, she had great sympathy for the less attractive twin. Barbarina's affection for the child was deep and possessive and Hyson was fascinated by the strangeness of Barbarina, who revealed herself more to the child than to anyone else. Hyson did not understand, but she was aware of the strangeness, and like Barbarina, learned to project herself into that make-believe world; Barbarina had hinted that she still lived and Hyson believed her; she believed that Barbarina would lure me to my death so that she might rest in her grave, according to the legend.

It was from Carrie we learned that Barbarina had sometimes gone to the music room and played the violin, and that she sang Ophelia's song; and that it was she who had waited for me to leave Polhorgan and had removed the sign on the cliffs in the hope that I, less sure-footed than those accustomed to the path, would have a fatal accident. She it was who had locked me in the vault, for the only other key to the vault had been in her possession; she had often paid secret visits to the vault as, according to Carrie, she told her she wanted to be with Barbarina. She would never have come to the vault had not Hyson been missing and she, guessing where she was, had decided to abandon that method of disposing of me, for the sake of the child. She had quietly unlocked the door before going to find Roc. Then she had tampered with the car and chance again had stepped in so that it was Morwenna who had had an accident.

Often I reflect how easily the legend of the brides might have gone on and on; for few people can have come as near to death as I did, and escape. If Barbarina had been a cold-blooded murderess, I should never have escaped; but she was not that; if she had been, she would have planned more carefully; but she was caught in her world of make-believe; she was living on two levels and she could not see where reality and the dream world merged. I discovered that she had trunks of Deborah's clothes and often wore them when she was in Devon. The Hansons were not aware of this, never having known Deborah, and when Carried called her Barbarina they merely thought that Carrie was a little weak in the head. And Barbarina could lightly step back into the character of Deborah to assure them that this was so.

What damage she would have done to Hyson if I had not come to Pendorric when I did; the child was neurotic, her head full of strange notions. She was already beginning to believe that she stood in the same relationship to Lowella as Deborah had to Barbarina. Barbarina had won her devotion by preferring her to her gayer sister; and that was when the damage began to be done.

But there again events worked against her. Hyson had endured the terrifying experience of being locked in the vault with me. She had known, because of the hints Barbarina loved to give the child, that something was going to happen that day. She believed that the figure she saw in the grave-yard, when she had hidden herself there, was the ghost of Barbarina. Barbarina had been unwise to involve the child, but, because she was already identifying Hyson with Deborah, could not stop doing so. And when Barbarina opened the door of the vault and sang the song which was to lure me inside, Hyson slipped in. Thus we were locked in together and from that moment Hyson began to understand the horror of death, that it did not come lightly, that there must be suffering before oblivion was reached.

Then she saw her mother in the hospital and she must have known that Morwenna was lying where I was intended to be.

Death was hateful; it was frightening; and it touched those she loved. Her own mother. And even for me she had some affection.

She was frightened; and when she saw me going off with Barbarina in the car, guessing for what purpose, she broke into hysteria, which so alarmed her father that he sent for Dr. Clement, but it was some time before they could understand the meaning of her incoherent words. Dr. Clement's first action was to telephone Roc; and Roc immediately drove to the Manor.

Yet although I lived so dangerously up to that night when Roc came to me in Devon, it was during the following months that I learned so much more of life than I ever had before; the months of safety and serenity.

For one thing, I learned the story of the boy who lived in Louisa Sellick's house on the moor. Morwenna must have grown up, too, because she confessed to Charles that he was hers. She had been afraid to do so before because the boy was the result of a brief passionate love affair which had occurred when she was seventeen.

Rachel Bective, who as a child had so longed to be asked to Pendorric that she had locked Morwenna in the vault in order to blackmail her into giving her an invitation, had proved a good friend. She had looked after Morwenna during her trouble and of course Roc had been at hand. It had been his idea to ask Louisa's help, and he and Rachel took the child to her; Louisa had been only too glad to do what she could for Petroc's children.

As Roc said to me: "I couldn't tell you the truth when I'd sworn to keep Morwenna's secret. But I did intend to persuade her that you should be brought in. The trouble was she was so afraid of Charles's knowing."

There had been fear and drama in Pendorric before I arrived.

During the last year we have gone a long way towards turning Polhorgan into a home for orphans. I am going to be very busy keeping an eye on this particular project as I shall be starting my own family. Rachel Bective is going to be a nursery governess to the orphans, and Dr. Clement will be at hand to advise when we need him. The Dawsons will stay on and although there may be a little friction now and then between them and Rachel, that is inevitable, I suppose. I don't like Rachel—I doubt whether I ever shall—but I have wronged her in my thoughts so much that I try very hard to change my opinion. She was merely enamored of a way of life which was not hers. The romantic big house must have been very appealing to an orphan, brought up by an aunt who had children of her own and didn't really want her. She saw her main opportunity in life when she was sent to a good school paid for with the money her parents had left with instructions that all of it be spent on their daughter's education. She had attached herself to Morwenna and clung; but she had been a good friend in Morwenna's trouble and often visited Bedivere House—as Roc did—to bring Morwenna news of a son she dared not see until she had confessed to Charles.

The twins have now gone to school—separate schools. Hyson had a holiday, a holiday at Bournemouth alone with her mother after Morwenna's recovery. They both needed to recuperate; and we feel that in time Hyson will grow away from that sinister influence which Barbarina cast about her. We shall have to be very careful in our treatment of Hyson.

This then, has been an illuminating year.

We all seem to have grown up, become wise; but then I suppose it is experiences such as these which make us learn our lessons quickly.

Morwenna has cast off the burden which, like Christian in the *Pilgrim's Progress,* she has carried for fourteen years, and Charles, she discovered, was less self-righteous than she had believed him to be. Indeed he was a little sad and reproachful that she had not trusted him all those years.

As a result Ennis and Louisa are often at Pendorric. Morwenna would not take the boy from Louisa, but she does want to share him, and I have an idea that in time he will be to Charles the son he did not have.

It may well be that one day we shall have to give up Pendorric as we know it. We shall probably have to throw it open to the public and have strangers walking through our rooms. We shall have our own apartments of course, but it will not be the same.

Roc is reconciled. "You can't fight the times," he says; "it would be like trying to fight the sea."

All the money I have will be used on Polhorgan and that is how Roc wishes it to be.

He often teases me, reminding me that I once thought he schemed to marry an heiress and then planned to murder her.

"And yet," he said, "you loved me . . . after your fashion."

He is right. During those months of danger I was deep in physical love with Roc; I knew only what I saw, what I heard, what I sensed.

But there are many facets of love and of these I am learning more every day; and so is he. And that is why when we walk down the cliff gardens to Pendorric Cove and look towards Polhorgan, high on the cliff, or to Cormorant Cottage, where Althea Grey once lived, we remember those doubts which, while they did not diminish our passion, yet were a sign that we had just begun that voyage of discovery which our life together will be.

*In Victorian England, a woman's place is
in the home. Susanna Pleydell
dares to be different.*

SECRET FOR A
NIGHTINGALE

by
Victoria Holt

Published by Fawcett Books.
Available wherever books are sold.